HIGH

by

Thomas Hinde

Chitty, Sir Thomas Willes, bart.

HODDER AND STOUGHTON

*The characters in this book are entirely imaginary and bear
no relation to any living person*

Copyright © 1968 by Thomas Hinde

First printed 1968

SBN 340 04302 4

Printed in Great Britain
for Hodder and Stoughton Limited
St. Paul's House, Warwick Lane, London E.C.4
by Willmer Brothers Limited, Birkenhead

Here, in his long-awaited successor to *The Village*, the author of *Mr Nicholas* reaches his full stature as one of the very few eminent British contemporary novelists.

Maurice Peterson has followed many another to Flatville, USA, lecturing on English literature and casting a hopeful eye on the young natives – in particular Jill who has no leanings towards the normality that Peterson sadly links with family life, at which he himself has hardly been a marked success. The air of Flatville is unexpectedly bracing, High, in several senses he realises when he is invited to embark on an expedition into the brave new world of sex. The possession of a flamboyant and totally unpredictable mistress appears at first as success; even all the splendours and miseries of romantic love, so surprisingly adapted to twentieth-century Flatville, until in the kingdom of the truly high, where the secret of life is about to be revealed, he makes a sentimental anti-Flatville choice which lands him back in square one. However, like all expatriate professors, Peterson is writing a *book* in which Peter Morrison, Olga Hopping and others bear a suspicious resemblance to the author and his circle; Peter Morrison, a rebel against the current fate of discarded lovers, designs a somewhat different end. Peterson, then, has a second chance, a fantasy success it seems. But ... is it? And does he?

With some, these complications might easily have become merely an ingenious conceit, but Thomas Hinde uses his mirrors so creatively that we are given an exciting prismatic view that could have been achieved in no other way. Grotesquely funny, improbable yet absolutely true, HIGH is easily the most original and exciting of Thomas Hinde's novels.

FOR CHARLES HODGSON

MORRISON WAS DEAD, Peterson wrote, at work on his third novel. To his own disgusted amazement – but secret delight that he should truly be the victim of such a sick joke – Peter Morrison (revised name) was at last dead.

That was the trouble, Maurice Peterson thought, nipping his ballpoint pen with his teeth till they made tiny pits in its shiny blue plastic, furrowing his forehead in what he imagined to be a look of profound concentration but in fact suggested a sheep which has taken a greedy nibble of hay, then detected a nasty smell, watching the scene focus into detail: the tree-shaded park – Sunshine Memorial Gardens – the well spaced graves with clumps of never-fade red plastic flowers, the middle-distant grey-stone gothic chapel – plastic too? – with attached furnace chimney; and beyond the trees, out in the less trim world, the used-car lot of rusting Chevies, Dodges, Fords, piled two deep in a five-hundred-foot wall, the neon sign flashing "Small Animal Clinic"; and over and around all, tugging at their hats, blowing dirt in their eyes, the humid air from the Gulf, rushing past in a great hot gale which had already crossed Louisiana, Mississippi, Kentucky, Tennessee, Kansas, Missouri, give or take a few, in its thousand-mile flow north ... The trouble was that although Morrison (invent new name) was finally screwed into that black and silver coffin with its four grey-suited carriers, an empty unconscious corpse, his consciousness pervaded the scene.

It was *his* scene. He had given it life – in at least one sense. It *should* give him life. His dead presence at something so proper was a contradiction.

At any moment he should prise up the lid, "Hi, you've got it all fucked up. Don't you know that Englishmen are buried with their shirts and ties reversed? What sort of savages *are* you?

7

And a big bow of ribbon – purple for mourning – tied to their penises. Just where *were* you dragged up?

"To placate the spirits? What sort of Red Injuns do you think we are? Tradition, ma'am. A way of life, based on the values of an older, wiser, less guilty, more guilt infested . . ." He was right up to them now, arms waving, finger poking, bush of carrotty beard far too close for hygiene, ". . . less dramatic if more melodramatic, more dead than alive, but still heroic . . ."

But of course he'd lost them, caught up by accident in parody – Doctor Jacobstein, thirty-three-year-old, head-cropped Harvard sociologist – had anyway only phased them for a moment before they were driving him back, minds closed, purses swinging, "Now you get right down in that casket, young man," managerial, hatted women, advancing at full shout, "You forgotten where you are? This is a Home of Rest," pausing only to scream back "Well aren't you going to *do* something?" to their grey men, paralysed with anxious hate.

And back he went, a step at a time, elbows raised in mock alarm, because, not only was this the best joke, since it was against himself, but to the end he would keep them guessing, not knowing whether the knocking they would presently hear was the rattle of earth clods on the coffin lid or some obscenity he was tapping to them from inside.

Lillian Morrison must be there too, Peterson realised – and their four daughters. At once he saw her, tall and pale, hadn't recognised her because of the ugly pill-box hat some friend had lent her, saw too, that it was for her, the injured wife, that they were aligned to beat him back into that casket, to punish him, and make him recognise that he was being punished. How did they know she was injured? Of course she was. To die on her was the ultimate injury, an act easily exceeding in offensiveness wooing her, marrying her, getting her four times with child and betraying her, each of which implied a degree of consent. Doubly offensive because not only had it been done without permission but it put him beyond their punishing reach.

But while they swung forward, their voices endlessly, effortlessly clacking, creating their own hysterical farmyard in which nothing quiet or wise could survive, she hung back, tearful, he thought at first, then he believed with some secret happiness, something beyond masochism, even pride that he should have arrived at this ultimate act of male defiance, like Sampson, have

8

had the courage to bring the temple down on himself. Better than Sampson because his reward wasn't in heaven but only in that last wild laugh at their instant of panic – before they could pretend it wasn't happening.

Because Olga was dead too, he was sure of that. Dead some weeks earlier, he thought, though just how and where he wasn't certain. Much easier to believe *her* dead. For her it was the ultimate kick, to which she'd been hurrying for at least half her twenty-odd years. A picture came to Peterson, of them both, toy-sized, in a giant bath, the plug out, the whirlpool beginning. As soon as she felt it tug at her feet she breathed out and shut her eyes and let it take her with a swift, never-to-be-bettered, orgasmic wriggle. But to the last Morrison was on the surface, swimming, laughing, fighting, pretending he didn't believe it, suggesting he could drink the bath dry, still clutching at the slimy pubic hairs on the brass cross-piece as he was sucked down with the final gurgle.

And whereas Olga had disappeared without trace, he'd reappeared, like a belch of sewer gas, to offend them once more.

It was typhoon, electric-storm weather, the end of June, hard to imagine on this sunny-blue, fresh October day. At least Peterson thought it was sunny-blue, was suddenly worried that his study window, like the top quarter of his car windshield, might be blue-tinted. You lived in a blue-tinted world, cut off from cold, heat, the depressing effects of grey sky, ear-plugged with Muzak in case there was ever a second's dangerous silence . . . Home they had gone, to console stereo, English china and barbecued T-bone in the air-conditioned picnic basement, no one, not even Lillian Morrison – or his four daughters – left where that humid gale still rushed through Sunshine Memorial Gardens, pulling at the red plastic flowers, flapping and creaking across those ten acres of used cars.

Darkness came, black clouds threatened, retreated, advanced again, and Morrison lay still under the straining full-leafed trees, under four feet of the world's most fertile soil. In a night of storm, black funnel-clouds moved across the prairie, dipping to suck up a barn here, tear down a stand of trees there, moved into a trailer park wrecking thirty-nine trailers, shifting one a hundred feet before it landed on its roof and exploded, killing a seventy-nine-year-old bed-ridden widower and hospitalising his forty-three-year-old unmarried daughter. Torrential rain fell,

9

A*

the ground hissed and steamed and several dozen tons of it were washed into the nearest sewer-polluted streams. But Morrison was dead, dead, four foot down in black earth, his carrotty beard still spreading like a frothy fungus, but slowly, then more slowly.

A blue-tinted world, Peterson thought, bluer than blue on fine fall days like today, and he thought of Olga Hopping dead too, though he wasn't certain how – and he thought of her inspiration, Gilda Hearn.

Gilda was her name on the class roster, a mistake by the computer, he'd guessed, because when he'd read the roll she'd called out "Jill". And that was how she'd signed herself on the questionnaire he'd given them that first day of class, the questionnaire on which, in answer to the last question, "Why did you sign for this course?" Miss Sherry Steiner had written, "Because in my courses so far I have not been exposed to much modern comparative literature and I reckoned this would be a fine opportunity to widen my knowledge in regard to this field." And on which she had written, "Because I like novels and I like Englishmen. Jill Hearn."

And in the after-class confusion round his desk – the add-slips to sign, Miss Sherry Steiner's three problems to evade – firstly, could she discuss with him a paper she'd written last semester on Northrop Frye's *Anatomy of Criticism*; secondly, just *where* in the Humanities Building was his office; thirdly, was he going to insist on typewritten papers, like he'd said, because this semester she had such a heavy load she reckoned she just wasn't going to make it – Gilda, or Jill, Hearn had passed behind the crush – though he hadn't known her then, seen only a wide-faced, short-haired girl with big round eyes – "Say, haven't I read something you've written?"

"I doubt it."

"You *have* written something?"

"Could be." But he'd disliked his own coyness. "Two novels, to be exact. You can't buy them in the States."

"Oh novels," she'd said, as if disappointed at such an obvious vote-catcher.

But from the classroom doorway she'd called, "Do you lend them?"

"I might."

"I *might* see you then," she'd called. And before he could

answer she'd gone down the stairs of the Schmitt Chemical Building with that bouncy walk he'd come to know so well.

He'd been left with an astonished chuckle inside himself – but an odd warmth too – glanced for someone to grin with and found only Miss Steiner. "About the way you were knocking archetypal criticism, Professor Peterson . . ."

Peterson left his notebook and stood at his study window. One of the few days in the year when you weren't forced to keep it shut against the icy winter winds which scoured the prairies, or the hot-house gusts of summer. He opened it and heard more clearly the Saturday-morning buzzing of rotary mowers from a dozen neat lawns on this and the neighbouring blocks. And saw more clearly against the cloudless blue sky, the oranger than orange leaves on the fall trees, a cardinal bird more scarlet than any natural bird on the top branch of his neighbour's maple. And smelt burning leaves, the smell of English autumns in London squares, with nanny, with mummy, with the poems of Shelley, and later still with Nancy. But the smoke somehow smelt wrong. Perhaps at forty his sense of smell was already decaying, or perhaps they pre-mixed the leaves with deodorant. The senses were censored here. Seeing : safe enough to be grotesquely exaggerated. Hearing and tasting : limited to the bland. Touching and smelling : dirty. It was a film cartoon world of bright vulgar shapes which couldn't hurt or touch you. Peterson left his window and came out of his study on to the brown upstairs landing of his brown rented house.

But now there was silence, not a hint downstairs of the sounds he'd heard of his three daughters working each other into hysterics . . . A week later the same round-faced girl had bounced into his office, sat on his visitor's chair, stretched out her legs, knees apart, hands in the lap of her orange-striped tent-dress. "I have a problem." She wore a thin wedding ring on her right hand.

"Haven't we all?"

"Hey, that's right. But you might be able to solve mine. By the way, I'm Jill Hearn."

"Hallo."

"It's about this Joyce paper I have. Compare *Ulysses*, Picasso's *Guernica*, and some junk by Bartok."

"Sounds like quite a course."

"Right, right. Seven students and three professors. You never

11

heard such bull. But kinda interesting bull. Hey, I suppose I shouldn't be talking like this." She stared at him with her big round eyes. "How do you like it here? Say, you *are* English?" as if she'd suddenly had an alarming doubt.

He laughed loudly.

"Well? You must have an opinion."

Accidentally, he seemed to have worried her. "I've lots of them. How do *you* like it?"

"Seems okay," she said. "I've only been here two weeks. About this paper. I reckon I have a line."

"You have?"

"On Picasso. And it should be easy to work in Bartok – I gotta listen to that. But I'm really light on *Ulysses*. Could you suggest a short critical summary?"

Peterson thought about it, relieved to retreat from the surprising intimacy into which she seemed to have rushed him, but disappointed that she now seemed to become less interested.

"You could begin by reading the book."

"You're kidding!" she said, leaving him uncertain whether this suggestion was absurdly obvious, or just absurd.

As he made other careful suggestions he found himself staring at her plump tan knees, which had come loose from her orange-striped dress. She'd begun to tip her chair, bending and straightening them, so that they developed a series of soft dimples. He noticed, too, her stubby tan feet in sandals which flapped at the back, but it was her knees which fascinated him and the strange way that, by continuously softly dimpling and filling, they suggested a movie he'd once seen of ant-lion sand traps. Presently he so lost the drift of what he was saying that he came to a complete halt. At this moment he found himself staring into her eyes and got the odd idea that they both knew what had happened. Perhaps this was why they gave each other big but slightly surprised grins. It seemed to bring them to an unspoken understanding that he needn't try to remember what he'd been saying about *Ulysses*.

"Say, you lending me your novel?" she said.

"When you're sure you won't be dropping my course, so I'll be sure I get it back."

"Oh I shan't drop *your* course," she said. "Can't afford to. I've dropped two already. Microbiology. Me! And Dance Three-One-Five! Can you beat it! So you do have a copy?"

12

With an unwillingness which wasn't entirely affected, he took his last but one copy of *Two, Four, Six, Heave* from a drawer and put it on his desk. It had been written eight years ago and he genuinely believed he wasn't proud of it.

She skimmed the blurb and the biographical note, holding it close to her face, so that he guessed she normally used glasses. "Oh, you're happily married?"

"If it says so."

"With one daughter?"

"That's out of date."

"Looks kinda interesting." She closed it, held it against her shoulder and stood.

He put out his hand for it.

"You don't honestly think you're getting *that* back?" she said, holding it tightly to her, grinning at him, but not moving away as if leaving herself the chance to turn what she was doing into a joke.

But now he shrugged, and after a second she went bouncing and flapping away from him. "You're a sport," she said, glancing back when she was half across the office. "I won't lose it," she said, turning fully round and backing through the doorway. "Thanks for the advice," she called, already beyond the landing corner but bending into sight, so that her head, shoulders and chest with his clasped novel, appeared three feet from the ground and almost parallel to it.

A second later she must have lost her balance, because she came staggering back several paces into view, still bent parallel to the ground. "Well, stuff me," she said, recovered, grinned, waved, and went finally out of sight. From the receding flapping and louder slaps of her sandals he knew that she was sometimes jumping several steps at a time as she ran whistling downstairs.

"Wow," Peterson had said, tipping his chair and giving several amazed laughs, then sitting completely still and thoughtful . . .

Not a sound below him, except the occasional hiss of water in the sink. What were they all doing down there behind the kitchen door? Had they heard him come out here on to the landing and were listening for what he would do next? There was a simple answer to that. Softly he went back into his study, closed the door and sat at his desk, leaving himself, as far as they knew, still poised threateningly out there above them . . .

Just a month ago, that had happened. All the way across

13

the sun-browned lawns of campus, all down the sidewalks of seven bosky suburban blocks, he'd chuckled at the visit of Jill Hearn, remembering details to tell Nancy. Two minutes from home he'd begun to think of her soft dimpled knees and rather weighty tan thighs going up inside that orange-striped tent-dress, which left them so much freedom to rub softly against each other. One minute from home he'd thought he might postpone telling Nancy about Jill Hearn, at least till a suitable moment came . . .

A noise for certain now, an astonishing outbreak of laughter, as if they must be swaying about, tears running down their faces, not knowing what to do to escape from this laughter which threatened to leave them spread out and gasping about the tables and benches. Incredible – till he understood : so they'd known he'd been standing out there on the landing, listening stupidly to their silence which he couldn't understand. They'd been holding back their giggles till they couldn't hold them any longer.

This time he'd outwit them, not come down, as they secretly hoped. He reopened his notebook. She was dead too, he read. Easier to believe about Olga Hopping. She had no twenty-years-on. Five, perhaps ten, but there wasn't a picture for anything later. It was as if she'd intentionally left herself no choice . . . already he was pleased by his strong concentration.

But now, as he failed to find new words to write, the fact that his attention had been distracted to think smugly about his strong concentration became just as irritating as their giggling. How could they do such a thing to him! Didn't they know he was writing . . . ! A new burst, just when he'd thought they'd stopped, ending in a shrill squeal : "No, no, NO." Out through his study door he came, picturing Jennifer bending away on the bench, both hands raised to protect her head, Carol kneeling above, both fists raised to pound her. Down his broad stairs he hurried, three at a time, but slowing. Speak to them firmly but gently, to show how they'd failed to anger him.

Determined but calm, he'd reached the last flight when he heard their loud hiss, "Quick"—rushed the final steps, stood in the kitchen doorway, watching them where they stood clustered at the door to the yard, caught before they could escape.

Jenny and Carol he accepted. But Myrtle too, his youngest, half their height, almost a baby, so that her balance when she ran still seemed unsure, looking up at them, then back at him, as if uncertain whether she should have been carried with them in their sudden rush, then at Nancy. Nancy was at the sink. She didn't turn or give any sign that she'd heard a thing.

"Jenny, didn't you know I was working?" His own voice calmed and pleased him. "You must be quiet when I'm working."

There they stood, only a quarter facing him, short dark girls with straight dark hair cut off at mid-ear length – Nancy's children. He was dark, too, but tall and thin. His face, wide at the top with high cheekbones, but frail and narrow at the jaw, giving him his pensive-sheep look, showed no connection with their small round faces. They had short legs, short arms, and often seemed to him like rubber children, undamageable.

"There aren't many rules, but what there are . . ." his fair and reasonable tone.

"It wasn't me, it was Carol. Why do you always pick on me?"

"Jenny, you happen to be the eldest."

"It *was* you."

"It wasn't."

"It was."

"You horrid pig."

"Pig pig yourself."

"Shut up, do you hear," he screamed at them.

But he was too late. Already their own shouting had brought back their hysterical giggles and they were going in a squealing rush, out through the door, Myrtle trailing, into the yard. "Look out, he's coming," from Carol, and "Temper, temper," from Jenny when she could pretend to believe she was too far away to be heard. A gentle fall breeze closed the yard door.

Nancy was drying her hands. Then she was coming past him, through the doorway he was half blocking, not looking at him. As she passed she said, "Didn't you know, your father's working!"

He was left alone in the empty kitchen. Success. A silent house. He went slowly upstairs. Her sarcasm amazed him. What had he done that was unreasonable?

He sat at his desk. The continuous snarling chatter of his neighbours' lawn mowers swelled and receded through his open study window, bringing with it occasional breaths of exhaust gas. But now there were other sounds out there. "You did. I

15

didn't. You did. I didn't. Can't catch *me*, can't catch *me*. Stop it Jenny. Jenny, stop it. STOP IT. I'll scream." He slammed the window shut.

Nancy managed them differently. Sometimes she'd chase them out of the house, poking at them with the handle of a broom, but till then she'd give no sign that she'd even heard them. There was no building of exasperation. No tongue clicking and failing of self-control. With Nancy it was nothing – followed by the broom handle. As a result even the broom handle wasn't too serious, more a charade in which they were all taking part, leaving only a charade resentment . . .

A week later she'd brought back his novel, *Two, Four, Six, Heave*. It certainly made him shudder.

"Hi, thanks," she said, and dumped it on his desk. She stood watching him. It was another hot late-summer day, but he was surprised to see that she wore no shoes. He noticed again her short wide feet, and saw now that they were narrower at the heel – duck-shaped.

"You're certainly an improvement on Joyce," she said.

"Thanks."

Her duck-shaped feet had grey stains round the toes from the day's sidewalks. She was wearing a white sweater which fitted tightly over large breasts – or padding, how could he tell?

"Did that really all happen to you?" she said.

"There's an answer to that but it's complicated."

The novel, his second, had been about the troubles of a sensitive young man during his National Service. Unlike his first novel – about a sensitive young man's troubles at his Public School, and much praised – this second had been reviewed less widely and with less enthusiasm. Her white sweater had no sleeves and showed the full length of her bare arms, and her bare tan shoulders, which were round and soft.

"How's the multi-media paper?"

"Oh that!" she said, as if it was too long ago to remember – or now too overdue to think about. Her short brown hair made a fringe close above her eyes and she stared at him from under this, as if trying to judge something about him – as if there was something else she'd talk about if he'd give her the right cue.

"See you then," she'd said, and gone round the bend on the landing with a wave, her bare feet this time making no retreating jumps down the stairs.

16

On his twenty-minute walk that evening between the neo-Georgian halls of campus, along the streets of white clapboard suburban houses among their maples and cypresses, he'd sometimes thought about Jill Hearn's soft brown shoulders and her big brown eyes under those brown bangs. But he'd thought more about his next day's class on *Saturday Night and Sunday Morning*.

Three mornings a week, for four weeks now, he'd seen her in class, though seen was almost the wrong word. Often the whole fifty minutes would pass with him only aware of her from the cloud of smoke which rose continuously from her front row desk. She'd never asked his permission to smoke. He always gave it – the rule was absurd – but he was surprised she hadn't asked.

When he did make himself look at her, she'd be lying back in her chair, wearing blue jeans, watching him through big dark-framed glasses. She never took notes and often didn't have the text. Sitting silently watching him like this, she seemed different from the bouncy girl who'd come to his office, but it was a difference he couldn't define.

Last Wednesday, for the first time, she'd cut class.

"Nice to have you back," he'd said to her, as she'd come hurrying in on Friday.

"Sorry about that," she'd said.

"Work trouble?"

"Well hell, nine o'clock," she'd said, and put on her big glasses and sat staring up at him, straightfaced, then grinning, then not. "Some people don't know when they're lucky," she'd said, quickly and not too loudly, so that he wasn't certain he'd heard.

Peterson pulled his chair to his desk, opened his notebook and began to pit the shiny blue rear of his ballpoint pen with his front teeth. After five minutes, slowly at first, then with increasing speed and carelessness, he began to write:

Silence in the dark house. But a silence alive, vibrating.

He was a caged animal. At any moment they expected some wild shrieking or chattering to begin up there. Or just a great roar as he strode about, rattling the bars, pretending to believe he was caged – then, bored with this act, burst on to the landing

17

at full shout. But he didn't come, just sat there, keeping them deliciously shivering, and knowing it. Morrison was at work.

His desk, deeply piled with papers, books, typescripts, coffee cups, descended in the shape of a crater to a central hollow, but even here was several layers deep. In this central hollow lay the only unused sheets – Morrison kneed himself away from them, tilted his swivel chair and sat with both shoes on the desk edge, gripping his carrotty beard on either side, tugging till it hurt. He'd had an idea.

It began with a book he'd once reviewed, published with a neat rectangular hole penetrating page 251 and the seven below, so disclosing several lines of page 267. A green hand-out from the author had explained that this was to enable readers to get a partial preview of a certain coming event. It had maddened him. What could he ever invent which would compete with that for self-conscious idiocy?

Now he thought of a book not merely with one hole but dozens, so that every page was more or less perforated, so that often you were turning a page with only one line – or none! So that you really did become confused, reading backwards and forwards, and there really was no present. For sixty seconds the idea wildly excited him. He gripped the chair arms, sat staring ahead with wide eyes – at the landlord's painting of a wispy nude changing her nylons, which he'd named The Crotch. His excitement decreased. The work it would need. A good insult must be casual, as if you couldn't care less whether or not it insulted. He thought with hatred of that group of metropolitan bugger-boys who believed they arbitrated taste. He opened his mouth and let escape a loud noise, "Nyaaa," half snarl, half jeer, as if he'd suddenly sighted them up in some mid-distant opera box. "NYAAA," he yelled, and sat listening to the echoes descending through the stone arches and iron grilles of his rented, mock-Spanish house.

In the kitchen his four daughters looked up quickly with alarm and delight, and his wife, Lillian, unloading the dishwasher, lifted her head to listen anxiously. Tall, with blue eyes and long fair hair, they were all Lillian's children.

Presently Kathy, aged three and youngest, began to go round the kitchen cabinets, putting her head inside them and roaring, in imitation of that astonishing noise upstairs, and Lillian came after her to hush and lift her, but Winnie, aged twelve and

18

eldest, knew how wrong this was because her father would want Kathy to do it.

Lillian Morrison, lifting Kathy, her youngest daughter, still softer and podgier than the others but soon to be long and thin too, reaching for a paper napkin to extract the gum someone had fed her, which she constantly expected to choke her especially when roaring, pictured her husband, crouched over his desk, crying out in some ecstacy of creation. The floor, as she often saw it through his open door – she wasn't allowed in – would be littered with scrumpled balls of paper, the waste basket overflowing with them. His beard would be near the desk, and in an odd way his left knee would be there too, as if also taking part in the creative process, jacked up by his left foot which he'd set on an open drawer. His right hand would be scribbling faster, faster, as it tried desperately to keep pace with his ideas, while his left hand, circling the knee, turned the finished sheets on to a growing heap on some peripheral plateau on papers. Lillian Morrison sighed.

Morrison, leaning back idly in his swivel chair, was surprised to see, in the opposite window of his neighbour's house, his neighbour's wife. Curlers, gripping and twisting her grey hair, encircled and dwarfed her baby-girl face. For a second they stared at each other from their seventy-two-degree incubators, across twenty-five feet of prairie air at ten below zero or roughly eighty degrees colder – it was late January, the coldest time of the year – before he put out his tongue.

For a shocked instant his neighbour's wife – married to the Chairman of the Home Economics Department – did nothing, before she whisked behind the drapes. With pleasure he remembered her, eighteen months before, leading him from window to window of her house, proving how little she could see into *his* house. "I'm just showing you so you know that even if we were nosey people there'd be just nothing we could do about it." Ever since then, each time he found her spying on him he remembered with delight, as he invented an obscene gesture, that there was just nothing she could do about it.

Each night and morning he undressed here, close to the undraped window, putting himself to some inconvenience solely for her pleasure. This idea, and his total failure to write a word all morning, now made him change into clean shirt, socks and underpants. Standing naked close to the window, a thinner and

19

less robust figure than his bushy beard suggested, he believed for a glorious moment that he was going to have a fine erection. But the thought of Mrs Grundig in her halo of curlers, and the idea that Mr Don Grundig, Chairman of Home Ec., presumably sometimes made love to her, was totally deflating. For a second he stood meditating – his long body topped by face with that sprouting beard suggesting some thin flower, a sort of orange cornflower – before he turned, parted his buttocks and farted sharply towards her, wherever she was, lurking in the shadows.

At this moment, disturbingly, the idea came to him that he wasn't a person at all, just a pose, a fantasy of someone else's – or his own – imagination. A compulsive puffed-up pretence, an inflated complex of gestures with no internal co-ordinating principle, directed entirely from outside, solely for the outside impression they'd make. He was exasperated at his own compulsively characterful behaviour . . .

Happier than he'd felt all morning, Peterson sat listening through his closed window to the pleasant purring of his neighbours' rotary mowers out in the bright fall sunshine. He stretched and wanted to go down and hug his daughters, and smile when they couldn't understand his calm warm friendliness. He wanted to find Nancy – the exciting dark girl he still sometimes found her.

Not at first. Sixteen years ago, watching her cautiously as she worked behind the counter of the provincial town library, where he'd often come as a change from the provincial university library, he'd found her thick wrists and black hair which curved inwards round her jaw suggesting a chain-mail helmet, curious but unpleasant. And thick ankles, which he'd seen whenever she'd helped him find a book – something even he had noticed that she often did. It was exactly these features which, a year later, he'd found most exciting.

It had needed a friend to bring them together.

"She's certainly got hot pants about you."

"The dark thick one. I don't even know her name."

"She knows yours."

The cinema. Dinners with wine. Parties given by her girl friends. His own even quieter parties for his colleagues and more mature students. After six months – to his retrospective astonishment that he must have been less naïve then than he now be-

20

lieved – they had even slept together several times before they were married. Then her soft ankles, then her strong but soft oval face on the pillow, her black hair lying around it ... A curious knocking below him in the house – some repair she was botching to punish him for not doing it – but even then he doubted whether she'd have gone to bed with him at eleven on a week-day morning.

Twelve hours later, the house dark, his daughters asleep, he knew she was willing the moment he pushed the bathroom door and saw her reflected in the big mirror, right hand holding up the front of her nightdress, left hand poking to fit her apparatus. A second when he might have stepped back, apologising, but tonight some sense that too much of his life he was apologising – however correctly – kept him there, staring at her short olive-skinned arms, the imprint in her big upper thigh of a stocking suspender.

"I happen to be using the bathroom," she said, reaching to the faucet to rinse the fingers she'd been poking with.

He could think of no answer.

'Deaf?' she said, passing him in a swirl of white nightdress, leaving his nose full of a strong and rather rank scent he'd given her last Christmas. He stood at the basin, cleaning his teeth, gargling and rinsing.

There she lay, propped on soft pillows, among nylon frills, a baby blue ribbon at the neck of her nightdress. As he came into the bedroom she half lowered the *Saturday Evening Post* she'd been supporting with her pretty olive arms, half turned her head and smiled at him. A smile which implied, we know I was joking.

Looking at her, propped there so soft and olive-skinned, her black hair which she still cut in that chain-mail shape, her wide neck and big soft wrists, he felt his stomach sink and open as he gave way to his longing for her. A second later he remembered how these parts of her had repelled him in the bathroom. He was amazed to find that he could alternate these feelings about every five seconds.

He switched off the light and made love to her. As he lay on her in the dark, their bellies sweating softly against each other, he had the strange fancy that she had become even broader and more spread out on the bed, her hips about four feet apart. Now he really wanted her, really loved her. Oh Nan,

21

Nan, he wanted to say. But tonight he made no sound, even when he came.

He lay still beside her, one arm across her chest. During the action he'd not only loved her but felt a great re-growth of confidence. This was something she needed and he could give her. Temporary, it might be, this break in her scorn for him, but real. For five minutes, one minute, he was shocking her out of it, giving her enjoyment, making her love him, forcing her to shut off her mind and go into some region of intuitive pleasure, undamaged by fear or disappointment – Why, then did she continually give little peevish grunts of complaint, which he heard more clearly tonight in his own silence, as if he was all the time clumsily hurting her.

Lying turned away from her in the quiet night, occasional police sirens wailing down distant streets, he thought of a resolution. Not one he could tell anyone. Not one he was even sure he meant to keep. An experimental resolution, to see how long it would last, and how soon she'd notice.

She began to snore. He snored, too, she told him. When he bumped her with his arse to wake her accidentally, or, this failing, poked cautiously with his knuckle at her kidneys, she'd say with no hesitation the moment she woke, "So were you." Repetition had made him believe it, so that in a few moments from now he imagined their two sheet-covered shapes, lying side by side in the black room, rasping away together, out of time and tune.

If only it wasn't a resolution he was nearly sure he'd made before.

Why had she ever wanted him, Peterson was wondering again, two days later, at four in the afternoon as he waited in his office for Miss Sherry Steiner to discuss her last semester's term paper on Northrop Frye.

Because, want him he was sure she had, and obtained him, with the clear-headed persistence he now knew well. Probably the difficulty of getting him had provoked her. But his published novel had been important. She'd believed in books – it was why she'd become a librarian; and why she'd despised her colleagues who treated them as disposable stock, and laughed at her for reading them. He'd been someone who not only cared about the inside of books, but had already written one. These were logical

22

explanations, but they never seemed the whole truth, had too little connection with the way, for many years now, almost everything she'd said or done had seemed to imply that he'd deceived her.

Especially in front of their children. "Your father wouldn't do a thing like *that*," she'd say, with sarcasm, knowing that he'd never quarrel with her where they could hear. And when they were alone and he'd answer her reasonably, she'd laugh as if it increased her irritation that he should be so good-tempered.

Miss Steiner arrived at the same time as another boy.

"I'm Ric," the boy said, coming forward, in front of Miss Steiner, holding out his hand. "Hi there. You *are* Professor Maurice Peterson?"

"That's right."

"Good, good. I have some questions for you."

"Unfortunately I've an appointment. Could you come back in half an hour?"

"Yeah, yeah," the boy said, but it checked him. "Yeah, I reckon I'll come back." For a second Peterson thought this answer offensively bitter, but it was too improbable.

Exactly half an hour later he came back.

"When you're sure it's a tragedy in the low mimetic mode," Peterson was saying, "how will this help you to enjoy the book? Or find its connection with life, with *your* life?"

"Isn't the point," said Miss Steiner, who wore her hair in a big black bun, held together by a vast tortoiseshell clasp, "that criticism needs a new methodology?"

"Don't quote at me," Peterson said, his voice rising to an unfortunate squeak in his exasperation. "Do you *believe* that?" He glanced quickly at Ric to show he'd noticed him, though it would have been difficult not to. Instead of waiting tactfully beyond the corner on the landing, occasionally showing an arm or a shoulder, he was standing in the centre of the doorway, watching and listening with a steady tolerant sneer. "I'm afraid we must stop now."

"So you're a writer," Ric said. He sat on the chair Miss Steiner had left – though not before making a new appointment – leaning forward, elbows on his knees, so that when he looked Peterson in the eyes – as he did occasionally, with a threatening intensity – he had to cock his neck sideways in a bird-like way. In other ways – his bald forehead, bent nose and general jerki-

23

ness – he suggested a bird, perhaps a young but already tatty jackdaw. Most of the time he stared at Peterson's shoes.

"That's right."

"So am I," Ric said.

When he could think of nothing better Peterson said, "Oh fine."

"It sure is good to meet a genuine person among this bunch of layabouts," Ric said.

"Are they?"

"Oh come off it," Ric said. "You been here over a year and not found that out? Don't give me that crap."

"Some of them, maybe."

Ric didn't answer, but stared threateningly.

"You *are* genuine, aren't you?" Ric said. "Maurice? May I call you Maurice? By the way, I'm Richard Schuster," he said, bitter again about something Peterson couldn't guess. "Forget that. Ric's good enough. Funny, the moment I saw you I knew you were the sort of guy I could call Maurice."

"Makes no difference to me," Peterson said, and felt that he'd just passed – but only just – some test. Ric stood and held out his hand which, in a reflex way, Peterson shook.

"Hi, Maurice," Ric said.

"Hallo, Ric," Peterson said, blushing and breaking into a hot sweat.

"Look, Maurice," Ric said, down on the chair again, elbows on his knees. "I'd like you to help me with my work. I'm a poet mainly. Have been for five years. I'd like to get back to some prose. Short stories and things. I've got a novel too – I'll be starting on that soon. You see, Maurice, I've been married. And divorced. But you don't want to hear about my troubles." He stood again, holding out his hand. "Thanks, Maurice. Be seeing you." He raised his eyebrows, winked, grinned, no need for words among such old friends, and was gone across the landing.

Again, as Peterson crossed campus on his way home, he wanted, then didn't want, to tell Nancy. Presently he saw that the reason might be similar because there had been something similar about Ric Schuster's visit and that first visit of Jill Hearn's. Both had left him feeling that by behaving slightly differently he could have kept his distance, but that he was glad he hadn't. He doubted whether he could explain this to Nancy. Both had given him the ill-defined sense that he had been

24

hustled, but that now this had happened he wasn't going to pretend it hadn't. It was alarming, but also relaxing, as if he'd swallowed something – indeed opened his mouth wide and gulped it – and there was now nothing to do but wait for its effect.

The poems were on his desk next morning, seventeen typed, and two in thick loopy handwriting. They were on several different sizes of paper and looked much handled, perhaps because they were the only copies.

At four that afternoon, as he reached his desk for his office hour, Ric was standing in the doorway. He was there so quickly, while Peterson's back was still turned, that it was as if he'd been lurking in some closet.

"You get them?"

"The poems? Yes."

"You like them?"

"Well I've only glanced at them," Peterson said – the truth, though with luck it would imply a complete first reading. "Could you leave them with me a couple of days?"

"Yeah yeah, that's okay," Ric said. "I know how it is."

"Today's my teaching day, but tomorrow I promise . . ."

"Yeah yeah, okay," Ric said, watching him steadily, his disappointment more and more obvious. "Say, Maurice, do you ever think about dying?"

"Well not right now," Peterson said, pleased with the clever way he'd turned that one.

Ric stared steadily at him, not the hint of a grin at this weak joke. Presently he sauntered to the visitor's chair and sat absentmindedly, his whole attention on their mutual dialectic.

"I do. All the time. Especially after screwing."

"Hence the Elizabethan double meaning," Peterson said.

Ric Schuster, who had begun to watch Peterson's shoes, looked up as if he didn't understand – or indeed understand why Peterson had spoken at all. "And let me tell you, I can get plenty of that," he said. "All the tail I can take, and more. But that's not what I'm after. Is that what you're after, Maurice? Eh Maurice?"

Peterson laughed and mumbled that there were times.

"Oh shit, times," Ric said. His hair was cut in short bristles and because of the way he sat, Peterson was often looking directly down on it. He realised that since yesterday he'd had the impression that somewhere among its front bristles there was a big

25

scar, but, looking for it now, he couldn't see it. "Bloody chicks," Ric said. "Hell, Maurice, I sure like discussing things with you. You're one of the few real good guys around this dump. You know that?"

Peterson made self-deprecating noises as Ric stood and left abruptly.

His office was connected by an internal door to the next office which was shared by Jo, a mediaevalist, and his wife, Marge, who taught hundred-level Art Appreciation courses. Neither of them ever shut the door so it was often possible to listen to them giving conferences to their students, or to guess that *they* were listening to his conferences. Now he went through this door and found them both there, correcting quizzes.

"Do you know that boy?" he asked.

"The one you just had in?"

"That's right. Ric Schuster."

They both looked up from their papers, shaking their heads. "He's amazing."

A third colleague, Bill, who taught the Modern Short Story, came through an open door from his office beyond. "Richard Schuster, did you say?"

"That's right."

"So he's found you?"

"Seems like it. Who is he?"

"Who's Richard Schuster?" Bill said, grinning with anticipation, as if he didn't know where to begin. Jo and his wife now watched and waited too. Turning to them, Bill said, "Who's Richard Schuster, eh Jo? Don't tell me you've forgotten Ric Schuster."

"Oh Richard *Schuster*!" Jo said.

All three of them now stared at him with bright-eyed enjoyment.

"Well who is he then?"

"Who *is* he?" they repeated.

"I guess he's just indescribable."

"You'll find out."

"Oh you'll find out all right."

"We've known Richard Schuster for a long time, haven't we, Jo?"

They wouldn't say more and presently Peterson smiled and went back to his office, closing the door.

26

Late the following night he read the poems. "Oh christ," he said aloud several times, holding his head and pulling painfully at his hair. "Where do we go from here?" he said as he finished them for the second time.

They were in free verse, of course. When he tried substituting different words, or breaking the lines in different places the effects seemed no different. He hunted for a single poem or stanza, or line or image to pick out for approval, but the idea that by praise he would produce repetition or magnification of any of them was daunting.

This one, for instance, in which the persona had been killed in an auto-accident and his short dark-haired girl passed by and waved and didn't notice he'd been squashed.

Or this one, about the persona as a piece of furniture, probably a bed, on which his short dark-haired girl was making out with another man.

"I like the second one," Peterson said, the following afternoon. "About the auto-accident and the girl."

" 'Green Eyed, She Passes By' " Ric said, correcting him for forgetting its title, and waited.

"I like its ironic tone. Nothing till we reach 'tomato pulpy red he lay' to suggest that this isn't just a normal meeting in the street between a girl and her boy."

"Ahha," Ric said and waited.

When he could think of nothing more, Peterson fumbled through the sheets. "I like 'Oh God Protect Her'. That's a nice idea." At once he imagined more and more nice ideas, persona as tables, chairs, dish-washers.

"Ahha," Ric said. He was like a dog asking for food. Throw him a lump of meat and he swallowed it at a gulp and stood perfectly still waiting for the next. The perfect stillness was to leave no hint that it had happened, and the single gulp to show its total inadequacy.

" 'White Dress Crabwise' . . ." Peterson began.

"What about the last ones?" Ric said, too impatient to wait any longer – getting his nose hungrily on to the table. "They're the two that really send me."

"There's a slight legibility problem," Peterson began.

"Show me."

He turned the sheets, ignoring Ric's hand reaching for them.

27

"Here, you want me to read 'em to you?"

"I think I can manage." He glanced at the half open door to Jo and Marge's office, and moved the sheets absentmindedly off the desk on to his knee, tilting back his chair.

But not far enough because Ric came after them, shifting his chair beneath him with one hand, getting a grip on them with the other. "Le'me read them to you."

For several seconds they stayed like this, Peterson occasionally muttering, "Where was it now?", Ric giving the sheets a succession of jerks, "Hey, le'me. Here, gi'me," till – affecting surprise to see that someone else had hold of them – Peterson moved them back on to his desk, looked up at Ric with frankness and concern and said, "Anyway, what's more important is that they worried me in another way. In several places I couldn't see what difference other phrases would have made, or other line divisions . . ."

Without a word, Ric moved his chair alongside Peterson at his desk.

"For instance . . ." Peterson gave examples.

Without a word Ric used a thick pencil to change what he'd written to the arbitrary alternatives Peterson suggested. "That better? You like it now?"

"I think so, but I picked those more as examples . . ."

"You think it all needs changing?"

"Well, not all . . ."

After half an hour Ric left. He paused in the doorway and gave a big rueful grin. "Try again," he said.

"Oh, it isn't like that," Peterson began, but Ric only grinned some more, the artist who knew that initial failure was his lot – though making a small reservation that a more perceptive critic might have discovered genius.

Jo and Marge went home, the office janitor pushed a trolley of cleaning equipment in at one door and out at the other, pausing to make a few broom strokes and tell him about his son's high school grades, then silence settled on the building except for the violent electrical clanging of the fifty-minute and hourly class bells. Did they ring all night, he wondered. They certainly did all day at the week-end. He pulled a wad of examination paper to the centre of his desk – "The giving or receiving of assistance during a Final Examination is a cause for summary dismissal from the university" – and began to write.

28

"That's quite a book," Olga Hopping said. She sat in the visitor's chair beside Morrison's desk, sometimes stretching her bare brown legs and bare dirty feet towards the room centre, showing him her fat brown knees and about eight inches of soft brown thigh, sometimes lifting her knees to her chest and hugging them, her head laid sideways on them, ogling him with big brown eyes.

On the desk between them was *The Joke Book*, Morrison's only published novel – if you could call it that – which, a year ago at thirty-five, after ten years bumming his talent round the world of London literary journalism, had earned him this cosy job in a new world. The reviewers had raved. He lifted the book and began to read in camp intonations from the back of the second imprint's dustjacket. "The joke is on Mr Morrison, because he has accidentally – or could it just possibly be by intention – written a novel which is no joke, but a provocative, disturbing, even moving, and above all serious comment on the contemporary human situation."

Morrison stopped and stared gloomily at the author's photo, with bristling beard and panama hat. "They're unbeatable," he said. "The only thing they wouldn't take seriously was the photo, and that's genuine. The sun – lack of protective pigment," he explained vaguely.

"And *did* Mr Morrison want to be taken seriously?" Olga asked, tilting her head even further, opening her big brown eyes still wider.

Morrison stared back, flicking his carrotty eyebrows and narrowing his eyes in a meaningful way, without much idea what he meant.

"Born in Battersea," Olga quoted. "Where's that?"

"South London. A little village . . ."

"Hey, how cute! Son of a CSM. What in hell?"

"Company Sergeant Major . . ." Morrison began, but there seemed no possible explanation. "Soldier. Special sort of soldier. Slope arms. Form fours," he said at random.

"Hey, how romantic."

"Accident of his old age."

"You don't say!"

Morrison glanced sharply at Olga Hopping, surprised by the idea that she might be laughing at him, but saw only her big

29

brown eyes, cocked sideways on those plump knees she was hugging, as she thought of her next innocent question.

Beyond the bend of the corridor, down a hundred feet of passage walled in oatmeal marble and floored with yellow plastic tile, a violent whistling began. It grew steadily louder and more obviously out of tune as it approached and he recognised the university football hymn, whistled with raucous irony.

As soon as the student came into sight he stopped whistling with a jerk of mock surprise to find himself so close to a member of the faculty, then strode on into Morrison's office, holding out his hand.

"Hi. You're Professor Morrison. I'm Butch. Maybe you don't know me. I'm just a card in an IBM machine. Look." He bent to drag from inside several furry windcheaters the left breast of a black T-shirt, pinned with a scarlet button : "Do not fold, bend, staple or mutiliate, this is a student."

"Too bad," Morrison said. "Can I help you?"

"Can you *help* me?" Butch said, as if it was some profound but not original question, like, what is the truth? "You're a writer, aren't you. Let's say I've come to *help you* with your writing. Would that make sense?"

"It certainly would," Morrison said, "so what I suggest is you fuck off, because I'm busy."

"If that's the way you see it . . ."

"That's the way I see it."

Peterson re-read this several times but nothing more happened. How could it? He stared out of his office window at the red glow in the sky beyond the university power station, where the sun was setting a hundred miles away across the prairie. "The sunsets are marvellous," was one of his answers when asked how he liked this place. And they were – though it was too early for the really marvellous sunsets of winter, icy still and clear, the sky lit up with a faraway black-red glow, the sun going down behind frozen, motionless trees – the local problem, of course, was to find the trees.

"Your supper's in the oven," Carol called downstairs as he shut his front door. "Mummy says it's probably spoiled. There's a message by the phone."

In the kitchen he ate the dry steak and peas – on which a metal cover had dripped condensed steam. Upstairs in one of the

30

bedrooms they were playing a game and there were bursts of high giggles. Though he didn't once hear Nancy's voice, he knew she was there. At home, without him, they were happy, spontaneous, gay. He knew that their gayness was spontaneous and that he was wrong to suspect that she had organised whatever they were doing up there as a demonstration. He read the message. "Please call Mr Richard Schuster. Urgent."

Using the downstairs phone, he called.

"Hi, Maurice," Ric said with loud sardonic cheeriness.

"Hallo."

"What cooks in that house of creation, eh? What's brewing in that old creative mind?"

It sounded offensive, but Peterson had already begun to trust the boy's liking for him and fit generous explanations to his rudeness. There was music in the background. Perhaps he was drunk.

"Did you want me?"

"Yeah, maybe we could get together sometime," Ric said, with heavy irony. "Fix an appointment. Any day'll do."

"Ric, why not drop round for a beer?"

"What, *now*?" Ric said, still sarcastic, but less certain.

"That's right."

"Maurice, I'd certainly appreciate that," Ric said, sincere and grateful. "See you then." He rang off.

Peterson brought beer from the icebox into his brown sitting room. Ric ripped the opening tab, raised his can with a wry smile, drank and sat, dramatically silent, staring at the carpet between his knees.

"I'm sorry I sounded discouraging about your poems," Peterson began, "because the point is . . ."

"Maurice," Ric interrupted, "we gotta be honest. Isn't that right? We all gotta try to be a little honest. I like you because you *try*. You really try."

"The point is, I believe . . ."

"Yeah yeah," Ric said. Clearly tonight the whole subject of his poems was an interruption.

When enough time had passed, Ric said, starting the scene properly again, "Maurice, I'm in bad trouble."

"What trouble's that, Ric?"

"I'm going to be thrown out of school."

As often in this country where he understood so little, Peterson

31

didn't laugh but suspended judgement. Anyway, his sympathy with whoever he was talking to, which sometimes seemed a gift and sometimes a pathological reflex, would have stopped him laughing as he watched Ric staring with gloomy drama towards a fifty-year-old colonial-antique wooden coal bucket.

"What's your subject?"

"Communications," Ric said, as if astonished that Peterson didn't know. " 'Narcissism in the Later Fellini', that's my dissertation," he said, bitterly, but perhaps with just a hint that he would have liked Peterson to cry out in admiration. Anyway, it was another interruption.

"I've got this chick," he began presently. And seemed not to know how to go on. "Judy. Hey, you must meet Judy, Maurice. I'd really like to get you and Judy together."

At this moment Nancy opened the door. She stood there, too much in shadow for Peterson to see her expression or even her exact attitude, then re-shut it and he heard her go with bumping feet upstairs. He was left with an impression of a grotesquely short dark figure in the doorway, and with an odd fancy – surely it was fancy – that in one hand she'd been holding a carving knife.

She'd hardly take that up to bed with her, he thought, to reassure himself, but this started still more worrying ideas. As a result he missed several of Ric's remarks, only aware of their general tone of amazement at the things which happened in this world.

"I really love that girl," he was saying. "And I have to sit and watch my goddam mother turning her into a replica of her own gross self."

"Can't you keep them apart?" Peterson said. A minute's misunderstanding followed before he realised that Ric was now talking, not about Judy his new chick, but about Susie his kid sister.

"Do you mind me telling you all this, Maurice?"

"Of course not."

"Christ, it's good to find someone you can really talk to. You know what? I get a funny feeling about you, Maurice. I think you're a damaged man too. Are you a damaged man, Maurice?"

"Aren't we all?" Peterson said, cautiously.

"I don't wanta pry, Maurice, but I get a feeling you've been

32

through something like this yourself. I see pain at the corners of your eyes – all right you don't have to tell me."

Peterson sat staring at a colonial-antique dry-sink unit, highly embarrassed, but at the same time half hoping that Ric might interpret this as a slightly damaged look, while his mind ranged over the last twenty years of his placid bourgeois life – marriage, children, house and mortgage, two novels – his mildly artistic, but hardly bohemian venture – teaching at a provincial university.

"Okay, Maurice, don't say. Where was I? Yeah, I love that girl. That's why I've been going home each week."

"Where's home?"

"Hickory Street," Ric said, to the surprise of Peterson who'd imagined a down state small town.

"Does that tear me up. I stand looking at that mound of flesh, thinking, christ, can that honestly be my mother? Well, she's teaching my kid sister to grow up just like herself. Gross in mind and body. Maurice, she's my mother and I wouldn't say these things unless I meant them. She's teaching her to despise her father, all ready so when she gets a husband she can start right in despising him without further practice. They go downtown together for no other reason than to spend his money. They come back and laugh together about how much they've spent. I've heard them. They don't need the things they buy. They do it for one goddam reason only: to humiliate him.

"So if he ever dares object, they turn on the hysterics. If there's some little thing he takes it into his head is the last straw, some little thing they not only don't need but they've actually got five or six of already, and he says 'no', my mother tell her, 'Honey, go on in and give it him'. I've heard her. And she does, too. Screams, tantrums, the lot.

"Okay, well a month ago she gets this squirrel bite. At least she thinks she does, though it needs a microscope to tell if the skin's broken. She's feeding it nuts and it nips her pinkie. You can't blame her. She thought it was a Walt Disney squirrel, fluffy and cuddlesome. All right, she's learned a lesson. Real squirrels may look fluffy but they nip. She still doesn't mind much. My mother soon puts that right. Squirrels are *unclean*. And if there's no evidence to the contrary we must assume that this one DIDN'T HAVE ITS RABIES SHOTS.

"Tears, panic, blame. 'You let the child out. You don't *love*

33

her. You don't love *me*.' What do you expect the kid to do except start howling as loud as the rest?"

Peterson listened with sympathy, and fetched more beer. When he came back Ric was moving along the bookshelves, reading the titles. His expression suggested, Just the sort of crap I'd expect, though I'm being tactful enough not to say so. Since the books were Peterson's landlord's he wasn't offended but he doubted if Ric knew this.

"So how did it end?"

"I walked out," Ric said. "Hell you didn't expect me to stay around." He seemed angry that Peterson hadn't guessed something so obvious.

"All right then," Ric said. "I meet this chick, Judy. I'm not a guy who bears a grudge. I send them a letter saying I'd much appreciate it if they'd agree to meet her. Hell, we may get married. I'm their son. So they may wanta see the girl their son's going to marry.

"That's a month ago. Not even a goddam acknowledgement. I send them a registered letter, asking if they got my previous letter. No answer. I cable them('Much appreciate reply to my communication of tenth October and my registered communication of twenty-first October'. That's the sort of language they understand. Not a fucking peep." He paused dramatically. So what d'you think's going on? Eh? They're trying to break it up."

"Why ever should they do that?" Peterson said, honestly surprised.

"*You* tell *me*. And what d'you think they're planning on doing if I go on seeing her? They're going to get me for statutory rape. That's right, she's seventeen and three-quarters. And I'm twenty-six. And we've made love. Twice," Ric said bitterly.

"You've actual evidence they're threatening to bring a case?"

"For godsake, doesn't it stand to reason?" Ric said, angry again. "What would you do in their place? Who're her bridge friends except all the shyster lawyers around town?"

Surprisingly, Peterson thought Ric might have real evidence for what he suspected, but be hiding it as a test of his belief in him.

"Certainly sounds bad."

"Bad!" Ric said, half gratified, half holding up this understatement as a quaint curiosity, in doubtful taste.

"Look, Ric, if there's anything I can do . . ."

"No no, I don't wanta involve you, Maurice," Ric said, draining his beer. "You gotta rotten enough pitch as it is." He shook his hand dramatically and in less than five seconds went out across the veranda into the dark street to rattle away on a two-stroke motor cycle.

Peterson climbed to his study, his mind occupied not with Ric Schuster's problem, but with the surprising idea that, to other people, he might seem to have a rotten pitch. Across the town in the dark night the railroad locomotives howled. Presently he began to write:

To Lillian Morrison they were the spirit of the prairie. Those long howls – which were less like warning hoots than like the straining groans of iron wheels on iron rails, as if hundreds of box cars were being pushed infinitely slowly round a vast curve – suggested to her an imprisoned spirit, the spirit of untamed America, now so thoroughly tamed. Lying on her back, long, pale and alone in the double bed, her fair hair limp on the pillow, tears came in the corners of her eyes.

Weirdest to wake and hear them at one in the morning and know that all through the night they must be a background to her dreams. Somehow they fitted what she'd been told about the uneven paving stones of the town's sidewalks, those great four-feet-square concrete slabs which were often tilted, so that their edges were inches above or below the next – making it impossible for her to wear high heels, as she'd often explained to Peter. They were being pushed up by the spirits of the murdered Indians.

Now rain came quickly, beating on the shrubs in her garden, filling the cold winter night. Through it, the railroad's howling became the foghorn of a great ship at sea, some liner in distress . . . a violent clatter and clang, ending in a heavy tumble, as of some big object falling several feet and coming apart, made her stiffen and break out in sweat. Peter in his study, a heart attack – but it had happened before.

At three, four in the morning he'd come to bed and she'd roll over and say some sleepy words, pretending she'd been asleep. How could she sleep when she was aware, through the walls, of his great irresponsible energy, shut up there? How could she want to sleep?

35

It was an accident which Peter Morrison did nothing to stop, though he plainly saw it start. The cleaning woman had got in that day. What else could he do but pace angrily about the vacuumed floor, accidentally barge a shelf of books, turn and watch them tip into space, crash to the floor, and slither with dented corners and splayed pages in three directions? The shelf, coming last, projected an end into the kneehole of his desk, and as he sat he gave several kicks to clear it from his feet which only wedged the other end under the runners of his chair.

His typewriter, he now noticed, had been placed at the centre of his desk – not just the cleaning woman but Lillian too! There it stood, fitted with a clean sheet of paper, ready for his genius! He stared at it, opening his eyes wider and wider in horror, reached quickly to flick up the rod to see if she'd actually typed "Chapter One" – fantastic enough for that – but no, just a beautiful idiotic blank sheet. A holy accusation . . . His head came up, his eyes narrowed, his gaze focussed on the distance. For sixty seconds he sat perfectly still, then squealed his tilt-chair close to his desk, the book shelf coming too among the runners.

"Dear Cuntface," he typed, to probably his closest friend – in a basement near Olympia, London. "What are you doing back there on that puritanical atoll – where every second person spends his day seeing the rest don't get tuppence they aren't entitled to?" and ran back the machine to "x" out the second half of the sentence. The longer he was away, the more a mean jealousy stood out as the national characteristic of that nation of ex-empire-builders, but put like this he detected a hint of seriousness, an influence of Germanic sociological pedantry – where could that have rubbed off? Restarting, he typed, "The most incredible thing has just happened . . ." and stopped.

For half an hour he stood in various parts of his study, pulling at his beard. He stomped downstairs to mix himself a bourbon. He stomped upstairs, and was surprised at the top to find that he was carrying a drained glass except for ice cubes. He set it in the mock Spanish recess beside the mock terracotta Don Quixote and went into the dark bedroom.

"Hallo dear," she said sleepily.

"Did you put my typewriter on my desk?"

"I may have . . ."

"With a clean sheet in it?"

"I can't remember."

Not a word he could say.

"Isn't that where it lives?"

"No it's *not* where it lives."

Now the bedside light went on and he saw her long fair arm which she'd reached from under the sheet to the switch. An erection! Immediate. Nothing he could do about it except put down a hand to adjust his pants to make it mechanically possible. That frail fair arm, with the wrist turned down, coming out of the white sheet, where he could now see her pale shoulder; her fair hair on the pillow as she turned her face away from the light – not fair but golden! The lamplight, shining through it, transformed it from its daytime mouse to a shining gold. He shrugged his shoulders, undid buckles and buttons and let his clothes fall in a heap around him. Stepping out of them, he circled the foot of the bed, switched out the light and got in beside her.

It was indecent, no other word for it. She didn't say another word, even when he dragged her sleeveless nightdress from under her arse, and heard it give a sharp rip. Not a grunt of complaint even when it somehow got stuck over her face for so long that she gasped for air when, after a ten second struggle, it came clear.

Had she no pride? He made love to her violently, entering her uncomfortably before she was ready. She kept quite still, only once stiffening with pain. It was like loving a slab of pale damp meat.

It was necrophiliac. More small gasps, not of complaint let alone pleasure, but of real pain which she couldn't hide. When his beard scraped her face she turned it sideways on the pillow to escape. He was filled with anger at the pity he felt for her. Anger that she didn't mind being pitied. He was sickened by the way this excited him.

Suddenly he knew that she'd gone away from him into some private place where he couldn't follow. She was still limp and meat-like but no longer being hurt. Nothing physical about it. Nothing to do with *him*, either. Pure spiritual masturbation. He quickened the pace, came, withdrew and switched on the light.

She turned her head away from its brightness without complaint. She lay there, eyes shut, a small happy smile on her face. After a moment she guessed he was watching her, half opened her eyes and made the smile bigger.

37

He didn't want her thanks for something he wasn't responsible for, a present she was now pretending he'd given her, but in fact she'd taken by herself. She needed him to send her into this cloud-land of hers as much as she needed a candle.

He lay there, staring with pop-eyed fury at her, (smiling with quiet happiness), mad with himself for what he'd done. That pale limp wrist, hung over the sheet top with the thin wedding ring, about which he now felt absolutely nothing. How had he ever been excited by her? How could he live with the certainty that in a couple of hours she'd excite him again?

Nic crosses quad . . . Peterson read, two days later, sitting in his office, winter closing in now, an early flurry of snow blown past his office window, though it was still two weeks to Thanksgiving. Down from Canada the icy winds came, pushing back for six months the humid gales from the Gulf, driving across the cornfield checkerboard of mid America, to reach the city of Flatville, a giant cow turd on the landscape, all breadth, no height, a concrete turd with psychedelic fringes of neon-lit gas stations, bowling alleys, drive-in hamburger joints . . . Nic crosses quad . . . Peterson came back to the typescript of Ric Schuster's first return to prose fiction after five years' voluntary absence:

It's fall, and the university band's practising. Nic once played in the band. He was seventeenth piccolo. But that's a long time ago. Nic's through with the band, has been for five years.

Just the same, he can't stop himself watching. There they go, left right left right, all one hundred and fifty of them, wheeling and marching, letting that little shit-arse on the top of his fifteen-foot ladder bawl them out.

They're good boys, the boys who play in the band. They like being bawled out. It's part of their training in citizenship. "Number one hundred twenty-two," shit-arse shouts through his megaphone, and his voice goes echoing between the buildings, tweny-two, tweny-two, tweny-two . . ." It even echoes way off campus, down Vine Avenue and Orchard Avenue and Elm Avenue, among all those crazy orange and scarlet maple leaves where Nic was born and where he can remember hearing it twenty years ago when he was a kid, and thinking it was some big-voiced monster they kept up there at the university and thinking that the one thing he, Nic, was never going to be so goddam stupid as do was let his momma and poppa send him

38

up there where that big monster lived. But Nic was a cunning young sod, even then, and he didn't tell them that was where he was never getting sent, oh no.

"Number one hundred tweny-two, just where in hell do you think you gotten to? gotten to? gotten to?" And number one hundred twenty-two's getting a real kick out of this because he believes he *deserves* to be bawled out. There's not the littlest flicker of resentment in his All-American breast. Now they've halted in formation, all facing that wooden step-ladder. The sixteen trombones are kneeling, and those great brass horns over their backs are making them look like they're sea slugs that have just come out from under their shells.

Left right, left right, off they go again, and now they're advancing right towards Nic, every instrument playing, cymbals clashing, big drum dragged on two little wheels, the drummer thumping it as he strides, the enormous brass tune filling the space between the buildings. And in front, leaning back like an acrobat, knees jumping as high as his chest, his baton still higher, comes the boy who'll be Chief on the day of the match.

"Just what toon are you playin', hundred twenty-two?" But now the music drowns him. On they come, right down the grass towards Nic, that great phallic baton jerking and jerking – they'll turn before they reach him, of course – but Nic turns away first. He's had enough of the University Football Band where some boy who had his name once played seventeenth piccolo.

Nic's going home and on his way he's going to pass The Girl. He can see her there ahead of him, with her twenty-five classmates, having her four o'clock class in golf. Nic stands by the chain-link fence and watches. The girl I love's majoring in golf, he thinks. Can you beat it! That's right, the slim one with the dark hair.

All right, she's not majoring in golf, but in recreation. All right, it's the Greek tradition. The cultivation of the whole man – or woman. Nic knows.

Look at them now. Raise the club. Strike girls, all twenty-five of you, not very straight he's sorry to see, fluttering up the field. Fluttering because they're not real balls but special lightweight plastic balls. An indecent parallel comes to Nic. Hey, maybe that's the way to keep the place sane : make all balls lightweight plastic, for practice only. Special issue . . .

"Hi, babe," Nic shouts, on inspiration. Real loud he shouts.

39

And she hears him. Oh yes, she hears him – but she wishes she hadn't.

"Hi," she calls, brave and cheery, but wishing he'd get to hell out and stop interrupting her four o'clock golf class.

"Watch out for those plastic balls," Nic bellows, and turns away leaving them all wondering whatever sort of girl could have a boy like that. The sound of little shit-arse on the ladder comes echoing across the field, "Didn't I say eighdy-eighd paces? eighd paces? eighd paces?"

Nic walks down Vine Avenue and Elm Avenue, and Orchard Avenue, under all those crazy paisley maple leaves to the house where, twenty-five years ago, his loving momma brought him into this great big loving world. Nic lurks on the sidewalk by the privet hedge. From here there are several things he can see.

He can see the metal swing in the yard where his kid sister used to swing till her mother dragged her away with some new distracting toy. She used to look nice there, just swinging away quietly by herself and smiling sometimes, till her mother saw her : "Hey, watcher doing out there swinging away all by yerself and not saying anything? It's goddam *morbid*. Come over here and look what I boughtcha and laugh and shout a bit cancha?"

And seeing that grassy back yard with the swing reminds Nic of how, another time he'd rather not remember, he and some friends had played football out there and how he'd gotten pushed into the flower bed and come inside with all that blood and dirt on his knee but not crying. And how his mother, watching his dad wash it, had said, with a catch in her big floppy throat, "Nic's all boy." And how Nic had known even then that this was said partly because she was proud of him but more to knock shit out of his dad – by comparison. And how Nic hadn't cared because what his momma had said had made him happier than he'd ever been in his whole life.

Beyond the yard, Nic sees the house. It's certainly time his parents got out of this rotten old clapboard house – which Nic can remember ever since he was a kid – and bought something in keeping with their status. But Nic isn't looking at the house. He's looking at that Buick Convertible parked by the sidewalk out front.

Now that's more like it, taken together with last year's Oldsmobile, which is still in the garage . . . Nic strolls up to the car.

40

He's leery about going too fast. And he's leery about going too slow. But most of all he's leery of what he's thinking. It's green, this Buick Convertible, and it's shiny and it's very new . . .

He's thinking of last night when he was with The Girl.

The Girl lives in a lodging house apartment with two roommates. She's too young, but the Dean of Women's given her permission because she's a special case because she's gotten a broken home – we needn't go into all that.

Her roommates are dating boys in the lodging house next door and those boys are in her apartment ALL DAY. Every single minute. Not only them but their friends too. And not only all *day*.

They're nice guys, these friends of The Girl's roommates, but last night Nic gets to asking The Girl if they can't go someplace where there aren't all these nice guys around all the time. Someplace they can be alone and have some real talk. Just for once.

"But I like them," The Girl says. "They're *my* friends too."

"Oh I *like* them," Nic says. "I like animals. But not twenty-four hours on end."

"Anyway, where?" The Girl says.

And that's a real problem, because it happens Nic hasn't got an apartment. He's given up his. It's cheaper that way. Sometimes he sleeps in a coalhole. Though there isn't any coal there now, thanks to the generosity of the landlord who's taken it out and burnt it. And there isn't any furniture, either. That's the address he gives to the Big University for their RECORDS, but more often he sleeps in friends' closets, when they aren't using them. And Nic hasn't any money either, not for the sort of things The Girl would like to do.

So Nic and The Girl go to a coffee bar full of jolly students who're singing and shouting and occasionally pouring beer over each other's heads.

"Why do you draw back every time I touch you?" Nic says to The Girl. "What do you expect me to do? Pretend I don't love you? Make it a game? Is that the only way you can take it? I'd despise myself if I did. We've had sex, haven't we?"

"Not here," The Girl says.

So they walk back to her apartment.

"Why can't we just be nice and easy?" The Girl says. "Why must we always be so intense?"

"But you love me for my intensity," Nic says.

41

So she tells Nic how she doesn't want to commit herself to the big thing yet because then it'll go, and there'll be nothing left. Nic's still digesting this information when they reach her apartment, full of all those nice guys – who Nic knows are just waiting to start dating The Girl as soon as he breaks up with her . . .

So now Nic's standing beside this new shiny green Buick Convertible, thinking how he'll be seeing The Girl tonight and how she'll maybe sulk because of the rude thing he shouted at her golf class this afternoon, or maybe not, because she's a good girl . . . When Nic sees something he hasn't seen before, something he's somehow *known* he's going to see, so that the moment he sees it he ducks his head away, and puts his arm across his eyes, like he's protecting them from an atom bomb flash, say. He sees that his father's left the keys in his new Buick Convertible.

Nic doesn't act after that. Things are done *to* him. He's literally pushed around. Before he knows what's happened The Pusher has pushed Nic into the seat of that car and lifted his hand to turn the key. And, goddam it, he's in such a fucking hurry, this Pusher, that Nic scarcely has time, as the automatic engages and swooshes him away from the curb in a single breath of power, to turn and wave his thanks to his old dad inside that old white house – and to see, instead of his old dad, his kid sister leaning out of a second floor window.

She's gaping – showing all the hardware her parents have had clamped on her teeth to make her a still more beautiful lady. She's so delighted to see Nic taking a spin in her dad's new convertible she just can't call out one single friendly word.

It's about three hours later now. Nic's been downtown, getting loaded. Not because he's frightened, but because this needs a little celebration. It's not often his father's kind enough to loan him his brand new car. And now it's dark and cold and Nic's standing on the sidewalk with The Girl, looking at it.

"Like it?" Nic says.

"It's lovely," she says. She really thinks so. It does things to her, this great vulgar machine with its built-in obsolescence and its buttons to raise and lower all the windows by power in case you haven't the strength, making you into a kind of tiny impotent brain in the middle of all those buttons, not *your* brain but *its* brain . . . This thing makes her stomach give a heave

42

and turn all wobbly. She puts out a hand to touch its green paint, all shining black under the street lights, then takes it back quickly as if she's afraid she'll annoy it.

"Where did you get it?" she says.

"My father loaned it me," Nic says casually. But he should have invented some crap about winning it in a breakfast food competition – she'd have believed that.

"You aren't speaking to your father." It's like he can hear her brain ticking. Tick, tick, tick. It's like he knows hours and hours before, just what's at the end of this ticking. And there isn't a goddam thing he can do.

"Oh, we get along fine sometimes," Nic says.

"Seems like it," she says.

That's not a statement, it's a question. Please explain more circumstantially, she's saying, because right now your story sounds a load of bull.

"Look, I call them up," Nic says. " 'Hi dad, I'm your son,' I say. 'Let's cut this crap about not speaking.' 'You're goddam right, son,' he says."

" 'And please borrow my new seven-thousand-dollar car'," The Girl interrupts him.

Nic says nothing. Tick, tick, tick. Nearly there now. And there isn't a goddam thing . . .

"Nic, I'm not coming in that car," The Girl says, "because you stole it."

"Borrowed," Nic shouts at her.

"Stole," she screams and begins to sob all over the place.

That's where they've reached when the squad car pulls up, all flashing red dome, and howling siren, and muscle-bound cops, like they can scarcely walk for the weight of the arsenal they're carrying on their hips and under their armpits, and probably in their crotches too from the way they stand with their thighs about six inches apart.

It's two hours later again, and Nic's still down at the station, where these big guys invited him. Nic has a problem – apart from the fact that he can't see out of one eye where one of their elbows accidentally jabbed him as they got him into the squad car, and the fact that he's wondering if he's got internal haemorrhage of the kidneys where one of their knees accidentally jolted him as they pulled him out. Nic's problem is, he's allowed *one* phone call. So who's it to be?

43

Normally he'd call his good old dad. Dad, your son's in bad trouble. Right now that doesn't seem to suit the case. So maybe he should call one of those shifty downtown lawyers, if he could remember any of their names, if every last one of them wasn't his dear old momma's best friend. And this leads Nic to wondering just how they picked him up so quickly and to remembering that farewell wave and a kiss his kid sister Susie had somehow forgotten to give him as he drove away – you just never knew your luck. And somehow this leads Nic to thinking of one of his teachers. A foreigner. A limey.

There's something about this teacher that makes Nic trust him. He's a walking innocent, of course, but that's maybe why he's about the only guy right now who can help Nic. No one else would be such a stupid fool.

Nic's head isn't so good, what with having only one functioning eye, and his back teeth having a lot of jagged edges they didn't have before, and some nasty thick stuff he keeps needing to swallow, but he'll just have to chance that.

"I need the phone book," he says.

"You're goddam right, you need the phone book," the patrolman says. It doesn't mean anything but it sounds tough and rough and threatening. This patrolman's got an image to live up to, a genuine personal hero figure to model himself on.

All the time it takes Nic to find the number and wonder how he's going to dial – with the kind of pulpy fingers he seems to have gotten some place – he's thinking of this teacher.

He's thinking here's a guy who's up to his knees in shit, and doesn't even know it. He believes he's still somewhere he can be honest and say what he thinks and people will love him for it. He doesn't realise that it scares the living daylights out of them, and they're trying their damndest to keep clear of him because it's not safe to mix with someone who's got such a load of bad luck coming to him for talking that way. He believes he can *afford* to be free and sincere with people and like them for what they are, not for their position or status. Right, he's a dangerous innocent, but Nic has the idea that even if he knew how stupid he was behaving he wouldn't change, because at bottom there's something good about this guy. Not tested, but good.

Peterson put the typescript sheet to the bottom, as he had the twelve previous sheets, and read on : Nic crosses Quad . . . He was back at the start and there was no more. The fifty-minute

44

bell had rung and he stared down at the packed side-walks, several thousand students hurrying to their next classes. The snow had stopped but they bent their shoulders and turned down their faces against the cold north wind. Earflaps and Russian fur hats were out early this year.

His back to his class – in Comparative Modern Novels – Peterson wrote on the board. "Next assignment: THE RAINBOW". They were still arriving, co-eds to sit neatly upright in their chair-desks, notebooks at the ready, boys to lay themselves on the smalls of their backs so that they seemed to face him principally with their big slumped knees, more prominent by far than their faces which sank to the level of their note-slabs. "Mid Semester hourly: Wednesday November 22,' he wrote. In the front row, Jill Hearn half lay in her seat, like one of the boys.

Her soft knees, which he remembered so well, now in faded blue jeans, were slumped forward and apart. Her duck-shaped feet, in Spanish rope-sandals, half blocked the gangway. She'd lit up already and, glancing above her, he saw that she'd blown a perfect smoke ring which was rising fast, with swirling internal rotation, towards the ceiling. It seemed to surprise and fascinate her, too, and for a second they both stared at it, then their eyes met, both realised what the other had been thinking and they gave each other big grins. The whole incident was so unexpected and confusing that it left him totally without the question he'd prepared to start this final class on Mailer's *An American Dream*.

He turned for help to the lecture notes on his desk. The sheet of paper he saw was entirely unfamiliar.

So he'd brought the wrong notes – or come to the wrong classroom, would see, when he looked up, thirty unknown laughing faces, sense behind him the laughing crew-cut professor whose class he'd accidentally arrived at. Postponing this unpleasant moment, he began to read it.

"Miss Sherry Steiner will likely MISS CLASS through Wednesday, reason being her CATand/or DOG ate her contact lenses and she CAN'T CROSS TRAFFIC without them. Signed, Sherry Steiner."

The explanation was easy: while he'd been writing on the board some friend of Miss Steiner had put it on his desk. It didn't entirely expunge the earlier moment of panic. Resolving to take extra coffee on lecture mornings, he moved to shut his classroom door, another foreign habit : his colleagues left theirs wide as they taught, so that, circling the corridors, he could pick up interesting ideas on *Moby Dick*, *The Miller's Tale*, *Troilus and Cressida*, *Moby Dick*, Poe, Donne, Differential Calculus, Faulkner, *Moby Dick*, and so on. Before he reached it, Ric Schuster was there.

"This your literature course?" He was breathless, as if he'd been running. "May I audit?" He seemed reluctant to wait in the doorway, as if he was the victim of some red-hot impulse about how he should live which mustn't be interrupted. Stop me and you'll only have yourself to blame, he implied. In one hand he carried a new red notebook.

"Of course." Peterson watched him sit at the back, fetch a ballpoint pen from his flapping khaki windcheater and wait, hand poised, a parody of the attentive student.

"One announcement," Peterson began, using it to clear his throat. At the same instant, into his mind, complete and formed as if he might have been planning it for days, came the idea that after class he'd ask Jill Hearn to coffee. "The office of Instructional Methods," he read, "is currently making facilities available for the tape-recording of class sessions," – Coming for coffee? he'd say. How ludicrously simple. How unbelievable that he hadn't thought of it before – "thus providing playback data of which students and instructors may avail themselves as background material for a planned programme of classroom technique improvement," he read, and stopped, deeply shocked to see Ric Schuster's pen ostentatiously at work recording this announcement.

"Who'd like a class session recorded?" – Her big brown eyes laughing up at him, she'd say, Hey, and about time too, he thought, counting hands, "Twenty-six, twenty-seven, a clear majority. I'll announce the time and place next week."

Now he began to draw a parallel between literature and conjuring. The most tempting, but ultimately least rewarding, way to study a conjuring trick was to find out how it was done. In the process you destroyed all wonder. Wasn't the same true about novels. Far from enhancing their value, systematic analysis made them as dull as an understood conjuring trick. Didn't this current critical trend *reduce* novels to tricks by ignoring the fact that,

46

unlike tricks, they were about life. When critics refused to value novels for their message, didn't they automatically fill this judgement gap with another standard which was appropriate *only* to conjuring tricks: their complicatedness. Wasn't this why *Ulysses* was at the centre of the canon and *Finnegan's Wake* might soon be – they were very complicated books – *i.e.* very tricky, or should he say tricksy? And incidentally were fine to teach since the teacher was in no danger of running out of things to say after a single class session.

A small titter told him that he hadn't completely lost them, but something dramatic was badly needed; glancing down on the front row he could see Miss Muller, a flat-faced girl with acne, actually writing ".... or maybe tricksy?" Peterson liked teaching and liked his class, so he was still more distressed to see, further back, Miss Foringer staring vacantly out of the window, her writing hand gone to sleep on her notebook; and Mr Dool fallen into his familiar stare in which he appeared hypnotised except for his continuously chewing half open mouth.

"What do you think, Mr Dool?"

Mr Dool, a slow boy, majoring in forestry, took time to hoist himself eighteen inches higher in his chair-desk and get the gum to one side of his mouth. "Well sure, that *is* just about what *I* think." A good laugh from the class.

Peterson quickly led the discussion from the abstract to the concrete – though he was glad to have excepted himself from a system which annually taught thousands of young Americans to hate books – fresh from high school they arrived, enthused about *Animal Farm, The Catcher in the Rye,* Camus; six years (and two hundred footnoted papers) later, they emerged, never wanting to read another printed page – "Are we agreed, then, that the book is an adolescent dream, half anxiety, half wish-fulfilment?"

Stirrings from Mr Dool, who perhaps hoped to repeat his success. Partly to prevent him, partly to forestall Mr Norbury, a psych. major, who might here be expected to introduce Jung as he had three weeks ago, creating much confusion, Peterson hurried on, "Hasn't everything in the book a dream quality about it? *The* male American dream. You murder your wife – because you can't satisfy her in bed – but prove your potency by a series of marvellous seductions of child-women whom you *do*

47

satisfy. You further insult your dead wife by buggering the German maid . . ."

Whenever sex became the subject he had their full attention. Not a sound in the classroom, thirty-five pairs of eyes focussed on him, a dozen hands waiting to rise – Like a blow in the kidneys, he realised that she might refuse. Sorry, I have a class, she'd say, and bounce away, waving a hand. Or perhaps faculty might be forbidden by university regulations to take students to coffee. There'd be an astonished silence as the others heard him ask her – Fighting his way back to Mailer, he realised that Jill Hearn herself had raised a hand, knew that he'd nodded to her with ludicrous quickness, which he tried too late to slow.

"I don't know about the *male* American dream . . ." she said. The class was delighted. Fifteen seconds before he could quiet them.

"Let me finish," he said, still grinning with them. "Why is buggery an insult? Because his wife is his mother and to *her* this is the dirtiest thing he can do because *she* potty-trained him . . .

No longer to be frustrated, Mr Norbury had a question on anal eroticism. Listening, Peterson knew that Jill Hearn's question had settled things. Her worldly amusement at his own innocence convinced him that he must never expose himself to her. Even if she had agreed to come, what would he have suggested next? An evening drink? But she'd have laughed at him for thinking an after-class coffee entitled him to date her. Coffee again on Monday? She'd have laughed at him for not having the courage to ask her to a drink. The whole prospect made him feel very tired and deeply grateful that he'd realised in time.

"Yes, I think we're in agreement," he said, curtailing Mr Norbury, whose question was growing into a speech, at the same time flattering him, and hiding the fact that he'd heard only about two sentences.

"One thing I did notice," Miss Percy said, without raising her hand, "was the use of moon symbolism." She had a slow careful delivery and seemed to communicate with her notebook rather than himself or the class. "Just how would you line that up?"

"I'll come to that," Peterson said pleasantly, "but first I'll suggest other wish-fulfilment elements of the dream: to be a tough hard-drinking guy, who can out-wisecrack the most wise-cracking cop, but also to have a cunning legal twist of mind to help you slither out of trouble. To be a show business name – *And* a psychologist – *And* a college professor – *And* a war hero who's destroyed single-handed two enemy machine-gun posts . . ." She was tall, certainly, Miss Foringer, but it suited her long fair hair, which she'd now swayed back over her shoulders; and her soft slim, but not too slim, legs – if only Mr Dool would clear the view by slumping to his original position on the small of his back. Compared with the long-haired, slim fairness of Mary Foringer, the chubby-cheeked, short-haired prettiness of Jill Hearn seemed suddenly crude and unattractive. Why had he never noticed Mary Foringer till today? Because of today's tent dress, with huge red strawberries and green vine leaves, which left her long arms bare to her shoulders and stopped half way down her slim thighs? Suppose she came to him after class with a question. That's an awkward one, Miss Foringer. Hang on a moment. Then, when the others had gone, Hey, why don't we discuss that one over some coffee?

"Well sir," Mr Hertzerton, a Jewish boy with frizzy hair, was saying, "If, like you say, you go for this book, how about all this adolescence crap?"

"Any suggestions?" Peterson asked the class, delighted, encouraging.

"Isn't it a question of the persona?" a dark girl he still hadn't named said.

You're the first teacher who's ever treated me like a human being, Mary Foringer would say, tears shining in her blue eyes . . .

"Well, *personally* . . ." Mr Dool said before Peterson could stop him, and paused for the laugh he knew he deserved this time. After five seconds' total silence, Mr Norbury groaned.

"You mean he's sending up all this bull?" Mr Hertzerton said.

"Isn't that possible?"

"Like we have another class on Woodrow Wilson," Miss Muller, the flat-faced girl with acne, began. Now he saw that what had seemed an improvement in her condition was a thick coating of skin-coloured make-up, some of which was starting to make scabby flakes. "Well, this may take a little time," she said with a small laugh of apology, "but anyway, you see Woodrow Wilson . . ."

Concentrating hard, Peterson listened for the tiniest hint of a path back to the theme of their discussion so that he could hurry forward with an encouraging call, pointing the way. His failure became complete when he saw Mary Foringer begin to pick her nose. Though she used the rest of her hand to hide it, she was definitely poking her little finger up her pretty nose to pick out snot. Dimly he heard Miss Percy begin, "Well wouldn't that fit right in with the moon imagery . . ." Helplessly, as he watched Mary Foringer shift her hand an inch down her face to nibble what she'd extracted, he heard other students making points about the hero myth, christ figures, sojourns in the underworld, which they'd industriously mined into the book ten days ago, saved through two and a half classes and now, before it was too late, must disclose.

Cutting off comments by turning sharply away, he began to stride backwards and forwards across the room, adopting a pose of deep, summary-creating thoughtfulness, but in fact trying to discover any coherence in what had been said.

"Let's go back to Miss Hearn's comment. The *male* American dream may be different from the female, but the two are inseparable. The hero of this novel is a direct extension of the Hemingway myth, tough, sexy, disillusioned, monosyllabic. But underneath, romantic and anxious. Anxious about prison and the electric chair. We don't need Mr Norbury's help to translate that. Anxious about his own courage. He's obsessed with courage. When he's walked once along three sides of a balcony with a thirty-storey drop to the street below, he's haunted by the fear that he hasn't the courage to do it again. But all he's saying is, Look mother, I've escaped from you, I'm a real man . . ." At this moment, for the first time for half an hour he noticed Ric Schuster, and for the whole of the remaining sixty seconds of the class, as he struggled to shape his conclusion, he was distracted by the astonishing faces he was making.

Sometimes he would open his mouth widely on the right side, keeping the left shut, and shutting his left eye, as if suffering acute toothache. A moment later he would reverse the whole arrangement, even dipping the closed-up side of his face to a few inches from his note slab. Was it some comment on the class? Or had he forgotten he was here?

"Look at the culminating anxiety," Peterson went on. "He's rescued his child-bride from the Mafia and her life of promis-

50

cuous sex. Then it turns out that for years and years she's been his father-in-law's mistress – who incidentally had also laid the German maid, as well as having an incestuous relationship with his own daughter. The poor fellow can't win. In the background is the haunting fear of a REAL MAN. Wherever he goes this man's been there before and done it better." Now Ric Schuster was staring directly at him with hard intensity, at the same time drawing in air through his teeth with an audible hissing whistle.

"So the real fear," Peterson concluded, raising his voice, reaching with relief a passage in his notes he'd drafted, "is of impotence. Back to Hemingway. No wonder the conclusion shows the hero taking off for the gambling West, where a man can be a man among MEN."

The bell rang . . .

"So why's impotence the basic fear? I suggest it's because of the American *female* dream. We'll expand that point next time," he concluded, and at once knew that he was going to ask Jill Hearn to coffee. Boldly upright, notes under his arm, he watched without panic for the moment, his mind bolstered by useful clichés, faint heart never won fair lady, you only live once – Unfortunately a small crowd of students were pressing round his desk. Mr Hertzerton came first. "This hourly exam, sir, will you be wanting feed-back? Or will they be think questions?"

"What do *you* think?" Peterson said. – Now she was stretching and yawning.

"I was afraid so," Mr Hertzerton said.

"Excuse me, sir," Miss Muller said, turning her back on the others to edge him into a private discussion. "I hope you didn't mind my mentioning that parallel . . ."

"No no," Peterson said, his mind groping. – Now she was standing, putting on a large blue cloak with scarlet lining.

"You see, President Wilson . . ."

"Fine fine," Peterson said. "Knowledge mustn't be kept in watertight boxes." – Now she was moving towards the door. "Excuse me."

He began to push between students. Totally blocking his way, he came on Miss Percy. She stood quite still, notebook open, reading carefully, collecting evidence to trap him. She gave off total confidence that, when her case was ready, he'd be waiting to be trapped. He hesitated – and this saved him.

Jill Hearn, already in the doorway, had turned to look back.

51

Another pace and he would have been there – when up to her, big shoulders hunched, elbows projecting, hands in the rib pockets of his wind-jacket, slouched Mr Dool. They smiled at each other and went out together.

Together they crossed the landing without seeming to say one word. Clearly they knew each other too well for that. Together they went downstairs.

Three minutes later, crushed by Miss Percy, he came out of the empty classroom. Hidden to the right of the door, Ric Schuster was waiting for him.

"In demand!" Ric said.

"Seems like it."

"All fixed for tomorrow night?"

"Tomorrow night?"

"Your date with me and Judy. Double date with your wife. Show you the low life of the town."

"Oh yes," Peterson said, trying to remember when he'd agreed to this. "That'll be fun," he said, sensing a gap which he should be filling with gratitude. "By the way, we must fix up a time to discuss your story . . ."

"Oh yeah!" Ric said with suspicious irony.

"Unless you'd rather finish it first."

"You think I should!" Ric said, and went abruptly down the stairs, hands in his pants pockets, whistling loudly. At the first bend he turned and shouted back, "Bye, Maurice."

Four miles out on the prairie, where the no-dancing-with-liquor law didn't apply, The Stardust stood beside the highway, a small, entirely windowless brick building in a treeless, flower-less, grassless, gravel parking lot, suggesting one of the utility buildings of a military depot, the laundry perhaps. East from town, it lay about midway along the umbilical which now more or less joined Flatville to its small satellite, Casablanca, beyond the numerous Flatville filling stations, drive-in steak and shake houses and bowling alleys, beyond the drive-in cinema and the three funeral homes, beyond the five trailer parks, but in sight of the estates of single-storey cracker-box houses which were creeping, or rather careering, out from Flatville across the prairie like a wonders-of-nature film of some plasterboard fungus. Here, cruising along at seventy, Peterson had often flashed past without noticing it, his attention at once diverted

52

by Casablanca's funeral home, drive-in cinema, trailer parks, filling stations, steak and shake houses and bowling alleys. On the one or two later occasions, when he did make himself see it, he was amazed that it could shrink by day to this small brick storehouse. By night it was quite different.

Down avenues of flashing, rotating, pulsating, red, pink, green and blue neon, the four of them drove to it. A giant puce hand filled the drive-in screen, holding delicately between its two-foot forefinger and thumb a wedding ring the size of a truck tyre. "EVEREADY FUNERAL PARLOUR" advertised in six-foot emerald gothic. A continuous line of multiple red tail-lights led them ahead and a line of quadruple headlights followed them, while another zipped past in the opposite lane. It was Saturday and the joint was jumping, as Ric Schuster said twice from the back seat. Oddly, he seemed to say it with a touch of wonder, and no irony.

Across a lot solid with shiny cars stretching away into the night, they came towards its ten-foot roof sign, a mauve neon cornucopia which projected the letters STARDUST mixed with stars in a glittering fountain. Ducking, they pushed into its orange grotto interior.

At once they came against a dark press of people, and a howling of song far too loud to speak above. Blocked in the narrow entrance, unable to hear or to see more than a few feet into the cavern beyond, they seemed deprived in an instant of their most important senses. Out of the orange smoke a manageress, menus under her arm, spectacles hanging by silver chains to her ears, slid towards them like a fish functioning easily in her underwater environment.

But she didn't offer the menus, and immediately a row began about Judy's ID card. It was the strangest row Peterson could remember, for though Ric and the manageress, and presently the manager, a young man with a naked pink head, and even Judy were soon obviously shouting at each other and he was only four feet away, their voices were tiny and far off. Still odder, the other doorway loungers, in floral cowboy shirts and leather thong ties, paid little attention, sometimes watching, more often still staring past them into the smoke-filled cavern beyond.

A moment later Peterson saw the manager and manageress each seize one of Ric's upper arms and begin to run him violently backwards, barging one of the lounging cowboys whose

53

beer whooped in a single curved slop over Ric's shoulder, down the front of his pants. He even noticed that the manageress was more courageous in her attack than the manager, who held his bald pink head back out of danger – before his English indignation at this two-against-one bullying shot him forward between them, arms raised, "Please stop at once."

For a second they seemed so surprised that they stopped, and there was time for him to wonder how to extend his success, and suffer a wave of impotence at the idea of being persuasive at the top of his voice, before, in a rush which almost toppled him over, all of them were stumbling backwards together. The force behind this new push seemed to have its source in the darkness beyond the manager and manageress, who came too, in a jerky suffering way, as if being injured in the smalls of their backs, while the imitation cowboy who'd lost his beer gave sharp kicks with his pointed suede boots at Ric's knees. Close beside Ric, Judy was so slight and short that at times her dark hair went out of sight. Though Peterson could have touched her, he was unable to raise his arms. Anyway, it was Nancy he should help, but she had completely disappeared. So he was surprised when they came stumbling out through the Stardust's doorway into the parking lot to see her standing slightly apart, watching them. Surprised, too, that only the four of them had been ejected.

They sat in his car and drove to the Golden Nite. Four and a half miles north of town, the Golden Nite lay a little more than half way along the umbilical which more or less connected Flatville to Peking, its satellite ... But the Golden Nite was out of fashion, only half full, with a country and western band of electric banjos and accordions, and tablecloths of check gingham, suggesting a social evening at an English village hall. The lights were brighter and they could hear each other speak.

There were occasional tables of students in plaid shirts, but more of young-middle-aged couples, the men too gross or bald to be properly one, too fresh and baby-faced to be the other, a category which seemed common here. Even his older students were often on the edge of this twenty-five-onwards phase. As for the women, at this point every suggestion that they'd ever been girls disappeared and they seemed already at the start of the blue-haired-matron phase.

"Look at them all," Ric called, loudly enough for the nearest

54

heads to turn. "From the pâté factory. Saturday night wife-swapping. Hi, Maurice, shall we do a wife-swap?

"Wasn't he great?" Ric said to Nancy. "Rushing into the fight like that."

For a minute the bottle-green-suited manager with tie of bottle-green velvet and heavy ruby ring, examining Judy's ID card, then gave it back and walked away.

"It's forged," Ric said loudly, while the manager still seemed likely to hear. "You don't think I'm going to let any fucking creep throw Judy out, do you?" he said, towards the bottle-green back, moving away through the tables, in a mutter which was at the same time a shout.

"Then why did the Stardust . . . ?"

"You wanta know?" But the reason now made Ric too angry to speak. The pleasant evening they'd begun seemed to be changing. It had begun unexpectedly pleasantly.

They'd been drinking beer in his sitting room when Nancy had come down. Ric had advanced, hand outstretched. "Good to meet you, Mrs Peterson."

He'd stood close in front of her, looking her up and down. "Jesus, you're a lucky woman, Mrs Peterson. Perhaps I shouldn't say it. That's the kind of guy I am."

And Nancy hadn't objected. "In what way?" she'd asked pleasantly. Peterson had been filled with gratitude.

"I reckon you know," Ric had said. "Hey, meet Judy."

In the pizza house, eating the red-hot circle of dried-up crust coated with cheese-flavoured glue which Americans called a pizza, he'd returned to the subject. "Gee, marriage is an odd thing, Mrs Peterson. When it's good it's the best thing in the world. Well, *you* should know." Later, he'd just stared at her, shaking his head in wonder, occasionally clicking his tongue. "Gee, Mrs Peterson."

When he and Nancy had sat together in the car's back seat, Peterson had heard him telling her the story of his own marriage. "At midnight, say, I'd get restless. Go out in the park. Sit on a bench. Stay there till three in the morning. She didn't like that. 'What do you *do* out there?' she'd say. 'Do I have to *do* anything?' I'd tell her. If she'd thought I was lying, that would have been one thing. Out for a quick lay. The trouble was she believed me. That terrified her, because she thought she'd married a goddam nut."

55

Suddenly Peterson had understood Ric's need always to drama-tise himself, and at the same time watch his audience with pre-judging suspicion. People rejected someone so tiresome. To be known to know him would make *them* odd. Nancy didn't reject him. A great warmth for her had filled him. She understood that the embarrassing admiration and trust Ric was giving her was only because of his own desperate need to be admired and trusted.

Now, raising his voice against, "Home, Home on the Range", crooned by a man whose flabby paleness suggested a Germanic Hawaiian rather than a cowboy, Ric began again. "He's just a fucking fine guy, your husband." He stared at Nancy. "You don't like me to say that, do you?"

"Say what you like."

"You think I should be more restrained. More English."

"Do I?"

A terrible suspicion came to Peterson that the whole evening she'd been drawing Ric on to see how idiotic he would make himself. He fought against the idea, broke in, to prevent her proving it to him: "Ric, there are a few things I'd like to say about your story, in case I forget . . ."

Ric still stared at Nancy.

"First, I really like it. But there are two small points . . ."

Ric turned his head to glare.

"The boy's name. Surely Hemingway . . ."

"That," Ric said, with elaborate clearness, "is the whole goddam irony."

"Oh yes, of course," Peterson said, genuinely grateful for an explanation he could accept.

"What else?"

"Well the general tone does have just the slightest Holden Caulfield flavour."

There were several seconds' total silence, in which he became aware of Judy listening.

"You think so?" Ric said.

"Only in places . . ."

"You really think so?"

"I'll show you on Monday . . ."

"He thinks my story's like *The Catcher in the* Fucking *Rye*," he said to Judy.

"I didn't say that."

56

"Maybe I wasn't listening . . ."

As so often in this country Peterson felt adrift without experience to help him. He knew that open manly rudeness was acceptable, but whether it should now lead to a fight, or to a future in which they never spoke to each other, or to a tomorrow in which they forgot it, because it was so usual and proper that it was totally unimportant, he'd no idea.

"Maurice," Ric said, leaning across the table, holding out his hand for him to shake, "you goddam idiot." They shook hands diagonally across Judy and Nancy. He felt like a doctor being thanked for some outsize pill, which has cured the patient but also just about choked him. The patient was grateful, but at the same time warning him not to try that sort of cure again. Glancing at Nancy, a more disturbing idea came to him: that she could hardly control her laughter at how foolish Ric was making him.

Suddenly he was gripped by exasperation at the way he was being asked to behave with outgoing response by Ric Schuster, and with detached English coldness by Nancy. There the boy sat, opening himself to him, asking him to do the same. There Nancy sat, laughing at the weak way he was treating this tiresome boy. When she and Judy went to the powder room, an attached corrugated lean-to, he felt an enormous weight lift. For a moment he need no longer play two parts to a split audience each of which hated him for trying to please the other. Moving to sit opposite Ric, leaning forward across the table to speak sympathetically, he asked, as he'd wanted to all evening, "Any developments?"

"Developments?" Ric said loudly, not looking at him.

"Your trouble about Judy?"

"Trouble with Judy?"

"Your parents. The charge. Statutory rape . . ."

"My parents are fine, thanks," Ric said. "Good people, my parents. Not a lot of imagination. Hell, what do you want with all that crap."

For the second time he felt the ground of solid experience tilt under him. This time it made the hair at the back of his neck stand on end. Casually putting up a hand, he felt an unexpectedly thick mat of it here, which he had apparently been living with but ignoring all his life.

"You said . . ."

57

"What did I say?" Ric said, loud and hearty, as if in a second he would give him a cheery slap.

Peterson shook his head, badly confused. A second later there was a new change. Ric's eyes narrowed, his shoulders hunched and he was staring across the dance floor. Turning, Peterson saw a dimly lit line of wall booths.

"The bastard," Rick said. He scarcely seemed to notice when Judy and Nancy came back. "The fucking bastard."

Now Peterson had the strange sense of a suffocating pillow descending over him. With an effort which seemed enormous, but he knew he must make, he stood and asked Judy to dance. They danced in an old-fashioned style, her dark hair level with his chest. She seemed even frailer than he'd expected and moved easily so that he had to use only the lightest pressure to turn her.

"How long have you known Ric?"

"Six weeks, I guess," she said, but didn't fill the gap he left her with any more information.

There was an odd self-possession about her which he liked better for that one moment at the Stardust when he'd seen her shouting at the top of her voice.

When they came back to the table Ric still glared across the room as if he and Nancy had sat like this in silence the whole time. Peterson now guessed that he was staring at a short, grey-haired, faintly familiar man sitting alone in a booth for four.

"Shit arsing, horse pissing bastard . . ." he said through shut teeth. "Hi there," he called with loud heartiness to Peterson and Judy.

"Hallo, Ric."

But already he was hunched and staring at the short grey-haired man. Now he made noises between a growl and a snarl.

"Who's that?"

With a bitter wrench, Ric said, "Dr Ivan Heinz," as if just to say his name was to lapse into treating him as human.

At once Peterson remembered the party where he'd met Dr Heinz and the story he'd heard about him. He was from Egypt, but born Russian-Jewish, an anthropologist – or was it an electrical engineer – who'd turned psychologist. Five years ago he'd lost his wife and child in a sailing accident.

Now Peterson watched him more carefully, sitting alone, stout but upright, both hands holding his drink. His grey hair was tufted and owl-like over his ears, but bushy on top. His eyes

58

were round and owl-like but too startled for an owl, as if he'd just been half amused, half frightened by some joke. They'd been sailing at night and capsized, and he'd clung to the up-turned boat while his wife had set out to swim to the shore with the boy. After quarter of an hour he'd heard screaming.

Suddenly the scene was vivid to Peterson; the cold black Canadian lake under moonlight. This thick little man clinging to his boat at water level, hair soaked, a kind of sea animal. Silence, then far away in the night this screaming. So inhuman that he'd thought for an instant it was some night bird.

Much too far to save them – but not too far to try? Had he tried? Would be, Peterson, have tried? He had no idea, because he knew that, if the same had happened to Nancy, at the heart of his horror, he would have felt relief.

Did he only feel this because his own marriage was often hard to bear? Because he secretly wished for the courage to face again his own loneliness. To feel again real desperation, real happiness. To be freed from this suburbia of the emotions ... Suddenly he was sure that whatever Dr Heinz had done when faced with this real problem of life, it was something he was not ashamed of. Whereas he, faced with no such problem, was all the time obscurely ashamed about his life.

"That guy thinks he's counselling me?" Ric said. "He got me my job, working nights at the City Hospital. Wheeling the patients into the operating theatre, wheeling out the stiffs."

Nancy gave a sharp laugh, as if something particularly ridiculous about this had made her break a promise to laugh only to herself.

Ric stared hard at her. "Say, Mrs Peterson, did I mention your husband to you?"

"I don't think so."

"Didn't I tell you what a fucking fine guy he is. Just the guy for a jolly evening on the town. Wife-swapping, the lot. Can't hold him back." He gulped the rest of his bourbon, spitting back an icecube into the glass, and took Judy to dance.

Sometimes Peterson could see them, dancing a twist or frug which Ric did clumsily, turning it into a parody, to his own obvious amusement. Once he caught him glancing towards their table to be sure that his funny performance was being watched. Nancy saw it too.

Left alone with her, he knew he should speak to her about

59

her behaviour to Ric, but suddenly he hated her in a way he'd never before admitted. There she sat, dark, amused – if rather sickened . . . He knew that this was something he shouldn't feel – just because *he* liked Ric, there was no reason why she need – but he knew too, that if he tried to argue calmly with her, admitting this point but asking for her tolerance, his hatred might come bubbling up, reducing him to stuttering incoherence.

"Hi, Maurice," Ric called, giving his shoulder a slap which made him choke on his bourbon, and sat looking round aggressively for the next amusing project. "So what the hell are we all doing here? What's Maurice Peterson, well-known British novelist, doing, pretending he's enjoying being taken to a crumby joint like this by some crumby student?"

It was hard to be sure whether he was now drunk, or with increasing determination acting drunk. Whichever it was, Peterson knew he must help.

"Look, Ric, maybe it's time . . ."

"Ay say, Ric . . ." Ric mimicked.

It curled him up with indignation. Before he could control this, Ric was hunched and snarling again. "What's that lonely fucker doing over there? He needs company. Let's go join him."

"Maybe another time . . ."

"I'm going to cheer up that lonely bastard."

"No, Ric," Judy said.

"I don't think you should," Peterson said.

Nancy watched, laughing to herself.

"Oh yes I am." He was like a child who has hunted all day for the noise which will madden its parents. At last he'd found it. His delight at the discovery competed with his anger that the hunt had taken so long. No sop or threat was going to distract him now, but there was no hurry either. He was going to enjoy every moment of it. "Oh yes I am," he said with thick anger and got slowly to his feet.

Judy held his arm. Peterson stood.

"So fine, we're all coming!"

"No we're not, Ric."

"I'm going to introduce you all to the loneliest fucker in town."

When he began to move, Judy went with him, still holding his arm but not struggling. Peterson came behind. Nancy stayed sitting.

The psychologist held out his hand. Ric didn't take it but

60

sat on the outside of his seat, penning him into the booth. Judy sat opposite. At once Ric began to speak to him, pushing his face within a few inches of his startled owl's face. A few seconds later he took him by the lapels of his jacket, closed them round his throat, and hoisted him to his feet, at the same time going on speaking with spitting anger close up against his face.

Short and thick, the psychologist stood there, gripped at the neck, but at the same time raising one arm out to his left, as if to call for a drink, as if this arm had no idea there was an angry man clinging to its lapels.

Things happened fast then. The bottle-green-suited manager came with helpers, jumped Ric out of the booth and ran him out through the entrance door, an arm twisted behind his shoulders. When it was over Peterson found himself nearer the wall booth but still only half way from their own table. Turning, he saw Nancy holding a big smile ready for him.

He crossed to Dr Heinz. "I'm Maurice Peterson." He held out his hand, American style.

"Please to meet you," Dr Heinz said, as if he knew there was no need to give his own name.

"Sorry about that."

"It is nothing."

"These things happen."

Now Dr Heinz gave no answer, partly as if he was not prepared to co-operate in meaningless politenesses, but more as if there was something specifically incorrect about this particular one. Oddly, this didn't annoy Peterson but filled him with gratitude. He wanted to thank Dr Heinz for reminding him that words had meaning. He wanted to stay here with him and discuss the real meaning which his own foolish politeness had hidden, and the real meaning of Dr Heinz' silence. But there was no time now, the problem of Ric pressing worryingly. Excusing himself, he went with Nancy and Judy out to the Golden Nite's parking lot. Ric wasn't in the car. They looked up and down several parking lanes, waited ten minutes then drove back to town.

"Oh gee," Judy said several times. "I guess I'm real sorry."

"You don't have to be," Peterson said, with quiet firmness.

"I guess he'll go to his room," Judy said.

"If he's got one," Peterson said, forgetting whether his room-less state was fact or fiction.

61

"Oh yes, of course," Judy said, as if loyally supporting something Ric had told her.

"Maybe he'll go to his parents," Peterson said.

"That's what scares me," she said.

"Isn't he reconciled with them?"

"He told you that?" she said, leaving him uncertain whether she was astonished at this news, or at this vast lie.

The girl surprised him more and more. Her concern made him realise that he'd come to expect Americans to drop difficult relationships like broken appliances. She sat beside him, not thinking, he believed, about how what had happened reflected on herself through her date, but about what might now be happening to Ric. He believed it was making her too worried to trouble to speak.

"He hates them," she said. "I didn't know you could hate so much."

Peterson parked under the street lamps outside her lodging house.

"Should we warn them?"

"Gee, I wish I knew," she said.

"Can we go home sometime?" Nancy said from the back seat. "My head's splitting."

"Is it?" Peterson said.

"What do you mean, 'Is it'?"

Peterson shrugged. "I'm surprised it started just now."

"Did I say it started just now?"

"Call me if I can help," Peterson said to Judy on the sidewalk.

"You're a friend," Judy said.

From the dark of the back seat, Nancy said, "You think people aren't capable of being in pain if they don't spill the fact all over the place."

Peterson restarted the car and turned for home. "Of course they're *capable* of it."

"What does that mean?"

Peterson realised that he didn't know. "Even if I was sure," he said, "I shouldn't tell you at pistol point."

"At pistol point!" she said, holding the absurd phrase up to ridicule. "Even if you were sure!" she said, suggesting that this, though less obviously absurd, was more maddeningly typical.

The house was hot after the cold night, the babysitter had set the thermostat at the top end of "Comfort range" : seventy-six. He sat in his shirt in his study, listening to Nancy going to bed. In the bathroom faucets hissed, plug holes gurgled and the lavatory cistern flushed three times, as if only a thorough cleansing could wash away the events of the evening. He thought of his tentative resolution of a fortnight ago which to his surprise he'd kept, and wondered if she'd noticed. Was she laughing at him for this too?

But, now that he couldn't see or hear her, and guessed she was propped up alone with the *Saturday Evening Post* in the double bed, he felt pity for her. Like a revelation, he saw that everything she'd done that night had been the result of fear. Fear that she would be disliked by other people, fear of her own emotions, in case they showed her that she was a different person from the one she wanted to be. It gave him a vision of a world entirely filled with people living in fear of each other, none able to see that their own self-centred anxiety was universal and that they therefore had nothing to fear.

At times as he stirred and dreamed through the hot night these unhappy people, Nancy, Ric, seemed to come to him expecting something, and go away angry and disappointed. But now the worry this might have caused him seemed to drop right away from him and he felt that he could never again be hurt by them when he understood so well why they needed to hurt him.

In a way he could not explain, this new freedom which the unfortunate evening had brought him seemed connected with Dr Ivan Heinz.

There were two Schusters in the book. "Schuster, Vernon D., Schuster, Henry A.," he read, reaching over his chair, his physical world tilting today, after the bourbon of the evening before and his short, restless night. An instant later he'd miscalculated his balance and arrived, unhurt but astonished, on his knees behind the chair, his chin resting exactly on the top of its wooden back.

In this position, safest for the moment, he checked the addresses. He stood cautiously, put on his overcoat, and walked through the sunny but freezing winter Sunday morning towards the residence of Henry A. Schuster at 304 West Hickory.

The streets were deserted, the whole town quiet, even the metallic howls of the railroad locomotives gone far away with the daylight into the northern part of the town, and less pained,

63

as if exhausted by their long night. A strange sound ahead: flap, flap, clang – familiar but unplacable. Round the corner he came to it: a lone crew-cut boy of about ten on the concrete ramp to his garage, putting a basket ball into a ring above the garage doors.

All over town you saw them, bounce, bounce, clang and rattle of the head board. Lonely boys with this obsession. Peterson passed slowly but the boy gave no sign that he knew he was being watched. Later in the year you'd find them in pairs with baseball and catcher's mit. Chuck, slap, return. Chuck, slap, return, on and on, in front of fraternity houses, along suburban sidewalks, all dreaming, perhaps, the American sports-hero dream. The garden of the next house had been TP-ed.

From its freshness it must have happened in the night – Saturday night, of course. Every shrub and bush was wound or draped in pink toilet paper. It went in great circles round whole tree tops, like loosely wrapped bandage. Other lengths connected the front porch to the telephone wires. It was a practical joke of disapproval, he'd been told, but seemed more like the playful punch in the stomach of a friend. Often it was left there for weeks till the winds from the prairies carried it into the park, or over the house roofs right out of town. Look, they seemed to say, we've been TP-ed – doesn't that finally prove what good guys we are. He was surprised to find that it was the Schusters' garden.

At once he was worried that it might be connected with yesterday evening. He chimed their bell and watched uneasily a trailing pink end lift horizontally in a wind so light he couldn't feel it. He didn't hear the inner door and when he turned he was looking through the outer – of plain glass in an aluminum frame – at an enormous woman.

She seemed to be dressed in a padded bed quilt. Her size, and this glass frame, gave her the look of a giant playing-card queen.

"Hi," she said.

"I'm sorry to disturb you. My name's Peterson."

"Well, how do you do," she said. Her white bed-quilt was patterned with sprays of delicate blue flowers. Her big face was as wide at the double chin as at her forehead, and had a lightly greased look as if normally coated with make-up. But her hair was piled in a six-inch bouffant-style tower on top,

64

as if for an evening out. Peeping from below her bed-quilt, which reached almost to the ground, two little plump pink feet nestled in the pile carpet.

"Mrs Schuster?"

"Correct," she said, still not opening the glass door.

"This may sound impertinent . . ."

"Well let's give it a try," she said. Her grossness, immobility and slight ill temper all now suggested what Ric had led him to expect, that she'd recently made a night-meal of Mr Schuster and was suffering from indigestion.

"I was with your son last night. We lost him. Frankly he was a bit drunk. I was worried about the police . . ."

She didn't say another word but stepped aside so that, as if at some child's show, a new picture was revealed. Deeper in the house, on a higher level, through the open doorway to a kitchen, sat Ric Schuster. He was on a high stool at a break-fast table, and at the moment Peterson saw him was taking a spoonful of breakfast cereal, but at once he looked up, raised his spoon and called, "Hi, Maurice," with a slight milky splutter.

"Oh, you're all right . . ." Peterson began, and was stopped, partly by the idiotic obviousness of this remark, partly by its total failure to express his exasperation.

"Fine, thanks, Maurice," Ric yelled, slurping in some escaped matter. He seemed in enormously good humour.

"Good," Peterson said. There didn't seem another thing to say, but nor could he think how to leave.

"See you, Maurice," Ric called.

"Bye then," Mrs Schuster said, reappearing in the glass frame and shutting the inner door.

Classes were ending as Peterson came near to the Humanities Building at four next afternoon. A gush of winter-wrapped students was pouring down the steps from its doors, and from the doors of twenty other Neo-Georgian halls on all sides of the big grass campus. Each flow fed on to the concrete sidewalks, to join the thick streams already going in both directions. No one ever looked at each other here, someone had once told him. It was true.

The boys especially, passed, hands in pockets, shoulders hunched, notebooks gripped between elbows and ribs, watching

65

c

the concrete. Again Peterson saw around him a world of in-
turned people, frightened to be themselves. There was something
mole-like and short-sighted about them. Most surprising was
the idea that, till Saturday evening, he had been likely to live
the rest of his life without noticing that he was one of them.
Immediately he knew that he must give a party for the students
of his class.

The typescript was on his desk. It had no title and began at
page thirteen, but it wasn't till he began to read that he
recognised it.

While Nic's having this cosy chat with these nice policemen,
who happened to remind him of hairy apes, but that's not their
fault, and while he's getting the friendly loan of their telephone
book, and their friendly help to dial a number, because two
hours ago they accidentally trod on BOTH his hands, this
teacher who Nic's going to call is sitting in his cosy home. He
doesn't know about the call he's going to get from Nic, any
minute now, but that doesn't matter, because he's ready to help
anyone, all the time. That's the sort of guy he is.

But there's something else coming to this teacher which he
doesn't know about. Because The Girl – who's a good kid really
– hasn't been idle these two hours while Nic's been chatting
up the law. First hour and a half she's spent sitting in her
apartment, just about pulling her hair out, thinking what in hell
can she do to help her boy. Then she's thought of this limey
teacher, who Nic's always saying is such a fine guy, and found
where he lives and started to walk there all by herself through
the black city night – because she's a brave kid, too.

Knock knock. Come in. Hi there. So now they're sitting in
his cosy living room, talking over what they can do for this boy
Nic, who's got himself into such a shit awful mess.

After about half an hour of this cosy chat which brings them
so close together, both feeling so sorry and anxious about her
boy, The Teacher begins to notice that The Girl isn't bad looking. Somehow he's missed this before. It's quite a shock to this
two-faced, smart-arse limey teacher, who's so smart one side of
his mind doesn't know what the other slippery side's doing . . .

About to read on, Peterson stopped with a jerk and re-read
the last sentence. He read it twice more, hunting for possible

66

negatives or qualifications, or for some undetected sarcasm, or some different way of emphasising the words to produce a different meaning. He didn't find any. The words apparently meant what they said.

He began to pace his office. Phrases formed in his mind: "A joke's a joke . . ." "There's a limit . . ." phrases which he instinctively rejected but which insistently returned.

The moment Morrison cut the engine of his rusted red Triumph (Peterson wrote) he heard the party. "Where's the party tonight?" No need to ask, just stand on a high roof and take bearings on the noise. Any week-end night there'd be a dozen shaking, pulsating houses to choose from. They were like stars suddenly exploding into a phase of violent self-consuming activity, burning themselves to nothing in a couple of light years, Morrison thought, standing in the dark street, twisting a tuft of his beard as he judged the direction.

Some parties sounded shut-in, gave a sense that when you got inside you'd find a red-hot, beating core, loud but contained. This one had broken out. Though still at least two blocks away, the music was sharp and crackling, as if all the windows were up, and the noise was echoing about a wide area of streets and houses. It was warmer tonight, spring coming, not steadily but in a series of tepid surges. Tonight for the first time Morrison felt the year alive and kicking.

Up the black tunnel of the stairs he went, controlling an impulse to block his ears. The house itself seemed to be jumping about. As he climbed he heard a separate lower noise on the level of his head; the continuous thundering of bare feet on the floorboards. It sounded quite a party.

A total block of dark bodies at the stair head so that he couldn't even reach the top step. No one moved for him, probably because they couldn't, but he pushed on, squeezing himself, hips, belly and ribs, upwards and forwards, a few inches at a time. The four couples he worked himself past watched him, as if he was a new discomfort which they couldn't avoid so there was no point in resenting. They stood here, arms round each other, but not necking or drinking, content it seemed to be sardined together in this semi-deafening darkness. With a final wrench and wriggle, he penetrated them and reached a kitchen. Only about twenty people here, propped against walls or stirring

67

gently in a room designed for two to work comfortably in, and already filled by sink, cooker and vast ice-box.

Most were boys, staring with sullen discontent towards the doorway, through which nothing they were hoping for came. They held beer cans but occasionally one who didn't would push his way to the icebox, peer inside, shrug and close it again. It was empty. After a few moments the closest of them leaned up to his ear and shouted, "Jesus Christ!" Morrison nodded vigorously to avoid a more subtle shouted conversation.

Facing outwards from the doorway, he looked left and right down the blocked passage. Here a thick humourless man, the owner perhaps, was regularly forcing his way with six-packs of beer, which seemed to be arriving up the stairs over the heads of the block at the top. Because of the crush he carried them at arm's length above his head. He seemed to be establishing a cache in a far room and each time he returned was more surly and defiant about what he was doing. Sometimes he conducted short angry conversations, as if commissioning people to guard it.

Across the passage, through another door, Morrison could see the main party dancing in a tight jumping pack under a low ceiling. The noise which came from this room was so devastating that he was surprised each time he saw a face that it wasn't screwed up in agony. Instead they gaped with a sort of stupefied delight, gesturing to him to come and join. A low-intensity fight also smouldered in there. A short man with a sharp nose was speaking up with muttered anger at a tall boy with a droopy moustache. For several minutes they would be separated by joggling dancers, then a rapid shuffling would show they were together again and people were pushing back to leave them a few square feet to hit each other. Once a blow seemed to have been struck, because a group of a dozen or more came sideways together in a stumbling rush, as if the deck of their ship had tilted.

Putting his mouth up to Morrison's ear, the boy next to him shouted, "Not a goddam chick who turns me on."

Two minutes were all Morrison could bear of this gathering of male wallflowers, before he forced his way across the passage into the dancing room, ahead only the most uncertain glimpse of bare shoulders and long fair hair, appearing twice on the fringes of the dance, but to be pursued at any cost.

68

He'd thought the noise loud before but now it hit him like simultaneous deafening blows on both ears. The orgasm was reaching a periodic climax and the jumping house, floor and furniture was jolting the phonograph needle out of its grooves, so that it often took several at a time with a thunderous discord. Each time this happened many of the dancers screamed with excitement. He could see their mouths opening to scream but couldn't hear them.

Through this thick pulsating sound, he pursued, openly at first, taking her away from the tall crinkly-haired boy she'd been dancing with to dance with her himself. She danced with cool surprise, amusing herself by herself during this interruption of her evening. He danced with wild violence, stamped, swayed, flung his hair back and arms up, puffed out his cheeks, performed for half minutes at a time with knees bent and arse hung backwards over space as if at any moment he must collapse onto it. A small admiring space cleared round them, but in front of him she still pranced and wriggled with maddening detachment. Sometimes she laid out a bare arm to click her fingers to the music, then didn't, as if even this was a concession she wouldn't make to him.

"Thank you," she said, stopping at once when the music paused. "My date," she said, giving him her first quick smile, and her hair a neatening shake over her bare shoulders.

Standing at the far side of the room, he ogled her – where she now sat squashed on a sofa beside her tall boy – raising his eyebrows, winking and making obscene gestures. The first time she noticed he caught her neatly with one of these at the moment she began a reflex smile, saw it die and a bright blush spread.

For a quarter of an hour after that she ignored him, then for a minute stared at him to embarrass him, or exhaust his stock of obscenity – a bad miscalculation this – then for quarter of an hour she ignored him. She became so deliciously restless that she had to make her tall boy dance although he only wanted to sit squashed against her. When they came back, Morrison ogled her. So she turned her back, sitting uncomfortably on the outer edge of the sofa to face away from him towards her boy. But she'd no sooner done it than she glanced to be sure he'd noticed. At this moment he began a shouted conversation with an abandoned dumpy girl beside him. He shouted for several minutes

69

close to her ear, sure that that fair iceberg on the sofa was watching, fairly sure that this dumpy girl thought him insane.

An hour and more passed in this entertaining way. At one moment, when she was again dancing with her boy, ostentatiously hugging him, she passed close enough for Morrison to turn his back and give her arse a sharp pinch. He felt her wriggle of shock and even heard her gasp of disbelief. Then he lost her.

He hunted her, a step at a time, over legs, round squatting, leaning, clutching wedged-in bodies, sometimes stumbling, occasionally barged outwards by some dancing back or struck by some flying arm, but persistently. She wasn't in the dancing room.

Out into the passage – a glance into the kitchen of disappointed boys – then deeper into the apartment; at last he saw her in a dimly lit inner room. She stood beside her boy against a wall, their legs sloped out, not touching or speaking, as if they might be quarrelling.

He backed quickly into the passage and watched round the doorpost. What success if this was really his achievement! He became more and more excited. Now he must arrive at the right moment and with one swift remark or wink persuade her that every gesture she'd been making in his direction for the last hour had been sophisticated flirtation. He peeped again. Less than a foot from his face, he found himself staring into the pop-eyes of a round-faced girl with bangs.

She was so close that she almost obscured the shocking sight beyond of the tall crinkly-haired boy helping his blonde into her coat.

At once he thought of several bright introductions, but a moment later there was no need for any of them because he was astonished by an instant of total understanding with this new pop-eyed girl. He realised that she was peering round the doorpost for exactly the reason that he was: she was hunting. And he realised that *she* knew *he* was hunting. More, he realised that they both understood that this could be a misunderstanding – and so might this . . . in infinite regression. So all definition of what they understood about each other was not only futile but wrong, because their understanding was either nothing or everything – or indeed both: a total communication about

70

everything and therefore about nothing except total communication.

It was from this instant when they first met (Peterson wrote) that all else followed, because not only was it their first moment of total understanding, but it was also – with one possible exception – their last.

They stood there, grinning at each other with astonished delight. A second later, delicious chuckles started at Morrison's diaphragm and quickly spread to shake his shoulders – but now he was less sure she understood. Though she still grinned, there was a puzzled look in her funny pop-eyes.

"Say, come dance," she said, moving fully into the open, taking his hand. But the passage to the dance room was blocked again.

"Oh well," she said, and led him in the opposite direction, past the doorway where they'd met, round a bend. Immediately they were in this quieter place, she let go his hand and stood close to him, looking up into his eyes. With a shrug which there was only time to think, he began to kiss her. It grew more and more energetic. It grew into one of the most astonishing kisses he could remember. They came apart, panting.

"Gee," she said, as if he'd now really surprised her.

"Mmmm," he said.

"I'm Olga," she said. "Who're you?"

"I'm a marine biologist," he said, the idea arriving from the groping, sound-destroyed quality of the evening perhaps, or from his odd meeting with her, in low light, as if each peering round a projecting underwater rock.

"Oh, I've known some of *them*," she said.

"Let me tell you about the angler fish," he said. "This creature is thinly distributed over the world's oceans . . ."

"Say, you're English," she said. "That explains things."

"What things?"

"Oh, just things," she said. "Go on."

"Because of its sparsity, whenever a male angler encounters a female angler he realises that he mustn't miss his chance and hangs on. If another male encounters the same female he hangs on too. Sometimes you get six males with their teeth semi-permanently embedded in one female. I should have mentioned that they're about a twelfth her size."

"Sounds kinda crowded," she said.

71

"Now comes the exciting part. Whenever she ovulates they ejaculate. They do it automatically. A chemical signal passes from her blood to theirs – remember they're still biting her. So in practice they become nothing more than appended testes."

"Hey, that's cute." She stared up, big-eyed at him. "That really so?"

"I'm a marine biologist, didn't I tell you."

"Where do I apply?"

"For my course in marine genetics?"

"Hell no, to become a female angler fish. Do you know Al?"

"Al who?"

"I'm not sure. He's my roommate's boy. She's typing his thesis on carp. We call him The Carp."

Now they didn't talk but stared into each other's eyes, as if agreeing to drop this digression in favour of what they were really interested in. But a second later she was glancing sideways to the bend in the passage and the party beyond. A short grey-haired man of about fifty-five stood there. Morrison recognised a German psychologist whom he'd met at faculty parties.

"Do not let me interrupt you," he said.

He wore big dark-rimmed glasses with thick lenses, making it impossible to tell whether he was staring at them or generally surveying the corridor as if designing a new décor for it and only incidentally wondering whether they fitted.

"Come on," she said, taking his hand to turn him in the opposite direction. There were two doors off this passage and she opened the first. It was a bathroom. "Shit," she said and closed it.

She led him to the second. The room inside was dark but presently he made out a bed and on it a big stirring shape. "Aw, shit," she said, leading him out and shutting the door. "Some people have no consideration."

They moved back down the passage. The psychologist was still there.

"I am telling you, do not mind me," he said, taking off his big glasses and staring at them before going out of sight round the bend. As soon as he'd gone they burst out laughing, though exactly why Morrison was uncertain. He had the strange impression that the situation of a few minutes earlier had been reversed, Olga genuinely amused, himself puzzled. Later he even felt that there'd been some understanding between her and

this man, as if they knew each other; and that his invitation
not to mind him had more meaning than he had yet discovered.
At the time he was quickly distracted, watching her give the door
to the bathroom a hard stare through narrowed eyes.

"Well hardly!" she said. "Say, is all that fluff real?" looking
up at him.

"Try it and see."

She took a strong tugging grip of his right side beard. He
caught her wrist and in a single movement forced it down past
her side and up hard behind her back. "Hey, stop it," she said,
her face screwing up, her neck going back on her shoulders.
"More," she said, through barely open mouth.

At once they went into a new and even more surprising kiss.
Their mouths opened wider and wider, their tongues dipped,
quivered and twirled, and they lost their balance and
staggered against the bathroom door. Since this was unlatched
they stumbled together several paces inside and began to slither
about on its wet tiles.

"Phew," she said, when they'd recovered. "Gee!"

"Sorry about that," he said, feeling his right shoulder with
his left hand to judge the bruises, at the same time unobtrusively
using his right to adjust his throbbing erection.

"Don't *apologise*," she said.

"After you," he said, and they came out hand in hand.

They faced, at three feet, a stout young man wearing a
Donovan cap, familiar from the dancing room.

"Well, hi there," she said. "Meet my English friend. He's
a marine biologist. Just been showing me the bathroom, appropriate, eh? Jim Pool, my date. Meet . . ."

"Maurice Peterson," Morrison said cunningly. "How are you?"
holding out his hand.

The young man with the cap didn't take it. He stood still,
big hands hanging by his side, staring at Morrison and not at
Olga. "Having a good time?" he said.

"Splendid, thanks," she said, answering for him. "Say, let's
go home," and grabbed his arm to turn him.

For several seconds he resisted, still staring at Morrison.
"Nice knowing you, Mr Peterson," he said and let himself be
turned and led up the passage. At the bend she glanced back
and waved with her free hand. She didn't speak and he thought
that Jim Pool, plodding heavily beside her, hadn't noticed.

73

C*

Morrison returned to the party, and circled it twice, occasionally drinking from abandoned beer cans. When something soft came flopping against his lips and he realised that this one had become an ashtray for cigarette butts, he left.

Driving through the busy one am streets of swerving headlights and parking, date-decanting cars, every aspect of the party made him chuckle with delight and surprise. He ran his red Triumph up the ramp to his mock Spanish front door – of two-inch oak with heavy iron rivets, bolts and functionless knobs – entered and slammed it with a thunderous clang which shook the house. This reminded him of Lillian, lying upstairs with a bad headache, and of the grad student who'd invited him to the party and he'd never discovered there.

The only other person he'd recognised had been the German psychologist. But even if he and Olga did know each other the idea of asking his help to find her was for some obscure reason highly offensive. So the problem of rediscovering her became insoluble. His shoulders shook, his mouth opened and in a moment he was laughing aloud, the sound echoing round the house as he staggered about it. Now he was certain the joke was against himself. Hands on hips, he found himself bent double among the wrought iron occasional tables of the sitting room. Tears oozing from the corners of his eyes, he stood in the hall, staring up the stairs, right in the face of that poor sod Don Quixote in his niche.

Like the steady pouring of water from a height on to the earth, a moth fluttered against the inside of Peterson's study window, and he glanced to see if it was raining. But outside a bright blue day had come at last.

He pushed away his notebook to stretch magnificently and hunch at once, caught by a sharp pain below his heart which thumped heavily from his night of black coffee and no sleep. The moth still fluttered. How frighteningly futile because, a foot above it, was a two-inch gap to the bright free world. Peterson made himself a new promise.

All the way across campus he nursed it with its symbol and moment of certainty. He walked clumsily from exhaustion, sometimes stumbling as if a leg, trying to snatch some independent sleep, had forgotten to move forward to take his weight. He was

74

strangely insensitive to cold. What sort of class would he give this morning? But, worryingly, this too didn't worry him.

Days ago he'd sent the other invitations, but not hers, because he'd planned to ask her in person, so giving her the best chance to exclude Mr Dool. The days had passed and he hadn't asked her. Now this plan seemed so illogical that he couldn't believe his intelligence had passed it : she could exclude Mr Dool as easily from a written as from a verbal invitation.

Holding carefully to his promise, touching it occasionally to be sure it was safe, he came into the Humanities Building. The College of Humanities was in ferment. He saw them as a yard of clucking hens, who'd suddenly noticed that a fox was among them. The fox was the new Dean of Humanities.

They stood in pairs in low conversation, in classroom doorways, the corner by the staff mail-boxes, the pantry of the coffee room, their faces grave with indignation, falling into unexplained silence if he came close, because they weren't sure which side he was on. Nor were *they* sure. They took up a wide variety of carefully argued in-between positions, and spent much time defining them to each other, so that it often seemed to him that to give a group of academics an opportunity for political action was the ultimate practical joke.

Today, Bill, Jo and Marge were gathered in the centre office, big with news, and he listened while they told him how the Chairman of the English Department had walked out of the Committee on Curricula Rationalisation, and how the Dean's wife had said to Bud Phin (Yeats and Henry James) at the Dad's Day football game, that for two pins she'd get shot of the whole bunch of stiffnecked bastards. Then they were showing him a typed sheet.

"We, the undersigned . . . the committee proposal to reduce the whole seventeenth century to one multiple sectioned course on Milton . . ." He read its phrases of understated desperation with growing alarm. By the end he was sweating heavily.

"It isn't for *you* to sign," Jo said.

"Just thought you'd be interested," Bill said.

"I'd like to . . ." Peterson began.

"I wouldn't if I were you," Jo said.

"Why, it's not even your period," Bill said.

"Though you could say principles were involved," Marge

75

said with the tired thoughtfulness which sent her Art Appreciation classes to sleep.

Most worryingly, Peterson now realised how anxious they were for him to sign, or at least approve. He had a sense that they were forcing him to swell out and play the role of English referee. In the silence which followed, they'd all looked up from the paper to him. Straightening his shoulders from their usual hunch, staring back from one to the other, he said boldly, "Give me twenty-four hours to think it over," and left in a hurry.

Past the Women's Old Gym, left here from when the Humanities Building was shared by Physics and Recreation, where thirty bulky co-eds in skin-tight black were limbering up for Dance Two-Six-Seven, past the official notice board, his eye caught by a black-edged notice, SIX WAYS THE RELIGIOUS GROUP OF YOUR CHOICE CAN AID YOU, he came into the bright cold day. Long before he reached the Schmitt Chemistry Building, he saw how absurd it was for him – skinny, married and forty – to compete with such husky, virile boys of her own age as Jeff Dool.

Past the official notice board, his eye caught by an out-of-date notice in Dayglo orange DAD'S DAY PEP RALLY AND SNAKE DANCE. THEME : DADS AS LADS. CROWNING OF KING DAD. Up the wide stairs – long before he reached his third-floor classroom, he knew that he must hold tight to the conviction that he once *knew* what he must do. In ten seconds he would have spoken the words. In eight, seven, six, he would actually have done it. It was unbelievable . . .

The shock of finding her not alone, as he'd imagined, but one of a group of five students, easily stopped him. Impossible to ask her in front of several he hadn't invited. How ludicrous, anyway, to arrive up the stairs and come straight out with it, as if it were an important idea he'd been busying his mind with. And how idiotic not to give himself another fifty minutes to decide.

The class proceeded. Miss Sherry Steiner was back, her black bun gripped in that vast tortoiseshell comb, presumably with new contact lenses – or had she rinsed the old ones from her dog's/cat's faeces? Soon he was embattled with her over signs and symbols.

"Shouldn't you ask yourself : do I naturally see the world in terms of symbols, and if I do, is this a conscious or unconscious perception, and if I've been taught it, can I ever escape from it, and if I can't escape, does it become a proper part of my perception or an artificial part, which interferes with my proper unconscious perception? So you come back to square one, should I be asking myself this sort of question." – I will, because I once *knew*, he thought. I can't till I remember why I knew, he thought, staring at Miss Steiner, whom he'd apparently silenced by this fluent, though almost certainly meaningless answer, turning to Mr Dool, who was laughing aloud at what he knew must be a parody of academic thought.

"Take a personal example. This morning I saw a moth . . ." He stopped, appalled to realise where this would lead him, his eyes fixed on Mary Foringer's pale note-taking hand, asleep on her pad as she stared out of the window.

"Miss Foringer, will you give us a personal example," he said, recovering brilliantly, but with no spare margin – I will, he thought, I can't. Will, can't, will, and began a strange continuous shudder, half at the danger of asking, half at the cowardice of failing to ask.

Even more disturbing, he began to notice that the astonishing way he was conducting the class was getting him more and more of their attention. He had the idea that in a moment they would all stand together and walk out. This isn't teaching, they'd say as they went. The more he struggled to settle them back into reassuring boredom, the more interested they grew. He stumbled over words. His mind stumbled over ideas. As often when tired, it seemed able to retrieve them only from the past fifteen seconds and to lose all memory of anything before. At this moment, appallingly, Miss Percy's watch showed him that only five minutes of the class had passed. When at last the bell saved him he was soaked with sweat and collapsed in mind. Sitting on his desk, not trying to speak, he glanced up and saw Jill Hearn close ahead of him, standing by her seat. "Coming to my party?" he said.

"Sure thing, if I'm invited," she said, and when he'd told her the day and time went out across the landing, waving back to him.

He was crossing campus before he felt any excitement. He'd done it, he told himself, but it felt less like a deliberate choice than an abandonment of choice. It was as if, all these weeks

77

he'd been attempting something in a wrong way, and only now heard a voice telling him, Don't resist, go with it.

He'd reached the front lawn of his house when he heard singing. A single voice, distant but clear. The moment he heard it he seemed to remember what music was like, as if for months he'd been living in a world deprived of its most moving part. A force he had no will to resist drew him towards it, slowly at first, into the shrubs of the rectangular park, then hurrying, dodging between trees, with a growing happiness – and hardly bearable anxiety that he'd be too late.

There she was, not a machine as he'd half feared, but a real person. Slowly she made her way across the far side of the park, singing to herself, not softly or with embarrassment, nor loudly and defiantly for other people. Just as loudly as she and the song needed. Why did no one else notice? Passing in their cars, perhaps they couldn't hear, but why didn't the windows of all the houses round the park go up? It was as if she wasn't really there.

She was wearing an old brown cape with a cowl so that he could hardly see her face. She came to the road and stopped singing to cross. As soon as she reached the far side she began again, but after only a few steps a hedge hid her. It cut off her singing in an abrupt way, so that he wondered if she'd stopped. Then he caught a phrase again, and for several minutes he could still half hear her as she went further away.

The whole incident filled him with the sort of spontaneous happiness which for many years his reason seemed to have been blocking, but he could now clearly remember feeling as a child. He smiled at Nancy, eating toast with peanut butter and jelly in the kitchen, and went upstairs to his study.

He pulled down the top of the window to the sunny winter day and gently lifted the moth with both hands to the gap. He leaned forward to watch it, rising at once with astonishing speed for something so small, ten, twenty feet against the bright sky. A second later it happened, so quickly that at first he didn't understand: something black, coming from above the house, swerving in flight, then weaving out of sight among his neighbour's trees. It was so sudden that he went on screwing up his eyes to look for the moth where he'd last seen it, high, small and black against the bright sky, but it was no longer there.

The telephone rang.

"It's Judy Finch here. You probably don't remember me."

"I certainly do."

"Say, Mr Peterson, I don't like to trouble you, but I sure would like to visit with you."

"Of course."

Uncertain what it could mean, he rebuttoned his coat and went back through the kitchen.

"Where are you going now?" Nancy said.

He stared down at her black chain-mail hair, curving inwards around her big munching jaw, rejected every answer in turn because, without hurting her, none of them could explain how she was failing to hurt him. He could see so clearly why she needed to sit there, munching and reading a magazine, laughing at him for the way he let his students push him around.

After ten seconds she became aware of his stare and glanced up. "Well, for suffering christ," she said, and went back to her reading.

Without a word – though shaken – he left the house. He recrossed campus, walking now with steady exhaustion, every movement needing an effort to start it and another to prevent it miscarrying and landing him in a tangle on the sidewalk. Judy was already outside his office.

"I sure do appreciate the way you're helping Ric," she said, sitting in his visitor's chair, small, thin and dark.

He was surprised to learn that Judy, and presumably Ric, still believed he was helping him. "It's nothing," he said modestly, at the same time noting that it really didn't seem to have needed effort, but more a failure to make the emotional effort of telling the boy to go and stuff himself.

"And Ric sure appreciates it too. He thinks you're one of the finest people he's known."

Again Peterson had the sense of moving into an unreal world. It didn't seem possible that this was true, and yet it didn't seem possible that this small serious girl was being sarcastic.

"Frankly, I'm confused," he began.

"You can say that again," she said. "Oh, he's so demanding."

"He certainly is," Peterson said, but he thought they were agreeing about different things. In a moment they would try to define their sympathy and fail to find it.

"Not in the usual way," she said. "He's so giving."

It was the last word he'd expected.

79

"Take last night," she said. "He brings me this huge cheque. All those zeros. I didn't even count. He gives it me and just waits. I try to give it back. 'Keep it,' he says. 'But you don't have that money,' I say. 'And even if you did, I wouldn't take it.' 'You just keep it,' he says. So what's he doing? Laughing at me? Or mad with me? Or is he just plain off his head? Or would he really like to give me that crazy cheque with all those zeros? That's worst of all." She stopped and stared at Peterson, as if slightly shocked to find him listening to her.

He believed he understood. She was so unsure why the boy liked her that she didn't even know what part to play to please him. She was only sure that it couldn't be for something she was, but something he was giving her, something he needed to find and might just as well have given someone else.

" 'Do you want me to go away?' I asked him. 'Is that what it's for. To pay me to clear out?' That makes him real mad. For a whole hour he won't speak. Just keeps looking up at me and cursing under his breath."

Again she stared at him, but now he had the fantastic idea that she was watching to see how her story affected his attitude to herself. It was easy to dismiss this idea, which agreed with nothing he believed about her, but, in the way of fantastic ideas, an instant later it seemed to stand beside what he had believed as a complete and coherent alternative.

"Coffee?" he said, and suffered a dizzy sense that this suggestion was part of the same fantasy.

Sometimes as they crossed campus together to a coffee bar she said, "Oh gee," and sometimes just sighed. He was again surprised by her smallness which forced him to take slow steps to stay beside her. By the time they were sitting in the dimness of the coffee shop – an unfashionable one and nearly empty – the idea had receded.

"If he thinks he's going to break up with me . . ." she said, but stopped, too many complications interfering with what had started simple and assured.

Once more he knew as he'd known at the Golden Nite, that she was frightened and rather lost but not going to run away, as most American girls would have done, most girls anywhere perhaps. She had a quality which he couldn't easily name. Braveness was too simple. Just of staying with things that happened to her. It was less that she seemed to refuse easy

80

escapes than that she knew already at seventeen that there weren't any.

"Sometimes I really think I love him," she said.

"As a sort of helpless child?"

"I suppose so," but her hesitation told him that it hadn't seemed right.

"You want to mother him," he said, suddenly convinced he must shock her into understanding things about herself, for her own protection.

"Oh that, of course," she said. So it was the incompleteness of the idea that she hadn't accepted.

"I could never hope to be as intelligent as him."

He was depressed. He sensed that her understanding was patchy, sometimes far more adult than his own, sometimes childishly simple.

The door to the coffee bar swung and Ric came in. Peterson was half to his feet, "Hallo," almost spoken, when paralysis gripped him. His head began to spin and at the same time give a sense of drifting sideways. How better could he have confirmed the boy's paranoid suspicions that by being found here drinking coffee with Judy?

Nor did Ric speak, but crossed to the bar, bought beer and carried it to a table three away. He sat there, drinking it, sometimes looking round the room, sometimes looking casually at, or rather through, them, as if they were any pair of unknown people. But every gesture showed that he knew he was stage-centre. Glancing back at Judy, Peterson's mind suffered a new jolt to see that she apparently hadn't noticed, just sat thoughtfully stirring her coffee.

At once a new alarm hurried through his mind: was it really Ric? To ask her now – You may not have noticed but Ric's come in – at least I think he has – was unthinkable in his role as Ric's friend and counsellor, which he seemed again to have accepted. This idea lasted only a second before a still more disturbing one came. Had they planned the whole episode to-gether? Even if she was the honest girl he thought her, Ric might have forced her to do it.

"Gee, I wish I knew," Judy said.

And now in the most terrifying way, he began to hear Ric speaking.

"That's my girl over there," he said.

81

"Where's it going to end?" Judy said.

"And that's my friend she's with," Ric said.

Peterson sat rigid, shivering from his neck to his ankles.

"It scares me," Judy said.

"That's right," Ric said. "Maurice Petahson, the famous British writah. He's helping me with my problem."

Now Peterson had the impression that he was speaking to people at nearby tables, leaning towards them, pointing. It was impossible to turn and look. Sweat dripped below his arm as fast as a ticking clock.

"That's right," Ric said. "Not my writing problems. My psychic problems. And that's my girl he's got with him. She's helping me too. Funny, isn't it, both of them sitting there together!"

With a wrench which needed all his will, he turned, but Ric sat staring away towards the coffee bar, smiling and not speaking. Nor did any of the students at nearby tables seem to be paying him any attention.

"Sometimes I don't dare guess what might happen," Judy said.

"You mean . . . ?" Peterson said, with a dry croak which set him coughing.

"You might think they were enjoying themselves," Ric said. "That's where you'd get it all wrong. They're worried as hell to know how to help me."

"Pack it in," Peterson said.

"What's that?" Judy said.

"Nothing," Peterson said.

"Please tell me, is he plain crazy?" Judy said.

"D'yer hear that fellers?" Ric said. "*He's* telling *me* to pack it in."

"You're only hurting yourself," Peterson said.

Now Judy's black eyes grew wider and wider, and she stared at him as if she, too, had suddenly become terrified by what was happening.

"Hey, fellers," Ric said, "would you say that bastard had it coming to him?"

Peterson pushed back his chair and hurried from the coffee bar. The sun in the street was dazzling and he barged heavily into three people on his way to the corner. He was aware of

82

many others staring after him as long as his dodging back-view was in sight.

By eleven-fifteen Peterson knew that his party was a success. Like a fire, its hungry crackle suddenly told him there was no more need to feed it anxiously. Standing in the doorway between packed kitchen and packed sitting room, looking ahead through another doorway to blocked entrance hall and bar, and to dining recess beyond where twisting dancers appeared in succession, he had a happy sense of achievement, as he strained to listen to Dorothy Phin, pretty wife of Bud Phin, shouting, "So what do you *really* think of us?"

"You're very logical," he shouted. "You find an easy way to do something so you all do it, New England to New Mexico."

"Oh, I know that," she shouted.

A howl of group laughter from somewhere out of sight rose above the general yakety yak of the party.

"Your gridiron cities. You've found they're psychologically unhealthy so now they'll have crooked suburbs. Not *some* but *all.*"

"Yeah, yeah," she shouted. "No totalitarian state could produce greater uniformity." She took a big mouthful of ham sandwich, leaving a half circle of pink lipstick on the excluded bread. Surprised at her silence, he glanced and saw that her mouth was crammed and she was using the triangular tip of her little pink tongue to recover crumbs. At the same instant, through the doorway ahead of him, over the heads of fifteen or twenty drinking guests, he saw Jill Hearn pass slowly and alone down the bar.

"Drink?" he said to Dorothy Phin, and took her empty glass before she could clear her mouth.

He had fifteen feet to go. "Excuse me. Excuse me." He eased and pushed, holding both empty glasses high. Sometimes, at waist level, he saw his small dark daughters. They held plates of party eats and smiled before they were engulfed again. Once he caught a glimpse of Myrtle, his youngest, moving among a forest of legs, occasionally lurching into one, staggering with sleep but refusing to give up. He was filled with pity and love for her small obstinacy. Tonight they were on his side. "They can stay up," he'd said boldly, and waited with increasing surprise for Nancy's contradiction which hadn't come.

83

Immediately this side of the doorway, twisting to squeeze himself between the bright plaid shirts of two students, he found himself staring into the startled-owl face of Dr Ivan Heinz.

"Good evening," Dr Heinz said, as if he'd been watching his approach.

It was the first time they'd met since the Golden Nite. Surely some explanation was still needed, but Peterson had no idea what. More disturbing, he distinctly remembered deciding not to invite Dr Heinz to this party, because he'd invited Ric Schuster – yet here he was, as if by right. He felt a shiver of alarm at the idea that he'd not only taken this action quite unconsciously, but totally expunged any memory of doing it.

"Busy?" Dr Heinz said.

"Yes," Peterson said and glanced ahead for a chance to pass on with this excuse, but now his way was completely blocked. He became more and more worried by his position, stuck here staring closely into Dr Heinz' face with nothing to say to him, at the same time holding a glass in either hand, forward and above shoulder level, as if about to stick him with two bullfighter's banderillos. What really alarmed him was a sudden desire, perhaps because of his embarrassment, to do exactly this.

"I should warn you," he began, starting any conversation to distract himself, but now unsure whether it was about Ric Schuster, or about the danger of suddenly being struck on the head by two empty glasses that he must warn him. At the same moment, totally stopping him, came the picture of a cold Canadian lake under a high moon, an upturned boat, clinging to it Dr Heinz, sodden and shivering, only his shoulders and head with soaked grey hair above water, a dripping walrus . . . And far away across the lake that screaming which at first he'd thought some hideous night bird, but had been his wife and only son drowning . . .

"Excuse me." A gap had opened and he slipped through. The incident had so upset him that he stopped beyond the doorway, his back to the wall, separated by nine inches of brick and plaster from the short broad back of Dr Heinz. Most disturbing was the idea that he had wanted to pity Dr Heinz but not been able to because Dr Heinz wouldn't accept pity. In the most astonishing way he'd seemed actually to reflect it,

84

so that by even attempting to pity him, Peterson had made *himself* pitiable. This was why he'd hurried away, but why he now stayed here, strongly, almost desperately anxious to go back. Anyway, he'd again lost Jill Hearn.

She'd come an hour before, in her orange and yellow tent dress – with Jeff Dool. What a relief he'd felt. It was a definite, if small, advance, but one which still gave him time. In the presence of her boy there was clearly no chance to attempt anything – even if he'd known what he wanted to attempt.

But she hadn't stayed with Jeff Dool, begun instead a slow progress alone round the party, bourbon in one hand, picking at nuts and chips with the other, glancing from face to face. Wherever she'd gone he'd kept track of her.

Once he'd accidentally caught her eye, deeply embarrassed to guess that she'd known what he was doing. At another time he'd talked to her in a group of four or five. "What I need," she'd said, "is a small black slave to carry my bourbon."

"I'll see what I can do," he'd said.

"You will?" she'd said, looking up wide-eyed at him in a way he found most confusing. Before he could continue this surprising conversation Mr Dool had arrived, panting slightly, What could it mean?

But now he could see neither of them. Had they left? The idea of the rest of the party without her filled him with terrible boredom. Though he stood on the bottom stair and looked out over clustered heads, able to see all rooms except the kitchen, he couldn't find her. Instead he saw Ric.

He stood with one foot on a window seat and was speaking down at someone he hid. He made big gestures, sinking his head and putting up both hands up to grip his hair in despair, raising his chin to open his mouth wide in a hearty acted laugh, using forefinger and thumb to widen one eye. He changed feet, disclosing that the person on the bench was his daughter Jenny. She sat there, feet off the ground, plate of party food on her lap, like a polite child at a Victorian tea party.

Suddenly around him he saw everyone in the room asking desperately for something from someone else, and seldom finding it. He saw Ric asking for love and approval from this child because he couldn't get it anywhere else, but frightening her far too much by the way he was asking for her to give it him.

85

There was something appalling about her childish self-sufficiency in front of his humiliating adult need.

Beyond them he now saw Nancy, half facing another wife, but reduced to speechlessness by this loud party of ill-dressed students. She was asking everyone to realise that she wasn't responsible. He saw that by making her give this sort of party instead of one for his colleagues and the husbands of the women she played bowls with, he was forcing her to despise him.

A full glass in each hand, he elbowed his way back to the kitchen. Dorothy was waiting for him.

"I hate to go on about it," she shouted, "but you're an intelligent outsider. What do you *really* think of us?"

"You're very tolerant," he shouted. "If an Englishman tells me I'm wrongly parked he's full of jealous moral disapproval. If an American tells me, he's trying to help me beat the cops."

"You try being American," she shouted, but with less hope that he would ever understand her question.

"You mean, what do I think of American women?"

"Yeah, yeah," she shouted. "It's a matriarchy."

"If so it's got a lot of discontented matriarchs."

"Are we discontented?" For the first time he seemed to have interested her. "You really think so? – Oh yeah, I know that." She turned her back on him. "Better than being in the harem."

A stir in the party brought Dr Heinz close. "Hi," she called, as if she knew him. "You met our tame English sociologist, Dr Peterson?" She kept her back to him.

"Oh yes, he is writing a novel about us," Dr Heinz said.

It was the sort of guess any facetious middle-European might have made to a writer at a party, but the totally unfacetious way he said it, as if he *knew*, gave Peterson a bad shock. It was as if, at some party he'd quite forgotten, he'd had a long confessional conversation with Dr Heinz.

"Novelists are victims of their experiences," he said, to escape his embarrassment, adding a mysterious smile.

"Is it not often the case," Dr Heinz said, "that these experiences you mention are victims of the novelist? I ask you. As a rule I am not reading novels."

"Depends how he treats them," Peterson said. "Dr Heinz, we were talking about American women," he went on, confirming his escape. "You should be able to tell us" – and was at once appalled by the tactlessness of what he'd said, which

86

might seem to refer not to Dr Heinz' expertise as psychologist but to his dead American wife.

"I do not talk of the way they write about these experiences," Dr Heinz said, "but of the way they live with them before writing. To be more precise, the way they fail to live with them."

"That's right, tell us what you really think of us," Dorothy said, brightly substituting new hope for her disappointment.

Dr Heinz allowed such a long pause to develop that Peterson became convinced he hadn't heard, and was wondering how to help Dorothy re-start the subject when he took a sharp breath into his wide squat chest and said, "The Female Orgasm."

It was as if he were announcing the title of an academic paper, and he now left another long gap, as if before the text, in which Peterson saw Dorothy begin and suppress a giggle.

"What other civilisation has put such importance on this thing?" Dr Heinz said. "Name me. Who has ever heard of it? It is your special invention. I would like to say your contribution to Western Civilisation, but this I cannot."

To hear him, Peterson and Dorothy had to bend their heads close to him. Dr Heinz didn't bend and Peterson was conscious of the odd pyramid they must form, his grey haired owl-face at the top.

"The way you talk, we might all be nymphomaniacs," Dorothy said.

Dr Heinz observed this interruption steadily, before going on, "Because I am thinking this sex may be a limited form of human activity. What do we have? Six books – of a technical nature. Forty-nine positions. Look now at cookery. Six thousand, perhaps even sixty thousand books. As for recipes – forty-nine million."

When Peterson laughed Dr Heinz' tufted owl-face became wide-eyed and innocent.

"I speak of the female orgasm and its effect on the American male," he went on. "If you say to him, look, here is woman, take her, how many can do? They are suffering initial impotence. Why? Because they do not believe they can please their women. Because they have been required to attempt this thing at an earlier and earlier age. Not only to their high school young ladies, but many many years sooner, to their mothers."

"Oh not that!" Dorothy said and wandered away, as if unable to bear this new disappointment. But she went on staring back at Dr Heinz, wrinkling her nose and once putting out her little pink tongue at him as she receded into the party. Dr Heinz stared innocently after her.

"As I am saying," he began when she was finally out of sight, "already one novel has been written about this campus."

Had he been saying it? Peterson was almost sure he hadn't. He had a sudden desire to escape from what he was going to be told, because it now occurred to him that Dr Heinz had planned this whole conversation, and that the last minutes had been deliberately invented to drive Dorothy away so that they could have it alone.

"To my mind, it is not a good novel" Dr Heinz said, "but I am no expert, and you will give a professional judgement. It is called *The Singing Priests*."

At once Peterson remembered hearing of this book, though when he wasn't sure. For no reason he could explain, his alarm at what Dr Heinz was going to tell him increased. During the last minutes he'd become conscious of Miss Sherry Steiner, invited in a moment of euphoric compassion, close on his other side, sandwiching her podgy hands between her arse and the wall. She held her fine black-haired head upright and, even through the party noise, he occasionally heard her great tortoise-shell clasp squeaking on the shiny wallpaint. Now he turned to her with relief. "Hallo there."

"Hi, Professor Peterson."

"Did you want something?"

"Not *me*," she said, watching him with her black eyes. Tonight for the party she was wearing a huge white blouse, which surrounded her upper half in a cloth balloon, as if continually inflated by some breathy atmosphere inside, and fell forward in white floppy cuffs over her hands.

"I thought . . ."

"It's none of my business, Professor Peterson," she said, squeaking her comb, "but I reckon you should do something about Jill."

"Jill Hearn?" he said, his heart giving a violent thump.

But now Sherry Steiner just looked at him as if at a heap of one of her menagerie's vomit.

"Is she ill?"

"Not that I know."

88

"I thought . . ."

"Well go talk with her or something, for christsake," Sherry Steiner said.

At once he understood. For hours the whole party had been watching with amazement his unbelievable obtuseness. Only Sherry Steiner, with her blunt kindness, had been insensitive enough to tell him. He wanted to grasp her great frilly inflated upper half and hug her. Hope filled him, but at the same time, looking quickly round the party and still failing to find Jill Hearn, rage at his own stupidity and desperation at the possibility that she'd gone.

"Excuse me," he said, starting forward, but Dr Heinz stood in front of him, with Dorothy again, as if attracted back against her will, and another faculty wife, small, dark, with straightened Jewish nose. At the same moment doubt came to him. Did Miss Steiner's message merely mean that Jill Hearn had some specific thing to say to him – about a paper perhaps – or, worse still, about an extension for Mr Dool's paper on *Hard Times*, now seven weeks overdue?

"May I introduce Sherry Steiner," he said, with quick ingenuity. Now he had no desire to search before he'd prepared himself for such a disappointment.

"Pleased to meet you," the two wives said. Dr Heinz observed her but didn't speak.

"By Martha West?" Dorothy said.

"Who's she?" Peterson said, glad to rejoin their conversation about this novel, the impossible optimism of the moment when Sherry Steiner had spoken now making him flush hotly. Thank god he'd saved himself from some mad, self-exposing rush round the party, asking for her with laughable anxiety and hope.

"You mean who *was* she," the small dark wife said. "She took her life."

"You have read?" Dr Heinz said.

"Oh yes," she said.

"Why did she do that?" Dorothy asked.

"You have *not* read?" Dr Heinz said.

"Sure," Dorothy said, but in a way which suggested that, if she had, the traces were slight.

"It's about the Markham case," the dark wife explained to Peterson.

"No no, it's about the Schlitz affair," Dorothy said.

89

"Haven't you met Karl West?" the dark one asked Peterson.
"Is he still around?" Dorothy said.
"He certainly is. He's a dean now."
"Well for heavensake," Dorothy said.

"I'd certainly like to read it," Peterson said abstractedly, because now a new possibility was making him sweat with embarrassment. Had his care to hide his continuous awareness of her made him seem to ignore her more than anyone else? Had she, and everyone else, noticed this rudeness? Did she merely want him to explain : Tell me what I've done?

"It is a difficult book to obtain," Dr Heinz said. "We are living in a paradise for litigants," he said, with the first hint Peterson had detected of annoyance. Again he believed that the subject was being kept alive for himself. In an instant Dr Heinz would tell him what it was he feared. The man's stare grew bigger and bigger, giving him a terrifying sense of being drawn into it. But before Dr Heinz could speak, still another explanation of Sherry Steiner's message and of Jill's disappearance for the last fifteen minutes came to him. She was not merely in the bathroom. She'd got shut in.

"However, I am in possession of one copy," Dr Heinz said.

"Excuse me. Must go." Now Peterson escaped, but, dodging his way through the party, he was near panic. The more he thought of it the more possible it seemed. All this time she'd been locked in there. Everyone except himself had known. "Go talk with her for christsake." Now the meaning seemed obvious. She was half hysterical in there. Needed his comfort and reassurance. This missed chance to calm and rescue her. Master of the house, advancing through them, gathered uselessly outside, axe in hand – his revenge on his landlord, incidentally. Stand back. Crash. Three manly blows. Flying splinters of timber . . .

No crowd round the half bath beside the back door. Up the stairs he strode. But straight across the landing was the open bathroom door and brightly lit white lavatory.

Too late, someone else had rescued her – Jeff Dool? – to take her home in his big husky arms. But doubt now fell on the whole idea. Surely he would have heard noise. Slowly he came downstairs, more confused than disappointed. He'd reached the third step from bottom when, right ahead of him, the front door opened and Jill Hearn came in.

90

"Hi," she said.

"Oh, hallo," he said, back for a moment of wild hope with his explanation – it was himself she'd wanted to rescue her, for him that she was now returning – came forward both hands held out. "Are you all right?"

"Well sure," she said, taking his hands in both of hers, but looking at him with surprise. Terrible doubt filled him again, but it was far too late.

"Come and dance," he said.

"Sure thing," she said, still looking at him most oddly, but smiling and coming willingly. Confused as he was himself, he began to get the pleasant idea that he'd accidentally confused her.

They danced close together, moving at once in time, without the knee-knocking, toe-treading apologies which he always expected.

"Well, Professor Peterson!" she said, holding her head back and on one side to look up at him and flutter her big brown eyes under her brown bangs.

"Yes?" he asked innocently, pulling her close again, increasingly sure that he'd accidentally astonished her by his dashing forwardness.

"Your arms are cold," he said, taking hold of both her wrists – surprisingly small and soft – to swing her carefully.

"Boy, you may not have noticed but it's winter out there," she said.

"You been out there long?" he said, edging towards his question.

"As long as it takes to say good-night to one athletic date. He needs his beauty sleep. University archery squad."

"But you came back," Peterson said, his inside knotted with happy laughter at the trick he'd played on himself.

"I came back," she said and smiled at him with a meaning he didn't dare guess.

For an hour they danced or sat beside each other in the brown window seat behind the dry-sinks, wooden coal buckets and other New England artifacts.

They asked each other their ages.

"Thirty-six," she guessed.

"Afraid not," he said.

"Forty-six," she guessed.

91

"Forty," he said, to prevent anything worse.

"You don't look it," she said. "You don't look any age. You could be twenty-five or fifty."

"Twenty-two," he guessed.

She shook her head. "Twenty-seven."

"You certainly don't look that."

"Oh I don't change,' she said. "I looked like this at seventeen. I probably always shall."

When they talked they looked into each other's eyes. When they danced he held her hand to lead her out, and once experimentally put an arm round her waist to lead her back.

She asked where he came from.

"A real Englishman," she said.

"That's the way it is."

"Whereabouts?"

"Nowhere special. I'm a displaced person, like all the southern English lower upper middle classes."

"Hey, that's the way I feel," she said. "I'm from a State City suburb, but it doesn't mean a thing."

If she ever glanced away his eyes went down to her dimpled brown knees, which her orange and yellow dress didn't cover. He longed to touch them. Quite soon as they danced she kicked off her shoes, and tonight her bare rather broad feet seemed cleaner – or perhaps it was the dim light.

The party, though thinner, was rising to a series of separate but excited climaxes. In several places faculty were talking to students.

Big noisy groups were gathered at the centre of this room, but in corners through doorways he could see pairs talking together in a new way, at once relaxed but acutely attentive, as if interest had at last replaced politeness. All over the party he believed surprising things were happening in these quiet corners. Even Nancy and Judy Finch were talking together in a way which seemed to hesitate on the edge of sympathy. Again he saw the desperate and obvious need of all these people. All day they carried it round with them, but only at an occasional party, when half drunk, did they dare ask openly for love – or give it.

He asked her how she'd come to this odd place on the prairies.

"I met a boy," she said. "But that's all over."

"Jeff Dool?"

92

"Christ no," she said, staring at him as if he'd really alarmed her. "An Italian boy," she said dreamily. "Raphaelo."

"I don't believe it."

"Too good to be true, isn't it. Raphaelo Bandini. He's useless."

"You came here after him."

"I was in love with him for five whole months," she said. "Ever heard of such a thing! Do you know what he says the first time I bump into him at the Union? 'What the fucking hell are you doing here?'."

"Sounds charming."

"Oh he is. No, really, that's just what he is – when he can be bothered. But utterly useless. We're all through now. Want to know what happened? Well, we have coffee together, me buying the coffee, of course. He's lost every cent at poker the night before – Hey, maybe that's why he was in such a bad temper. Never thought of that," she said as if the idea really was new. "Too late," she said.

"Well there he sits, looking bored as hell while I keep saying things to amuse him and he doesn't even answer. I may as well not be there – except I bought him his coffee. It's just as if he knows he needn't do a thing except sit and let people see how beautiful he is. He is, too. That's what's so sickening. 'So what do you really think of me?' I ask him. 'You're a good lay,' he says. That does it. I come round the table and hit him, right in the stomach, as hard as I can. What else can I do? Didn't he ask for it? I've never seen someone so surprised. That really finished it. We're just good chums now."

"Sounds like it."

"Oh yes, he's nice to me now he's sure I'm not after him."

Peterson took her to dance, and now to his amazement she sometimes laid her head on his shoulder. When she did this, or raised it, their cheeks touched softly and they began to prolong this moment. As they danced he recognised one of the other pairs of dancers: his small soft hand set in the middle of her big white back, collapsing her billowing blouse, his other holding hers out and up, above shoulder level, so that their two short still arms seemed glued in this position, like some nautical signal, Dr Ivan Heinz was dancing with Sherry Steiner.

The music stopped and Peterson watched him guide her away, his small hand still set amid her white billows. An unkind

93

suspicion came to him that Dr Heinz was giving a live demonstration of a recent theoretical point.

"And you've really written two whole books?" Jill said.

He nodded.

"And I've read one."

"Want to see the other?"

"What would you guess?"

Together they hurried upstairs. When it was almost too late he remembered to glance for Nancy. With relief – and slight surprise which he quickly suppressed – he saw that she seemed to be listening with even more attention to Judy Finch. Together they came into his study.

He sat in his chair to reach for the copy. She went on her knees to turn it and hunt for the author's photograph. When she looked up, to compare this to the original, with a spontaneousness which amazed him, he took her face between his hands and kissed her.

At this moment, as he heard his novel slip to the floor and knew that he didn't care whether it had blunted its corners, he dimly understood that for the last hour, while they'd apparently been exchanging ideas on various interesting subjects, something entirely different had been happening. Uneasily, as he also reached a kneeling position and took her more firmly into his arms, he wondered if all his life two parallel successions of events had been going on and he'd only been noticing one of them.

After a minute they came apart but stayed kneeling, staring with happy astonishment into each other's eyes. Automatically his mind began to search for an appropriate comment, but, failing to find one, he suddenly knew that there was no need to search because she wasn't searching. More clearly he saw life divided into parallel streams, and realised that she naturally lived in the other. To her, every word was part of a game she agreed to play because other people seemed to want it, but quite superficial, nothing to do with her real world. All his life he'd believed that people meant most of the things they said. Now he guessed that the opposite might be the truth.

To her, words might *never* seem true, because even if they'd been true at the moment they were spoken, speaking them destroyed their truth. For the first time in his life he didn't want to speak. He wanted with desperate longing to join her in her

94

real unverbal world. By this time they were sitting on the floor, their legs going opposite ways, their mouths tight together and so wide open that their tongues seemed to twirl in an undefined area, neither in one nor the other. They came apart breathlessly.

"Professor Peterson!" she said.

"Hi there," he said, with besotted gentleness.

"Eight weeks!" she said dreamily.

"Till when?" he said, wondering if it was a guess at the remaining part of the semester.

"*From* when, stupid," she said, and they held hands, staring dopily into each other's eyes. "Must be a record."

"I'm not even drunk," he said, with smug astonishment.

"Silly," she said, putting up a hand to rumple his hair. "Hey, let's give you bangs. No. Doesn't suit. Did anyone ever tell you you were beautiful?"

"Not as far as I can remember," he said, trying seriously to think.

"Gee," she said, shaking her head in wonder, but whether at his answer, or at the general situation he wasn't sure.

They danced again. They went into the kitchen and he put a devilled date into her mouth and she put a roll of smoked salmon into his. When they were unexpectedly alone – and their mouths were empty – they kissed with quick violence between the portable dishwasher and the icebox. Someone was coming and they hurried on to the side porch and kissed in the darkness out there till they swayed against the insect netting, and came quickly inside. He was shivering continuously, he noticed, but had no sense of being cold. They were dancing again, her hands on his shoulders, his clasped behind her back, looking into each other's eyes from six inches, when someone tapped his shoulder.

A cold shudder ran down him. Nancy? Some friend of hers to threaten him. But it was Dr Heinz.

"We leave."

"Oh, I'm so sorry."

"Why?"

"Well, you know, good party ..." Peterson said vaguely, letting the loud music cover his confusion.

"I will lend you," Dr Heinz said. "Or perhaps you do not want to read."

"Oh yes, I'd like to," Peterson said, now openly promising

95

himself that he wouldn't, the way Dr Heinz was forcing him an ample excuse. Beyond him he saw Sherry Steiner, standing sideways in a doorway, sandwiching her podgy, white-frilled hands against it.

"I lift Sherry," Dr Heinz said.

"Oh . . ." Peterson could think of no answer, believing this must describe some acrobatic dance which Dr Heinz had been performing with her – an achievement so satisfying that he had to keep telling people.

"You got room for another?" Jill asked.

"Indeed yes."

Later Peterson believed that it was his confusion about Dr Heinz' meaning that had paralysed him. The arrangement was made before he'd thought of offering to take her in his own car. How much harder to do it then! How it would have drawn Dr Heinz' look of owl-surprise! Thirty seconds later it was already happening. Time only for a passionate kiss among the coats in the television room, to emerge under the eye of Sherry Steiner, heaving herself into a great fur wrap – suggesting a legacy from a grandmother in some Lithuanian forest, made perhaps from a bear or two.

"This it?" he said, holding up Jill's red-lined cloak.

"Certainly is," she said and let him help her into it, as they tried, not very hard, to hide their giggles. But all the time he was wondering whether he dared say it. "Hey, let me drive you home," or whether she would understand that, as host, he had a duty to the tail end of his party. Then they'd gone, her face a pale shape at the back window of Dr Heinz' car, as he drove it away with three convulsive lurches, leaving a faint white cloud in the night of condensing water vapour and oil smoke.

A fine fall day, perhaps the last before winter again froze the prairies, fires of burning leaves by the sidewalks, bony lantern-jawed Abraham Lincolns tending them under the bare branches of maple and oak, in scarlet Dayglo hunting caps. Peterson's daughters persuaded him to take them camping. They drove five hundred miles south to a warmer climate. Logically, he knew it was the best thing that could have happened. With every mile he suffered more pain and despair.

Classes had ended for Thanksgiving at one o'clock the day before – the day after his party – and wouldn't meet again till

96

one o'clock next Monday. He wouldn't meet his own class till nine o'clock on Wednesday. Seven whole days. How could he bear it?

A month ago he remembered promising this last trip of the year, if the weather allowed. Then he believed that he, too, had thought he would enjoy it. It was impossible to remember this state of mind. He looked forward to seven days of terrible boredom.

They camped on a sunny hilltop over a mile-long artificial lake. More long-jawed Americans in scarlet Dayglo caps, with steel fishing rods, and reels nine inches in diameter of precision-engineered stainless steel and black plastic; or just sitting in the sun in the doorways of their trailers, in sky blue aluminum folding chairs. What would she be doing all these seven days?

He didn't even know if she was in town. Perhaps she was with Jeff Dool. Somehow he felt sure that she wasn't alone. All Tuesday he'd wondered whether he should call her.

But he hadn't even asked her number. His bungling inexperience appalled him. Late in the afternoon he'd set out for the Union enquiry desk.

"I thought vacation had started," Nancy said, baking brownies for the Flower Arranging Interest Group of the Faculty Wives Club.

"I accidentally made an appointment."

All the way to campus he looked down cross-streets and glanced behind him and ahead in case he passed her – but he didn't even know on which side of campus she lived.

The broad concrete sidewalks across the grass were deserted, the bells still ringing but no crowds pouring out. The Union passages were empty. He found her number, carried it to his office and sat staring at his phone.

What should he say? It was as if the successful achievement of getting her number had left him with no energy for this far worse problem. Desperately he lifted the receiver. Something would come. He put it down before the first ring. Suppose nothing came.

Just called to see you got home safely. As soon as this bright invention came to him he re-dialled and listened to the long unanswered ringing. He dialled again in case he'd made a mistake. Still no answer. He forced himself to walk all round the deserted passages of the Humanities Building – SIX WAYS

97

THE RELIGIOUS GROUP OF YOUR CHOICE CAN AID YOU – before he dialled again. As he reached the last number he forgot what he was going to say and hurriedly put down the receiver. Anyway, how lucky he'd already been. What would he have said if, instead of Jill, some friend or roommate had answered?

Early next morning he left the house and called from a coin box in the nearest shopping centre. No answer.

"Where have you been?" Nancy said, handing out breakfast of toast with peanut butter and jelly to his daughters.

"You should try it," he said, avoiding a direct excuse with cunning obliqueness. "Spring's coming."

"Please can we go camping?" his three daughters said, in the sort of prepared chorus he most detested.

"Why not?" he said, with desperate cheeriness – to prove something to Nancy, and perhaps to himself, though he was unsure what.

In the sitting room he'd taken the Beatles, the Monkees and the Animals from the phonograph and started *Rigoletto*. All the time they'd packed the tent and sleeping bags and hamburger equipment he'd listened to its marvellous but despairing sound which filled the house, giving deep but hidden sighs, on the edge of tears.

Sitting now on the sunny hilltop, arms round his knees, looking down on the blue lake with its small fishing boats, each with bristle of rods, listening to the sounds of Nancy and the girls gathering sticks in the wood behind him, the whole evening seemed less and less to be trusted. Turning the pages of the student register at the Union, he'd even known for several seconds that he wasn't going to find her name. But there it had been, HEARN, GILDA ARAMINT – the computer would only accept twenty units – with address and number, reassuringly similar to the other thirty-three thousand.

Her ringing unanswered phone had made him doubt again, not exactly whether it had happened, but why. He found it harder and harder to believe that to her it had been important. Just the friendly way she always behaved at parties. Perhaps next day she'd been mildly ashamed because she'd been a little drunk. Worse still – he broke out in sweat at the idea – could it have been a bet with Mr Dool, who'd been secretly watching from the drive?

98

Far more certain was the brown paper parcel in the tent at the foot of his air-bed. He'd found it inside his front porch as he'd come out for the last time. This was a door they seldom used, so it had probably been there since the day before.

It was an odd parcel, the brown paper not containing it in the efficient way of a mail package, but wrapped loosely round it with many creases, the string making many loose loops, all going the same way. It had suggested an abandoned baby, and perhaps because of this he'd meant to leave it there till he returned. Carol, coming last down the steps, had brought it out triumphantly. "Parcel for Daddy."

At their first halt he'd seen the sheet of green paper, tucked into the string, pulled it out and read, "I am finding only this one copy. Ivan Heinz."

When their tent was pitched he'd put the parcel under the foot of his bed. Increasingly, since his party, he'd felt that Dr Heinz had provoked what had happened, that he had reacted with comical promptness, as if to some button which Dr Heinz had pushed. But whether in a way Dr Heinz would approve, he was unsure, because he now sensed that it had been a testing sort of provocation and imagined Dr Heinz watching the result with owl-eyed innocence, or, if he disappointed him, with alarming indifference. Until he knew the answer to this problem he wanted to postpone the still more difficult one of why Dr Heinz had so insistently lent him this novel.

All day he thought of her. If he saw a tree or a bird or a hill, he still thought of her. Whenever he spoke to Nancy or his daughters, she was in his mind. He thought of her with every mouthful he ate and every twig he fed on to the fire. Immediately he woke in the morning he thought of her and of the time which still remained before he would see her. When there were two days left he felt no closer to seeing her. Two whole days and nights. How could he ever live through them?

Often he walked alone among the trees where he could sigh deeply without being seen. At night he couldn't sleep but, when the others were breathing or snoring steadily, dressed in a warm sweater and walked about the silent camp. Because it was late in the year there were only three other tents, pale two-dimensional shapes in the moonlight, but in the nearby park there were twelve or fifteen trailers. Here, under the camp's overhead lighting, they stood in their allotted spaces, each plugged by an electric umbilical to the power supply. Since dusk their owners had been shut up in these little boxes, and wouldn't emerge till the sun grew warm next mid-morning. They were trapped, it seemed, in these hot hutches between the urge to be tough axe-wielding frontiersmen, and the determination never in their lives to suffer a moment's discomfort or inconvenience. Peterson sighed and walked on into the moonlit wood. For the tenth or fifteenth time, every word they had said to each other went through his mind and he broke into hot sweats of alarm at the new ways she might have misunderstood him, or of frustration at the wittier answers he might have given.

Next morning, the day before they were to leave, they had planned a long hike and a picnic. Now, as he wandered in an anxious dream, he found himself again limping, as he'd occasionally limped all day, preparing this excuse for not coming. A whole day of their cheery company, identifying flowers and trees and birds, would be more than he could bear.

Sometimes he listened to them in astonishment. Could these things really be all that was happening in their heads? Surely there must be ideas there which they cared more about. How terrible if there weren't.

But he'd loved them better these days than for many months. Even Jenny and Carol. Myrtle he always loved – still too young to be continuously on the edge of idiotic giggles, as the others seemed. This new love for his family seemed not just a side-effect of a single party flirtation, however delightful, but the flowering of some understanding which had been growing in him all fall.

Nancy, too, he could have loved. He saw again her good sense and calm. He found her pretty. But just when his feelings for her had changed so encouragingly, freeing him from guilt that he didn't love her as he should, they were blocked by a worse frustration. Because the first need of this new love was to trust her with all his thoughts and hopes, and unfortunately these were exclusively about Jill.

In the end he said he must work. Standing outside the tent, he watched them disappear, feet first, down the slope towards the lake. Sometimes he waved and sometimes they waved. Jenny pushed Carol, she shot forward, half stumbling, and they sank out of sight in screaming pursuit of each other. Nancy and

Myrtle plodded after them, descending into the grass, Myrtle first, then Nancy, waist, shoulders, head. The excuse suggested the idea. He propped car cushions against a tree, fetched his notebooks and sat with them on his knees.

He sits at his desk, working with concentrated attention (Peterson wrote). Sometimes he changes position to get an elbow further on to the desk top, and sometimes he alters the angle of the paper. Sometimes he holds back his head to admire what he's written. He's written, "Peter Morrison, peter Morrison, PETER MORRISON, Peter morrison," all down the paper, in many different styles . . .

Or is she with her Italian? Peterson thought. Was it to be nice to him for an evening that she'd pretended she no longer cared about this boy? Or to comfort herself? Raphaelo! He forced his attention to his notebook.

Notes for character: Morrison's friendships are warm, giving, spontaneous, without reserve for private comment. He likes people at once, and shows it. He takes no emotional precautions in case tomorrow, next week, next year, he may no longer like them. Because they at once see that he likes them, they at once like him. But he likes them because he likes liking, not for anything they can give back. He is a giver of love, not a loaner in the hope of a return with interest.

When he looks at people they positively please him. Almost all of them. The fleshy legs of plump girls. The emaciated legs of dark ones. The powdery wrinkles of middle-aged women's faces, the muscular shoulders of young boys. He is not all the time finding them repulsive. The way they move, or rest when they think they aren't being watched—he watches everything with delight, with pleasure. Pleasure occasionally *increased* by a shudder.

Instinctively he loves animals. His whole family love them, want to give them love, go on their knees to coo over them. Even in a timid way, his wife Lillian . . .

"Eight weeks," she'd said. Could this possibly mean the time she'd been hoping? He didn't dare believe it.

101

Today for the first time he saw his central problem. Relentlessly, Morrison appeared, sitting at that deeply littered desk, staring at a blank sheet of paper or – new development – doodling on it. His own novel would only make sense when he discovered what Morrison's novel was about. At present he was a hollow character, a huge preoccupation missing, unconsciously his principal preoccupation. Even if he couldn't actually bring himself to write it, the preoccupation must be there, a great misshapen baby he couldn't face delivering.

Though he saw this central problem more clearly, it seemed today to exist in a shadowy world which he had to force his mind to visit. An hour had passed – another four or five before they would return. He stood in the tent mouth. Presently his eyes became used to its green dusk and he could see that wrapped shape half hidden by the foot of his air-bed. Quickly he went on his knees to unwrap it.

It was a typescript – that explained its bulk, but left many more things unexplained. How did Dr Heinz have a typescript of a novel by this woman – who had apparently committed suicide? Had he known her? If so, why hadn't he said so? Peterson carried it to his seat in the sun.

THE SINGING PRIESTS

(scratched through above this was an earlier title: YOU CAN'T GET TO HEAVEN WITHOUT US.)

This morning my husband Karl (here the writer had noted: invent name) called out that he wanted to speak to me. I was in the basement doing the laundry. I came upstairs to the living room and there he was, pacing about by the window, looking grey and tired. The moment I saw him I started to shiver all over. I couldn't help it. He was my father, of course.

He didn't look me in the eyes – I'm used to that. He just went on pacing about, looking at the carpet, or occasionally, when it seemed he might speak, managing to get a glance as far as my feet.

There was a special reason for my shivering this morning when I saw my husband Karl pacing about in front of me like my father. Two hours before, I'd been looking on Karl's desk. I knew that at this time he'd been on campus. I knew that I hadn't touched a thing, just stood above it, looking down with scarcely bearable hope at what I saw there. I was still terrified by the idea that somehow Karl had found out.

It's only at bad times that I start to look on Karl's desk.

"I've withdrawn my name," he said suddenly.

"Your name?" I said, uncertainly, but I wasn't uncertain. I just needed time to think. The moment he spoke I knew with terrible certainty what he meant.

I needed to think back over the last weeks, every day of which I'd expected this to happen, though he'd never said a word which suggested it. I'd expected it with such steady fear, that, now it had happened, I felt something close to relief. I'd expected it ever since that hot summer morning when he'd come down to coffee and said, without warning, "I shall sign."

All the arguing was over then. I'd won. Because although we'd discussed it impartially, each taking either side in turn to see what we could make for it, I'd never doubted what I believed he should do. So I was happy for myself. But *he'd* won too; his true self had won. All that time of arguing I'd hidden from him my partiality, so that when and if he won, it would truly be *his* victory. So I was still more happy for my husband Karl.

Before that morning of his victory I'd lived in the greatest anxiety. Time and again it had seemed to me that caution, the life of academic non-involvement, or some specious argument resting on these bases would defeat him. It had been as much as I could bear not to cry out in my fear but to go on steadily and impartially repeating the evidence for each side in turn, waiting and hoping and, yes, actually praying for him: not to god, of course, but I know of no other word to express my sense of utter helplessness, because the decision seemed neither in my hands nor in Karl's.

What I hadn't realised was that by comparison the time after he'd made his good decision was to be ten times worse. Because the argument hadn't ended. It went on. Every day it went on in his head. The only difference was that I couldn't take part. I was totally precluded from admitting even that I knew it was still going on.

I knew by his grey face, by his awful, perpetual preoccupation, by the way I had to say things to him three times before he'd hear. Once when I said to him, "Well, it certainly will be a

103

strange experience, job hunting after all these years," he looked at me as if he couldn't think what I meant. I actually had to explain to him that the moment his resignation was accepted, even if it was one among two hundred and thirty-seven others, he, personally, would be out of a job and we'd be moving home. Signs like these would have told me by themselves.

But even without them I'd have known. After twenty years I know the way his mind works. A decision isn't a decision to Karl, it's a hypothesis, a point to argue *from*, not to reach with gratitude so that the argument can be forgotten. It's his strength as an academic. He doubts his own conclusions as much as everyone else's. They are always exploratory, revisable. He cannot understand that the decisions of life are *unrevisable*.

"Oh god," I said when my thoughts reached this point – and was terrified to find that I'd spoken aloud.

"What's that?" Karl said.

How fortunate I'd been. He'd only half heard. "Can you do that?" I began in my most reasonable way. "Surely the letter has been sent. Surely you can't *unresign*. It just isn't possible." I stopped, fearful that a hint of what I felt might be escaping.

"Of course it's possible," Karl said. "Don't tell me Markham wouldn't welcome back anyone who retracts."

"But do you want to be welcomed back?" I said. "Wasn't the whole point of our decision that we couldn't bear to serve under a man whose treatment of a responsible student – whose antediluvian sexual mores . . ." Again I had to stop myself, sensing the passion that was infecting my words, sick with myself for the bad way I was arguing the case, putting first what should have been an ultimate appeal. And then an awful thing happened. I knew that I couldn't go through it all over. I knew that I just hadn't the strength, day after day, to watch him hesitate and hesitate while I pretended I didn't know what was happening. "Oh Karl, how could you?" I cried and burst into tears.

It was the worst thing I could have done. I should have known – I did know – Karl better. It froze him, as it always does. He just won't argue. For an awful moment I even thought he'd go away, leaving me there alone, as he sometimes has when I've cried. Tears are an argument he can never accept.

More than this, they repel him. Occasionally when I've cried – and I certainly avoid it whenever I can – I've seen him, if he thinks I'm too distressed to notice, give me the most hideous

104

looks. And I've known what at other times I've only feared, that he hates me. That he'd like to get me on a shovel and toss me right out the door and never see me again.

Oh, I know why Karl looks at me like this when I cry. Tears make him feel. Karl never wants to feel again. Ever. I can't tell him this. Karl believes he's an angry rebel. He believes he's spreading left wing views among his bourgeois students, sowing agnosticism in the children of methodists. The incredible conceit of this belief of his! He's as arrogant as any reactionary, as smug as any religious bigot. As sure he's right. But Karl is a *dead* rebel.

Nothing he believes hurts him any more. He has anaesthetised every problem by reason and talk. Nothing, nothing is from the heart. At best he can dimly remember the feelings he used to have. His good liberal, anti-racist views — does he ever ask himself if he really *cares* about negroes, the poor, peace in Southeast Asia. I don't believes so. The answer would be far too disturbing, and Karl has insulated himself against disturbance. That is why he cannot bear my tears.

I think of Bobby Thwaite (that's what I'll call him). Somehow the thought occurs as a direct successor to these thoughts of Karl as he is now, and Karl as he used to be. Because Karl used to feel. Oh yes, I haven't forgotten that. It's because Karl felt so painfully that he's built himself this perfect insulation. I think of Bobby Thwaite as he is now and Bobby Thwaite as he may be one day — but I don't believe it. I won't believe it.

Bobby Thwaite is in Karl's graduate seminar. Oh Bobby, Bobby ...

How can Karl have a boy like Bobby in his class and not see again what he used to be. Bobby is a mess. A great sprawl of a boy, made up of loose ends and exposed nerves. You can hardly speak to Bobby but you know you're hurting him. But Bobby's alive. Bobby's a human being. How can Karl meet him for four hours a week and not see by comparison what a tiny withered stick he has become, a self-enclosed sterile point, an anti-human being?

I've known Bobby for three months.

Since half way through last semester, when Karl invited him to one of our informal At Homes. One of those terribly formal occasions when we believe we're promoting staff-student relations, and we sit around with a dozen students sipping weak

D*

punch and Karl plays the relaxed professor. How I hate those Sunday evenings. Bobby was different. He didn't say "sir" to Karl. Instead of listening to him he interrupted, or just wandered away and started to examine Karl's books, occasionally picking one out and looking at it as if it was just the sort of phony book he'd have expected Karl to own. I could see how mad it was making Karl, all the madder because he knew it shouldn't make him mad. Because Bobby was showing him that when he asks his students to an informal At Home he's really asking them to an extension seminar.

Oh Bobby . . .

A week ago I let him take my rhetoric class. Teaching methods is one of the things he has theories about. We've discussed them not only on that first evening but on many others when he's been our guest. He was marvellous. Quite marvellous. I learnt more in one hour that morning about how to teach a class than I've learned in twenty years of grinding practice.

He was better than his theories, far better.

He was quite natural. I sat in one of the side desks under the window and in two minutes he'd forgotten I was there. I saw him turn to ask me a question, thinking I was a student he'd been failing to include, and his shock when he noticed who I was and then that quick smile of his which I could never describe – so open, but not brashly open, and at the same time self-mocking, and gone almost before it has begun.

Oh, you should have seen how they talked to him, how they opened up in a way they never do for me, how in about five minutes he had them questioning half the beliefs they've been stuffed with by their parents or high school teachers.

"How do you know?" he kept asking them. And, "Is that what you really *believe*?" Before the class was half finished they were asking *him*.

I had coffee with him afterwards at the "Y". I think I disappointed him. I think he wanted reassurance. I couldn't give it. The only words I could think of were hopelessly inadequate.

He's so fine. Sometimes I caught myself not attending to a thing he was saying and realised that for five minutes – more for all I know – I'd just been watching him. The way he speaks, that hunched-up look he has as if the world has hurt

106

him too badly for him ever to trust it again – and then out comes an idea so beautiful it makes me gasp . . .

It took me five minutes to stop snivelling and feel sure that when I started to speak to Karl I shouldn't break down again. That would have been fatal. Part of this time Karl paced about. Part of it he stood looking out of the window. Finally he sat on the Danish settee and opened Harpers.

"But Karl," I said and stood there, swallowing and swallowing, the tears right behind my eyes, knowing I *mustn't* let them come. "But why Karl, oh why?"

I suppose he stopped reading, though he gave no sign. Presently, still not looking up, he said, "Hopefully, we needn't go over all that again."

"Yes Karl, hopefully we shall. We *must*."

"All right then," he said after another long pause. "I've had time to get things in better proportion. To see them more calmly . . ."

"But what makes you think this calm proportion is better than the excited proportion you saw them in before?"

"Please let me speak. If we win and Markham goes we shall almost for sure get someone worse. If we lose and *we* go, he'll be freer than ever to behave as he pleases, instead of still having our restraining influence . . ."

"Oh Karl, I didn't think you could be so naïve."

"Naïve!"

"It's the oldest trap. Stay in power in the hope of doing good later. It's the excuse of every despicable politician. It's the way any Catholic priest justifies the mumblings he doesn't believe."

"Please let me finish. These principles you talk about, even if they're as important as we think, we're employed as teachers, not as . . ."

"Not to set the moral tone of our community," I interrupted him with hopeless sarcasm. "How can you say that, Karl? How can you suggest that teachers have no moral responsibility, that somehow when they become teachers they *lose* an ordinary human being's responsibility for the morality of his society instead of taking on more."

"It wasn't what I was going to say," Karl interrupted, but I was far too excited to stop.

"Don't you see that it's coming," I cried. "This freedom to love. It must. It will. The whole of our society, of our live young society, is desperate for it. All we do is make ourselves absurd by not helping. By pretending we can stand aside and watch when the official position is so hopelessly out of touch with what half our students practise and the other half would if they had the chance. You say we shall keep our influence, but who with? The faculty? The administration? Is that what you want? Are we employed, as you put it, to teach *them*? Or to teach our students – in the proper sense of the word. How shall we teach them if we utterly lose their trust?" I stopped, breathless. "What were you going to say?"

"It doesn't matter."

That's a trick of his which drives me madder than any other. It means, if this is the emotional, illogical way you're going to argue there's no point in my taking part. It makes me want to strike him, to do anything to force him to speak to me, not cut me off in this cold despising way. I'm excusing myself for what I said next.

"What about that letter on your desk?"

It shook him. It gave me a vicious pleasure to see him actually look up from his magazine – as well as a shock of fear that I'd somehow hurt him so much that he would do something violent to me – my father again of course. It only lasted a moment. Karl will never do anything violent to me. Even the impulse doesn't come now. A moment later I wished I'd hurt him more.

"You've been in my study," he said.

"Oh no, I can see through walls."

"If you want to know, that letter made up my mind. It wasn't till I'd written it that I saw how we'd got this thing out of proportion."

The letter had been a personal statement, in part attacking Markham for the unconstitutional way he'd dismissed a student editor without any of the normal consultative processes, but in greater part putting the case for the substance of the editorial: a less hypocritical attitude to love and sex on campus. I can't remember his words. I can only remember how well it was argued. How persuasive it seemed, not just to myself, who didn't need persuading, but to the bigots who did. And the feeling of hope I could scarcely bear which I'd had as I read it on Karl's desk. The letter had begun, "Dear sir," and I'd guessed it was meant for a newspaper.

108

"But Karl, you believe these things."

"How do you know?"

"You've told me. If you live with someone for twenty years . . ."

"How do you know what I believe?"

"Oh Karl, be reasonable."

"What would you say if I told you that the person whose love I was thinking of when I wrote that letter was Bobby Thwaite?"

The shock was terrible. What did he know? What had he guessed? What was the truth, anyway, and how had he exaggerated it? It was nothing to the shock I was to suffer in a moment.

"You mean me," I stammered. "Me and Bobby?"

"I mean *me* and Bobby," Karl said, mimicking my bad grammar with angry bitterness.

My world spun. In the instant that he told me this I became physically dizzy. But right in the centre of my spinning world was the total conviction that it was true – that I'd been blind not to see it because now I understood a hundred things about Karl I'd never understood before: the cool way he comes to my bedroom once a fortnight to make love, the shower he takes immediately afterwards as if to clean away contact, the weeks which pass when he won't touch me, when I long for his touch, for any human touch.

"And suppose I told you that it wasn't just coincidence, but that I'm interested in him *because* you are. Because you're in love with him, though you may not know it."

Never have I known anything like the hatred I felt then. Because as soon as Karl said this I saw the horrible trick he'd played on me. So it *wasn't* true. My conviction of a moment before was totally reversed, and replaced by the conviction that this was just the sort of trick Karl would play on me. He'd wanted to bump me out of my theoretical position by the most horrid shock he could think of – how well he'd succeeded. But to him it was just a cold hypothetical example, which I must accept if my position was to be logical.

I cried. I screamed. "You don't love him. If only you *did* love him." I ran to my bedroom.

It's where I've been ever since. What do I believe now? Oh god, oh god, what *can* I believe?

Peterson drove his family home. The sky clouded and the wind grew icy as they came north. Grey puddles stood in the parking lots of drive-in hamburger joints. Around five, low over the prairie, the sun shone briefly between black clouds against a strip of vivid yellow, then set in a glow of red and purple which for half an hour made a gaudy picture postcard of a hundred and fifty degrees of western sky. It was long after dark when they came to Flatville and Nancy and the girls went to bed. Peterson sat in his study, his heart pounding from the black coffee he'd drunk to stop himself falling asleep while driving.

He began to write:

Two in the morning, his heart pounding from the black coffee he'd drunk to keep himself awake, Morrison screwed up the tenth sheet he'd drawn on, punctured with his pen or folded into paper airplanes, pulled the manuscript towards him and read:

THE SINGING PRIESTS (invent new title)

Her clear and luminous brow ...

Oh no, oh no. Almost at once he began to cry out in pain.

Her disturbing and penetrating stare ...

Christ save me. With one hand he dragged his head down to his desk by the hair, with the other held the manuscript above him at arm's length, as if in desperate prayer that a hand would descend from the ceiling and remove it. He returned it to his desk and began to read it from twenty inches away, as if afraid he might vomit over it.

The sharp yet serene line of her jaw ...

Oh my god. Too much. He shut it with a violent slam, felt the appropriate gesture gathering, slipped it below his arse, lowered himself carefully and farted. Supreme. Better than he could ever have expected. Loud, prolonged – at least three seconds – with that rubbery quality of a balloon set free to jet

110

itself across a room. He sat still, all his anger dissipated by such perfect timing.

Seriously, he thought, letting a little seep back, leaving it there in the fumes: the female academic in full narcissistic flight. The gaunt and bony braincase, self-exposed in the act of wish-fulfilment therapy . . . A slight sorrow came to him that there'd been no one here to see. Too perfect to repeat . . . He extracted the manuscript by lifting his knees, set it on them and began to turn its pages.

This morning she found a letter of mine on my desk. A draft. I don't understand why I failed to lock it away with this diary. Perhaps I wanted her to find it. (Think about this later.) Or perhaps I was distracted by the appointment I was going to keep.

If I'd known that she'd found it I might have chosen a better time to straighten out the Ellis affair. I blame myself severely for mismanaging this matter. But I had little choice. It was a mistake ever to tell her I'd given my support to the Faculty Ad Hoc Committee's protest – a result, I see clearly now, of my anger at the fact that for her sake I never could. Any day now the full list of names will be published and mine won't be there.

I'd gambled that as soon as she realised the academic suicide it implied for me (for both of us) she'd beg me to withdraw. The responsibility for my cowardice would then rest where it should. Just the opposite. I now suspect it is exactly the prospect of this suicide which so excites her. Perhaps there is academic jealousy here. Whatever the cause, in future I must be more careful.

The moment I'd spoken she became hysterical. The more clearly I explained to her the futility of sacrificing oneself in a petty skirmish instead of saving oneself for the important battle (an attitude I deplore), the more she cried and screamed. I suppose this irritated me and the final provocation was her mention of that draft letter, a mere doodle (check that I'm not deceiving myself here). I was irritated not that she'd been looking at my desk, something she often does, moving the little marking threads I place there, unconsciously making sure that I know, but at the sudden idea that I might have intentionally left it there for her to see so that she would at last see my (invented) danger and plead with me to withdraw (thus provoking me to send it).

I lost my head. No doubt the past hour had upset my judgement. I mentioned Bobby (revise name, Peterson noted). It seems crazy, but at that moment I was overpowered by a need not merely to expose my feelings but to boast about them.

To distract her attention I blundered again by disclosing that I had observed her own preoccupation with him. (Can I really be jealous of her?) Astonishing that she could think it secret. Perhaps I spoke because, privately, I can't believe this.

She claimed, ultimately, to reject my confession and I see now that she can't afford to accept it, but I wasn't counting on this. The fact that I know about *her* infatuation can no longer be put back in the closet.

I suppose the temptation to tell her that I know has been growing for several weeks. Not, of course, at first. There have been too many. At first I treated it in my usual way, by pretending not to notice, and at the same time making opportunities for them to meet, both secretly and in my presence. I've often suspected that her real desire is to make me throw them out. But I won't do that because a much more effective method is to let her play with her dangerous toy to excess, till she realises that we both realise that neither of us can take seriously the proposition that she takes *him* seriously. But for six or eight weeks now, ever since it ran beyond a normal month, I've known my treatment wasn't working.

For perhaps two more weeks I was safely sure that this was a measure of her desperation. That a mere contest of wills was involved. That this time she was determined to make me take her toy away from her (so proving my love for her), while I was equally determined to let her educate herself by admitting its boringness. Gradually I began to wonder whether this infatuation wasn't of a different quality because the boy was different.

I honestly believe I began with this purely intellectual curiosity. Whatever could she see in such a gauche and offensive person? This morning, just an hour after I'd left home, just an hour before the talk (I use the word ironically) which I'm describing, he came to my office. He brought me his first poem.

How can someone like this be the son of two of my dullest colleagues? The question, of course, provides its own answer.

Sometimes I feel that he is too innocent to live. That I cannot bear him ever to grow up.

It wasn't much. A mere impression. But it had promise. A metaphor here. An unexpected rhythm there. He sat in my office so attentive while I read it, so anxious I should like it. I was enchanted. When I made a suggestion he wrote it in, *there*, on the spot.

"Is that better?" he asked. "You like it now?"

My heart was full. I couldn't answer him. I could only look into his eyes and laugh inside with happiness.

Peterson stopped writing, disturbed by this weird development.

Three-forty next afternoon, time to go to his office, it's actually happening, he thought. In twenty minutes I'll be there. An hour later she'll come.

This afternoon he believed it. This morning, half way to campus, an idea had emerged which had never occurred to him in all the last nine days of hoping for this moment. Suppose she cut this first class after the break.

Suppose in the interval she'd dropped out of school. Or dropped his course, to avoid the embarrassment of ever seeing him again. Or just overslept. The awful needlessness of this last possibility had made him open his mouth and give a small high pitched groan, to the astonishment of two big-legged co-eds describing their Florida vacations to each other.

But she'd come, panting up the stairs behind him, at the moment when, failing to find her outside the doorway, he'd been looking anxiously into the classroom to see if she was already sitting.

"Hi, made it," she'd gasped. "Say, you wouldn't have a drag. No, *you* wouldn't. Oh, thanks," when a boy had lit one for her and she'd taken a deep suck into her lungs. "Gee, did I need that." And she'd leant back against the wall, puffing it out in a slow cloud, and started to watch him. "Hi," she'd said.

"Good party?" he'd said, watching her as he'd been the whole time, filled by happy relief at her arrival with this noise and confusion which had seemed to sweep aside all need for careful words and innuendoes, and carry them back at once to that evening nine days ago.

113

She'd raised her eyes to the ceiling as if considering the point. "I reckon so," she'd said. His heart had thundered at her meaning. She could only give this jokey answer to a question which could only have been meant as a joke.

The bell had rung. "You coming to see me?" he'd said. "In my office at five?" – a time he'd thoughtfully prepared.

"I reckon I might."

Standing now in his sitting room, he quickly lifted a bottle of bourbon from the antique dry-sink and slipped it inside his overcoat where he could grip it under his left arm. But it bulged conspicuously so he tried it inside the top of his pants, holding its neck through the lining of a pocket. He'd just re-buttoned his overcoat and discovered that in this position it jolted against his stomach with every step when he saw Nancy in the kitchen doorway.

"Whatever have you got there?"

"Nothing."

"Nothing!" she said, as if this really frightened her.

"It's a bottle," Carol said, coming from the television room where she did her homework. "I saw him put it there."

"That's right," he said defiantly. "A bottle of whisky."

For once Nancy seemed more shocked than she liked. "So that explains why you're hiding it in your pants! You look like" – she hesitated – "some senile incontinent."

"I'll hide it where I like," he said, "You may not know, but alcohol's forbidden on campus."

"So what suddenly makes you need alcohol on campus?"

"I don't *suddenly* need it," he said. "I've always needed it. Or rather, I *never* have – much. I need it now just as little – or rather just as much – as I always have. To put it simply, I don't *need* it but I resent not being allowed it."

"That really makes things clear," Nancy said, closer to her usual exasperation.

"I'm glad," he said, and went out, slamming the door.

After a block in which he gave the flesh over his left lower pelvis bone several dozen bruising blows, he glanced quickly back, no one in sight, and rearranged the bottle under his armpit. The incident had upset his plan and he paused next outside a supermarket, needing two glasses. But if he carried the whisky in with him he'd risk a charge of shoplifting – or have to pay again. He could hardly leave it standing alone out here on

114

the sidewalk. He went on across campus to his office, secreted the bottle in his lowest drawer, covering it with cards for reporting student absences to the Dean of Men/Women, and stole two paper cups from the department coffee room.

At five o'clock she came, feet flapping up the stairs so fast that he knew she was running, and sat in his visitor's chair. "Hey, you mind if I smoke?"

"Carry on," he said, moving past her to shut the outer door, then the door to Jo's office. "I thought we should have a little talk," he began, "about your term paper . . ." and, repassing her chair, lifted her into his arms.

They kissed and swayed, and paused to gasp and listen, and kissed again. At one moment she bent quickly to unzip and kick off her calf-length boots. At another she lodged her burning cigarette on his desk edge. When they finally paused it had charred half an inch of varnish.

"Gee, you're quite an actor," she said, still in his arms, alternatively looking up into his eyes and turning away to gasp for breath. "I thought you meant it."

"About your term paper?" he asked smugly.

She pushed him away and sat, still taking deep recovering breaths but watching him as if she'd really been frightened. "You know what I thought? You'd sent for me to bawl me out. Little girls must keep their hands off married professors."

"You really thought that?" He shook his head in wonder at how little she understood.

"Drink?" he asked.

"You're kidding!" she said.

They drank neat bourbon from the paper cups, standing them in his top drawer, ready to shut them inside if anyone else came. Between drinking they held hands across the corner of his desk, staring into each other's eyes.

"Did anyone tell you you were beautiful?" she said.

"You're pretty," he said, sincerely, but also pleased that he was learning to say it.

"Oh, come off it," she said. "My face is too round."

"I like it," he said, but sensed that this, though equally sincere, was less well judged.

"So you really enjoyed the party?" he said.

"I'll say. You think about it over vacation?"

"Ninety per cent of the time," he said.

115

"Me, all the time," she said.

They stared at each other in happy wonder – he was somehow pleased to have reserved that spare ten per cent.

"Did you call?" she said.

"Where were you?" he said.

"Minnesota. Thanksgiving with the parents."

"Yours?"

"Christ no. The forester's."

"Jeff Dool?" He was deeply depressed.

"He thinks he's going to marry me," she said. "It's all right, honey, he's not."

"How did he get that idea?"

"I suppose I gave it him. Oh shit, it's so confusing," she said cheerily. "And now you! Why do I get my life in such a mess?" She stared up at him, fluttering her eyelids under her bangs.

"I still don't quite follow," he began.

"There's nothing to follow. He just started talking as if it was going to happen and somehow I forgot to tell him nothing doing. I keep meaning to but I never get around to it. It was a kinda joke at first, and then it wasn't a joke. You see I really don't like scenes. It's all planned now. We're to live in a log cabin in some arctic forest, and he'll chop it down and hunt antelope with his long bow while I have lots of little foresters. Can you *see* me?"

Peterson supposed not.

"I ought to take it seriously, but somehow I just can't. The longer it goes on the harder it gets."

"But he takes it seriously?"

"You're telling me! You know what he says? 'If I ever catch you with another man I'll murder you.' He means it too," she said, not hiding the pleasant excitement the idea gave her.

"But if you don't like him, how did you get involved?"

"Oh I *like* him," she said. "He's a nice guy. He's not as stupid as he seems either. That's an act. He just bores the pants off me."

"Cheers," he said and they drank and leant over the desk corner, touching lips and giving each other delicious little whisky-tasting kisses.

"I still don't see why you got involved," he began.

"He's Raphaelo's roommate," she said, watching him sideways.

116

"Your Italian?"

"My Italian."

"You wanted to show him what he was missing?"

"Ah ha."

Peterson was badly depressed.

"Anyway, I reckoned I might do worse. He's really a nice guy. Got to get married again sometime," she said. "I guess."

"Again?"

"Oh yes. My husband's in a monastery in North Australia. How's that for an achievement?"

"What sent him *there*?"

"Oh it was a kick he was on anyway. Being married to me just helped."

"But you're divorced?"

"Yeah yeah," she said quickly, as if worried that he'd been unsure.

"Is that why you wear it on your other hand?" he said, lifting her right hand to show the thin wedding band. "To leave space for the next?"

"Never thought of that," she said brightly. "Hey, you may be right."

They finished their drinks and he poured more. She sat on his lap and they held their faces softly side by side. When she began to stop the circulation in his thighs she sat on his desk top and they stared into each other's eyes, putting their faces six inches apart, then drawing them back to laugh with happiness. With a scramble she sat in her seat and he shut his desk drawer as the janitor began to work his universal key into the lock. Sitting facing each other across the desk corner, they listened to him telling them about his son's high school grades while he leant on his cleaning trolley or occasionally made passes with a mop around their feet. As soon as he'd closed the door to Jo's office they fell into each other's arms, kissing with hard desperation as if they'd been separated for days, hugging each other as if in some frantic desire to become a single person.

"Mustn't let that happen too often," she said.

They sat across the desk corner, staring at each other, sighing.

"I'm afraid I'm expected," he said. "Family supper."

"Me too," she said. "The brutal forester."

"If I could fix it, would you come out one evening?"

"Well now, that's a very forward suggestion, Professor

117

Peterson," she said, getting back into her calf-length boots and bouncing towards the office door. "But I dare say it could be arranged."

When she'd gone, waving at the corner, "*Ciao*", flapping down the stairs, he sat in a haze of astonished happiness. At the far side of the dark campus, wrapped in his overcoat against the icy night, he thought, here he was, half way home, and he couldn't remember a single moment in the process of getting here. For ten minutes he must have been dressing, coming downstairs, walking . . .

The bright stars, this strange bare lamplit quad, everything he saw or heard made him ecstatically happy. He could never remember feeling like this before – unless perhaps long ago when he was a small child.

He could remember seeing or hearing beautiful things but for many years he hadn't responded to them as he should. Always there'd been some veil between him and them through which he could see or hear but only half feel. Now the veil had gone, and he could give himself to them. To the ugly as well, because in a sense they were equally beautiful.

For many years, if ever he'd been happy, he'd needed to put himself outside this feeling, observing it – and so destroying it. Tonight he was happy with such force that he could know about it and stay inside it. He could live in the present. He didn't want to retreat from it by describing it. To do this seemed a shameful confession of failure. Those who can, live, he thought with atonished smugness. Those who can't, write about it. He was sure that even when life became painful, as perhaps it must, he would never again be capable of such shameful retreat.

Patronisingly, he pictured the half alive person who'd crossed campus two hours before, wrapped in an overcoat which he didn't fill, shrivelled spiritually as well as physically against the cold world. He was astonished at the speed of the change – and slightly uneasy. Once or twice she'd said things which had seemed to hurry him forward faster than he'd wanted – till he saw that his success was perhaps the result of his own fairly persistent eight-week pursuit. Gradually he felt more certain that on that first afternoon when she'd come to his office, he'd made a deliberate, almost courageous choice to take what she'd offered him. The disappointments of the weeks between had been merely his impatience.

118

The sense of being hurried was also pleasantly flattering, suggesting that he was loved, marginally, more than he loved. "Ninety per cent of the time." It was an understatement which increasingly pleased him.

In the kitchen they were finishing fried chicken and salad. They ate in silence, making him guess at things Nancy had been saying when she heard him coming.

"Good drink?" she said.

"Delightful," he said, with amusement that he could be so truthful and at the same time so sure that she'd take it for a defiant lie. I feel no guilt, he thought. How can I, about something which seems so intrinsically good? I begin to understand a new and more important meaning for the word. Good for life. Good for my life and so, frankly, good for all life, he thought — and ran upstairs to his study, unable to bear the sight of his family which he'd needed and used and was now betraying.

In the underwater gloom of the Stardust they sat together two nights later, holding hands and sighing.

"Gee, it's good to be with you again."

"It sure is." He felt a deep relief which these words could express only because they both understand what laughable understatements they were.

Sometimes he'd thought he couldn't bear the interval, must hurry at once to her room. All day he'd walked about his house dreaming about her, sighing — when no one was looking — and playing Verdi. Whenever he'd walked to campus he'd made a detour past her address, a small red-brick apartment house, hoping to meet her. He never had.

Whenever he'd driven downtown he'd circled along her street, watching the sidewalks for a hundred yards before and after, once hitting the curb with his right front tyre and so frightening a bicycling student that he'd tumbled into the gutter in a shower of notes and textbooks.

"What the hell's the matter with you?" Nancy had said.

"Nothing that I know of," he'd said, lifting the student by an arm, dusting down his pants, hoping even now that Jill might pass — perhaps give help — for the secret looks they could exchange. She hadn't.

"You'll end up being sued," Nancy had said.

"Perhaps we all shall," he said, pleased with this enigmatic

119

answer which she certainly wouldn't understand since he didn't – though slightly worried by the way she stared at him, sadly shaking her head.

This morning lecturing to his class, including Jeff Dool, he'd twice let himself catch her eye. She'd watched him, puffing smoke, with a faint smile which sent him into ecstacies of love for her. What a girl! Passing close by her on the way out he'd said quickly, "Eight-thirty." And she'd raised her eyebrows as if she couldn't think what he meant and almost at the same instant winked. Every move or gesture she made seemed perfect, filled him with happiness.

At eight-thirty he'd met her on the third floor of the library and they'd followed each other, ten yards apart, to his car.

"Where does he think you are now?"

"In the library. I've become a serious student. He likes that. He used to be worried by my flippancy. He thinks he's converting me."

"What happens if he comes and looks?"

"He won't. He's drinking beer with his chums."

"Just suppose."

"I'd tell him I was in the john. Don't worry, darling. I'll fix him. I'm good at that."

He grinned at her, hiding a slight uneasiness at how good at it she seemed to be.

"And where's Professor Peterson tonight?"

"Attending a department seminar on 'Retention of Tone in a College English Department'," he said, pleased but at the same time rueful at this effective excuse.

"Well if you don't mind my saying so, Professor Peterson, you're sure making a real contribution towards that project."

They laughed, delighted.

They danced, and drank bourbon, and sat holding hands. She smoked and sometimes he took one.

The orange underwater gloom of the Stardust was emptier tonight, at first only a dozen tables occupied, some by couples, others by pairs of girls or pairs of imitation cowboys. Sometimes these united. Once he watched the whole incident, from the arrival in quick succession of a pair of each, looking round the room as if for friends, to their amalgamation, sixty seconds later. "Mind if we move over?" He was amazed. Had this sort of thing always been happening around him? Gradually more people came and after a couple of hours a guitar group replaced the juke box with noisy pop.

At about this time, in a far recess of the room, he thought he saw Dr Ivan Heinz. Certainly someone like him was sitting there, but the more he stared, the less sure he became. When he got his features clear he became even less sure, as if till now he'd only looked at Dr Heinz' eyes and avoided the rest of his face. Half reluctantly, when they danced, he moved her in his direction. They came opposite the compartment. It was empty. Perhaps he'd gone to the john, or perhaps he'd mistaken the compartment for another. But when they sat, he could again see him there, far across the room, lit up in his own little pool of orange light.

As at his party, he felt both anxious to try again and glad he'd failed. Anxious because Dr Heinz gave him acutely the sense all Europeans gave him of a deeper understanding and sympathy than he could feel with any American. Glad he'd failed because of the sense Dr Heinz gave him of understanding him too well, as if he was a programmed puppet, who could never surprise him, least of all by the desire to try to.

"Is that Dr Heinz?" he asked her. "The man who took you home after the party."

She peered. "Out of my range," she said and turned away. Though it was probably true, he had the impression that she might have been glad of this excuse.

"How did you like him?"

She shrugged. "I reckon I was in no condition to notice much."

He grinned, but persisted. "He worries me . . ."

"Honey, don't let him," she said. "Say," she said, turning to him – while he was still wondering whether her odd seriousness had been meant or ironic – taking his hand in both of hers, looking up at him and pausing, "do I get to go to bed with you?"

A new delight rushed through him at the way, with a simple sentence, she'd helped him solve this next problem, which had seemed so formidable that he'd barely admitted it. Narrowing his eyes, drawing back his head as if to consider his answer, he said, "Could be," and felt with astonished pleasure, the warm squeeze she gave his hand.

Now they seemed to dance with new excitement. Sometimes

121

he held her small soft wrists and swung her away from him. Sometimes, still holding them, he moved them past her hips and behind her, so that they crossed in the small of her back. Dancing like this, his arms round her, her breasts pressed against his chest, his tall erection sandwiched tightly between their bellies, nothing it seemed to protect her, his excitement grew unbearable.

If I can feel it, then so must she, he argued, but this logical warning, far from deflating him in embarrassment, hardened his throbbing excitement. He twisted her arms more tightly. Her head went back, her eyes shut, her mouth opened.

"Sadist," she whispered.

He loosened his twist.

"Hey, what did I do wrong?" she said, opening her eyes.

Presently he told her he must go.

"Oh shit," she said.

"That coffee reception can't last much beyond midnight."

"Christ, the library shuts at eleven!" she said, her eyes bright with alarm.

"What'll you say?"

"Oh, I'll think of something," she said. "I'd sure better."

They hurried to his car and drove back through the four miles of neon fringe to the centre of town.

"Where will he be?" he asked.

"At my apartment, unless he's gone away in a rage."

"Do you sleep with him?"

"We share a bed," she said, "most nights. Hell, we're going to get married! But I haven't made love to him, not since your party – well only once, I suppose, and that was horrible. Hey, darling," she said, coming close to him, taking hold of his driving arm above the elbow with both hands, looking up at him in the darkness. "You gotta believe that."

"All through vacation?" he said. But he believed her.

"That was my period."

"Doesn't he suspect? I mean, if he's used to it."

"I don't think so. Most nights he won't anyway, because of his training. Got to keep up his strength for all that bowbending next day. And when he's not shooting he usually comes back too full of beer to be interested and I just tuck him up. Frankly, I get pretty horny. That's what happens the other night. Then a thought seems to strike him. 'Hey, don't you

122

wanta make love to me?' he says and begins to climb all over me. Just nothing I can do. About half way through, I get the idea something mighty funny's going on. He seems to have stopped and when I open my eyes there's this terrible look on his face. 'I think I'm going to vomit,' he says. Christ! I just give him one great shove, right off me up against the wall. And what do you think there is alongside my bed against the wall? A scalding hot central-heating pipe. He lies there for a bit, not noticing. And then, oh boy, does he yell. He jumps right off that bed and into the bathroom.

"And I just lie there, not knowing whether to laugh or be mad at him, or terrified of what he'll do when he comes back. After a while I can hear him in there vomiting, but when he does come he doesn't do a thing. Just goes straight to sleep. We don't speak for twenty-four hours. Not even while I'm dabbing ointment on that three-inch blister on his arse. Oh, gee, was that scarey. I thought he was waiting for the moment when he could *really* beat me up."

"Does he do that?"

"Sure, when he's ticked off about something."

"And you like it?"

"I used to think it was just what I'd been looking for. Frankly, it's becoming a bore."

He listened with interest and wonder. "But you slept together at first?" he asked, pursuing the subject in case it was impossible to start again.

"Sure, that was the whole point. As soon as he starts making a pass at me I get this bright idea. Oh boy, I think, you don't know what's coming to you. I take him home to the apartment and then, do I use my nails!" The memory of it stopped her with wonder. "All that blood. As deep as I can. He just doesn't know what's hit him.

"Next time I'm in their room, playing gin-rummy with Raphaelo, I suddenly see Raphaelo looking at me. And I look round and realise the forester's in the bathroom doorway with a towel round his waist and his shirt off. Jesus Christ, those scars. I can't really believe I've done all those myself. Right from his shoulder to his arse. But Raphaelo believes it. Oh yes, he's quick at that sort of thing. Gee, oh gee, that sure was a good moment."

They stopped at the end of her street, clutching each other

123

in a last desperate kiss, till they slipped and became entangled with the steering wheel.

"Give me a call if you need help. I'll come and beat *him* up."

"You'd better not. He's six foot, and two-twenty pounds."

"Too bad," he said gallantly, but mildly hurt at the comparison.

"It would be for you. So he reports us to the Dean of Women and you get the big push. Me too. Oh yes, dating a student, strictly against university regulations. Hell, it might prejudice you when you grade my papers."

Again he had the feeling that she enjoyed their danger and he tried, not entirely successfully, to enjoy it too.

"Where's Professor Peterson tonight?" she said, three nights later, as they half sat, half lay across her apartment bed with their shoes off, drinking bourbon.

"At a party," he said.

"Doesn't your wife go to parties?"

"Not this one. It's given by a student she doesn't like: Ric Schuster," he said, blocking his mind against guilt, pleased at how inventive he'd again been, surprised and alarmed to find himself shaken by a heavy shudder.

Her bed was a double mattress on the floor, pushed against the wall. "I tossed my roommate," she explained. "Mattress or bed spring." He'd already inflamed the back of one arm by laying it against the central-heating pipe.

"Where's the forester?"

"In his room. I told him I had to work all night on your term paper."

That doesn't seem too safe, he thought, but he didn't say it. Instead he kissed her for several exhausting minutes, getting more and more on top of her, forcing her head back over a pillow.

"Hey, let up, lover," she gasped, and they lay against the wall, panting. With his rather skinny grey toes he tickled the upper sides of her soft tan feet.

"You know, I believe he's beginning to suspect," she said cheerily. "Not you, darling. Just in general. He keeps giving me very odd looks. And he's started saying we ought to get married right away."

"What'll you do about that?"

124

"Tell him I have to graduate first, otherwise I shan't feel a person in my own right. He'll like that."

"You sure?"

"Or say my divorce hasn't come through."

"But it has?"

"Well that's a bit complicated. Anyway, I never told him it had. Funny, I must have kept that back as a precaution even when I was trying my hardest to love him. I don't remember meaning to, but I must have."

"Surely divorce only takes a few weeks here."

"Sure sure," she said. "Then I'll tell him something else. You got him wrong, honey. He's not really a suspicious guy. If I promise him something he'll believe me. He can't afford not to. That would destroy the image. Anyway, I'm a good liar."

"You certainly seem to be."

"Not to you, darling. Honest, I don't tell you lies. Don't know why. Just don't. I haven't told you a single lie," she said, thinking back. "Oh yes, just one."

"What was that?"

She watched him, as if wondering whether it was safe to say. "Guess."

"Can't possibly."

"How old do you reckon I am?"

"Oh, I see," he said, surprised. "Well, twenty-nine?"

"No no," she said, taking him by the hair and giving his head a surprisingly violent shake. "Twenty-one. I reckoned you might think I was just a little girl and not take me seriously."

"You were certainly wrong there," he said, feeling the sore side of his scalp. "But you have been married?" he asked, surprised she'd had time for this and a return to the totally unmarried feeling she now gave him.

"Oh sure," she said. "At eighteen. Always an advanced child."

"Tell me about it."

"Not now, honey. Too depressing."

Progressing quickly in suspicion, he wondered whether to believe her. It was as if another covering had been removed from his familiar world, showing him this new one where lies should be expected. A pattern seemed to be emerging which he soon might know and thought he might like. He thought he might like it a lot.

125

Around two o'clock, the bottle three-quarters empty, they agreed to go to bed.

"About precautions . . ." he began.

"No need to worry, honey. The Pill. My life depends on it."

But she went to the bathroom and came back quickly in a sky blue nightdress. This ballooned around her, coming in closely at her knees, suggesting a sky blue pumpkin; a story-book, walking pumpkin, her pretty round face at the top, tan arms looking childishly small at the sides, soft dimpled knees and short soft legs at the bottom.

"Like it?" she said.

Kneeling, they kissed. "I certainly do." His heart pounded and his belly sighed with love for her as he hugged her to him, collapsing the pumpkin.

"One thing, darling," she said, holding his face in her hands, looking into his eyes. "Be rough with me."

"I will," he said, the words emerging with a bold lack of calculation which astonished him.

A moment later she had the nightdress off and lay naked on the bed. A strange thing happened then. Her mouth dropped open and down at the sides in a look he hadn't seen before, and she began to shiver and move her thighs about in odd convulsive spasms. What surprised him was the controlled way she switched on these changes. Slightly disconcerted, he lay naked beside her, and began to kiss her with sighs and gasps.

But unfortunately, when he tried to enter her, after a few rubber pushes, his bright strong erection collapsed.

And though he tried several more times during the next hours, each time the same thing happened.

They lay in each other's arms, sometimes in a drunken doze, sometimes laughing rather hysterical at this failure, so wrong that it could only be a sick joke.

When they were noisiest, her roommate beat on the wall behind their heads and, getting on one elbow, Jill beat back. "Clot! Slob!"

"Don't worry, darling," she said, snuggling close to him. "I've been thinking, I value sensuality more than sexuality."

He was pleased she should say this, though he knew it was for his comfort. Despite their laughter, his failure badly depressed him.

"Darling," she said, touching the end of his nose with the tip

126

of her pink tongue, "I love you far too much to let a little thing like this come between us."

He hugged and kissed her.

"Darling," she said, "I suggest you lay off the bourbon."

In the icy black morning, five am, not a sign of dawn in the sky, he drove home, cutting his engine half a block before his house so that he would drift silently up his garage ramp, but losing momentum half way and having to restart it with noisy revs and several loud clangs of the emergency brake.

All week his failure was with him. He knew about it. He was worried by it. But in a strange way he wasn't worried by it. Successfully he put it in a compartment, awful if true, but not to be thought about till proved.

Monday, Wednesday and Friday they saw each other for his nine am classes – in the presence of Mr Dool. But they exchanged notes, and presently made a plan.

Her first, waiting in his mail-box on Monday morning before his class, read, "Darling, I love you."

As the class ended he leant casually across his desk and passed her the copy of his first novel – which she'd accidentally left behind at his party. "I believe you wanted to borrow this," he said. He'd wrapped it in the jacket of a book club edition of *A Short Walk in the Hindu Kush*. Inside he'd written, "For my most advanced student. With love, Maurice."

In his mail-box before his Wednesday lecture was a new paperback of Yeats' poems. A note inside read, "Anyone I adore *must* read W. B. Yeats."

Returning her paper on *Last Exit to Brooklyn* as the class began, he watched her turn to the final sheet where he'd written, "A persuasive – if not entirely original – argument. A plus. I love you." And watched her chuckle for several minutes, occasionally giving him a quick grin which flooded him with happiness.

All week, all day he thought about her and about their plan which might or might not work, but which he could do little to influence. Nancy and the children had been invited for the week-end by a non-relation in State City.

The non-relation, Mrs Morton Percival Peterson, had written to him in England two years ago when her son-in-law, Junior Dean of the College of Commerce and Business Administration, had read in the *Flatville Messenger* and reported to her that a visiting English lecturer named Peterson had been appointed. She had offered, among many other things, to send a check list of two hundred American Petersons living in her state alone. "I just can't tell you how happy we shall be to have some English 'cousins' visit with us and show them something of our country." She and Nancy had corresponded since, sometimes arranging, sometimes postponing a visit to her home in a State City suburb. Fortunately this had made her Nancy's friend, and though Peterson was invited, there had been doubt from the start about whether he would go. He must keep this possibility open, thus promoting the plan, but, at a moment too late for Nancy to change her mind, say, not so emphatically that she would be suspicious, that he must stay and work.

All week Nancy hesitated. Whenever they sat for a meal she started the subject.

"Oh Mummy, why need we go?" Jenny would say.

"Why ever not?" Nancy would say, watching him.

And he'd chew silently, knowing that he mustn't say a word, pretending to be only half listening.

"What do we want with a lot more silly old Petersons?" Carol would say.

"Your father must decide that," Nancy would say, watching him.

And he'd chew silently, not knowing what to pretend. Was this hesitation like her? Sometimes he had the horrifying idea that she was secretly convulsed with laughter at the way she was keeping him in doubt.

At other times, walking about the house in his private dream, he would stop in sudden horror. What was he doing? Was it he who was behaving like this? It seemed to be, and yet it couldn't be. Because the only person he recognised as himself . . .

He saw her pain. He saw this brittle skin of rough tough behaviour she'd built to protect herself and below it her need. He felt it as if he were she. Yet he was doing the worst thing he could possibly do to her. He went on and on doing it.

One evening they went together to a faculty dinner party. Sitting listening to the mini-lectures which Americans believed to be conversation, he hadn't a single idea he wanted to add. When they paused, as they sometimes remembered to, asking to be lectured back at, he seemed to have to climb with terrible

128

effort through his boredom to answer one word. "Is that really so," he'd say, once, in a desperate effort to sound interested, artificially wobbling his intonation so that even this professor of plant genetics noticed with alarm.

Next night they were to play bridge. "I must correct papers," he said, creating this useful evidence of overwork for the week-end . . . Her coffee parties, wives' interest groups, women's bowling mornings, which filled her day – could they really make her happy? They seemed less like life than an absence of it. A sort of walking, speaking nothingness. How could she bear to let her only life pass in this way? But now he guessed that they were symptoms of her mistaken pride and that in a wider sense than he'd yet understood, he'd driven her to them.

When Nancy had gone and he was alone, he could only walk from room to room, appalled by the slowness of time passing. At some moments he thought of Jill with such intensity and knew so certainly that she was thinking of him, that he was astonished that they shouldn't be in actual contact. It seemed as if they ought to be – not in a moral sense, but in a scientific sense – as if something which should have been included in the physical universe had been mistakenly left out.

At eleven, no chance that he could sleep till Nancy returned and not much then, he took the baby-like brown paper parcel of manuscript from a shelf in his study, unwrapped it and began to read:

Today I have made a terrible discovery. I am shattered. And yet I believe it's good that I should be shattered – even though I've spent the last four hours in my bedroom, too numb with shock even to cry. Because right at the bottom of my terror and disillusion I see new hope. No, I don't see it yet. But I sense that it may be there. It *must* be there.

I believe, now, there is just the faintest chance, so remote that the word chance itself is an exaggeration, that my husband and I may save our life together.

Today was my day to see Him. I shan't name Him. He'll know. And He'll understand why.

I went to ask Him what I was to believe about Karl and Bobby. Was it true, or had Karl said it only to torture me? He's capable of that, even though he might at the same time be hurting himself. Because, of course, he *wouldn't* be hurting him-

129

self. He'd be so absorbed in the intricate and pleasing trap he was devising to torture me that he just wouldn't notice. Pleasing. That's as close as Karl can get to happiness. What a terrible insulating word. But it's true – oh god, it's true.

I had to go over old ground. I never mind doing that for Him. He just sits there with his wise round face and bright attentive eyes, occasionally making a note on his yellow paper. All the assurance of an older, wiser civilisation seems behind those eyes – and yet all the wonder at life of a young one. How have we managed to lose both? His eyes are so bright and young that sometimes it is a shock to look up and see His bush of grey hair. I talked and talked. This is my pleasure. I don't rate it as high as happiness. Just a temporary, blessed ending of pain.

I had to explain to Him – though of course really to myself – my feelings for Karl: just how it was that I could neither believe nor disbelieve him, but seemed trapped in a state of shocked uncertainty. In a true relationship my certainty of his love for me would have given me strength to reject what he'd told me at once. In a truly bad one I should have believed him, or else have known for certain that it was a vicious lie. I could do none of these.

I had to tell Him, as I'd often told Him, how Karl and I had married when we were graduate students. How I'd loved and admired him. Never had I met someone so intelligent and sensitive, and yet with such a fearless determination to be honest with himself. How, without ever saying a directly persuasive word, he'd made the Catholicism of my childhood seem ludicrous. How we'd planned to build a life together based not on superstition and subservience, but on reason and mutual respect. How for ten years I'd known we were the happiest married couple among all our friends. And then how I'd suddenly known that we weren't.

It wasn't really sudden, of course. All that was sudden was my discovery that I could no longer put out of my mind all the disappointing things about Karl which for years I'd been noticing . . .

We should have had children. Oh, what a silly explanation this is. Of course we should have had children, and of course it's important that we haven't. But the fact that we failed shouldn't have destroyed us. We're intelligent people, not animals. We should be able to adjust. Of course it's an occasional sorrow. You might as well say we should have had three legs, to avoid the occasional sorrow of tripping up.

Yes yes, our lack of children concentrated our attention on our relationship, made us attentive to its finer nuances. This should have made it strong, not weak – At least He's never advised me to keep a dog. I'd have walked right out of His consulting room.

What I began to notice about Karl was that his colleagues were getting to trust him. He was being elected to committees. He was made an assistant professor before either of us expected. Each year I saw him becoming more like them. It terrified me.

And he worked, oh god, did he work. "Publish or perish" ceased to be a joke between us. Though he never said so, I knew, because he ceased to say the things we'd always said about American college teachers : how their careers come first, their wives second and their students a poor third. How they're like priests in the mediaeval church, who've lost all interest in the cure of souls and care only about climbing in the church hierarchy. How Rome is the Ivy League. How they can only afford this incredible arrogance because no middleclass – or lowerclass – American can get to his middleclass heaven without the college degrees they dispense.

Perhaps he still thought he believed these ideas. Certainly he still thought I believed he believed them. But I knew he didn't.

Sometimes I'd say to him, why don't we get out of this dump before we've put down such deep roots we'd die. And sometimes he'd say it had a good library, and sometimes that he had a particular series of articles to finish. And sometimes he'd agree that we should, but do nothing. I knew the real reason. Karl *liked it* here. With his house and mortgage and tenure, and chance of becoming department chairman.

For five terrible years I fought him. I grew ill with fighting him. It was more frightful than I can describe. I began an absurd affair with one of his younger colleagues, to force him to move us away. He laughed at me. I told him the prairie climate affected my sinuses. It really did start to. He offered me surgery with the best surgeon in the state. When I dropped the subject he kept bringing it up. "We must get that surgery fixed for you." I even planned to set fire to the house and leave us homeless, all those awful papers he was working on burnt up. I stood in the cellar one dreadful night, the matches in my

131

hand, two of our bed-sheets soaked in gas heaped against the wall. And there he was, behind me on the cellar stairs, watching. He'd smelt the gas. Or he'd just known. God knows how, but I believe he'd just known. It wouldn't have worked anyway. It would have been exactly the sort of challenge Karl would have liked. He'd have rented a new house next day and begun all over on those horrible papers.

Divorce? Of course we spoke of divorce. Often. At first it was an ultimate threat either of us might use and so gain a temporary victory – because neither of us really wanted it. I think we came to realise this, because we came to use the threat more and more often. If I overspent on the Hoover repairs, he'd divorce me. If he insisted on non-drip-dry shirts because they were smarter, he could go find some other wife to iron them. The way we seemed to leap to this ultimate solution terrified me. I was terrified when he threatened me. I was terrified when *I* threatened *him*. I used to shiver with fear in case we might mean these words, *and* because we *didn't* really mean them. Somehow this was more terrifying, as if it invited a judgement to fall on us.

I gave up. Yes, I was beaten. But that wasn't why I gave up. I really began to admire this self-sufficient obstinacy of Karl's. He wasn't the man I'd married. I couldn't ever again give the love and hope to him which I'd given to that man, because he'd died. But I came to admire this new man, even when I hated what he stood for, and even to believe that one day, in a different way, I might love him.

I saw that my life – perhaps all our lives – would be neither a victory nor a defeat but a campaign. I thought of myself as no longer an amateur soldier, who hopes to end the war with every battle, but as a professional for whom there is no end to war – who doesn't want one. My aim should be never to be finally defeated. I must fight at every point, but if by going on fighting I risked total defeat, then I must make a temporary retreat. It worked. I was almost happy again, fighting my unending campaign to stop Karl turning into one of his own dead papers.

What has happened to turn me back into a silly amateur, who must win each battle or die fighting?

Several things, but, most important, I have come to see what a terrible way this is to live. That it isn't a marriage but an

132

unmarriage. As the years have passed I've compared it more often, not less often, with the hopes I had before I married Karl. How I'd imagined us fighting together against a philistine world. I've seen that what I thought was my perpetual struggle was my perpetual defeat. I cannot bear to fight against my husband when we should be allies.

Perhaps I was in this state of mind before the Markham affair. Perhaps it would anyway have seemed an issue on which there could be no compromise? Then Bobby. Oh god, why did it all have to happen at once ...?

Two days ago he gave me a lift in his car. He chanced to pass me walking, and stopped. That's the sort of person he is. *Car*, did I say? Don't make me laugh.

One buckled wing, a gaping black triangular slit where the hood won't close, the whole machine as if it has received some enormous blow which has turned its plan from a rectangle to a parallelogram. When it moves its back wheels don't follow the front but travel in a parallel path, nine inches to the left. I had to use the rear seat – springs and foam rubber were coming from the front passenger seat – but I wasn't allowed to use the right rear door. I might have trodden through the floor. The gap was filled by a loose metal plate, but I could see the road on all sides so I can't imagine what held it up. When he slammed the passenger door – which I'd mistakenly opened – the glass fell out of sight with a single heavy swish – like a guillotine blade. So out he got with a screwdriver – he had it ready so that I knew this was something which often happened – and spent the next five minutes unscrewing the door panel and getting the window back in place. I'd have been home ten minutes earlier if I'd walked – but how much poorer. When he got the glass up again it was a really nice unbroken piece which you could *see through* – new wine in old bottles – unlike the window on the driver's side which bulged two inches inwards at the front lower corner where a rock seemed to have hit it, and was patterned all over with a spider's web of cracks.

But the radio worked. How truly American! And we drove on listening—between Campbell soup commercials—to the United Nations President predicting a third world war, and our own president's plan for the *military* to take over *pacification*. How crazy can you get? And Bobby singing, to a tune of his own,

133

"When they stop their war, we'll stop our war, when they stop their war . . ."

Oh yes, and half way a bump in the road brought a shower of groceries down on my back from a shelf where they'd been lodged. He was taking them home to his wife.

Why have I forgotten till now to mention Bobby's wife? Because she's not important. A dull little girl. Because I often *do* forget her. She's just a small weak part of him – which doesn't matter to the human being he really is.

I came up the stairs that morning, filled with the sort of wild happiness any contact with him brings me. I passed my full-length mirror on the way to my desk. I knew I shouldn't look. I looked. There I was, thin, haggard, worried. The happiness I felt didn't *begin* to show. I tried smiling at myself. It was a skeleton grinning. With a conviction that couldn't ever be debated, I knew that Bobby was *being kind* to me. His friendly kindness overflowed and he could spare me some, just as he could spare his wife some. I never wanted to see him again. At that moment I could have killed him for this terrible automatic kindness which had nothing to do with me.

That awful grin. No one, I knew, could love that. No one who hadn't known me when I was younger and prettier – yes, really quite pretty. How could I bear to go the rest of my life without ever again being loved? Never never never never.

Karl? . . . Karl and Bobby. This morning I told Him what Karl had told me about himself and Bobby. He listened. I told Him I didn't believe it. I told Him I would make Karl admit that it wasn't true. As I spoke to Him my conviction grew stronger. He seemed to give me strength to believe. Even my anger with Karl for this mean trick grew less. I would tell Karl that I knew, but that I forgave him. I rose to go. He held out His hand.

Sometimes we shake hands after my consultations. Sometimes we don't. It's really for me to decide. Sometimes I want to, and sometimes not. This time I wanted to. But did he hold out his hand just an instant before he could have known that I wanted to? And was there just a shade of insistence about the way he kept it there, waiting for me to take it?

My hand was in his, warm, soft and comforting. I looked down past it. There on his desk was a big grey file and written boldly across the front "KARL WEST".

134

I tore my hand away. I ran from the room. I didn't stop running down the sidewalk till I found a cab to take me home.

Was it planned or an accident? How can I tell? He will never tell me. I can imagine asking, and Him just watching me, not even thinking about the answer but wondering why I needed to ask.

I think He stood as I ran from his room. I think he called "Martha". Was he shocked at his carelessness? Or shocked at my overly violent reaction to something which had been carefully planned? Either way it fits.

So Karl, too, is consulting Him. And what consultations, judging by the thickness of that grey file.

I'm not merely shattered because I now know for certain that what Karl told me about himself and Bobby is true. Why else would he be consulting Him? It's more than that. It's the fact that Karl needs to consult *anyone* that appals me. Never have I thought this possible.

Here is my seed of hope: we are both in the same boat. The danger is worse but at least we share it. Here is my task: to make Karl see that we are together again. Desperate but together.

Together together ... We love ... I have a plan ...

The manuscript here was much corrected, and only these words survived among heavy black erasings.

A bad day today, Morrison read (Peterson wrote). She accused me of writing a novel about her. It took me an hour of patient questioning to discover where this idea came from.

Tonight (as always in future) I have had to make sure that she is in bed and heavily sedated before I start my diary. She lay there on her back in the low yellow light of her bedroom (she'll never sleep in total darkness) her eyes closed, breathing evenly. The lids of her eyes are grey when closed. This is what she'll look like when she is dead. Hard to believe that I shall one day see that.

Was she pretending? Impossible to tell. Like a child, she will act with her whole being. Her total strength and ingenuity go into every tiny incident of her daily life. Adults learn to care more about some things than others, or they would die of exhaustion. Martha (change name) has never learned. I left the room and came to my study. Five minutes later I took off my shoes and crept back. She lay on her back in the yellow dusk,

135

breathing evenly. Was she still acting? Had she realised that I would have patience to come back in five minutes, but not in ten? Always I fear that she is a step ahead of me, not because she is cleverer but because of her single-mindedness – the single-mindedness of a child.

As a result I take a risk as I write now and expect any moment to turn and find her standing in the doorway . . .

It began at supper. She wouldn't speak. I refused, of course, to notice, but I could scarcely keep down my rising temper at what I knew she was planning for this evening – when I had completed a hard day's teaching, and hoped to work.

We sat in the living room, sipping coffee. I wanted to take the offensive, to say, Martha, I won't be treated this way . . . Then she started.

"How's it going, Karl?"

I refused to answer.

"Anything interesting today?"

Could she really be asking about my classes? It was just sufficiently possible for me to tell her about an intelligent student's question.

"No, have *I* done anything interesting?" she interrupted. She was shivering, her coffee cup making a delicate rattle in its saucer as she held them close to her face to sip – always a bad sign.

"You tell *me*,' I said.

"No, you tell *me*."

"Well, you've cooked me the usual lousy supper," I joked.

Certainly I doubted the timing of this sally – but I didn't expect to have to sit for ten minutes waiting for her tears to stop. They ran down her face and dripped on to the front of her dress. There was a time when I used to want to take her in my arms and comfort her when she cried. Not now. I just sat there, reading the *Prairie Gazette*, while she shook and sobbed and occasionally called out in a blubbery voice, "How can you *do* this to me? How do you *dare*?"

Her tears filled me with a terrible anger that she should resort to something so unfair. An anger that made my own hands shake – as I found myself skimming over and over the same letter on the correspondence page. I have it here:

"Each Decoration Day I put flowers on my deceased husband's

136

grave and this year, as cut flowers from our yard were scarce, I bought a plastic plant.

"It was a beautiful but different plant – a maroon hibiscus, supported by a piece of brown rustic wood, in a white plastic vase, held down by straight pins to stop it blowing away. Three days later when I went again to my deceased husband's grave the plant was gone, vase, pins, the lot.

"I think it is wicked to steal from graves and I hope the evil person who did this gets sick to his stomach when he reads my letter. Can't this poor man, who suffered so in his life, have a few plants on his grave now he's dead without some evil person stealing them?"

"Each Decoration Day I put flowers on my deceased husband's grave . . ."

"What is it then?" I asked, when I was calmer, resigned now to a wasted evening.

"Nothing."

I restrained myself from remarking that it was a pretty goddam noisy nothing.

"Why should I tell you? You don't care."

"I certainly care."

"You sure make a fine job of hiding it. I sit here crying my heart out and you read the newspaper."

For some reason this argument made me madder than any yet. "All right, I don't care, but I'm still curious to know what's upset you."

"Curious," she said in a rising scream. (I knew the word was a mistake as soon as it came to me, but deliberately didn't change it.) "My husband is curious about me!" No tears this time but what she believed to be terrible injured bitterness.

"Yes, I'm curious." I'm long past being unfairly silenced by this trick of repeating something I've said. Though still shaking with fury, I raised the newspaper again. This time I became intrigued by a Mitsy Quail letter.
"Dear Mitsy,

"My daughter is twelve but she looks like five years older. My sister's husband, Jo, has a crush on her, and I'm afraid she has one on him too.

"About five nights a week Uncle Jo drops by to talk old cars with my husband. He always starts with, 'Well, what's under the hood today?' and that ends the old car talk.

137

E*

"My daughter kisses her Uncle Jo on the neck and takes his socks off to massage his feet to help him relax. She sits on his lap to watch TV, and a couple of nights ago they start to dance the Monkey and the Jerk together and then do some 'fun wrestling' on the floor. Mitsy, I don't like the way this relationship is shaping up, but my husband says I'm just dirty minded. Would you say I was dirty minded, Mitsy?

"Yours, Worried Crazy as Hell."

"Dear Worried,

"It's your husband who's crazy if he can't see what's happening right under his nose. Because your daughter's heading for bad trouble. And plenty. Tell Uncle Jo to take his monkey tricks back where they belong – to the jungle, and say I said so. And tell your daughter to get stuck into her homework. And how."

I was calmed by this letter which had helped me not to hear several of Martha's remarks. I saw that here lay the explanation of why these scenes so distress me. As soon as I cease to hear her *self*-pity, my own pity and love for her begins to return. The moment I can hear it I remember all that I've done for her which she deliberately ignores. The way I've worked to make us financially secure. The way I've become a different person to calm her suppressed bourgeois instincts, above all, the way (to give her life the firm basis it needs and prevent her becoming a raving hysteric) I've forgone a dozen chances of academic distinction to stay rotting in this sink of mediocrity. The way she has persistently tried to interfere with the one aspect of my life for which I can still respect myself : my scholarship.

So I emerged from the *Gazette*, refreshed with pity, and spoke quickly before I started to hear what she was saying. "Martha, honey, I only want to be told . . ."

"Why are you writing a book about me?"

The two-step question. I controlled the sarcasm I invoke for a student who does this to me. "I can hardly tell you *why*," I said, smiling quietly, "when it's something which I'm *not* doing!"

"Look at you now, laughing away," she said, "because I've said something you think so hilarious that you'll be able to use it."

"Honey . . ." I said more sternly.

"What do you keep in that locked drawer?"

"I don't have a locked drawer – or if I do," I said (wondering

138

if I'd automatically locked it, though it was now empty) "there isn't a novel about you in it." I could say this safely because I've loaned my diary to "I". Indeed, the idea of keeping it was his. (Find new place to hide these fresh sheets.) Solemnly we went upstairs, myself in front, Martha behind. (What made the flesh between my shoulder blades creep as she came upstairs behind me? The fact that she should come so willingly to what she must have known would be a defeat?) I opened and showed her all my drawers.

She scarcely looked in them. "You've hidden it." She had had this prepared.

I shook my head, genuinely sad to deceive her.

"I know you have. Why do you *do* this to me?" Her tears were coming again. "Why can't you leave me alone to lead my own life?"

"That's not what you want," I said, astonished at this new contradiction – but she wasn't listening, determined now to shock me with what she had discovered : that I've been seeing "I". (I blame myself for being careless, though I can't think when.)

I was spying on her. The fact that I might or might not be writing a novel about her wasn't what she really cared about, she said, from my study armchair where she now sat crumpled up in a sobbing bundle, but that I had exposed this private part of her life on which she had been building a new self-respect.

Certainly it's the second time I've done this in a week. But I know she only invents these things in order that I shall discover them. In this sense it is my duty to discover them, even though, of course, I unconsciously also do it to destroy her.

At first I was safely sure that I had this double motive for seeing "I". To help me keep Martha sane (or to drive her insane) I needed all the facts. Most of all, I needed those she wouldn't tell me. But something has happened to my relationship with "I". More and more we have become patient and doctor, instead of fellow consultants on a difficult case.

A short while ago he sent me an account. I paid it at once, telling myself, as far as I let myself think about it, that it was for *her* consultations, addressed to me accidentally, or because he thought I'd occasionally like to pay for her. But I know now that this account was for *my* consultations. I can picture the sheet, with *my* name written there, where I must have read it but refused to understand it.

And I remember now (how have I watched it for weeks without understanding its implications?) that when I stand to leave him he calls Jessie, his secretary, and she stands between us, checking possible dates and hours for my next visit.

Still more significant, there are visits when Martha is never mentioned – when we talk entirely about myself (with the unspoken understanding between us, of course, that I am a vital part of Martha's problem). But for weeks now there's also been the unspoken understanding between us that this is *not* why we are talking about myself.

Ever since I told him about Bobby.

I told him not because I was troubled or in fear – but from a desperate need to tell someone. The words seemed to be bubbling at the lip of my mind. I was inflated with the desire to describe, and so in a sense give thanks for my love. For the way it had changed my life. Unless I told someone I would burst.

A few mornings ago, as I crossed campus, I saw that my whole life has been distorted by the ease with which my eyes water. I have only to say something I care about and the tears form. My character has been shaped by the need to forestall these shameful tears – an Anglo Saxon sickness, no doubt: the feminine gesture of tears has become shameful to us in proportion to our decreasing assurance about our masculinity.

But suppose I no longer thought tears shameful. Suppose there *is* nothing shameful about them. What if I let them run down my face and know that when others laugh it is *their* shame. Because they are still afraid of their tears. What if I cry in class as I read aloud the passages from *Piers Plowman* which move me. (I dismiss a picture of them going away to snicker at this lachrymose old fool). What if I cry with sympathy at movies, with anger at department meetings, most of all with pity when I guide and help Martha.

These remain unfulfilled possibilities, but that morning of spring sunshine I could at least conceive of them. "I" listens, and understands that Bobby has brought me this new maturity.

I have told "I" that I don't, of course, want to sleep with this boy. The idea of thrusting my erect person up his anus disgusts me. But I have told him, too, that all my life the only

140

dreams in which I have reached climax have been about boys – apart, of course, from those in which I am being tortured.

Morrison skipped several chapters. He read :

What is this new mad scheme which my wife Martha has got into her head? At first I didn't take it seriously. Now I know that I must take it VERY seriously.

Yipee, Morrison whispered aloud, widening his eyes and passing his tongue in a circle round the inner, bacon-flavoured, hairs of his carrotty moustache and beard. Carefully, he closed the book to deprive himself of the delicious disgust of this new episode in psychic masturbation.

On Thursday Peterson had a more important message to send. He wrote it quickly, listening for any noise below him in the house.
"All fixed for Friday, darling."
He crossed campus late that afternoon in the first heavy snow of winter and dropped it in her mail-box – The week before he'd discovered that she didn't live in that small brick apartment house he'd so often stared up at, but in a large rectangular concrete building on the next block – he'd mis-remembered the number by a hundred.
That lunch time Nancy had decided to go. Had she simply grown bored with provoking this public display of his indecision? Had it suddenly seemed unendurable that she could find him so interesting? He hoped so. Because, the moment she'd said, "I shall take the children, whatever you do," the alarming alter-native had occurred to him that she'd found somewhere to stay in town so that she could watch him.
Next morning a folded pink sheet in his mail-box read, "Friday Friday!"
That afternoon, shivering with his family on the station plat-form, light snow still drifting out of a grey sky and being swirled along the concrete by gusts of icy wind to form drifts against posts, bunkers, even his shoes, watching the stairway for her, he was astonished when she arrived in scarlet anarak, carrying a pair of skis.
She stood waiting fifty yards along, but whether or not he

141

was beyond her range of vision he couldn't tell. What an odd defenceless feeling she must live with, he thought, and regretted that they hadn't arranged some signal – an owl's hoot perhaps – which he could have casually turned his back on his family and given, to reassure her that he was here. Then the train was arriving and he could only see those skis waving about above the heads of a crowd round the stairway to a carriage.

"Byee," Carol called from her window.

"Byee," Jenny mimicked.

"Byee," "Byee," they began to scream at each other, entirely forgetting him.

But he was preoccupied with a new horrifying fear : that she was really going to get on to this train and ride away.

"For Godsake!" Nancy shouted, straddled on the carriage steps, one hand stretched upwards to hold Myrtle into the train by the collar of her windcheater, the other stretched down for a case she couldn't reach.

"So sorry . . ." Away she'd go. Invitation I couldn't refuse. Why else the skis? See you Monday. Proving how little he meant to her.

"Byee," "Byee," "Byee," Carol and Jenny screamed, now beginning to punch each other.

"When you've quite finished with someone else's luggage," Nancy shouted.

"Oh, so sorry." It was true, he'd picked up the white doeskin case of a blue-rinsed matron who was now forgiving him.

"Young man, don't mention it. If there's one thing I've gotten used to in my travels it's having strangers take a fancy to my luggage."

"Byee," "Byee," "Pig," "Swine," "Spotted swine," "Hairy hog . . ."

Two and a half empty days to fill while she raced down Minnesota slopes in a gay party of laughing students of her own age – Now the locomotive howled, the carriages jerked into motion, and he waved, but none of them saw, Carol and Jenny locked in a clinch at the far side of the compartment, Nancy bent to mop at Myrtle's mouth so that she rode past with skirted arse to the window . . . A lifetime of empty days. He wouldn't look till the last carriage had rumbled by. He turned – there she was, scarlet anarak and skis, standing alone by the trackside.

142

"You certainly believe in making yourself conspicuous."

"Aren't I brilliant?" she said. "You should have heard the forester coaching me. He's the most convinced deserted fornicator in town."

They went into a big breathless kiss which left them gasping and sweating inside their padded clothes.

"Gee, lover."

But he glanced round uneasily, had a picture of them high up and alone on this snowy platform which could be seen from many surrounding streets, in a tight clinch, the two skis seeming to peer down on them, as if surprised at what they'd got involved in.

"Where is he now?"

"Working at his elementary French. He's got an hourly due. Frankly, he's not shit hot at elementary French. It's a big sadness in his life."

"Didn't he offer to carry these up?"

"Sure, he offered. I said I hated good-byes. I do, too."

But immediately ahead of them as they came out into the railroad yard was the forester's old-gold Mustang. They hurried back into the waiting room and put the skis into the baggage check. She reversed her anarak, emerald green lining outwards.

"What's he doing there?"

"Stocking up on peanut brittle, maybe. That's another thing that worries him. Having too many peaks and troughs in his calorie intake. At least, the troughs worry him. Since Dr Strangelove he believes anti-fattening-food propaganda's a commie plot to weaken us."

"I thought you said he was intelligent."

"Oh he is. He just has gaps. Someone once taught him to say, 'Well, how do you *know*?' and he thinks when he's said that he doesn't have to listen any more because he's won. The surprising thing is, he often has."

When they grew impatient they hurried to his car and she crouched on the front seat where he dragged a blanket over her. They drove across town, and, before he thought it safe, she threw off the blanket. Right beside campus, halted at the Lincoln Street lights, she moved close and began to mumble the side of his neck with her teeth.

"We'll crash," he said, pushing her away to make space to shift.

143

She sat apart from him, wriggling in her seat with happiness. "More than likely," she said.

"Wouldn't that make good headlines!"

"Stoopid," she said, leaning quickly across to lick the inside of his ear. "Hey, it's really happening. I can't believe it."

A block from his home he dropped her on the sidewalk so that she could arrive on foot, a student keeping an appointment.

"Okay, honey, they're *your* neighbours."

"Do come in, Miss Hearn," he said, holding the front door open, bowing slightly. "It's the Beowulf you're worried about?"

She ran at him, making a strange brrrring noise, throwing her arms round his neck, giving him violent kisses on the cheek. He staggered back several places, spreading his hands to the passage walls to save himself. Again he had the sense that things were happening which he didn't understand and couldn't ask about. He thought she'd really wanted to knock him off his feet, and see him land in an absurd shambles on the passage floor – though a moment later she would have been sorry for him and sorry for what she'd done – and at the same time find it hard not to giggle.

They dressed to go out to dinner.

"Hey, you look good. First time I've seen you out of those silly old English tweeds."

"*You* look good."

She wore a slim black dress, with a wide collar that went once round her neck then hung down her back in a broad tail.

"I'll tell you a secret. Had to borrow it from my roommate."

"For the ski party dances?'"

"*Oh rather,*" she said with heavy sarcasm at the idea of herself on a community outing.

They ate at a plastic-Tudor steak house, the best in town, attached to a bowling alley. There were black plastic hay racks on the walls, seashell-pink plastic cornucopia of lilies above the tables and golden plastic carthorse brasses over the constantly flaming natural-gas log fire. Three-inch-diameter candles from the Danish shop stood in oval mauve candle glasses from the Swedish shop and the whole was lit by a concealed pink ceiling glow to ancient-passage dimness – till a table of six dark-suited, crew-cut, baby-clean executives complained of the glare and it was turned down to the brightness of an outdoor starlit night.

They stared into each other's eyes and held hands under the table.

"You sure he wouldn't come here?"

"Who d'you think I'm marrying, a millionaire?"

They sat in a movie house, his arm round her shoulder, her hand in his lap.

"Does he ever go to the movies?"

"Hell no, not with all that elementary French. Anyway, we saw this one, Monday."

They drove home, forgetting to let her walk the last block, and drank a bottle of domestic sauterne. They turned up the heating to eighty and went to bed in the double bed. Again she lay naked, her mouth dropping at the sides in that strange way, her thighs jerking. Again after two or three passionate attempts to enter her, which told him he was drunker than he realised, he collapsed and lay still beside her.

"Don't worry, darling."

He said nothing. He *did* worry but there was nothing to say. It was a joke, but like any repeated joke, less hilarious. She smoked on her back and he lay still, his face against her soft tan shoulder and big soft breast.

Around two he woke, soaked in sweat, sweat sticking their flesh together wherever they touched. Without a word he climbed on top of her. Her knees came up – though he thought she was still half asleep. He shoved and shoved, his heart beating so hard that he almost expected a heart attack. After sixty seconds, to his delight and astonishment, half a glorious inch at a time, he made it.

"Oh yes, oh yes, oh yes," she cried out, gripping his shoulders and scratching them painfully.

They lay in each other's arms, rubbing noses and licking each other's ears. Oh the happiness. A black cloud lifted from his mind. Now that it was lifting he saw how black it had been and how it had overshadowed all his thoughts.

He couldn't sleep, though he could hear her breathing evenly beside him. Around five he climbed on top of her.

"Hey, lover," she said, as if to protest, then stopped with a small gasp as he slid into her with a slithery ease, and male confidence, that amazed him.

Now she writhed and bumped about below him with greater violence, and, since it took him longer to come, this continued

145

for several minutes. She gripped and scratched his shoulders with her nails in the same places but more painfully, till he caught her wrists and held them down on the pillow above her head.

"Oh yes, oh yes," she cried. "Oh baby, oh baby, oh yes, Oh yes, OH YES."

He rolled free. He could only laugh aloud with delight.

"Gee," she gasped.

Amazing. Quite amazing. The first time might not have been love at all. Each time he regained his breath and looked at her they broke into new astonished laughter.

"I knew it," she said. "I just knew it."

"What?"

"That you were sexy too."

"Did you?" he said with smug surprise.

"Just fancy, a stoopid old Englishman," she said, rumpling his hair.

"You know what?" he said. "Nothing like that's ever happened to me before."

"Well there you are," she said. "Come to America and see the world."

He went on shaking his head in astonishment. "Has it to you?"

"Don't fish," she said. "Phew, air, cigarette," pushing him away, fumbling beside the bed, lighting up. "Frankly," she said, sucking deeply and blowing a cloud of smoke at him, "NO."

They stayed in bed till midday, when he closed all the drapes and wandered about the house naked, making coffee. Through cracks he could see a pure blue sky and bright sunlight on white snow under trees in the park. The outside thermometer read ten degrees, but inside he kept it at seventy-six. Upstairs she lay in a hot bath, smoking, reading his first novel, and, when he brought her a cup, sipping coffee.

She read at great speed. Looking down at her fine breasts and slightly plump tan body on its back in the bath where she lay reading through those big dark-framed glasses, he was amazed by the speed at which she turned the pages. There was a suggestion that she was eating the book which worried him: eating it rather impatiently. Propped there, her feet together, her hands raised to hold it above the water, she suggested a big-eyed reading fish.

146

"Hey, what you thinking?" she said, without looking up.

"Just good-coffee thoughts," he said and took a sip which scalded his tongue.

"You know what I'd like?" she said. "Oysters Rockefeller and champagne. Served by a great lecherous Negro in a white coat." She licked her lips and squirmed in the bath, her underwater flesh squeaking on the enamel.

He played Verdi on the phonograph. "What's that crap?" she shouted from upstairs.

"*Rigoletto*. Why?" He turned it low and came up to the bathroom.

"I'm spooked by that goddam opera," she said. "My husband had a sentimental thing about it, after he discovered I was named from it. Gilda. Thank christ it makes Jill and no one knows."

"I like Gilda."

"You try living with it."

"What made them choose it?"

"My mother was a singer. That was how they met, back-stage somewhere. My father was an electrician. As soon as they got married she never sang another note. That makes me really despise her."

"But if you don't like it . . ."

"Well *I* don't have to like it, for christsake. But *she* liked it. Fancy having talent and not using it. That makes me spew. You can't say I do that, can you, lover? Hey, soap my back. Oooo. Mmmm. Gee, honey, you sure can soap a back."

He went downstairs and took off *Rigoletto*, still whispering his full-throated song of love for his ill-fated, but incautious, daughter. He was relieved. As soon as he'd heard its marvellous despair he'd known he'd played it out of loyalty to a time two weeks ago which he could scarcely remember.

"Put on something jolly," she shouted. A moment later there was a loud rap on the glass of the front door. He kept quite still, determined not to make a sound.

But suppose it was Nancy. She'd have to knock because he'd locked the latch from inside. Suddenly he knew that this was why she'd gone away so willingly – with that mocking smile which he could sense even though he couldn't see it : to come back a day early.

Even if he kept her out he must discover. Slipping on an

147

overcoat, he stood close inside the door, bending and peering round the edges of its drape. He found himself staring at the waists of two overcoated figures, one bulkly and probably female, the other thin and male. They were so near that, though he squinted up, their faces were only pale distorted splodges.

"Hi," the female shouted, shocking him upright. His own peering face must have been visible.

"One moment," he called. "Lock trouble." And with a lot of unnecessary clicking and rattling, opened the door.

"We don't mean to disturb you," she began. She was familiar, and seemed to expect to be recognised, but at what dinner party or reception he'd met her he couldn't remember.

"No, we sure don't mean to disturb you," the man said, his eyes flicking to Peterson's bare grey feet and bare hairy legs.

"Come in," Peterson said, one hand holding his coat together, the other fumbling at the buttons to close its collar over his bare chest.

"If you'd rather we called another time," the woman said, stepping into the narrow front hall, backing him up against the wall.

"Yes, sure, we'll call again," the man said, staying outside.

"Why should you, now you're here?" Peterson said as a small icy breeze swirled dry snow round the inside of his porch and carried several frigid leaves to settle against his toes where they started to melt. "Do come in."

"It's just that we're worried crazy about our son, and we know you've been helping him – well come in, Henry, for christ-sake if he tells you," the woman said.

"Yes, we're sure worried as hell," the man said, squeezing himself against the unmoving bulk of the woman to give Peterson space to shut the door.

"Let me take your coats," Peterson said, in automatic re-action to them standing in his sitting room dressed against subzero temperatures – both wore fur-lined helmets, suggesting a pair of pre-war intercontinental air pilots.

"Oh, we're not planning on staying," the woman said. "Henry, help Mr Peterson with *his* coat."

"No, really," Peterson said, backing away. "I have a cold."

"You have a cold and you go around all day with no shoes," the woman said. "Well I'd call that downright Chinese."

148

"Yeah! Say – I mean, not at all," the man said, astonishing himself.

"Not English but downright Chinese," the woman said, laughing harshly at her joke and watching Peterson with increasing suspicion, now that he wasn't joining in the good humoured atmosphere she was creating. "Go on Henry, get his coat." Suddenly he knew her: Ric Schuster's mother.

His stomach gave a lurch of alarm. Keeping Mr Schuster away with one hand, still working to close his collar buttons with the other, he said, "Has something happened?"

"Not that we're aware," Mrs Schuster said.

"Unless you know something," Mr Schuster said.

"You know something then?" Mrs Schuster said.

"Oh no," Peterson said quickly. "I haven't seen your son for days."

A loud splosh of water, following by the echoing thud of a wet foot on hollow metal sounded from above, as if she'd half slipped as she got out. All three of them turned to look through the open arch towards the stairs.

"In the bath . . ." Peterson began vaguely.

"Oh please don't trouble Mrs Peterson," Mrs Schuster said. "Let's see now, you have several daughters. Our son has told us what lovely people your family are. One day I'd just adore to meet your wife and daughters."

"Playing," Peterson said vaguely, but hardly attending as he listened for more sounds on the upstairs landing. Suppose she came down to see what was happening. Absurdly rash though this would be, he had an idea that she might invent some plausible reason for doing it because she secretly wanted to increase the danger of their affair. He could already picture her here among them, wrapped in a big towel, her round eyes big with innocent surprise. The next moment a stopping car in the street told him for certain that Nancy was coming. At this culminating accident his mind paralysed. It was as if there was nothing in his head but thick jelly.

No children's gay cries in the street. Perhaps it hadn't been Nancy. Not another sound from the second floor. Slowly the jelly melted.

"Strictly it's none of our business," Mr Schuster was saying.

"We're not the sort of folks who bring up a son to twenty-one

149

then just dump him into an unkind world," Mrs Schuster was saying.

"No, we're not folk like that," Mr Schuster said. "In many ways our son Ric has had a raw deal."

"What's that you say?" Mrs Schuster said, turning on him.

"Raw deal . . ." Mr Schuster murmured.

"As my husband says," Mrs Schuster said, still staring down on him, tucking a straying curl into her flying helmet, a gesture more alarming for its cool restraint than any yet, "our son has had a raw deal. And the goddamedest thing is, the people who've claimed they were helping him most are the ones who've given him the rawest deal."

No one spoke.

"Well it sure has been nice getting to know you better, Mr Peterson," she said, holding out a hand. A minute later they'd gone.

Their visit worried him badly. He hadn't treated them as he would have liked. The presence of Jill upstairs in the bath had been far too disturbing. Even now he wanted to run after them and begin the serious talk with them about Ric which they seemed to want. A few days ago, it was what he would have welcomed most and his inconsistency shocked him.

Presently he went slowly upstairs. Or had they come for that? By the time he was at the half way landing he'd thought of an alternative : they'd come to threaten him.

By the top he believed it. So she'd been threatening him. Well she'd find out he wasn't a person to be threatened by any Mrs Schuster from Hickory Street. He became more and more convinced that this defiant attitude had been present unconsciously behind everything he'd said. I told them it was weeks since I'd seen their boring son, he thought, ready to tell Jill. By the time he'd reached the bathroom he'd forgotten Mr and Mrs Schuster.

She was standing beside the bath, Nancy's large orange towel pressed to her lower face, her big brown eyes staring at him over it.

He pushed it aside and kissed her. She was shivering but also lightly steaming. He dropped his coat in a heap and held her closely. She was warm but wet. Taking her by the wrist he led her on to the landing.

"Hey, I'm all soapy."

150

He gripped her wrist more tightly, feeling her give a gasp of pain, led her to the bedroom and pushed her on to the bed. She struggled but by an accidental movement swung her legs neatly up there too. They made love.

Although he wanted her passionately he took even longer to come.

"Oh baby, oh baby," she cried, and writhed so violently that she threw him out.

"Oh Jesus, Jesus," she cried, when, after a tiresomely interrupting fumble, he'd got back. "Oh don't leave me, darling. Don't ever leave me."

At last he made it. They lay gasping and laughing.

"You know what," she said, up on an elbow to smoke and stare at him. "It's becoming a habit."

"Could be," he said modestly.

"No, me," she said. "I came."

"Did you?" he said, as if interested, but not too surprised. Still greater happiness flooded him. "This morning too?"

"Sure," she said. "That makes twice. Only twice."

The achievement seemed totally apart from him. He shook his head with wonder and smiled at her. But he said nothing. He was learning.

A riddle he remembered from thirty years ago at preparatory school kept running merrily through his head. "If a French breakfast's toast and coffee, what's an American one? A roll in bed with honey." He told her.

"Oh you English," she said. "A funny poem for every occasion."

"That so?" he said uneasily.

"It sure is," she said. "You forget, I was half married to one. Or rather, married to half one."

"How's that?"

"He was half Indian. Didn't I tell you? Red Indian."

Though he quickly fitted these surprises into his picture of her, he could think of no comment, so he said, "Don't most occasions demand it?"

"Yeah yeah, but not all," she said. "You've got to be serious about something. Aren't I?"

"Three guesses what?" he said. Already, faintly, his desire for her stirred again as he carefully bit her neck.

Next evening before he drove her home they warmed a

151

casserole which he found in the ice box and realised that Nancy had left for him. The meat was fibrous and tasteless, and the carrots so undercooked that they were like little circles of pulpy wood.

"What *is* it?" she said, wrinkling her nose in disgust, peering and poking at the heap on her plate.

"Beef casserole," he said flatly.

"You're kidding!" She swilled down her mouthful with water. "Urgh," and pushed the rest away. "Hey lover, why the gloom?"

"It isn't very nice, is it," he said unhappily. It was true—her meat dishes especially were often disgusting, as if she refused to learn to cook because she still resented her reduction to a home-making female ... without telling him, she'd prepared and cooked it for him ...

Winter settled on the country. Snow covered the land for a hundred miles in every direction, only the grain elevators rising above it – cathedrals of the prairie, as some myopic romantic had called them. There they stood, little upright points at the end of twenty miles of straight flat highway. Ten minutes later, there they still stood, at the end of ten miles of straight highway. Gradually they grew taller and at last disappeared above the car roof, ugly, rectangular, utilitarian. Had the description been symbolic, he explained to his class, it might have been good. Cathedrals for the worship of the golden corn. In town the cars rolled softly on a padded carpet of dry white snow – for an hour each morning till the city mechanical brushes and ploughs piled it into grey mounds on the sidewalks.

A week later a surge of tepid air from the Gulf turned it to grey slush.

Each day they met with love and parted with despair. But the danger was constant and the places they could go limited. Sometimes it seemed to him that most of their affair was conducted in his car, he driving, she beside him on the front seat, hidden under a blanket. Or, more often than he liked, sitting up out of it, her big brown eyes glancing all round with excited alarm.

"You remind me of an animal," he said. "A small furry rodent."

"Thanks a lot."

"A bush baby."

152

"What in shit's name's that?"

"Comes from Africa. It's nocturnal and has big round eyes and a long tail, and clings to things by suction pads which it keeps moist by dripping urine on them."

"You sure know how to flatter a girl."

"I know an ex-colonial who keeps one in his topee. Not at night of course. It hunts then."

"Why do all my men turn me into animals?" she said. "Except for Raphaelo. I'm just a good lay to him."

It had certainly hurt her.

"Well it needs feeding, this bush baby," she said. "And it eats steak."

So they drove eight miles out of town to a steak house at Carthage.

Three days a week he saw her at his lectures, and they exchanged looks of sentimental yearning, but afterwards the forester took her away to coffee. There was something about the great hand, backed with ginger hairs, which he sometimes used to grip her elbow and direct her, which particularly distressed Peterson.

Lunch she took with the forester, and in the evening she cooked supper for the forester, Raphaelo and two Sicilians. Just a friendly arrangement, she told him, which earned her a free meal.

Nights, she was needed to sit with the forester while he worked. But twice she came to the library, and he met her there and they drank and danced at the Stardust. Though these times were their happiest, the forester forgotten, he was half relieved that they happened no more often or his new keenness for evening lectures, with coffee receptions which lasted beyond midnight, might have made Nancy suspicious.

Whenever they dared, usually in the afternoons when the forester was at target practice, they went to her apartment and bolted the door. It was a half basement. By day he realised that it suggested a fish tank. Six feet above the floor, there was a long window opening on a sidewalk where the legs of pedestrians passed continuously. Outside there, these humans were in the sunlight of an airy world while here inside she lived in the permanent underwater orange of electric bulbs.

"Oughtn't we to draw the curtain?" he said as they lay on her mattress in a breathless tongue-sucking clinch.

153

"Hell, no," she said. "They can't see a thing."

"Shouldn't we turn out the light?" he said, as she lay, a night later, naked on the bed, and he sat beside her, twisting her arm behind her back and giving her plump arse occasional hard, though still tentative, slaps.

"Hell no," she said. "They never look."

She wrote the score on the wall beside her bed.

"M.P." she wrote and awarded him a stroke each time. "Seventeen," she said. "Gee, oh gee."

"OTHERS", she wrote below, and awarded it a half.

"You still not making love to him?"

"No sir!" she said. "I'm a faithful little bitch. You don't realise."

"What do you tell him?"

"I've developed principles," she said. "No more bed till marriage."

"How long will that last?"

"Oh ages," she said. "It suits him really. He's a clean American boy at heart. He only tolerates me because he loves me."

"So he should," Peterson said.

"Hey, lover, love me," she said.

Presently, when she cried out, her roommate beat on the wall. Since they were upside down she stamped with the flat of her foot. "Jealous bitch."

Her roommate was a small dark Persian girl he sometimes passed in the passage on his way to the bathroom.

"Hasn't she got a boy friend?"

"Oh, she's got him," she said. "But she won't let him. Oriental attitudes and all that. Hey, I almost forgot. Eighteen, NINETEEN. Oh gee, whoever said anything against Englishmen? Hey, darling, it's hungry."

"The bush baby?"

She dressed in the orange striped dress he'd first seen her in. "Shall I tell you something. I like being a mistress. I think it suits me." She bounced about the room, turning her face over her shoulder to look in the mirror, then to kiss him. "Who wants to be a wife?"

One morning she wasn't at his lecture. Alarm and fear filled him. At least Jeff Dool was there. He lectured brilliantly, darting questions from student to student, wittily summarising their

154

answers. "Miss Foringer, are you saying . . . ?" "Yes, sir I guess that *is just what I am* saying."

The class ended, down the stairs he stalked the forester, overhearing, "Say, what was all *that* about?", far too worried to think what it could mean. With relief he saw him turn towards the Union. He hurried to her apartment. No answer when he knocked. He knocked again, and close inside in a sharp voice he hardly recognised, she said, "Who's there?"

"Me, Maurice."

The door opened. "Come in, quick."

She was wrapped in a sheet but under it naked. She took him by the wrist, led him into her room, stumbled quickly back into bed and heaved a bundle of sheet and blanket over her head.

"Wha's time?" she said, head still under them.

"Ten-five."

"Christ," she said and there was silence as if she'd gone back to sleep.

Unexpectedly she got out of bed, stumbled past him to the bathroom, stumbled back past him and got straight down into bed in the same position. All the way she kept her eyes shut. On the way out a black undergarment got caught round her foot and she gave several irritated kicks, but it was still attached when she came back. "The Pill," she said as she went out.

"Second nature," she said as she came back.

"Not enough sleep?" he asked brightly.

After several seconds she said, "Mmm," from down underneath.

He came close to her, knelt and worked in his face to nuzzle her soft neck. She didn't object.

"Shall I come in?" he asked, his heart pounding with excitement at the surprising idea that it might happen so soon.

"Mmmm," she said.

He lay across her, kissing her, holding out her arms, drawing his nail from the inside of her wrist up to her armpits.

"Oh, that's good." She squirmed and half opened her eyes. "Do you do that to all your girls?"

"Could be." He remembered the friend in England who, five years ago, had recommended this erotic technique, and how he'd tried it on Nancy who'd opened her eyes and asked him what books he'd been reading.

155

He leant away from her and drew his nail up the insides of her thighs.

"Oh, that's *good*," she said. "Now, come on, now, NOW."

He slipped into her so quickly that she gasped at its delicious pain. He lay still and happy. Never before had he made love at ten-twenty am. "Good fuck?" he asked her.

"Oh, you English, you're impossible," she said.

"It's an old Anglo-Saxon word."

"It hasn't the right American associations."

"Miss Hearn," he said, up on his elbows, "you missed my lecture."

"I missed you. Period," she said.

"What happened?"

"I got drunk," she said. "And stayed up till five, playing poker with Raphaelo."

"And the forester?"

"*Not* the forester," she said. "The forester and I are having a coolness."

"And you've got a hangover," he said, understanding now from experience the periods of abstraction she kept lapsing into.

"And I lost fifty bucks," she said. "Christ! I lost *fifty bucks*." The memory of it really seemed to brighten her. "Where the hell am I to get fifty bucks? Sometimes I think I'm crazy, I really do. So there, lover, that's your doing."

"You mean because of me . . ."

"I mean I got a bit desperate, so when I'd got drunk on the forester's bourbon I told him to go and stuff himself and played poker with my old chum Raphaelo. Just poker, honey, nothing more. He wouldn't have me now, not if I offered myself naked on a tray, right beside his couch."

"How do you know?"

"You can't live with a guy for three months and not find out a thing or two. Oh yes, didn't I tell you? In State City. You know what? After the first time – he was stoned then – we didn't once make love with him on top."

"Really?" Peterson said.

"You know what he says to me one night when I'm horny as hell and starting to make up to him. "Shit, now you've got me all sexually excited. Roll over, for christsake and let me fix it." And he does, right there beside me. After a couple of minutes he gets up, cool as you like, and takes a shower and comes back and goes straight to sleep, right beside me."

"Delightful fellow," he said.

"Oh he is," she said, with worrying dreaminess. "But hopeless. Quite hopeless," she said, with reassuring decisiveness.

"You know what I like about Raphaelo?" she said. "He's a real slob. You couldn't have two real slobs marrying. We'd never get out of bed.

"You know what?" she said. "Raphaelo's the only guy I could ever marry, because basically he doesn't give a shit about me. He'd keep me on my toes."

"You need that?"

"Do I need that!" she said. "Fifty bucks," she said. "Christ, I *must* be crazy. Say, it's feeling better. Let's try feeding it." They drove to a pizza house at Peking.

Next afternoon, as they lay side by side on her mattress in the dusty orange light of her fish-tank room, her mouth drooping as she asked for it, his naked leg already across her, the phone rang.

"Shift over," she said, disentangling herself with an abruptness which surprised him, reaching up a naked arm. "Hi," she answered.

She held the earpiece close so that he could hear only confined crackling.

"That's okay," she answered.

More crackling, continuing for a long time.

"No, not right now," she said.

Crackle.

" 'Fraid not."

Crackle.

"Honey, I wouldn't be very good company."

Long pause. Crackle crackle.

"*Ciao*, darling."

"The forester," she said. They lay quietly, not making love. "He called to apologise. Oh shit, why's it all so confusing?"

"Isn't that the way you like it?"

"Do I?" she said. "He sounded so sad."

Peterson shrugged.

"Christ what a bitch I am," she said, more brightly, getting on to an elbow to look down at him. "Do you think I'm a bitch? Hey, answer, damn you."

157

"Well," Peterson began.

"No, you wouldn't," she said, flopping flat. "You don't have to."

He gripped her wrist and twisted it above her head.

"Sometimes I think you take your privileges for granted, Professor Peterson," she said, through teeth closed for the pain.

They made love.

"Christ alive," she gasped. "Twice. Do you realise. I came *twice*. Hey, quick, gimme," and she reached for the pencil they now kept ready.

"Shall I tell you something?" she said, lying still and smoking. "I love you.

"I'll tell you something else, Professor Peterson," she said. "You've got me for good. So you needn't think you're going to escape back to that little old island of yours because I'll be right there after you." She turned her head and stared at him with an odd intensity he hadn't seen before.

"Christ, you turn me on," she said.

"For life," she said. "Get that?"

The snow returned, and in these icy days before Christmas there was a rightness about Peterson's world which he'd never known, though it was a state of mind he'd heard described. The snow in the streets was right. Right when it blew in powdery white drifts. Right when it was grey slush. The little rabies-carrying squirrels in the park were right. It was right that they should carry rabies. Acceptable, was perhaps a better word. Everything was right because it was acceptable, and everything was acceptable because it was right.

Jill was right, of course, but in a different way. She was a source of this rightness but not part of it. Because she was too close he didn't try to understand her, and understand was perhaps the best word. What he truly understood he couldn't think less than acceptable and right.

At first his family seemed the only exception to this sense of rightness everything gave him, and he blocked them off in a separate corner of his mind. Each time he imagined Nancy discovering he felt new horror, though now he understood that this wasn't because she might shout and scream at him, but because she might *not*. Because the brittle exterior she needed to live by might crumple up, showing the mushy inside, and

158

he would know it was his doing. But one day he understood that he might come to accept even the sinking guilt which this gave him. An instant later he seemed to gulp it, swallow it with a shudder and feel better.

Next day he did it again – with less of a shudder.

The morning after he did it as he dressed – locked in the bathroom to hide the long black lines of scratch scabs on his back – and again at breakfast, making him jolt coffee into his saucer. He half sensed that he was coming to enjoy these spasms of self-hate – but blocked this new horror into a separate corner of his mind.

In the next office, he understood, almost loved, Jo, Marge and Bill, explaining to each other their delighted dismay at the philistinisms of the Dean of Humanities, falling into silence as he arrived, politely offering each other the pleasure of telling him his latest monstrous course-rationalisation proposals.

"He won't have a department left," Jo said.

"He'll have a department but no staff," Bill said.

"You'd think his wife would tell him," Marge said with pained anxiety to make everyone happy again.

"Excuse me," Peterson said, closing the inner door to answer a knock at his outer door. It was Ric Schuster's small dark girl, Judy Finch.

He began to shut her out. His arm actually moved his door several inches towards her, though fortunately not so far that he couldn't simulate an accidental lurch and reopen it wide. It was a door which, in a sense, he'd been keeping shut for several weeks, but knew now that he no longer could.

"He wants me to marry him," she said, a yard inside his office, before he was even back at his desk. "What shall I do?" and she began to cry.

At once the whole conceited concept of his acceptance of a right world collapsed. Only the understanding remained – and it didn't help.

He understood again how frightened she was by this boy who, for his own need, was making her someone she wasn't, and who at any moment must discover his mistake. Who was perhaps doing it because he *needed* to discover his mistake and so destroy her. He understood her obstinate courage which wouldn't let her run away. He understood his own desire to say, "Leave him, he isn't worth it," and his irritation that she might refuse be-

159

cause to be obstinate and self-destructive might be *her* need. All of it pained him without seeming right.

Most clearly, he understood that he'd offered them help, and given it only until he'd found a more interesting diversion.

"But his parents," he began. "Aren't they threatening a case?"

"I don't know," she said.

"He told me . . ."

"Oh, he told *me*," she said bitterly. It wasn't really bitter. He could list the boy's absurdities and she'd agree with every one and at the end nothing she thought about him would have changed.

"Let me take your coat," he said.

"Anyway, he's over age, he doesn't need their permission," she said. "Anyway, I have to give him an answer." She shook her head, keeping her coat, but sat in his chair, her hands in its pockets. She cried some more, but quietly, to herself. She didn't take them out to wipe her face and some tears stayed on her cheeks.

"What about yours?" he said.

"I've only got one. She'd say yes if I asked could I jump under a bus.

"He's dropped his thesis," she said, and for some reason this produced a burst of louder tears. He opened his top drawer, was alarmed to see the two empty bourbon cups, pushed them to the back and offered Kleenex. Bill had advised this his first week at Flatville. "Why even *I* have to keep some, and I'm American. First whimper and I open the drawer and sit back till they've got it done with. Once let them discover it works and you'll be mopping up day and night."

"Narcissism in Early Fellini," Peterson said, pleased to show he remembered.

She stared at him, her eyes expanding in alarm, as if suspecting he might have gone out of his mind.

"His thesis," he explained quickly.

"Oh, 'Pop Art and the TV Commercial'," she said. "Oh, what's he going to do with his life? He's got so much talent. Why can't he use it? Why does he have to go around despising everybody?"

"Perhaps that's his real talent," Peterson said. Somehow her desire to programme him was disappointing. "I'm serious," he went on. "It's not necessarily negative."

160

She stared at him but wasn't listening.

"It was so marvellous at first," she said. "I'd never met anyone like him. Gee he was good to me."

"I can imagine," Peterson said.

"You can't, you can't possibly." She wiped her eyes on the sleeve of her coat and stood. "Why are you so kind to people?"

"I'm not, particularly."

"Yes you are," she said, staring at him as if now giving him her full attention. "You're a real friend. Funny, I didn't expect that."

"I just listen," he said.

She shook her head slightly, as if it was too far from the truth to be interesting, but went on staring as if some explanation escaped her. Why was it that gradually, as she watched him, he sensed that whatever she was discovering was turning out nastier than she'd expected?

"Bye," she said, holding out her small grey hand. "Friend."

Partially reassured, he closed the door behind her and allowed himself a cautious glow of self-satisfaction. He stood at his window, looking down at student hordes streaming across sun-lit snow – a block beyond, hidden by Kappa Delta Sigma and the "Y", was her apartment. What was she doing? Not sitting quietly there. Somehow that was impossible. Even the half hour she might take to gulp a book didn't fit that description. He felt a desperate need to be with her, a physical ache in his testicles from his need to make love to her – as he hadn't for at least twenty-four hours – an indignant fear that it would cause him internal damage if neglected. There was a loud knock at his door.

It was Ric Schuster. "Hi," he said. "Am I welcome?"

"Of course."

"You never know your luck."

Peterson sat at his desk, and Ric sat in the visitor's chair.

"Well!" he said, after ten seconds' silence.

"Well?" Peterson said. He felt tired by these multiple sarcasms, and the implication that he should interpret them.

"Seems there isn't much to say," Ric Schuster said after fifteen more seconds' silence.

Peterson shrugged.

"Maurice, are you crazy? Why in hell did you ask me to your party?"

161

A desperate temptation came to Peterson – as if this were the last time when it might be possible – to lead Ric Schuster to the stairs, put a shoe to his arse and kick him down them.

"Because I wanted to, Ric."

"You *are* crazy, Maurice."

"Did you enjoy it?"

"Yeah, yeah, I enjoyed it," Ric said. "As far as a condemned man can."

Peterson ignored this and hunted for a new idea. "I hear you've changed your thesis."

"Who told you that?"

"Judy."

"Women!" he said.

"Isn't it true?"

"Of course it's true."

"What's the subject now?"

Ric Schuster gave a loud sneering laugh, and didn't answer.

"I've got a question for you, Maurice. Suppose you had a cat you loved. A little furry kitten."

"Yes."

"And suppose someone, every time this little furry kitten came in the house, wiped its anus with a strong solution of lye in case it had crapped in the yard and was bringing in germs. What would you do?"

"I suppose I'd try laughing."

"I suppose *you* would!" Ric said, staring unpleasantly. "Well, that's my mom."

There seemed no answer.

"You know the phase, 'Out to get your man'?" Ric asked.

"I think so."

"That's an English expression, eh?"

"We use it."

"Well that's my loving mom."

"You mean ...?"

"Yeah, that's what I mean. She's the cop and I'm the man."

"You're quite sure ...?"

"What you mean, quite sure? She's my mother, ain't she?"

"She came to see me ..."

"I know."

"Oh," Peterson said, surprised.

"You know what she thinks? She thinks I'm going to rape

162

her. Oh yes she does. You heard of an Oedipus complex. Well so's she, but they didn't explain it right to her so she's got it arse about face. She thinks her little Oedipus is going to despoil her, and it gives her screaming hysterics, so she won't feel safe till he's locked up behind bars."

"I won't say I liked her," Peterson said, "but she did seem genuinely concerned..."

"Of course she's goddam genuinely concerned. Wouldn't you be if all day you were expecting a tap at the door and there was your babe in arms with a great hard a yard high with a scarlet end the size of a garden sprinkler, all ready to impregnate you with his filthy incestuous sperm? Wouldn't it give you the heebie jeebies...?"

"Maybe..."

"You heard of a cuckoo complex? Well that's what she's got, and she won't rest quiet till she's tipped her little cuckoo chick right out the nest..."

Peterson gave a small laugh.

"What you laughing for?" He seemed really angry now. "You can goddam laugh!" He stopped, too angry to arrange his words. "So shall I tell you what this little cuckoo chick's going to do? Eh? You like to know? Tip *himself* out."

"What does that mean?" Peterson said, with sharp alarm.

"That frightened you," Ric said with satisfaction. "You'd like to know, wouldn't you?"

"Of course."

"Well you'll have to find out, won't you?"

"I wouldn't do anything foolish..."

"You wouldn't? You really wouldn't? How do you know what you'd do if you were me? Do you have the smallest goddam idea?"

"Ric, you're hurting yourself."

"Ay say, Ric old boy, you're hurting yerself," he mimicked.

They sat glaring at each other. Perhaps, Peterson thought, he'd at last shocked himself by his own offensiveness.

"You know why I'm telling you all this crap?" Ric said.

"Is it crap?"

"Don't say you believe what I've been telling you? Don't say you've been taking these little psychotic ravings seriously?"

"I honestly don't know," Peterson said, with warm relief that for a single answer he could be totally honest.

163

"I'll tell you then. They're for your book."

"What book?"

"That beats all," Ric said, sitting back and giving a succession of bitter artificial laughs, first open-mouthed and raucous, then high and hysterical, then low and snarling. "The book you're writing about *me*."

Peterson knew better than to shake his head, thus convincing him that it was true. Also he was shocked into wondering whether he'd accidentally left notes on his desk where Ric had seen them. Perhaps he was even now staring at them, but he knew better than to glance round with guilty alarm.

"You are, aren't you?"

"What can I say? If I deny it you'll think I'm lying. If I say yes, you'll believe me."

"Correct, correct," Ric said, sitting back and slapping his knee with satisfaction. "I'm not a person to you at all. I'm just a performing object. That why I'm sure fucking you up right now. Because your performing object's got off the stage, begun to protest . . ."

"Aren't we all each other's performing objects . . .?"

"Because you can't pin it down and stop it hurting you. That's what you want to do. Put it on paper, pinned down where you can keep your distance from it and watch it. 'Say, guys, look what I've caught.' Where you needn't feel about it any more. 'Look, guys, it's squirming. It must be still alive. Maybe that's the pin I jabbed through it'."

"It's yourself you're hurting," Peterson said, but it no longer made sense, even to him.

"I sure am glad you think so," Ric Schuster said.

The note was on his desk early next morning. How it had got there he didn't understand because his office door was locked till he arrived. The envelope was marked, "Personal and important".

"To Professor Maurice Peterson,

"Unless Professor Peterson stops two-timing Richard Schuster with the girl he's engaged to marry, Richard Schuster will report this breach of university regulations to the appropriate authorities.

"Signed, Richard V. Schuster."

Peterson searched for Dr Ivan Heinz.

Crossing campus on his way to the Psychology Department, the full irony came to him. He was in danger of losing his job for something he hadn't done – but was in fact doing all the time. His danger was more real because there was therefore no way to stop doing it. Nothing exists except in the mind, he thought, but this phenomenon in the mind of Ric Schuster now had an alarming existence in his own mind.

If he spoke to Ric Schuster, if he could find him, he might make himself absurd in three ways. By taking him seriously when it was a joke. By not taking him seriously when it wasn't a joke. Or by showing that he didn't know which way to take him. "That really got you worried," he could imagine Ric saying. "You really thought I'd *do* that." And he still wouldn't know.

Dr Heinz was out of town, his secretary said, but almost sure to be at home for his own party this evening. A sense of urgency now oppressed Peterson but it wasn't till nine that night that he was making his way down a dark sidewalk, past front lawns decorated by the State Power Company for Christmas, with cut-out Christmas trees outlined in green neon and cut-out Father Christmases outlined in orange neon. Along a gable a four-foot line of neon-lit Mickey Mouses, Donald Ducks and Bambis gambolled after each other, and in many porches red and green bulbs flashed from bunches of plastic holly.

Surprisingly, there seemed to be a bunch of genuine mistletoe in Dr Heinz' porch—the first he'd seen in America—though it wasn't lit and was hard to see in the shadows. No one answered the bell so he moved into a front room where a small overflow of the party stood, drinking and eyeing each other. A fairly loud party noise came from a further room, but he paused here, suddenly worried that he must have an answer for Dr Heinz if he asked about *The Singing Priests*.

Why, most difficult, had he lent it to him? As a warning against Ric? Somehow this explanation was far too simple. As a comment on the proper connection between life and writing about it? As a comment which the lives of these strange knotted-up people would make on his own life? As soon as he had this idea its greatest improbability – that Dr Heinz either knew or cared enough about him – seemed to become the strongest argument in its favour. Like a revelation which he'd

165

closed his mind to, he believed that Dr Heinz might both know and care.

He'd reached this point when Bud Phin (Yeats and Henry James), wife of pretty Dorothy Phin, was introducing him to a grey middle-aged couple and leaving him with them.

"Hi," they said. "So you're an English writer. Well what you going to write about us?"

A second grey couple sidled up and were introduced, interrupting his gathering ideas.

"So you're from England," they said. "Well what do you think of us here at Flatville?"

"Would you know a Mrs Sidegate from Newcastle-on-Tyne?" a blotchy faced, grey-curled woman who'd been eavesdropping asked him and giggled at the absurdity of her question, but listened anxiously for his answer.

"'Fraid not," Peterson said, and asked, obliquely, whether they thought the campus novel an incestuous literary genre.

They stared at him with vacant good humour.

"Like making love to your mother while she's suckling you," he explained.

"Well for heavensake," one of the grey women said. None of the others spoke and he realised that the women were shocked and the men uneasy about whether or not they should strike him for insulting their wives.

"Among other things," he hurried on, to prove how academic the subject was, "doesn't it lead to the writing of 'teachable' books, full of obscure symbol, myth and double meaning? Do *you* enjoy campus novels?"

A terrified look of giggly alarm came on the face of the woman he'd asked, turning her in an instant from middle-aged matron back into the dumb girl of the class who's been picked on when asleep.

"Isn't there a novel about this campus?" he asked, anxiously letting her off the hook.

"Say, I believe that's so," one of the grey men said.

"Oh yeah?" one of the women said.

"Is *that so*!" the other grey man said.

Through a doorway, with a relief he'd never felt so strongly, Peterson saw Dr Ivan Heinz, Russian Jew, educated in Egypt, fellow European. "Excuse me." He moved swiftly towards him.

But, half blocking the doorway, was Dorothy Phin.

166

"Hi," she grinned.

"Hallo," he said, some of his happy relief at the sight of Dr Heinz getting into his answer, and some of his pleasure at seeing any pretty woman at a faculty party.

"If it isn't our visiting Englishman."

"Right, right," he said, imitating the keen-as-mustard, ask-me-the-next, manner of Americans. They stood grinning at each other, each perfectly aware, he believed, of the one thing she mustn't ask him.

"Now look, Englishman," she said, laughing at her own absurdity. "Stop holding out on me. What do you really think of us Americans?" She stopped laughing to listen keenly for the answer, then laughed at herself for listening keenly. "What's that?" she asked sharply, in case she'd missed it.

"Let's ask Dr Heinz."

"That old moralist," she said.

At the same instant he noticed that there was indeed one student at this party: Miss Sherry Steiner. No one else could own that black bun gripped in that great tortoiseshell clasp, which he now saw across the room by an indoor Christmas tree, where she was bending alone to examine a candle.

He was surprised, almost terrified, to find her here. Had Dr Heinz always known her, or had this affair, if it was an affair, developed since his party. The whole matter gave him a sense that things were happening which he didn't know about, not in a casual arbitrary way, but according to some plan, and that he was somehow at the centre of this plan, a sort of test-tube organism.

"Go on then," Dorothy was saying and he found himself moving towards Dr Heinz. She wouldn't follow and when he was beyond hearing put out her little pink tongue at him which he'd last seen at his party, aimed at Dr Heinz.

"They have this semen problem," Dr Heinz was saying to the blotchy woman with the friend in Newcastle-on-Tyne.

"Well, wha'd'you know," she said, glancing left and right for an escape.

"I do not joke. They are believing they have this limited supply. When it is used up, bang, they die. Oh yes, no question. You have been to India?"

"Not to *India*," the woman said. "I thought you meant *Red Indians*." The discovery seemed to bring her great relief. "Well

167

fancy," she said several times, while Dr Heinz watched her, so unnerving her that she began to repeat herself at increasing speed, looking at the carpet. "Just fancy, he'd didn't mean Red Indians, he meant *Indian* Indians. Well, wha'd'you know."

"Brown Indians," Dr Heinz said and laughed a lot at his own joke.

"You hear what he said?" the blotchy woman asked Peterson. "Oh . . ." and she hurried away – "Excuse me" – at the idea that she'd been about to give a full account of the Indian problem which Dr Heinz had been describing.

"Hallo," Peterson said.

"Hallo," Dr Heinz said, as if surprised at this formality because Peterson should have known that he'd been aware of him ever since he'd arrived. But though he still had no drink, Dr Heinz didn't offer him one. This added to the impression that the party wasn't his. It was as if it was an experiment which he'd started but was now entitled to stand and watch. An interesting part of the experiment might be to see what his guests would do when no one opened the door to them or offered them a drink.

"Why did you lend me that book?" Peterson asked, with an abruptness which surprised him.

"You are reading?"

"Of course," he said, staring at Dr Heinz, determined this time to remember his face, because it seemed that unless he could do this he would remain a performing child to Dr Heinz. But now, though he looked from feature to feature, trying to fix them in his mind, they became unrelated, nose, mouth, eyes, hair. Individually, each seemed grotesque. How fantastic that a human being should have such blobs stuck on to him and gaps cut into him. How could he ever have thought Dr Heinz owl-like – but what did he look like? Because now the features came together not in a single face but in one face after another. Each time he blinked it changed. It changed as he watched, the features seeming to slip and slither in relation to each other, some swelling while others shrank – till suddenly they became that innocent, startled owl again, a parody of central European owl-psychologists.

"You are interested in my novel?"

"Of course I'm interested," Peterson said, and at once a still more astonishing possibility occurred to him : that Dr Heinz

168

himself had written it. That he was asking for a professional opinion. It would explain the typescript – and the use of real names which had later, presumably, been altered.

"You have finished?"

"Will that make a difference?"

"It will make a difference." Dr Heinz said, smiling smuggly.

"But is it a novel?" Peterson said, glancing round, surprised and alarmed to see Sherry Steiner still by the Christmas tree, watching them.

Now, in the weirdest way, he became aware of an intense connection between her, standing there watching them, and himself and Dr Heinz here talking together. She was certainly too far away to hear them, even partly hidden by other guests, but they seemed a faded background to this intense awareness between the three of them, which he knew existed, although he'd not once seen Dr Heinz look towards her. Still stranger, it seemed to consist of pure awareness, unconnected with thought or information. Even when he turned back to Dr Heinz, he knew it was continuing, intense, powerful but passive. He seemed to be becoming merged in this vivid watchfulness, which held the essence of power without action. He struggled against it. In a moment he would cease to want to question Dr Heinz.

"Even if it's a novel," he said, "how much of it's true? How real are the people? Is the man really still here on campus? How can he bear to be? And who wrote it? Did she? Was it a therapeutic exercise you set her? Can I assume that you're the man she consults? Or did *you* write it?" As he talked he became more and more preoccupied with the problem.

"And why do strange things start to happen to me every time I read it? that's what worries me most. I feel compelled to write a second part to it. And into this I feed real people so that I can no longer judge whether they're real in the original or not. Did you know this would happen – how could you? Is that why you lent it me?"

"Many questions," Dr Heinz said. "I am breathless."

"Take the last first," he said.

"I am thinking that as a novelist you are having an interest in another novel, written about a background you will perhaps use."

"Did she kill herself?"

"You speak about a real or fictional death?" Dr Heinz said.

169

"More important, who are you asking? Myself, or a fictional character you believe to be me? Or indeed a fellow artist? You see, I, too, can be ingenious. Whichever is the case, there could be a question of professional confidence."

"Then it's hardly confidential to lend me the book."

"Which book? The book a real person has written about an invented character, or the book you say I have written about real character? You are seeing what an irresponsible act this writing of a novel can be if it is leading to such confusion."

"The student," Peterson said, ignoring obstinately the way Dr Heinz was now chuckling at his own cleverness. "Is *he* why you lent it me? Is the obvious guess about him correct?"

But now Dr Heinz would only grin with infuriating mystery. He seemed to have manoeuvred Peterson into a position he remembered from early childhood when he could ask and ask but his mother wouldn't tell him. The more he asked the more pleasure she had seemed to get from not telling him.

"You can't treat him like this," he said. "It isn't a game. He's a human being. If you know something about him you should tell me. I think he may be in bad trouble."

"You speak about a real or fictional boy?" Dr Heinz said.

"It isn't a joke."

"No? Perhaps you are learning . . ."

As rudely as he could, Peterson turned away from Dr Heinz. He snorted in his nose with anger as he went through the party. At the same time, as soon as he was away from him, he suffered a maddening desire to go back, and a maddening gratitude that he might unintentionally be earning Dr Heinz approval by this defiant rudeness.

As he passed the Christmas tree on his way out of the room, Sherry Steiner was close in front of him. "Good evening, Professor Peterson."

What did that mean? Was her formality ironic, implying all the awareness he'd believed they'd been sharing? Or had the whole thing been his imagination? Suddenly he was desperate and frightened. Would he ever again know anything for certain without at the same moment knowing *and* believing its exact opposite? For the first time in his life his mind seemed momentarily out of his control and he felt terror at this tiny fragment of madness.

He read students' papers in his study, but at ten there were no more to read. Only half an hour now till he must meet her at the library, and still not a sound of Nancy going to bed. Tonight he must wait till she went, because, with alarming absentmindedness, he'd used the excuse he'd prepared – a student reading of anti-war poetry – the night before when he might have told the truth.

At last she was going – but what an age she took. The number of journeys from bedroom to bathroom – unbelievable. He began to note them : nine, ten, eleven. It must be a joke. Out there she must be laughing at the way each time she went into the bedroom he hoped – actually wanted to pray – that she'd finally climbed into bed . . . Again. It just wasn't possible. Plomp, plomp, plomp, her soft bare feet on the brown carpet. *Twelve* double journeys, he thought, as he scored a twelfth red cross – and noticed that he'd decorated Miss Foringer's paper on *Tender is the Night* with twelve red kisses. He began to scrub at them with typing eraser.

Silence. Five minutes. Ten minutes. How soon did he dare? At last he went on his toes down through the house, out on to his icy drive, drifted his car down his sloping ramp and sang all the way to the campus.

"Lemon tree very pretty, lemon tree very sweet." It was a calypso he'd learned from her.

"But the fruit of the poor lemon isn't very nice to eat."

Lying on her back on her mattress-bed, kicking up her legs, showing all her plump tan thighs and some sky blue pantie, he'd found her singing it one afternoon.

"I spent that summer lost in love, beneath the lemon tree."

"But it isn't summer," he'd said.

"Fix it, lover, would you," she'd said, reaching up a hand, but instead of letting him pull her up, pulling him down on top of her . . .

She wasn't at her usual table in the Humanities Library. He'd been so sure he'd find her there that he could only stand gaping at the empty place. The explanation must be simple : he was twenty minutes late and she'd gone to the john, or to look for a book to read, in place of the notebook she usually laid open in front of her while she watched passing boys. Few boys at this time of night, except for one who's fallen asleep across his dime-in-the-slot-typewriter, his big arm on the roller,

171

his forehead resting on it, so that his face seemed jammed into the keys. He was so perfect – the impoverished student, no more dimes, the great thesis unfinished – that Peterson, sure that any moment she'd emerge from the john, found a big idiot smile on his face. And there, standing right in its path, dressed in frilly black, another acting-box costume, stood Sherry Steiner, behind the checking desk.

"Oh hallo," he gasped, letting the smile fade too fast.

She didn't speak, reminding him sternly of the library rule of silence and of who was in charge here, but went on watching him as she'd clearly been doing since he'd arrived. It must be her part-time job. When she came out from the desk and moved towards him, he had an astonishing inclination to run.

"Can I help you, Professor Peterson?" she said in a husky whisper.

"Looking for a book," he whispered desperately. *"A Short Walk in the Hindu Kush*. Would you have it up here?" he hurried on when he realised from the way she was staring at him that he'd suggested he'd been expecting it to appear in the air in front of him.

Beckoning to him with a podgy forefinger with big ornate ring – where had that come from? – she led him to the catalogue. She pointed to the appropriate card. She showed him how to fill out a borrowing slip and led him to the shelves. What had he done to make her treat him like an imbecile?

Round each line of shelves he expected to see Jill. Looking back to the reading tables, while Miss Steiner moved along the books, poking them with her plump forefinger with that huge orange-stoned ring, he expected any moment to see her appear from the john. If only Miss Steiner would finish his lesson – though he had little idea what to do next.

Disastrously, she couldn't find it. For ten minutes he followed her between the shelves, the catalogue drawers, the trays of borrowing slips. It *was* recorded in the catalogue. It *wasn't* checked out. And it *wasn't* in the shelves. So where was it? Not on the reserve shelves. Not abandoned on a reading table – he followed her down twelve lines of them. Periodically she stood still, frowning and working the blunt end of a black pen into the black hair above her temple, before setting out in a new direction, or to recheck an old one.

At another time he would have been pleased to find this

172

weakness in her. The unexplained loss made a serious hole in her world. Someone might have actually borrowed it without handing in a borrowing slip. Or was she, like Nancy, like so many people it seemed, playing some elaborate joke on him? At the last minute, the library closing, the book still lost, he became convinced of this when she took two quite different and heavy books from the shelf and gave them to him.

"You'll certainly want to be reading these," she said, her back to him as she filled out the slips.

"Oh thanks."

"Sign here," she said, pointing with her black pen. Though he tried to catch her eye to grin to show he guessed her joke, she never looked up, and as soon as he'd signed became entirely preoccupied with library-closing routine, filing the slips, locking cabinets.

"Thanks a lot," he said.

"You're very welcome," she said, slamming a drawer, examining a white fingernail she'd nicked.

Not till he was half a flight from the ground floor did he guess what had happened. Jill had left a message with Sherry Steiner, just as she'd used her to carry one at his party, and Sherry, in an excess of secret service zeal, had passed it to him in these books. He stood flicking the pages, inverting them in in turn, tapping their spines. No note fluttered out. For the first time he read their titles. *The Worst Journey in the World* by Apsley Cherry-Garrard, and *Sailing alone Round the World,* by Joshua Slocum. Glancing up, disturbed by a persistent jangle, he saw a university policeman standing by the expanding metal gates at the stair foot. Clearly he was waiting to lock them. He swung a bunch of keys with his left hand while he kept his right on the butt of his revolver, its fingers impatiently tapping its leather holster. He hurried out past him into the night.

For half an hour he moved from entrance to entrance of the closed library – she'd been delayed, any moment she'd come, breathless, apologising. But she didn't and his cheeks turned numb with the cold.

He stood in a phone-booth – no dimes. He bought gum at a drugstore and called her number – engaged. He called again – no answer. It rang and rang. Had he mis-dialled the first time? If not, how could there be no one there now if someone had been using it before? He dialled three more times. No answer. He circled the library. He stood and thought and noticed that he'd lost the feeling in his ears.

Were they still there? His gloves seemed to make contact with projections of a sort. Perhaps they'd already turned brittle, so that if he wasn't careful he'd start to snap bits off. There was something surprisingly disagreeable about these unfeeling appendages on the sides of his head. He turned towards her apartment.

The door opened a crack, his heart bounded with hope, a misunderstanding, all would be explained. A vertical section of the face of her small dark Persian roommate showed above a door chain.

"Is Jill in?"

She went and looked. "I guess not."

"Has she been in?"

"Not that I know."

"You've no idea where she could be?"

"Nope."

Was she sourer than usual, suggesting a lie? Was she hiding Jill in there?"

"Excuse my asking, but were you on the phone a short while ago?"

"I could have been."

"The first time I called it was engaged but the next time there was no answer."

"Seems odd," she said, with less hostility.

"It certainly does. You're sure you didn't hear it ringing and not answer it?"

"Don't think so."

"Almost as soon as you'd put it down."

"Put what down?"

"The call you were making."

"Who says I was making a call?"

"I thought you said . . ."

"I said I could have been," she said. "I just can't remember. Do *you* remember all your calls?"

He was terrified that his desperate need for help should be blocked by her quite unconnected need to claim an extensive love live.

174

"Well?" she said, when the silence had gone on for thirty seconds.

"There isn't a note for me? You see, we were to meet."

"Oh, she stood you up," the girl said, as if all was now explained. She grew much friendlier. She made movements inside the door, as if she might even take it off the chain – though she didn't.

"Could you go and look?"

"Sure," she said and went. "Nope," she said.

"Thanks."

"You're very welcome."

Peterson sat in his car. His mind raced and jumped. His hands reached to do things and he noticed them reaching and wondered why. All these weeks – all three of them – had she, too, been laughing at him?

He tested all the things she'd said, giving them sarcastic undertones.

"Gee, you're beautiful." It fitted.

"Hey, you're big." Of course it fitted. How utterly blind he'd been.

"Surely not *that* big?" Worse and worse, that he'd gone lumbering after her flattery with pathetic gratitude – and desire for more. His hair stood on end, hot sweat broke out behind his ears and fell in cold drops under his arms. How she must have laughed.

"Take it from me, lover, by American standards you're *enormous,* and I've seen a few. No one's ever touched bottom before. Of course it could be a question of angle." Did it really fit? Surely there's been something genuine about these details.

He started the car and drove home. "Twice. TWICE. Do you hear!" It didn't, it *couldn't* fit. Then why, oh why? he thought, and crossed a stop sign without stopping, bringing quadruple headlights to a screeching halt two yards from his left wing. A crew-cut, baby-man was getting out, deeply cigar sucking, spitting. "Hey, you with a face." Peterson shifted gear and drove away.

"Ten-thirty," he'd said.

"Library," she'd said.

"Friday," he'd said.

"Friday – I love you," she'd said. What possible misunderstanding did that leave space for? A light was shining from his

175

bedroom window. It had been dark when he left – he was almost sure.

His absence discovered – lucky, he thought bitterly, that he was returning now and not at three in the morning, Miss Steiner's library books such a perfect excuse that he felt almost apologetic as he came upstairs with them prominent, but not too obviously prominent, under his arm.

As soon as he reached the landing Nancy came on to it. "Where have you been?" she said, and went into the bathroom, as if sorry she'd bothered to ask.

Not too promptly, as if preoccupied with other thoughts – and how! – he said, "Library."

No answer from the bathroom, then an oddly powerful hissing, as if some small pressurised container had sprung a big leak. "At this time of night?"

"Needed some books."

The toilet flushed and she came out.

Absentmindedly, still in his study doorway, he held them back to her. Silence. Much more silence than she needed to read the titles. "You read them?" he asked, still not turning – ahead on his desk Miss Foringer's paper, crossed by a roughened red smear. Days ago, it seemed . . .

"Have I *read* them!" she said.

How oddly American she was becoming. The strange emphasis she used, so that he sometimes didn't understand her and suspected that she didn't understand herself but had spoken for the sound. When he turned she was still holding the books, staring at him with disbelief – he understood that. But he didn't dare notice, took them from her and shut himself in his study.

One o'clock. To his astonishment, a whole hour had passed. Now he knew that she loved him. It was some ludicrous mistake. He mustn't show that he'd ever doubted.

Another hour, at least, must have passed – his desk clock had stopped and said only five past. Now he knew he was her biggest joke: the besotted teacher she'd had this ridiculous affair with. It was how she'd describe him to her future lovers.

Suddenly he saw himself this way. Middle-aged, decaying, as lovesick as an adolescent for a student twenty years younger. He thought of some dignified old dog, trotting about with his nose to the arse of a bitch puppy. And he saw *her*, too, as others must see her : just an easy lay, neither especially pretty nor

176

intelligent, who talked too much. Even his successful seduction seemed diminished.

At three – his clock mysteriously going again – he began to write. He wrote till six and slept an hour on his couch, then wrote more. At intervals through Saturday, a day of driving snow and howling winds, he wrote again. Sometimes, sitting at his desk, he gripped his hair till tears came in his eyes and he let them fall. Why, oh why? Sometimes the grey snow-filled day and howling wind made him wildly happy – five hundred miles of blizzard, driving across the prairie. Three times, when the house was empty, he called her apartment. Twice there was no answer. Once the roommate answered.

"Is that Mr Peterson?"

"Yes."

"She's still out."

Why did she need to be sure it was him before she said it? Her pleasure was easier to understand.

He planned to call again at six, but now he was writing faster, with more excitement, and Nancy and the children came home from skating before he expected them. The phone-booth was seven blocks away. Tonight he didn't dare risk a new suspicious excuse. Anyway, he seemed to have mislaid his small change.

All Sunday he wrote, the sky clearing, the wind swirling the snow into high drifts against the houses. Across the white city the railroad locomotives howled on their iron rails. Sometimes a snowbrush ground and hissed past on the soft roads. At eleven, Nancy and the children at church, his phone rang.

"Peterson speaking."

Hideous childish laughter. More than one child, he thought. He held on, wondering what it meant, waiting for it to pause. There was something appalling about the way it never stopped, giving him no chance even to question it. It was abruptly cut off.

He held the receiver for several seconds, listening to the silence. He put it down. His hand was shaking. A joke? His daughters from the church centre, excited by after-service spud-nuts? He'd challenge them. "I insist you tell me . . ." But the more pompous he became the better they'd know they'd suc-ceeded. Not his daughters but other children? Not a planned joke, but a spontaneous reaction, the name "Peterson" now so intrinsically ludicrous that anyone who heard it, said in his

177

pedantic way, could only laugh helplessly? His phone rang.
Blocking his mind against its terrible ringing, he wrote on:

Summer had come, not with a whimper but a bang,
Morrison thought, as he crossed campus on a fetid ninety-two-
degree afternoon. Sweat drenched him as he waded forward
through the hot damp air, as thick as liquid, which lapped
around him and seeped into his mind. It was a summer of protest meetings, student marches and flower folk outings.

On the grass below the Union another was assembling. A new
species of student had emerged, as if from cobwebby cellars
where, deprived of light, they'd been sprouting etiolated but
sooty hair. To his left, fifty or sixty of these were playing ball
across a string of belts tied between two saplings. Wherever
their big red ball went they followed in a surge of bare feet
and beards to punch it back. They played on and on, without
intervals, scores or apparent rules. It was Game, with all unpleasant competition removed, reduced to its good qualities:
the innocent pleasures of Running After and Punching Ball.
Morrison was depressed.

Along the concrete sidewalks where he now passed, many
others were drawing in pink and green chalk – "Make Love
Not War", "De Gaulle is a Fairy", "Love the Student Disci-
plinary Committee" – putting flowers in each other's hair, pat-
ting coloured balloons, building with children's bricks and blowing soap bubbles. Slightly apart, a lone young man with softly
combed shoulder-length black hair, sat crosslegged on the grass,
staring at a single red rose fixed upright in the ground. Here
he presently accepted a sugar cube offered him by a mousey
girl in a two-piece costume which would have suited a suburban
coffee-party, who was handing them round in an IGA jumbo
pack. The big university was certainly learning.

Charming, he thought, such a headlong pursuit of East and
West, by this great Germanic belly of the continent. The true
American inability to underdo anything. The whole country
in a series of backwards and forwards surges from Puritanism
to Hedonism to Buddhism — they were like that ball game, all
rushing headlong in one direction after another, no one even
wanting to watch sardonically, all denying the need for an um-
pire – but secretly desperate for one. Outside his office a round
faced, pop-eyed, faintly familiar girl was waiting. Christ! Olga.

178

"Found you at last," she said.

"Come right in," Morrison said. "You've certainly taken your time."

"You certainly make it easy for a girl." She sat in his visitor's chair, staring bright-eyed at him. "Marine biologist!"

"A keen hobby of mine."

"Mr Maurice Peterson!"

"A slight identity problem I have."

"If you knew the marine biologists I've been wasting my time on."

The astonishing idea came to Morrison that it might be true.

"What have you got there?" he said, noticing the book she was carrying.

She put it on his desk: *The Joke Book*, by Peter Morrison.

"I don't always waste my time," she said. "Once I know what I'm looking for."

They were interrupted by a wild howling, ending in a wilder shrieking from the far side of the building. Out there he knew that they'd reached the big-circle stage, several hundreds of them in a ring, all rushing towards the centre with a great cry of love and togetherness.

"That's quite a book," she said, slipping her arse forward on his chair, stretching her bare brown legs and bare grubby feet towards the room centre, showing him her fat brown knees and about eight inches of soft brown thigh, then lifting these to her chest to hug them, head laid sideways on them, ogling him with her big brown eyes.

Morrison lifted, with distaste, his first and only published novel – if you could call it that . . .

"Did Mr Morrison really want to be taken seriously?" she asked, tilting her head even further, opening her big brown eyes still wider . . .

Beyond the bend of the corridor, down a hundred feet of passage walled in oatmeal marble and floored with yellow plastic tile, a violent whistling began. It grew steadily louder and more obviously out of tune as it approached and he recognised the university football hymn, whistled with raucous irony . . .

"Hi. You must be Professor Morrison, I'm Butch. Maybe you don't know me. I'm just a card in an IBM machine . . ."

"Too bad," Morrison said. "Can I help you."

179

"...Let's say I've come to *help you* with *your* writing. Would that make sense?"

"It certainly would," Morrison said, "so what I suggest is, you fuck off . . ."

"If that's the way you see it . . ."

"Who was that?" Olga said, against the same raucous whistle receding with a sense of injured threat down a hundred feet of oatmeal marble passage.

"A student of mine."

"He didn't seem to know you."

"That's *his* joke."

"A pretty odd joke. What's his line?"

"A thesis on English PhD theses," Morrison said. "Variations in approach and choice of subject over the years, by state, college, ethnic group. Rise and decline of interest in Rudyard Kipling, Arnold Bennett, Mrs Wharton . . . The possibilities are infinite."

"Sounds incestuous to me."

"Rise and decline of theses studying English PhD theses," Morrison went on, becoming increasingly excited. "Rise and decline of interest in theses studying the rise and decline of interest in theses studying the early non-chauvinistic poems of Rudyard Kipling, just think of that. In Western Minnesota," he added, ecstatic at this final touch. "So what's wrong with some good healthy incest?"

"Oh, you're sweet," she said.

Morrison sat up sharply and watched her more carefully.

"You certainly know how to get rid of people," she said as if she hadn't made her last remark. She seemed genuinely impressed, and stopped hugging her knees to sit on the edge of her chair. "Well, it was sure nice getting to know you again."

"Nice for us all," he said, wondering what on earth was happening now.

"By the way," she said, standing, "would you let me audit your course?"

"In elementary marine biology, sure . . ."

"No no," she said, but frowned, he was glad to see, as if for a moment he'd worried her. "The modern British novel."

"I suppose so."

"Fine, just fine," she said. "Be seeing you then."

"So it seems," he said, more and more astonished. "Hey,

180

what're you doing with that?" reaching for his first and only novel.

"Taking it back to the person I borrowed it from. Can't deprive other people. Seems there's quite a waiting list."

It was the most worrying thing she'd said. Listening to the flap and pad of her retreating bare feet down the corridor, he wondered what it meant. It was worrying if she'd invented it, but more worrying if it was true. Happiness returned. His morning class tomorrow, he remembered, was cancelled. Rarely had he felt so smugly pleased with his subconscious. And he still didn't know her name. Arriving, bright-eyed – and bare-footed – at nine am to listen to her sweet professor, she'd find an empty classroom. It was almost worth hiding in a closet to watch. Tomorrow his class was meeting at three pm in the laboratory of the Instructional Techniques Department, for a tape-recording session.

Morrison barely had time to begin to enjoy these two delicious prospects before Butch Steiner was again at his open door, knocking with exaggerated politeness, tiptoeing to his desk with ridiculous caution, laying there a printed form and printed envelope.

"What's that?"

"A job recommendation form, sir," Butch said with elaborate casualness. "If you ever had a moment to glance at it."

"Job?" Morrison asked sharply. "I thought you were in school for another year.

"I was, sir," Butch said. "Look, sir, don't you worry. If it's a trouble I'll go find someone else. You never know, I might be lucky." He reached for the form.

Morrison set a hand on it. "What's this job?"

"Oh shit, forget it, sir."

"What's this job?"

"Look, sir, I know how pressed you are. The last thing I want is to make myself a pain in the arse to you. It's just that I've a personal introduction to the head of this organisation which aids our Indian Fellow Citizens, and he'll be putting me into quite a fine job – if I can get a good college recommendation . . . Forget it, sir. He probably didn't mean it. It's just that I was planning on getting out of this goddam shithouse of learning, excuse my language, sir. Get down there and give my marriage

181

another go. But you don't want to worry yourself about that, sir."

"You leave that form and get out before I kick you out," Morrison said.

"Oh sir," Butch Steiner said, taking his hand coyly away, as if it had become too hot to touch. "Oh, it sure is good of you, sir." At the door he turned and gave one quick grin, perhaps as close to a grin of friendship and trust – go easy – as Butch Steiner ever came.

For an hour Morrison amused himself by jotting pencil answers.

"If you had a job of work to do, would you like to have the candidate help you (a) very much, (b) reasonably, (c) if there was no other help available, (d) under no circumstances?" That was an easy one. "Check appropriately and explain." "Because the candidate is still at the breaking, not making age."

"In your opinion, is the candidate emotionally (a) very stable, (b) reasonably stable, (c) stable, (d) less than stable?" "What is less than stable?" Morrison jotted. "Dog-house?" – and groaned aloud.

There were several reasons why he began to write these answers – in erasable pencil – on the form itself. He was continuously distracted by his office mate, Sammy the Smile (Dylan Thomas and Robert Graves), who had now come to sit back to back with him, often tilting his chair to read aloud news items from the the *New York Times* – "Well, get this Pete." And, in the few seconds of silence which Sammy left him, he had begun to think with astonished, almost indignant, lust of Olga's soft brown knees, oh my . . . But perhaps he really did it to experience vicariously the shock the programme director would feel when he opened a really stinking form of unrecommendation.

"Say, Pete, this cartoonist guy, he signs his daughter's name just dozens of times in every goddam cartoon he draws. He's real ingenious. I always see how many I can find."

"Is the candidate in your opinion (a) highly motivated, (b) averagely motivated, (c) motivated, (d) undermotivated . . . ?" "Does he indeed?" Morrison said.

"I got twelve today. Here, Pete, you have a go? I try it every day. Fills an hour just nicely after lunch."

"Not today, thanks," Morrison said.

"Hey, Pete, don't be like that. You really oughta."

182

"Because this boy is as close to a paranoid schizoid as you'll find outside a nuthouse," Morrison wrote. He sat back to admire his work. It was becoming impressive. Every multiple-guess question a (d). As for the personalised message content . . . Just to give himself the kick of pretending he'd really send it, he signed it on page four, folded it and sealed it into its stamped addressed envelope. As usual the envelope gum's raspberry-candy flavour made his stomach lurch upwards and project vomit dangerously into his throat.

"The book's not decent," Morrison lectured to his class. "The man's a masochist."

The book was *The Rainbow*. The lecture was being recorded by a big worried man at a corner desk, wearing earphones, hunched over turning tapes, for subsequent class discussion and analysis. The class, slumped like puddings over their notebooks, wrote it down – "Man a masochist" – their usual untalkativeness reduced to nil by the idea that they might have to rehear and analyse it. If there was one thing which irked Morrison it was this sense that they were making him into a human being at the expense of their own pudding-life, reducing themselves to memories with connected ears, flappers and notebooks – except for Olga.

Christ! Olga! There she'd been, the first person he'd seen the moment he'd arrived, sitting in the front row, her bright pop-eyes smiling merrily up at him, saying as plainly as words, if you thought you could pull that one on me, think again, professor. Olga didn't take a note, hadn't even brought a book, just put on big dark-framed glasses to watch him, so that the whole fifty minutes he knew she was grinning away inside them. Compared to those other puddings . . . Come on there, entertain *me,* he thought of saying. Convince me that I'm not wasting *my* time.

"Come on there," he shouted. "Convince me that *I* shouldn't drop this course."

There was a small titter. As a joke it was a failure. The big hunched man at his machine kept his eyes down on his tapes, listening intently, as if he'd detected a worrying technical fault.

"He thinks he's deploring the triumph of the female," Morrison lectured, "but he's celebrating it. What do his Annas

183

and Ursulas do except eat up their men? And their men aren't given a chance because they *like* being eaten. They get a real thrill out of hearing their bones being crunched up between those great female thighs."

Morrison enjoyed teaching. To help destroy in embryo so many phony book-lovers. It was a worthy vocation. To make them loathe books. Regularly he gave them quizzes – "Name three left-handed characters..." "Is the plot inconsistent (a) because the author got in a muddle, (b) because he was an inconsistent person...?"

He enjoyed especially teaching D. H. Lawrence. To sow distrust of this current holy of holies – A week ago Sammy the Smile had described meeting him in a dream. His eyes had been damp as he'd told how the Great Man had watched him with compassion but silence. "Honest to god, Pete, he just wouldn't answer me. Would you believe it? To get so close and then have the guy refuse to open his stoopid mouth."

"Well, maybe you like it too?" Morrison asked them desperately. "Maybe they give *you* a thrill, these 'almost superb' females with their dark yearning souls. Tell me," he ranged over them, enjoying this moment of provoking in the quarter who weren't still noting "yearning souls" a small secretion of adrenalin "Mr Vorster?"

Total silence. If Mr Vorster had been having beautiful thoughts, he was keeping them to himself. "Mr Goffer?"

"Well sir, I reckon I'm a bit confused sir. You see, this teacher I had last semester..."

But Morrison's attention strayed to the big worried man with the earphones. He was staring across the class with an expression of wide-eyed horror. No other word for it. What had happened? Had he suddenly started to hear something appalling on his earphones? Some really terrifying message from space. Or was this just the natural expression his face fell into when for a moment he stopped concentrating with worried optimism on his job...His speech of welcome: "Here at Bigg University, we're mighty lucky to have facilities available to have you do a real first-class job on your classroom instructional techniques..." It was a speech no Englishman could have made, so totally free from apology, doubt, protective alignment with the doubt of others. It reeked with confidence that there *was* a right way to do things and that if you systematically

184

tried, you were *more* – not equally or less – likely to discover it. And now, there he was, staring across the classroom in total but unexplained horror . . .

"Well, I reckon I got a bit confused," Mr Goffer ended, "but that's more or less the line he took."

"Thank you," Morrison said with a bright smile. "Did your last semester instructor agree with the line taken by Mr Goffer's last semester instructor Miss Cox?" Miss Cox sat upright with a jolt.

The class progressed. Sometimes Morrison swore and waved his arms about. The class tittered. Sometimes he shouted and pulled his beard and made fat-cheeked bear-faces. The class smirked. Presently he drew an obscene diagram on the board and sat on the lecturing table pointing out its meaning, and slipped sideways to get his foot wedged in the metal trash can. The class snickered. It was like pushing an enormous weight uphill. Sweating and desperate, he heard the bell with fury. He'd just been warming up. "A seven-hundred-word critical summary of Lawrence's *Fantasia of the Unconscious* by Friday," he told them and hurried for the door.

To top his misfortune, the worried recording man was already there, blocking his escape – must have sprinted from his corner – greatest of sick jokes that the world's fate should be in the hands of a nation of them, the madness of total logic followed by the vacant-eyed horror of wondering if they were wrong – "Just sign here, Mr Morrison. You're very welcome. And here. It's certainly been a pleasure. And once again, if you don't mind. All righty. We'll have those tapes knocking at your office door first thing tomorrow morning . . ."

And there she stood, grinning in the doorway as she waited for him.

"Well no, Mr Morrison. I couldn't let you have them till I've checked them for continuity" – his hands tightening protectively on the one he was holding, as if afraid it might be grabbed . . .

Her arse in those arse-tight white levis, deliciously plumper than he'd realised.

"Well, that's what I'm paid for, Mr Morrison. I'll be through well before midnight."

Free at last, they came together out of the air-conditioned laboratory into the fetid ninety-four-degree afternoon. It

185

swooshed around them, a physical shock which brought him out in a new gush of sweat. But she didn't seem to notice, bounced and danced beside him. "Oh you were delightful. Just delightful."

"Not sweet?" Morrison asked.

"Of course," she said, grinning wider.

They came to a halt on the sidewalk, in front of the Lutheran reading rooms, below the paladian columns of Theta Delta Kappa, facing Charlie's Chuck Inn.

"We *could* have a Coke," he said.

"You're putting me on," she said.

"You suggesting there's something else we might do?" he said.

"You have the brightest ideas," she said.

"Hardly at my place."

"Nor mine," she said sadly.

"Why not?"

"There's a great footballer there."

They stood watching each other, caught between wild excitement and terrible frustration.

"Can't you throw him out?"

"Not really, seeing it's me he's waiting for."

"The lecherous brute."

"I've an idea," she said and gripped his hand. "Come on." And she began to drag him along the sidewalk, through crowds of students, thinning now as the electric bells jangled in twenty neo-Georgian halls for the next classes and they were sucked in thousands, as if with drowning gurgles, into several hundred sterile classrooms.

"Where's this?"

They came up narrow stairs, though a front door to which she had the key, into a room littered with books, papers and records, with a big yellow punchball hanging from the ceiling in one corner.

"A friend's."

"Where's the friend?"

"Out," she said. "Honest, honey, you don't think I'd lie to you."

Morrison had scarcely time to let that one pass before they went into a desperate kiss.

They came out gasping and laughing and before they'd re-

186

covered went into another. But she pushed him away – "Hey, come on, quick," pulled him through a door into a bedroom, and pushed him past her to shut and lock it. Standing with her back to it, she began to let her clothes fall around her, though some didn't come cleanly free.

"Give a girl some help," she said after several seconds' frustrating struggles, plump arms twisted up behind to her bra strap, but when he only watched she stopped struggling and stood with her back to the door, her hands laid flat against it beside her plump bare buttocks, her ankles still snared together in a heap of white levi. Her face drooped and she began to take deep heaving breaths in her chest. "Love me, honey, oh love me."

Morrison did. It was one of the nicest things he'd done for a long time.

They lay still, laughing at each other and putting out their tongues so that the very tips touched. "Your silly old English beard," she said, grinning at it from six inches.

"Accommodating friend you have."

"Sure, sure," she said. "So he should be."

"It's a he?"

"Of course it's a he."

"And when's he due back?"

"Oh not for hours yet," she said. "He's faithful as hell. That's his trouble."

Understanding came to Morrison. "A date . . . ?"

"Yeah yeah, didn't I tell you."

More understanding. "A football player, waiting in your room?"

"Honey, give over," she said at his slowness. "YES," she said, as he rolled her on her front and twisted her arm painfully behind her back.

"You know what you deserve?" he said, getting the other arm there, hearing a joint creak as he bent its plump wrist.

"Yes, yes, quick," she said.

Morrison loved her again. He lay in a delicious torpor of exhaustion. Seldom before – indeed never that he could remember . . .

Up on her elbow, smoking and puffing, she was now bright and explanatory. "Hey, you've met him, of course. Jimmy

187

Pool. My date at that party. You see I'm kinda engaged to him."

"So that's why he ought to be accommodating?"

"Sure, sure, a guy must pay for his privileges."

Marvellous. She really meant it.

"Nice apartment he has. We should leave him a thank-you note."

"Oh it's not all his. He shares it with this Greek: Socrates."

"Another friend?"

"Mmm," she said with delicious humility. What can a girl do? she implied.

"But that's way in the past. A month at least," she said, and remembered a second too late to smile. "Gee, oh gee, was I in love with Socrates. You know why it ended? I had laughing hysterics one day. I just said to myself, honest to god, you *can't* be in love with a Greek called Socrates. It's grotesque. Let alone when he's a great fat slob like Socrates."

"Poor Socrates."

"Sure, sure," she said dreamily. "And right about that time he falls in love with me. That really finishes it."

"And how do you know Socrates isn't going to come home around now?"

From six inches she stared at him with widening eyes. "I never thought of that."

"It's his apartment too, isn't it?"

"That's right."

"Whose bed do we happen to be in?"

"SOCRATES!" she said. "You know what?" she said with increasing wonder at her self-discovery. "I reckon that *might* be what I was wanting to happen."

Morrison got out of bed and dressed. "Oh, it might be, might it!"

"Honey, don't be mad," she called, her plump face looking anxiously up at him above the sheet as she sat, knees up, holding it to her mouth. "It was my unconscious."

"Is that what I've been to bed with?"

"Hey, honey, I'll cry." They froze into silence. The outer door of the apartment had opened.

Together, she still stark naked, they edged up the window an inch at a time. Sometimes they had to stop, helpless with giggles. When it was up they went into a thirty-second, breast-

188

crushing kiss, then he climbed down the outside iron fire ladder. Had her unconscious thought of that too?

He returned to his office, sometimes giving bursts of delighted laughter in the hot evening, sometimes snarling. Butch Steiner was lounging close to his closed door.

"Hallo, there, come right in." A vague uneasiness infected his mind.

"Thought I'd just drop by," Butch Steiner began, "to check if you'd had a spare moment . . . Hey!" noticing the envelope. "Say!" picking it up and finding it was sealed. No words were adequate. He could only stare, his eyes damp with gratitude – or shock that for once he'd been too cynical.

"That's real good of you."

"No trouble," Morrison said, staring with dismay at the envelope which Butch held close in front of his chest, gripping it for safety with both hands.

"Real good of you," he murmured.

"I'll mail it first thing tomorrow morning," Morrison said, casually holding out a hand for the envelope.

"Shit no, I realise when I've imposed enough on a guy," Butch said.

Morrison cursed himself for his lack of subtlety. "What about a beer?" he began, deviously.

"Who'd have thought it," Butch murmured, a little of his normal nastiness seeping back. But he came, still tightly gripping the envelope. Together they strolled down campus, Butch still occasionally giving him glances of patronising amazement. A red and blue mail-box appeared close ahead. "Just look at that," Morrison shouted, pointing in another direction.

"What the hell?" Butch said, startled and irritated. Together they spent several minutes peering into the upper branches of a young oak. "Hummingbird," Morrison said with conviction. "Don't often see them round here. Not the rare white-eared."

The post office next, closed thank god – but a mail-box right outside. "We'll cross here," Morrison called firmly, saved by five seconds – but at the road centre, with astonishment close to disbelief, he saw another directly ahead on the far sidewalk – Never had he realised how the place was littered with them. The waste of federal money . . . With a cry of pain he began to hop and stumble.

189

"Christ, what is it?" Butch said, holding him up by an elbow. Cars screeched to a halt as they limped across.

"Thorn," Morrison said when they were safely ten yards beyond the box. He sat against a parking meter, taking off his shoe and sock, and together they searched the sole of his foot.

"Where in hell could a thing like that have come from?" Butch said.

Temporarily safe, they sat in a booth in Charlie's Chuck Inn, drinking weak iced beer. The envelope lay on the table end, totally distracting.

"Really?" Morrison said, as Butch told him about his marriage, divorce and proposed remarriage, and how a guy only found one or two real friends in life and he ought to take darn good care not to lose them. All the time that envelope loomed in the corner of Morrison's eye. Presently it seemed to grow in size. Now it was two feet long, now three. His answers became wilder. Sooner or later he knew that he was going to give up all attempt to answer and just sit there staring at it. Oddly, he felt that then Butch, too, would sit staring at it, as if all the time it had also been looming in the corner of his eye. Together they would look from it to each other, and from each other to it . . ."Excuse me."

He hurried to the men's room. Vital to be alone to make a plan.

But, pissing steamily below the twenty-five-cent prophylactic machine, he could only think with astonishment of where he'd been half an hour ago. He fed in a precautionary quarter, pocketed the packet and came back into the bar without a plan.

The bolder the better, he thought, half way to the booth. I'll just slip out and mail that, he'd say, in case we get so sloshed we forget it. And he'd mail it into his pocket. Or, better still, into some deeper recess of his underclothing if he could think of a safe one – a distracting picture came to him of it emerging an inch at a time at ankle level from the leg of his pants . . . The envelope had gone from the table end.

"Thought I ought to get that mailed," Butch said, seeing him staring with disbelief at the empty place.

"In case we get so sloshed . . ." Morrison murmured.

"Right, right," Butch said. "My turn. Waiter."

Sometimes in the next three hours, Morrison tried to peer into Butch's hip and breast pockets. He saw no envelope. Sometimes he went on his knees under the table, as if in pursuit of beer-nuts. No white envelope corner was peeping at ankle level from the bottom of Butch's pants. He hadn't expected one. But he still thought Butch might have it. As their jolly evening progressed, he became more and more certain that the special quality of Butch's friendly joviality *couldn't* derive from his discovery of a real friend, but from anticipation of the moment, now coming closer and closer, when he would go home and steam open the envelope and find just what sort of a friend he had discovered.

"Butch, you know what I was thinking," Morrison said, around ten, swallowing hard to keep down beery vomit, leaning his head on his hands in a desperate attempt to remember what he'd been meaning to say. Miraculously it returned. "Thinking you might have mailed that envelope *into your pocket.*" Suddenly it seemed the funniest idea. "So you could go home" – he shook with laughter, "and steam it open" – tears ran down his cheeks, "and read what I'd said about you."

"Gee, Pete," Butch said. "You really thought that! Just what sort of a twisted bastard *are* you?"

And he still didn't know.

"So!" Dr Hans Ifitz said, taking Morrison's hand in his small damp white one and holding it unnecessarily long. "We have already met."

So they had, Morrison remembered: in a passage at that party, when he'd come unclasped from that first devastating kiss with Olga, to find this faintly familiar German psychologist watching them through dark-framed glasses, as if wondering whether they fitted the passage decor he was designing. But whether Dr Ifitz was also remembering this occasion, or some earlier one, he had no idea. He hadn't made this connection when Dr Ifitz had called to invite him. "We are two foreigners. We must be getting togezer." "Delighted, I'm sure." "I give a little entertainment, any day now." "Splendid." "Let me see, zis Saturday evening?" Dr Ifitz had said, suggesting that until that moment he hadn't fixed the party date – or that the party had been fixed but he'd only now decided to ask Morrison.

Dr Ifitz was half Iranian and had been educated in Germany – or was it Poland? – he remembered, as he introduced Lillian.

"A pleasure, Mrs Morrison," Dr Ifitz said, taking off his

191

big dark-framed glasses for the first time, showing little round pink eyes. "Come into my aquarium."

It wasn't a joke. Fish tanks lined several shelves. In a three-foot bowl on a central table, big brown crayfish crawled over each other. The room was lit a deep green. A new memory came to Morrison: fashionably, Dr Ifitz' research was inter-disciplinary: the relationship between psychology and marine biology.

"These are my fishy friends," Dr Ifitz said, and laughed a lot. "You see: fishy for zeir specialisation, and fishy, not so honest as zey might be. Yes, even Olga here."

And there she was, bent forward, peering pop-eyed from close to the glass into a green wall-tank where a lugubrious brown fish with barbels, suspended over a rocky bed, stared back. The evening lurched.

"Oh yes, she takes one of my courses," Dr Ifitz said. "Olga, meet Professor and Mrs Morrison."

"Hi," Morrison called and moved away in a daze.

At once, between a terrarium of sea tortoises and a tank of sea horses he was involved with a tall gentle man who began to tell him about mouth-breeding talapia.

"That's why we call them mouth-breeders. Well, strictly the cycle commences with the nest building activities of the male. Right about the time he gets done, the female swims around his nest ovulating and the male follows ejaculating. Then back she comes and picks up all the eggs in her mouth and keeps them there till they hatch. After that she lets them swim along in a cloud in front of her till a predator approaches, then she just opens her mouth and they pop back in. Isn't that the neatest thing! And oh my, have they got a conversion ratio. Last April I initiated six point five pounds breed stock and just one hundred thirty days later I checked out twelve hundred seventeen pounds."

"It's not true!" Morrison said.

"What you mean, it's not true?" the man asked sharply.

"I mean . . ." Morrison said, but it was too complicated and he escaped hurriedly to a glass porch, jungly with rubber plants and avocado trees, set with many shallow stone gold-fish tanks. Olga was gazing down into one of them.

"For christsake, what are *you* doing here?" he began.

"Well, I like that," she said, gripping his arm above the

192

elbow, pulling him in among the foliage. "After you gave me all that trouble," pouting at him so close that he felt her breath. "You mean you really signed for one of his biology/psychology courses?" He saw the explanation. Dr Ifitz an incident in her search for a bearded marine biologist. Somehow it was no less disturbing.

But now she wouldn't answer, just watched him, mouth slightly open, the tip of her tongue sometimes appearing to quiver between her lips.

Morrison twisted his arm free and escaped to the main party. Dr Ifitz was talking to Lillian and he came close with fascination but an odd fear.

"You are judging lower class people as if zey were upper class," Dr Ifitz was saying. "You mistake zem because zey harf money. If you were talking to an Italian butcher you would not expect him to be making civilised conversations. Zese people are butchers who harf won ze lottery. Every one."

"I suppose so," Lillian said. Americans frightened and depressed her, but somehow it distressed her more to have them so well explained.

"As I was saying," Dr Ifitz went on – with no justification that Morrison had heard – "you must study ze words. Ze woman lays ze man, not ze ozer way round. Ze woman dates ze man. Ze woman makes ze proposals, of marriage, love, of anysing you like to say. Ze man is reduced to nozing. A drone. She uses him to make her home, her child, zen, poof, she blow him away. He is not a man. He is her appointment wiz ze fertiliser."

"I suppose so?" Lillian said, tall pale and worried.

"Oh look, oh look," several people called from a group round the central table.

"Yes, look," Dr Ifitz said.

Uncertainly, Lillian went. It seemed that one of the larger crayfish was gnawing a leg off one of the smaller.

"You harf a very intelligent wife," Dr Ifitz said.

"But she didn't say a thing," Morrison said. And you leave her innocent mind alone, he wanted to add. "She just stood gaping while *you* talked."

"Zat was while *you* were present," Dr Ifitz said.

What right have you, Morrison wanted to shout at him, to imply that I think my wife simple – but he'd deny it. To invite

193

that girl to your party – but she'd probably invited herself. To probe about with your psychological tentacles in my private life – but there was really no evidence of that. My sex life's my own business, he wanted to shout at him. Zat is why it is so interesting, he imagined Dr Ifitz saying.

Lillian wanted to go home. She said she was tired, but he believed the crayfish had upset her. They said goodbye, and thanked Dr Ifitz.

"You will make yourself free of my house? Please. Yes?"

"Delighted, I'm sure," Morrison lied.

"We strangers must adhere to each other."

"Stick together ... " Morrison murmured.

"Also I harf some interesting papers you might like to be seeing."

"Sure sure," Morrison said, now really disturbed. "I warn you, I'm no judge. No judge at all. Read far too many."

"I did not say zese were my own papers," Dr Ifitz said. "Let us say zey are by a friend."

"Oh sure," Morrison said. "Goodbye," escaping by starting to shake hands arbitrarily with nearby guests. Once started there seemed no logical end to this. "Goodbye, goodbye, it sure has been a pleasure. Goodbye, goodbye, so sorry we didn't get a chance ... "

Olga. "Goodbye Professor Morrison." A small square of paper stayed in his hand.

An instant when he might have let it flutter to the ground, then he'd gripped it and transferred it to his pocket.

"Urgent. 1223 South White, Apt 67," he read, standing in his study, listening to the faint knockings and flushings of Lillian going to bed. Now he did throw it away. To make certain, he picked it from his trash basket and carried it down to the kitchen garbage eater, which, with a heavy shuddering, ground it up and washed it away. But it stayed in his memory.

He said the number aloud, mixed up, back to front, half wrong half right. On a paper napkin, he wrote sets of quite other numbers. "Nine, Oh, Eleven, Apartment Oh Seven," he sang – and stopped with shock at the idea of this sound carrying to Lillian in bed. Clear and exact in his mind he saw her note: "Urgent. 1223 South White, Apt 67."

He stood in the bedroom doorway. "I must go out."

"Oh, aren't you tired, dear?" She sat propped by pillows,

194

using the tips of her fingers and a lot of shiny grease to work the worried creases of the day out of her face.

"Got to," he said and hurried downstairs. Ten steps down he remembered his excuse, stopped and called up. "Experimental play I'm helping with." But like so much else this evening, it seemed alarmingly distorted – fine if muttered abstractedly at the bedroom door, an absurd lie if shouted up the stairs, so that he could only imagine her hearing it with worse fear. "Title: 'Nine, Oh, Eleven, Apartment Oh Seven'." he shouted up with inspiration.

Silence.

Then, as he reached the front door, which he'd tiptoed to, he heard her faint voice up there, not raised, showing she still believed he was on the stairs: "What a funny name."

Number 1223 South White had been a defiantly modern apartment block fifteen years ago, much discussed as one of the first high buildings in a town which then – and still – was spreading like a flat but garish scab across limitless America. Five storeys of bright pink brick were topped by one of Elizabethan beam and plaster, so that it suggested a child's game of Consequences, say a unicorn's head on an emu's neck. He gaped up at it in the shadows above the street lights, then rose into it, five floors by elevator. Here the country's talent for built-in obsolesence was more obvious. Cheap pine showed where plaster had cracked. A flapping chronium rail hung by a single-screw. Outside the temperature had fallen to the mid-eighties but this block, heated all day by the sun on its under-insulated roof, was still an oven. Coming from the elevator, he held his breath against air well above blood temperature and he was close to panic in the windowless yellow passage before he found the varnished door of apartment sixty-seven.

At once it was opened by a six-foot blonde in Bermuda shorts and hair curlers. "Hi," she said, giving him a big warm smile. "I'm Sally." Her face was wet all over, as if she'd just showered, but he realised it was sweat.

"Olga?" he began.

"Come right in," Sally said, led him to an inner door, and pushed him through with a surprisingly sharp jolt in the kidneys and a little high giggle.

Olga was in bed. She lay facing the wall, covered to her head by a sheet so that only her short brown hair showed.

195

"Bastard," she said bitterly, without moving.

"And why?" Morrison said.

"Why do you think?" she said, throwing back the sheet, showing she was completely dressed except her shoes, running to stand close in front of him and take a painful hold of both sides of his beard.

He gripped her wrists to break them away, and quite soon they were both naked on the bed, slippery with sweat, making violent love. Olga gasped and howled, and bit his wrist, and scratched his back till it bled from the small to the shoulder-blades, and lay still with a happy smile.

"Oh my, oh my, where did you learn? Just *where did you learn?*"

"I took several extra-mural classes – hey," he yelled as she bit his stomach.

"Well?" he said presently. "What was the problem?"

"Problem?"

"Trouble? Need?" he said. "What was urgent," smiling at the idea that it hadn't proved particularly urgent.

"Honey, what was *urgent*!"

"You mean . . .?"

"Well wasn't it?" she said, licking his adam's apple. "Urgh. Hairy."

Had again, Morrison thought. But to leave in protest might become monotonous. Anyway he must spend a more convincing time on that experimental verse tragedy . . .

They drank Coke and bourbon and played calypsos and went to a midnight movie. They returned to her attic apartment and made deliciously sweaty love.

"Where's our friend the footballer?"

"Home with Mom and Dad. It's terrible. I'm sure he's getting their permission to marry me."

"Aren't *you* needed, as an exhibit?"

"I think he's preparing the way. He has a problem. Divorced woman. They won't like that."

"So?" Morrison said.

"Oh that's a long story," she said. "Oh why do I always get my life in such a muddle?"

"Who's Sally?" he asked.

"Now then, hands off," Olga said, gripping his hair, forcing back his head to stare into his eyes with clenched teeth.

"You don't think I'm interested in a bunch of curlers."

196

"Good," she said sternly, but letting go.

"Aren't American women marvellous. When they wear curlers men aren't allowed to look. When they want stuffing their men can obediently look, rise and stuff."

"Don't you like American women?" Olga said, beginning to pout.

"They're marvellous."

"Sally's a whole lot of fun," Olga said. "We're going clothes-stealing on Saturday. Carson Pirie's. Easy as pie. Always a crowd on Saturdays. Take them into the fitting closet and put them on underneath. They can't possibly count how much you take in. Hell, they're not going to undress you as you go out."

"Sounds great."

"Oh it is. We've done it before, but only casually. This time we're going to be systematic. Make out a shopping list. The real thing."

"If you call me from jail I shan't come."

"Darling don't be silly," she said, but watched him as if it had made her think of something. "You know what? Apart from gambling, it's the nearest thing to sex I know."

"That's saying something."

"Mmm," she said, and forgot to laugh.

"Hell, a girl's got to *have* clothes," she said. "I can't let a great slob like Socrates say I look like I dress at the Salvation Army."

Around five-thirty on Saturday afternoon, at work in his cool study on *An American Dream*, a deplorable book for which he had a warm liking, Morrison's phone rang.

"Hi, it's Olga."

"Sorry, wrong number," he said and put it down.

He stared out of the window. It looked leafy, fresh and fragrant out there in the sunny park, but it wasn't. There wasn't air out there but a tepid substance like liquid cotton wool. He had a picture of the whole town rushing desperately through this vile stuff from island to island of air-conditioned coolness. They lived like moles, scurrying between dark holes. Out there it lapped against the walls, seeped through cracks – as soon as you gave it a chance it seeped into *you*, setting up infections in your sinuses. His phone rang.

"I'm in trouble," she began before he could speak.

197

"Just listen to this," he read desperately: " 'And then I heard from clear across the city, over the Hudson in the Jersey yards, one fierce whistle of a locomotive which took me to a train late at night hurling through the middle of the West, its iron shriek blasting the darkness. One hundred years before, some first trains had torn through the prairie and their warning had congealed the nerve. "Beware," said the sound. "Freeze in your route. Behind this machine comes a century of maniacs and a heat which looks like to consume the earth." What a rustling those first animals must have known ...' "

"Honey. Darling. Listen. Please *listen*," she tried to interrupt him several times, but he read on. When he stopped, there was complete silence. Perhaps she'd rung off.

"What's the trouble?" he asked sharply.

"Finished?"

"There's a lot more."

"I need help."

"We know all about that ..."

"No, honey, this is for real."

"Yes, and it's *urgent*."

"I need somewhere to go. Bad."

"Well you can't come here."

"Can I come to your office? Look, I'll explain. I'm not putting you on. I really *am* desperate."

His hand over the mouthpiece, Morrison groaned.

"Hi, are you there?" she called.

"See you in seven minutes," he said.

They reached his office door at the same moment. All the time he was unlocking it she was glancing behind her. Inside she pushed it shut, and stood against it taking some deep panting breaths. "Gee, thank god for that," she said. "They had me real scared." She put a bulging zip bag against the wall.

"Who did?"

"That goddam store. Christ!" she said, growing indignant. "Who do they think they are? I shan't ever deal with them again." She came close. "Kiss me, honey."

Morrison kissed her. "Hey, what's up?" He kissed her properly.

"What did they do?"

But now she was unzipping the bag, pulling out clothes, holding them up to herself with excitement. "Hey, look at this.

198

Ain't this cute? Oh, I just can't wait to get into *this*." She hung them over chairs, dropped them across his couch, tossed them among the papers on his desk. "Oh that's horrid, they can take that right back where it came from," dangling it away from her, dropping it in a heap.

"You mean you walked out carrying that case?"

"You're telling me! And *were they* suspicious. Look. Two swimsuits. This is the one I like, but I thought you might not, so I got another just in case. Oh honey, what a mess I'm making of your room."

"What do you mean, suspicious?"

"They made me give my name and address. They near as dammit made me open the case."

"You mean they *didn't* make you open it?"

"Honey, I need to use your closet."

"Sure, sure, help yourself. They'll probably take an hour or so to trace you . . ."

But instead of carrying in the clothes, as he'd expected, she went in herself, and through its half closed door he could see her undressing.

"Hey, look at this," she called, and with a bare arm dangled out a pair of silver net tights. "A bit fancy, but one can't be choosey – no, don't come. There's a surprise – I didn't *let* them open it. I threatened to sue them. False accusation. You should have seen the way I looked at them. Goddam wild, I was. There." And she flung wide the door to show herself, naked except for black lace panties and an astonishing black lace bra with a scarlet stand-up frill mounted round the top of each glorious breast.

"Like it? Oh, come arn, you gotta."

Morrison shook his head helplessly. "It's marvellous."

"It had better be." She ran on her toes to sit on his lap and give him an enormous mouth-sucking kiss. They'd been occupied with this for a minute or two, no sound in the room except her occasional moans as he chewed her lips, when there was a loud knock at his door.

Working silently, they cleared the room in fifteen seconds. Her arms heaped with clothes, more around her feet, she squeezed into the closet and he shut its door. "Come in," he called. It was Butch Steiner.

"Thought I saw your little red bug," he said.

For a second Morrison thought this a jocular reference to Olga, then he recognised it as a playfully offensive description of his TR2 parked outside.

"Doing some quiet work?" Butch said. "Home life not conducive?"

"My home life's fine."

Butch seemed in no hurry to come to his point. Indeed, during the next forty minutes he often denied that he had a point, except to call on a friend – If he'd had a scientific education, Morrison thought, he could have calculated how long the air inside a three by four by nine foot closet would support one human being. Sometimes he heard mouse-like rustlings. What could she be doing in there? Had she already slumped to the floor and were these the final scrapings of her fingers against the crack below the door? – Student's body found in visiting lecturer's closet.

But oddly, whenever Butch said he must leave, Morrison felt compelled to start a new subject. Somehow it had become an endurance test, and he suffered an athlete's hysterical compulsion to break more and more records. How long could he extend this delicate situation. Till eight. Till midnight. ALL night. He began to toy with the fantasy of having her permanently locked in there, dressed just as she was now in that incredible bra. If she ever screamed he would assure his students that he could hear nothing . . .

"Funny thing," Butch said, watching him closely. "No word about that job yet."

"Really?"

"Perhaps the form went astray. You think that could have happened?"

"It's your country. You tell me."

"Just thought I'd drop by and let you know," Butch said, and left quickly.

She came out seething, "I always knew you were a bastard," the effect perhaps spoiled by that bra, now suggesting a pair of vast black eyes with scarlet eyebrows. The hideousness of this idea made him laugh and she tried to slap his face and he caught her wrist and they tumbled sideways on to Sammy's desk. Already he'd half worked those lace panties over her plump hips when there was a jangling of janitor's keys down the passage.

200

"If you think I'm going in *there* again," she said, dressing quickly.

Using his key to the department office, Morrison checked his mail-box, checked the Department Chairman's office door, found it open and sat in his chair. Feet on his desk, dialling home, he began, "Mr Morrison, I reckon you leave me no alternative but to take a vurry vurry serious view of your case. Had the 'tumbling' – to use your quaint Elizabethan phrase – taken place *off* university premises—Hello, that you Winnie?" recognising the adenoidal voice of his tall pale eldest daughter, "Tell Mummy I'm having trouble with that play. Right, the one with the funny name – how did *you* know? Oh, she told you, did she?"

Sitting opposite him, Olga took notes. "Would you mind checking that last sentence Dr Offenbach – your left hand happened to be *inside* my skirt, and when that occurs I just *can't* concentrate." Keys jangled distantly, as if pursuing them, just time to draw an alert whiskery rodent on his DONT FORGET pad and write "Guess who?" before they ran, slamming doors, hand in hand, out into the tepid evening, scampered for his car, collapsed into it with helpless giggles and fell into a passionate kiss.

But tonight they could find no diversion. The movie was about the trauma-infested suburban life of a Jewish Belsen victim. They walked out. They were desperate.

"We can't go to my place," she said. "Even if the footballer isn't there, the cops may be. I didn't even dare go there to call you."

"We can't go to my place."

"We can't go to Socrates' place. Hell, honey, we did make rather a mess last time. Why don't you have a proper size car?"

"We could check in at a motel," he said. "No, no," they shouted together, appalled at this bourgeois device.

"Got it," Morrison said.

They drove to Jefferson Place, the covered, seventy-two-degree-winter-and-summer, pride-of-the-chamber-of-commerce, shopping centre.

"Hey, what's the idea?"

"Wait and see."

"This is where I was this afternoon."

"That so?"

201

Slipping through the foyer of the connected hotel, they came into the cool covered streets, as deserted as a lifesize museum exhibit. Not a customer, not even a cleaner in sight, the big glass doors shut against the hot black night outside. The Danish shop, the Swedish shop, the phoney Victoriana shop, the steadily flaring gas lamps. And there, right at the centre of the cross-roads, a child's giant play-porpoise.

"Quick." Taking her hand he ran with her – oh she was fine, the way she shut her eyes and plunged at life – for the first time he felt a disturbing second of admiration for her. Glancing left and right, still not a person to be seen, they ducked through the porpoise's iron anus and came into its hollow black belly.

"Gee, I love you," she gasped, giving him a huge kiss. She undressed. Every time she knocked its iron walls an echo rang along those bare hygienic streets outside. "Excuse me. The washing." She reached out of its mouth to hang her black and scarlet bra from its snout. She laid herself on the cold iron floor of its belly. They made love quickly, with desperate need.

They lay sideways across its belly, their feet on its roof, smoking. He pictured little puffs of smoke rising outside from each of its orifices.

"Let's set up house here," she said.

"Get it registered with the University," he said. "Number one, the Porpoise."

"Hi, Mr Postman," she called, leaning out through its iron jaws – "christ a man!"

Side by side, kneeling together, they poked out their heads. He was a long way off, near the hotel doorway.

"Is it a cleaner?" she said. "He's just a blur to me."

"Not sure." For several seconds Morrison thought so, then he seemed more like a hotel guest who'd strayed. He was short and grey haired and round faced. He wore big dark-framed glasses. Gradually a far more offensive conviction grew. It was Dr Hans Ifitz.

"This is serious." They dressed in a hurry. "Now." One from each end, they came out and ran howling at him. For a moment he seemed to stand petrified with horror at this vision of un-natural parturition, then he threw up his short arms, turned and fled into the hotel.

Through it they followed at a run, out into the hot night. Ahead his compact was pulling out of the park.

202

"I'll fix that snooping bastard." Engine roaring, tyres howling, Morrison drove in pursuit. Quickly he was level, crowding him from the outside into the sidewalk. "You know what? He *bugs* me."

"So that's why you're going to murder him?"

Already he seemed shaken, was accelerating away but at the same time making jerking swerves from side to side.

"Correct," Morrison shouted, shifting down to roar in pursuit. And he really might. He'd meant only to scare him, could remember only a determination to terrify this snooping bastard, a familiar sense of being outer-directed, less a person than someone else's mad conception of one. But because he'd accidentally said it he now believed he had a good chance of doing it. Closing again on his tail lights, he flashed, hooted, howled past.

"You know what he is? The original Central European BUG."

"Gee, you're crazy," Olga said, gaping up at him, as if she'd discovered some new and unexpected quality to wonder at. "Real crazy," she said, as he jabbed the brakes, throwing them both at the dashboard – and he saw the following headlights rush dangerously close, swerve, screech and shudder to a stop. At once he accelerated away.

"You know what he's done to me?" Morrison shouted. "Sent me a three-hundred-page manuscript to read."

"That explains everything."

"And it's disgusting. About two of his miserable patients. May even be their confessions. Doesn't matter because it's *his* confession," Morrison shouted and, howling to a stop, revved backwards into a side street to pause five seconds till the compact shot past, then roar on to its tail again.

"You know what he's doing?" Morrison shouted, accelerating to seventy, now out in the city's neon fringe, close to open country, "He's trying to tell me how I should live. *Him. Me.* Hey, you there," drawing level, rolling down his window, forcing his head out into the hot slipstream. "Just climb off my back, you goddam impotent voyeur."

"Oh, I doubt that," Olga said, as if this was a subject she had a serious opinion about.

A final set of lights, a screaming halt on his inside flank. "You there, Mr Psychologist." He bent lower, screwed up his eyes to peer harder. The face in the other car was totally strange.

And it was dark with emotion. Two hands gripped the wheel

203

in a rigid convulsion of terrified fury, went on gripping them as the face turned. "You crazy bastard . . ."

"Sorry, wrong number," Morrison gasped faintly, let in the clutch with a jolt and ran the lights.

They made love in a roadside cornfield. It was fine, but had been finer.

"Just how could that have happened?" he said, lying quietly by her, looking up at the sky of bright stars.

Olga didn't answer, squirmed on to one side then the other to brush imbedded earth from her soft buttocks. She put on her panties then took them off to hunt for scratchy grass seed.

"Was it ever him?" Morrison said. Olga didn't know.

They drove back to town. "All that goddam open air," Olga said. She didn't seem cheerful again till they were well into the neon fringe.

Four days passed. A chilly wind, the last feeble breath of winter, blew down from the Canadian Rockies. Sometimes Morrison had an impulse – guilt? responsibility? – to call her. He didn't. First, she wouldn't expect it. Second, it would interfere with the delicious, used and abandoned feelings she must be having.

On the fifth day he didn't see why he should go on allowing her her marvellous used and abandoned feelings. Four whole days! That was greedy. He called her, but she was out. An hour later she called.

"You're in trouble?"

"How *did* you guess?"

"I'll be right round."

"Darling, it isn't that easy. Can we meet at the 'Y'?" . . .

" 'I'll be out to supper, dear,' " his three older tall pale daughters sang in uneven chorus as he came into the kitchen.

"That's right," he said, shaken.

"Tell us what it means, Daddy."

"What's it about, Daddy?"

"You mean . . .?"

"Nine, Oh, Eleven, Apartment Oh Seven," they chorused more accurately, suggesting to his dismay that it had become a jingle which was running all day in their heads: "Where's Winne?" "Nine Oh Eleven, Apartment Oh Seven." "What's

Kathy doing?" "Nine Oh Eleven, Apartment Oh Seven," not even funny any more it was so automatic.

"Come on Daddy."

"Tell us, Daddy."

"Is it really called that?"

"Of course it is. He told Mummy."

Among them at the kitchen table, Lillian frowned with pain at this crescendo of the continuous squealing, shouting, squabbling noise she lived with – and loved.

"Top secret," Morrison said. "But just for you, it's a tragic who-done-it – in blank verse. It's about a college president, but he never appears. No one can find anyone who's ever met him. Everyone talks about him, but it turns out they're just describing their own idea of what he *ought to* be like."

They listened, fascinated and disbelieving.

"He may have been murdered. Or he may have been kidnapped and put in this apartment – that's what the title means. The chief suspect, of course, is the college computer. In the final scene the president's been rescued and everyone's watching the door for him to come in, but the audience is expecting nothing, or perhaps a puff of white smoke. The tragedy is that he *does* come. He's real."

"That's silly," Melinda said. "No it's not," Winnie said. "Where's his wife?" Vicky said, while Kathy, catching the excitement, beat with a teaspoon on her plate, flinging several gobs of soft boiled egg on to the table and floor.

"He hasn't got a wife, he's a fairy," Morrison said.

"Oh Peter," Lillian said, as he left her sinking amid a new wave of noisy enquiry. But the really disturbing thing was what he'd noticed a second before. While his children were questioning, noisy, egg-destroying, Lillian had been watching him with a faint faraway smile of admiration and – god, yes – love.

"You wait till I get my hands on him," Olga said, apparently furious, but perhaps slightly less than she'd like him to think.

"Who?"

"Socrates. What do you think that great flabby Greek god's gone and done? Told the footballer about the souvenirs we left in his bed."

"How do you know?"

"Why else should he call me up, wild as hell and say he's *coming round to discuss something.*"

205

Morrison was delightfully unconvinced. Only now did he understand the deprivation he'd been suffering these last four days, back in a boring logical world.

"Couldn't he have been coming to ask you to marry him?"

"Hardly, honey, he did that yesterday."

"What did you say?"

She wouldn't answer, just looked at him with pain at his unkindness.

"You sure he hasn't seen us around together? I mean, we have been pretty cautious. No movies. No public bars. Secret rendezvous. Look at the way I always put you under a blanket on my front seat."

"Honey, I just *know* that great Greek slob. The fact is, I took fifty bucks off him at gin rummy the last couple of nights. Fifty bucks! Hey, we're rich. What shall we do?"

"There's that," he said, pointing to a gay red and green poster advertising the campus fair: "Support BIGGamy, your student summer fair."

Together they groaned.

"Come arn then," she said. "Well you couldn't get much squarer, could you?"

"Isn't it just the place for the footballer?" he said suspiciously.

"Oh him," she said, as if she hadn't thought about him for a week.

"Isn't he hunting for you, mad with jealous passion?"

The subject plainly bored her. "Honey, he doesn't know for sure. Socrates isn't that crude. He's just suspicious. Enough to make him stay home and grind his teeth. Look, if he doesn't know what a lover's quarrel is yet, it's time he learned."

But to Morrison as they moved between the screaming professional rides and the fraternity stalls it seemed more and more the sort of place for the footballer.

Ten cents for three throws, and even if you missed every time you won a coloured paper necklace. Hit twice and you won a red swagger cane with black and white plastic dice-handle. Hit three times, three times in succession and you won a toy doggie. And here were four broad-faced, piggy-eyed boys, obviously footballers out of season, who'd hit three times, three times in succession, time after time. Under each arm they carried two or even three large toy poodles.

These, in contrast to their red crew-cut heads, were glossy

206

white, with tinkly silver bells on silver collars, still wrapped in crinkly transparent paper, as if fresh from an expensive toy store. Expanding their already wide shoulders, they made them seem even shorter, wider and stronger than they anyway were. Kneeing them further into their armpits, or stacking them temporarily in piles, they jeered at each other as they threw. They didn't say words but let their mouths fall open in mocking grunts and yowls. They seemed bloated with their winnings, as if some enormous meal had reduced their appetite even for this jolly acquisitive fun. Why win another doggie? But they went on, their bull necks deeply sunk in circles of coloured paper necklaces, their free hands gripping clusters of red canes. Morrison gaped and led her past, but his head kept turning back.

Now they were opposite a Heath Robinson device for pouring buckets of porridge over two shivering students. Get a ball down a hole, and you started a weight falling which tilted a beam which spun a bicycle wheel which inclined a lavatory seat which set a device like a dredger's chain of scoops travelling up an incline like a roller coaster structure, and the highest bucket tipped out several quarts of sludgy oatmeal. This fell on to their heads where they sat, the girl on the boy's lap, but more on to the girl's head than the boy's so she scooped some from her shirt and smeared it over his hair and flapped it on the back of his neck. Sometimes they smiled, but more often they held their mouths tight shut to stop their teeth chattering. Morrison and Olga moved past, but their heads kept turning back.

Past the sideshow where a well directed dart could project a co-ed down a chute, waist deep into a bath of iced tomato juice, past a moon exploration rocket which students in a thin line were waiting to enter, they paused opposite the two old cars, donated by the University Chevrolet Company, which you could hit six times with a seven pound hammer for twenty-five cents. Apart from their glassless windows, the cars seemed surprisingly undamaged. This sideshow, at the end of the line, was dimly lit in the dusk, and ill patronised. Two student ticket collectors watched their single client, a lone thin six-foot boy, striking with slow regularity, a blow every five seconds. He seemed close to exhaustion but still determined. Sixteen," one of the ticket collectors counted. "Seventeen . . ."

"He's got sixty-six," the other told Morrison. "Sixty paid for, and six free bonus." – Glancing up, beyond the further windowless car, Morrison saw his wife, Lillian, walking with Vicky and carrying Kathy, approaching out of the darkness.

"This way, quick." A forgotten – how forgotten? – memory of their family plan to visit the fair tonight came to him as he hurried Olga away. But now, ahead, he saw Winnie and Melinda, his two elder daughters, each already with a red cane. Typically, they were duelling, and he almost plunged forward, "Do you want to poke your eyes out?" swung sideways to save himself and join the line for the moon rocket.

"Excuse us, we have an appointment." Not waiting for their permission, gripping and dragging Olga by the wrist, he squeezed up the steps to the entrance.

Slowly they passed down its plush-carpeted interior. Muzak hummed. Glass cases showed moon survival suits and a three dimensional model of Cape Kennedy. Marvellous. Astonishing. Man's ingenuity and persistence. Near the front a small plate screwed to the hull and almost hidden by the cases, read, "Warhead attachment bolts."

"All right, Professor Morrison, so just what in hell are we doing here?" Olga asked presently, pressing close to him, looking up pop-eyed at his beard, absent-mindedly working a hand into his pants pocket and moving it around searchingly.

"Someone I'd rather not meet."

"Hey, what *do* we find?" she said, taking a grip – "Oh, there was, was there?" hearing what he'd said, removing her hand. Delighted, he realised that she'd guessed it was some girl from his past he'd had to avoid. Now they lingered over a case of steak sandwiches, dehydrated to the size of sugar cubes. "Just fancy." "Who'd have thought."

"Excuse me, sir, we have quite a line out back," the uniformed youth encouraged them, and they were pushed out of this office-smooth metal sausage into the chilly fairground. Darkness had finally come while they'd been inside and now they moved cautiously among glittering coloured lights. Half left, a pop group was screaming on a raised platform. Ahead, his whole family advanced on him.

"Excuse me." Abandoning her as he now must to save them both from the humiliating discovery, he dodged into a narrow alley between stalls.

"Yes, *sir,* and what can we do for you?"

"I just wondered if you ever needed volunteers . . ."

"Hey, Chuck, he wants to volunteer." Quickly three or four muscular boys in comic hats were around him. "Give him the shirt, Dave." "We'll mind your jacket, sir" – and he realised – perhaps had always realised – that it was the porridge-bucket stall.

A drenched, big-chested girl, her sodden T-shirt clinging to her large breasts, led him forward by a porridgy hand, put him on the stool and sat squadgily on his lap. Out beyond the lights there was a small laugh from the thin crowd for his obvious unacted unhappiness. Encouraged, she put a sodden arm round his neck and laid a fat slimy cheek against his beard. A clanging of the mechanism and, with surprising weight, several quarts of porridge fell on to his head, jarring his neck. But, through it all, he was delighted with the perfect escape he'd so instantaneously invented, as he used a free hand to spread the dripping sludge over his face and into his beard. The big girl squirmed and gave a small squeal when he cleverly scooped a handful down the inside front of her T-shirt ... Disastrously, he sensed an erection.

She was sitting on it. How to get her off without explaining? Lift her bodily, if he could, and release it in a single bold jerk? Splosh. Another soggy load struck him, some getting into his eyes. Preoccupied with this double problem, at the same time getting a hand inside the top of her slacks to fondle her deliciously soft wet fleshy hips, Morrison found himself staring straight ahead at Winnie and Melinda.

They gaped. Their mouths had dropped open. They didn't know whether to believe what they were seeing or not. It was their father – but it *couldn't* be – but it *was*. They were so appalled that they'd quite forgotten each other. Their duelling canes hung limp. Again the mechanism began to creak and, recognising its warning now, he moved his head away. As a result a full load of vomity porridge fell on his forehead and splattered and dribbled down his nose and face. Through this slimy curtain he saw something still more disturbing: it was Olga who was rolling the balls.

Surely that was her there to his left, laughing with delight as she went away backwards into the crowd. Quickly he dropped his knees from under the big girl, saw her try to stand but her feet slipped in the goo around them, saw her topple and throw up her arms to save herself then land on her arse and elbows, as he stumbled into the side alley.

Here the four boys in comic hats were killing themselves with laughter. It was the best five minutes of the evening. They bent double, hands on hips, and rolled their chests about. "You were great, sir, just great." He grabbed his jacket and hurried away.

Now he saw no one he knew as he moved quickly about the dark fairground, looking for Olga, looking left and right to avoid his family. But they all knew him. They stared and laughed and moved aside as he came towards them. It was as if every one of them, far more than possible, had been in front of that stall watching him. They drew away from this lurching, porridge-covered figure, as if to avoid touching the filth, but as if there was something else about him which frightened and disgusted them. In his hurry, he'd forgotten to return the T-shirt, or to ask where to shower. He certainly wasn't going back. For ten minutes, increasingly uncertain what he should do and astonished to have got himself into a situation which truly hurt him, he moved around or stood looking about him uncertainly, until he saw her below a distant ferris wheel. She was alone when he reached her, though he'd had the impression that she'd been talking to a boy.

She stared at him. "You're crazy, you really are." Her eyes shone. She seemed half delighted with him but half horrified, as if undecided which to let win.

"I need a shower."

"You sure do."

They drove to her apartment. Sally, the roommate from Texas, stood in her doorway and shrieked with laughter. "Oh gee, just look at him!" Out of curlers, her blonde hair fell in two page-boy sweeps over her strong shoulders, but the rest of her again seemed compressed into too tight garments, big breasts inflating a pink T-shirt, huge fair knees four or five inches wide coming out of skin-tight Bermuda shorts. "Oh my, oh my," she screamed, swaying about, a tyre of white flesh escaping between shirt bottom and shorts top, and shut her door quickly as if, now she'd established her amusement, she could stay away from something so insanitary. Morrison stuck out his tongue at her, showered and sat on Olga's bed in his underpants and one of Olga's shirts, his bare sandy-haired legs thrust into the room.

"You sure are a nut," Olga said, mixing him a whisky sour, getting on to his knees, snuffling her nose into his beard. "That's better." She closed her eyes and began to gasp a little. She slid off his lap, dropped her skirt in a circle round her feet and slid back. "So's that," and she settled her soft mouth on his. There was a sharp knock at the apartment door.

They came apart and listened. She padded out of the room and he followed.

"Who's that?" she called.

At the same moment he noticed, behind him, that Sally had opened her door half an inch to listen.

"Jim," a voice outside said.

"The footballer?" he whispered.

"You're telling me," she whispered.

They stared at each other, appalled at this disaster. For a moment they believed there was nothing to be done.

"It's me, Jim," he said, outside.

"Oh Jim, it's you," she said brightly, but it didn't help. She threw open her hands. She put them to the back of her head and gripped her hair as if to pull it out in handfuls, at the same time opening her eyes as wide as they'd go.

"Jim, I can't see you right now."

After several seconds' pause, in a lower tone, he said, "Well whad'yer know!"

"Jim, I'll explain, I really will."

She tiptoed about the apartment, making gestures of despair and giving gulps of quickly suppressed laughter. "What shall I *do*?" she whispered.

"You're doing fine," he whispered.

Outside the door, Jim the footballer said, "I reckon you could do some explaining now."

She hurried to the door. "Jim, I can't. I'm working real hard. I just don't dare break off."

"Else I'm coming right in through this door," and it was struck an enormous blow which echoed round the apartment like a gun shot and made it jump inwards two inches at the bottom.

"Jim don't." She struggled with her skirt.

Bang. Bang.

"Jim, I'm coming." She ran at Morrison, pushing him back-

211

wards through Sally's door, closing it quickly. Outside he heard her unclick the apartment door.

Bumps and footsteps but no words. What could they be doing? He stood facing Sally, less than a foot away, both quite still, listening. Disconcertingly, she was at least an inch the taller.

Beyond the door Jim said, "You know what I reckoned? that you had some other guy in here," and there were more bumps and knocks.

"He's searching the apartment," Sally whispered.

"He'll look in here next," Morrison whispered.

"Hey, we gotta embarrass him."

She pulled back her sheet, Morrison got quickly under it and she came after him. She lay on top of him, propping herself by her elbows which she placed painfully on each of his shoulders. A second later there was a knock at the door.

"Who's that?" she called.

Morrison heard the door open, a pause, then very close above his head a voice say, "I sure am sorry," in that nicest of American tones: real apology for a well meant fuck-up. They were at their very best, he thought, when they said, in this humble way, look what a clot I've been again . . . But he couldn't see this nice boy because the top of his head was towards the door, and because, as soon as Sally had called, "Who's that?" she'd put her face down on to his and began to act an enormous kiss. Morrison heard Jim Pool close the door but perhaps Sally hadn't heard because she still kissed him. A minute later she was still kissing him.

What, you had enough! she seemed to imply when they'd been kissing for several minutes and he squirmed an inch or two to free his squashed nose so that he could breathe. Outside in the flat he distantly heard the door of Olga's room shut and beyond it, Jim the footballer shout, "Whose glass is this?"

But now they were wrestling with a violence which seemed to have less connection with love than the gymnasium. At the same time, in the most astonishing co-operative way, they were each struggling with their free hands, she to get her Bermuda shorts off, he to get his underpants down.

"You're not doing the shit on me by any chance?" they heard the footballer shout through two doors, and a small piece of furniture – perhaps the phonograph – hit the floor and broke noisily.

Christ, was she strong – and heavy. Never had he met a girl who was really strong, not merely strong enough to flatter *his* strength. The struggle, now they were half naked, had become specific: who was to end on top. But soon Morrison understood that it had changed – the question was no longer whether he would be able to throw off this hundred-and-seventy-pound girl but whether he wanted to. His will seemed to fluctuate – now he knew he must, now he knew that his truest act would be to fail. Whichever he did, he saw the result as more and more important – though why he had little idea – as they strained and heaved at each other.

"If I ever catch you with another guy," they heard the footballer shout faintly.

Most amazing was the grunting silence in which they fought. Now she had both his wrists in the grip of her mansize hands. Now he'd twisted them free and gripped hers. They were vast. His fingers and thumbs wouldn't meet round them. With all his strength he crushed them, felt rather than saw her mouth against his face twist in pain. So what the hell's happening to me? he thought. This gesture, which had had complex but logical causes – to lay this curler-wearer, to prove his independence from Olga – and incidentally show that she couldn't throw balls to bring down buckets of porridge on him without punishment – which at least had been his own, now seemed hopelessly out of his control. Next door Olga was in real trouble, making her back into the human being he realised he'd been refusing to believe her. And here *he* was in real trouble, fighting desperately not to be consumed – that was the only word which seemed to fit.

A moment came when he knew he could win. His hands were on her throat, a bubbly gurgle starting there, her great carcase going limp. But now his need to take her became uncontrollable and he entered her from below – at the same time allowing her just enough air to breathe.

Great bones up there, independent of her limp weight, seemed to grip and twist his penis. He had the strangest picture of this normally fine organ, grown thinner – though still erect – as easily bendable as a soggy twig. Desperately he thrust with this poor thing into her vast dark cavity guarded at its entrance

213

by these rolling, soft but at the same time rock strong bones, and came quickly.

They lay still, exhausted. No one had won.

He crept to the shower and dressed in his jacket and porridgy pants. He drove to K-mart, bought a new pair, dropped the old ones into the town creek – to join the sewage outflow trickling softly among ice boxes, auto tyres and dead dogs – and went home. His house was silent, his family asleep and he crept to bed. Close to him in the darkness Lillian stirred but didn't wake.

"Darling, I sure am sorry about last night." It was Olga. It was ten to nine next morning and Morrison stood by his office desk, answering his phone with one hand, a jumble of lecture notes in his other, about to leave for his class.

"You are?"

"Darling, don't be bitter. What could I do?"

She sounded faint and far away. With surprise, he realised that she knew nothing – or was pretending to know nothing – of what had happened in the next room, and with more surprise that he'd been expecting that she would, when this was most unlikely.

"Honey, he's six foot two."

Even if he'd known what to say there was the problem of Sammy the Smile, close behind him, also collecting notes for his class, but with yesterday's *New York Times* folded ready on his desk – just a chance of slipping in a quick news quote before the bell.

"Honey, he doesn't look it because he's about five foot eleven *wide, too*. Don't blame me. That's why I don't blame you for not rescuing me. Darling, could we get together. There's something I need to see you about rather urgently."

Nothing had changed.

Or had it? Because, when she said this he no longer wanted to laugh at her – or wanted to laugh in a different way. Now, whenever she called to say she must see him urgently, as she did increasingly during the following days, it was a joke *with* her rather than against her. It was as if some preliminary skirmish to a battle was over, neither side winning, but both learning. The chief thing they'd learned was that there was going to be a battle. Both could now look back and laugh

214

at their previous misconception that there might be only a skirmish.

Probably, he decided, she didn't know what had happened with Sally from Texas, but suspected. By suspecting, but not telling him, she turned his gesture of escape into one which involved him more decisively – she needn't show offence, but at the same time could show him that she understood why he'd needed to make it.

In the days which followed they met as arbitrarily, and went to bed with neither more nor less magnificent cries. And there were neither more nor less moments after he'd loved her when he watched her padding about the room with astonishment at what he'd done. At these times her big lozenge-shaped buttocks and thighs and the flippery way she let her hands dangle from her wrists gave her a seal-like look. They passed as miraculously.

But they met more often, less and less carefully. They seemed to fall into competition : who could force the other into not daring to do something. "Where's the footballer tonight?" "At the Moon Bowl, swilling beer." "Hey, I've an idea, why don't we go to that nice joint the Moon Bowl?" "Darling, let's. You know what that sweet boy showed me today? A nine-inch flick knife. He keeps it in a red cowboy handkerchief – no finger-prints. He gets me up to his room to tell me he's sorry he was so suspicious the other night. It's just 'cos he loves me so. Then he shows me this knife. When I turn vomit green he says, 'Cute, ain't it'."

And Morrison's work with the Experimental Drama Group became more exacting. Each time he told his children, he saw them grow more confused between this improbable story and the sincere way he told it. They seemed to watch him anxiously for a hint that he was joking. He wouldn't give it. It was as if he was under some compulsion to allow himself no way out of this lie except their final discovery that he really had been lying and they couldn't trust him again. Lillian had guessed already. He was glad. To punish her for the way she went on pretending she hadn't guessed? Maybe.

Sometimes their affair seemed a continuous public scamper, hand in hand down the busiest campus sidewalks. Or she'd bounce ahead, turn, eyes shining, "Oh, you're delightful, just delightful. Your silly old English beard" – as after his public poetry reading to the English Department.

215

He came late, read Dylan Thomas in a Peter Sellers' Indian accent, invented a Significant New Young English Poet called Sinkington, read several invented extracts and stood damp-eyed with emotion. Clearing his throat from the sob he'd been choking back, he asked for questions.

"Mr Morrison, would you say there was any intrinsic difference between prose and poetry?"

He couldn't answer, puffed out his cheeks, too marvellous, stared pop-eyed – for one terrible moment he thought the man was laughing at *him*. Sadly no. At last he couldn't resist telling them what they wanted to hear. "Why, of course not."

"Mr Morrison, would you say Bob Dylan was a poet?"

"Who?" He pretended not to hear, leant forward, hand to his ear. "Who did you say?" "Bob Dylan." He still couldn't hear, looked round the audience for help, already they were tittering. "Terribly sorry," raising his other hand to his other ear.

"Oh HIM." But he gave no answer, just stood there, looking down at his lectern, as if nibbling small nuts. Now they laughed aloud. He looked up, still nibbling. They howled. Every move he made . . . He opened his mouth to speak but no words came. They roared – but they hated him for it.

Presently he said quietly to his lectern, "What can I say?" More howls.

At once he shouted at them, intense, passionate, "WELL IS HE?"

Shocked silence.

"I'm asking *you*," the sharp young instructor who'd put the questions said.

"I was afraid so." He recited from memory what he remembered of "The Gates of Eden", applauded himself, shouted "more" distantly in the back left corner of his beard, invented more.

"Do you like it?"

Mumblings, then the sharp young instructor said, "Yes."

"Good," Morrison said seriously. He really was glad. Suddenly, and as seriously as he knew how, he felt that it would have been a far worse thing than he'd intended if this keen young man had said no.

"Just delightful," Olga said, gripping his hand to drag him faster.

A moment of bad depression hit him. "It stank."

She stopped, staring up at him. "Hey, I believe you *mean* that. Quick, quick." Now she really dragged him, faster, faster, towards her apartment. "This is serious."

At other times they seemed to sit hour after hour, over iced bourbon at the Moon Bowl, the Old Forty Niner, the Glo Worm, touching each other, then not letting themselves, playing deliciously at erotic postponement, while she told him about her life.

"That was before I met Socrates," she said. "I had a job modelling at an art school. Oh boy, was that *bad*. We have this cool Life Class teacher. Well, I can't have him staring lecherously at me six hours a day while I stand there stark naked and not get ideas. Added to the fact he's beautiful, he really is. It's his wife's the trouble."

"He had one of those?"

"First thing I know, she arrives in class one day and starts attacking me. I don't even know who she is, just some mad dame screaming and hitting me with a clothes hanger. Must have picked it up as she ran out the house. Well you try having a fight when you're stark naked in front of thirty art students. The Life Class teacher? He doesn't do a thing. Just stands there, holding his head in his hands, and crying out, 'Oh no, Oh no.'

"Soon as I get the idea I make a dash for the dressing room and lock myself in. I can hear this mad dame beating away on the door with her clothes hanger. What she doesn't know is, there's a back way out. I don't even stop off at the office for my pay – *and* they never send it. Meanies.

"That was before I worked for this entymologist. I was desperate, I can tell you. Not a dime. Out on the dunes all day, collecting grasshoppers. All that goddam sandy country, and this keen, grey-haired young guy with his nets and pots and killing bottles. I can't decide if I like him or he's just the spookiest thing I've seen. Well, I haven't planned anything quite so quick, but by afternoon I'm in a real bad way. The day seems to have gone on for about a year already. Bored? I didn't know what the word meant. So I lie in wait for him behind some horrible prickly bush and pounce. You know, undo a zipper or two, to give him the idea. Jeez, does that scare him! I don't think he's noticed me before. At first he just stares at what I'm temptingly exposing like it's a ghost he's seeing.

217

Then he comes for me with a great roar. No kidding. He really roars. I run, I can tell you. I still don't know if he planned on raping or murdering me. I didn't wait to see. Well, honey, he must have been pretty odd, because I'm not generally like that. Well am I?

"That was after I had this real good job buying space for an agency. Oh yes, they had it all planned for me to become a proper executive. They were expanding or something. You might not think it, but I'm really efficient when I try. I reckon I let them down rather. Well, can you *see* me as a career executive? Yeah, the pay was good. Yeah, I stood it for a time. The fact is, that was when Socrates came along," she said dreamily.

"You know what?" she said. "I've had thirty-seven jobs – not counting wife, *or* mistress. Reckoned them up the other night."

Sometimes Morrison believed her. He was especially surprised one day in her apartment to find a corroborative letter pad with the printed heading, "From the desk of Olga Hopping".

"Met him at the racetrack," she said. "That was love at first sight, if you like it. I just moved in. I can be pushy in a kinda way when I want. He has this apartment in State City where he's living with this half coloured girl. I soon fix her. Tell her he's doping her food so he can get her pregnant because he has this thing about having a quarter black baby. She's gone before I finish telling her. What does he do? Oh he asks where she's got to once or twice and I tell him she's fixing an abortion for herself. He doesn't want to hear any more after that. Anyway, I reckon he was getting bored with her.

"Christ, was I innocent. I thought all I had to do was get him into bed and I was made. He really taught me, Socrates did. I was just a little girl till I met him. Yeah, I'd been married. So what. I was just innocent as hell.

"I tried every goddam thing. Even religion. One day I buy a gold cross on a gold chain and about eleven on Sunday morning I get up and dress – that's about four hours before we usually get up. Presently he rolls over.

" 'What's going on?' he says.

" 'Getting dressed,' I say.

" 'What in hell for?' he says.

" 'Church,' I say, as innocent as I know how.

218

" 'What *is* this?' he says, as if the world's really going crazy. It takes him about thirty seconds to get it. Then, 'Ah ha, you needn't think that'll work,' he says and he rolls over and goes to sleep again. Jeez, I could have murdered him.

"Yeah, I went a couple of times. Had to, after that. I rather liked it. But not that early in the morning. If they had afternoon services. Hell no, *he* doesn't go. I just thought he might be hung up on little girls who did. Well, it was worth a try. I tell you, I was desperate.

"Anyway I fixed him. Took his Marshall Field's credit card next day and charged him a sixty dollar bill for underwear. Signed it in the name of his wife. Not as far as I know, but this half coloured girl was pretending to be and she'd made him fix it so she could sign too. Anyhow, it worked. But was I scared they'd ask for my ID card. They gave me some pretty odd looks. I think what convinced them was I bought this egg poacher too. Now wasn't that smart of me?

"Never found out, as far as I know," she said, losing interest. "Anyway he was paying them off at ten per cent a month so I don't suppose he knew the total from one month to the next. Anyway he'd given them a false address – and just to make sure he got a lawyer uncle of his to write and say he'd last been heard of on his way to Afghanistan. Every Greek has a lawyer uncle.

"Yeah, yeah, I tried leaving him, that was the first bright idea. But of course I had to keep coming back and having a peek to see if he'd noticed. What's the good of leaving someone who doesn't even *notice*. Tried it as soon as we got down here. That was a real sell," she said, remembering it with delight.

"I meet this French boy on the jumpers' stall on Student Activities Day. So I join. What could be better? I can keep telling Socrates all about my day's parachuting and looking wistful – he'll soon guess the rest. Anyway, this French boy is real nice – I think. Well hell, you can't afford to throw up chances, can you.

"Jeez, do those jumpers screw! Oh, that's crude. Several of them have these trailers and as soon as they arrive, in they go and sometimes they don't come out till it's time to go home. That's all the jumping *they* do. The cute thing is, these trailers are all lined up and you can tell just what's going on inside from

219

the way every few minutes one of them gets a great sway on all by itself, for no reason at all.

"You never know from one week-end to the next who'll be with who. Sometimes they even swap around at lunch time. Well, it *is* a bit animal. Funny," she said, in puzzled self-discovery. "Wouldn't have thought I'd have minded.

"The French boy? That was the big sell. Turns out he's a faggot. I just can't believe it. Most times I can tell but there weren't any of the usual signs. Do I feel a fool! I keep wondering why the charm isn't working. I think he's shy or something, or a bit odd because he's French. Christ, it's so obvious afterwards. He's always taking up this Javanese boy, or getting taken up by him. They're having a marvellous time, I suppose, trying to kill each other, and I just don't see it.

"Well about the third week I manoeuvre him into an empty trailer. Tell him I need some help with my harness. As soon as he's inside I shut the door and go and sit on the bed and start undoing more than my harness. Oh boy, am I horny. Three weeks without a lay – that was part of the plan to get Socrates curious. I keep watching him, waiting for him to get the idea. Do you know what he does? Just gives an enormous horrid French laugh. Doesn't even try to escape. Just stands there laughing at me.

"Does that make me mad! I try to scratch him. The trouble is, by this time my jeans are undone and I have to hold them up with one hand. Anyway, he's waiting for that, and catches me by the wrist and twists it, and when that makes me scratch at him with my other hand my jeans fall down. So he gives me a cracking great slap on the arse and walks out.

"I didn't go near that place again. Walked right out after him and straight back to campus. Yeah, nine miles. Oh no, I forgot." She paused, thoughtfully. "Not all nine. About one, in fact . . ." She smiled distantly. "I got a lift. From an Armenian boy. Forgot about him."

"So the day ended well?"

"Honey do you blame me?" she says. "Three weeks!"

"Those places give me the creeps," she said, driving north to the Glo Worm, past the Esmeralda Home of Rest, advertised in six-foot green neon gothic. "I was just a high school kid and he was working his way through college as a funeral parlour night ambulance driver.

"He has a room in the house but he shares it with the other driver, so we make out in the back of the ambulance. As soon as the other guy gets the call he runs downstairs and thumps on the outside and we bundle out and they drive down the road to pick up the boss – or anyhow get instructions from him before they go for the stiff.

"Well one night the first we know, the boss is coming screaming across the yard, what the hell's the delay. So Johnny jumps out the back saying he's just fixing the oxygen. I suppose the other guy must have slept right through the call because next thing the boss is shouting how he won't wait another second and off we go down town to get the body, him and Johnny in front, me still in the back.

"Do I panic. As soon as I'm properly dressed I hunt around to see if there's anywhere to hide, but once they take the stretcher out there isn't a goddam place. Anyway, I don't fancy being bounced around in there alongside a stiff even if they don't notice me. And the biggest joke is, the boss is a personal friend of my parents.

"Eventually I work out a plan. I wrap this big scarf I'm wearing all round my face except my eyes, and the minute he stops and opens the back doors I step out and walk right past him away down the street. You should see the look he gives me. He just stands paralysed. I suppose he doesn't dare create a scene in front of the customer's house. Or else he thought it was resurrection day.

"So what do you think happens next? Johnny suggests we use the laying-out theatre. He says there's a nice convenient bed right in the centre. That's the table where they put the stiffs. Made to tilt, he says. Not to mention with a gutter round the edge for the blood. First thing they do, they make two great cuts right up the chest and right across to drain it all out so they can pump in the formaldyhyde."

"He must have been keen on you."

"I told him what he could do with that!" she said. "Hey, did I tell you I'd been a nurse?"

"Really?" Morrison said, parking the car, cutting the engine, and turning to listen with full attention, at the same time working a hand up her skirt between her soft warm thighs.

"Yeah ... Oooo," she said, squirming. "For a week. That was real spookey – hey, do you want to hear about my life or

221

don't you?" And for five minutes they lay on top of each other in a tight limb-crushing kiss between the front seat and the steering wheel.

"The very first patient I get is this nice boy from Kansas City. Jeez, why does it always happen to me? He isn't bright but he's real nice. How am I to know what he's in there for? Well we kinda get chummy. Yeah, he's married, so what? Then I find he's due to have this brain surgery. He gets terrible headaches and a couple of fancy specialists who're making a reputation for themselves for how neatly they can chop up brains are going to try cutting a piece out. I wonder why all the other nurses are looking at him kinda odd. It's because the chances are he'll wake up a lettuce and stay that way the rest of his life. I couldn't take that. I quit. Right that afternoon."

"Doesn't seem quite your vocation," Morrison said.

"Maybe," she said distantly. "The fact is," she said with a faint distant smile, "there was this young doctor . . .

"It's my mother I get my pushyness from," she said. "Picks out this poor little guy she's seen day after day going up in the elevator, thinks, that's the guy for me. She's told me. Oh, she doesn't actually say it that way, but I can tell it's what she means. I could *kill* her.

"Hell yes, she proposes to him. Wha'd yer think? Of course he accepts her. Doesn't occur to him to do anything else. He just takes things as they come. He's really rather sweet, I suppose, if he wasn't so goddam hopeless.

"She was good for him in a way. Built him up. Just as far as she wanted and no further. She gave him permission to be her husband, then sat down in the shade of what she'd done and decided she needn't do any more for *him*. She's got what she wants. How can she want it? that's what bugs me. Cooking, bridge twice a week, coffee parties. Christ, it's scarey.

"That's right, only child . . .

"That's the one thing she didn't interfere with. Let him do whatever job he liked. Soon as they're married he tells her he's always wanted to be a farmer. I suppose he hadn't had the courage to admit it before. So he tries that, and does he make a mess of it. Then he's in real estate. God no, not in a big way. Just big enough to lose all the money he's made from a lucky deal in dried fruit. That's when he was an importer. Then he tells her the thing he's always wanted to be is an oil prospector.

222

So he goes to night school and gets qualified, but there aren't any jobs for oil prospectors, so he sells bicycles. Christ, doesn't that show you? Only my father would try to sell *bicycles* to *Americans*.

"Hell yes, you name it, we've lived there. Florida, Maine, Washington State . . .

"She just sits back and lets him have his head. When we're really broke she teaches school, but she doesn't *like* teaching. As soon as he's working again she packs it in. And now he works in a life insurance office and lives in a State City suburb. Right back where he began. That's what she's waiting for. Twenty-five years it takes her to let him prove to himself that's all he's worth. Gee, oh gee, is she patient. And could I kill her, slowly and painfully.

"You know what," she said, taking several quick sucks at her cigarette to surround herself with a dense cloud of smoke, peering at him bright-eyed through it. "Last night I started checking up on the men I've been to bed with. Was that scarey! When I got to thirty-three I quit. Each time I thought I'd got the lot I'd think of another. Then two or three would come in a bunch. I reckon I'm just a little whore," she said, and waited, perhaps for him to deny it.

"Who likes her work," he said.

"Right, right," she said, delighted. "A whore who likes her work," and she sucked deeply. "That really what you think?" she asked sharply.

At this time Morrison made love to her, head to feet, from back and front, all ways up and in as many other ways and positions as he could remember from a long-ago reading of Kraft-Ebbing. "We're breaking state law," she'd sometimes gasp happily.

He made love to her in various characters. As the footballer, of course.

"No, honey, you haven't got it right. More grunts and groans."

"More as if he's having a great shit?"

"How did you *guess*? – oh hell, he's a nice guy really. Why don't we try someone else?"

As the leader of the university football band, humming the university football hymn distantly in his beard as he laboured to its rhythm.

As Sammy the Smile. "Say, isn't this just a whole bunch of fun?" Bounce, bounce, bounce. "Isn't this the jolliest, cosiest thing you've done in your *whole life*?"

As Butch Steiner.

"Who's he?"

"A problem student of mine. The one who kept you in the closet."

Half way, Morrison withdrew and lay on his back.

"What's up?"

"That'll teach you, American bitch."

"Hey, that's NOT FUNNY," she shouted and dragged him back on top.

As a nervous English novelist-teacher, having his first mistress on an American campus. "Darling, you sure I'm not hurting you. Darling, doesn't this remind you of Paul Morel and Clara." She grew hysterical with giggles, then desperate. Most often she ended the act this way, trying to make him sincere, half angry, half frightened when, whatever she said or did, he wouldn't come out of his part. "Gee, you're weird, you really are."

"Honey," she said, "What about Dr Ifitz?"

"Too disgusting."

"Come arn, come arn."

"Too depressing." But he did it, lecturing her continuously. "Zis problem of ze orgasm, zey are totally preoccupied wiz it ..." Even at the climax, "Miss Hopping, I harf seen you and your loffer in ze beeg feesh. Ha ha, very symbolic," till in desperation, humping and bouncing under him, she put up both hands to try to close his mouth. "You do zat – I bite," he said, and bit.

Smoking, recovering, she said, "Christ, I sometimes really don't know who you are."

"I'm no one," he said, and was disturbed at the possible truth in this answer which he'd made without thought.

"What I like about you," she said, "is you don't want to *do* anything about everything that's wrong. If any American was half as cynical as you he'd be around twenty-four hours a day, putting it all right."

"Who's cynical?" he said.

"One thing's for sure," she said, "you're not in love with me."

224

"Well frankly," Morrison began.

"Honey, you don't have to answer," she said, holding down his shoulders and kissing him.

He was glad. For the second time in two minutes he'd been about to tell the truth: that he never had been in love and wasn't sure what the phrase meant.

"Honey, I'm in trouble."

"Hold it five minutes, can you?"

"Honey, this is for real."

Driving to campus, he remembered how she'd said it, with the start of a laugh but no more, as if the joke this time was that it *wasn't* a joke. But she was bright and fully dressed when she opened her door.

"We're going to a party."

"Was that the trouble?"

"Shit no. They've just called me." For a second she seemed to remember something. "Shit, that can wait. My friends are giving a party."

"Will the footballer be there?"

"Say, *yes*," she said, as if she hadn't thought of it. "Tell you what, we won't know each other."

"Then at the end he can take you home."

"I'll fix that honey, I'm good at that sort of thing. Hell, they're my *friends*, don't you want to meet them? That slob Socrates? All these names I've been boring you with?"

The party spread through the lower floor of a clapboard lodging house. The lights were low, in one room there was dancing, in others low sofas but no dancing, and in the darkness on the floor just inside the front door a couple were copulating. They were there when he arrived, a minute after her, and still there an hour later when his slow circle of the party returned to its start. Now that his eyes were used to the gloom he could see portions of bare flesh, oddly disconnected, and one long bare leg. Her face was covered to her nose with the bottom of her skirt. As he watched, the boy began to work on her again, but no one else seemed to notice.

"Don't they have a room?" he whispered to Olga, passing her in a dark corner.

"They prefer it here," she whispered. "More chummy."

All through the rest of the house, an alert noticing quality

225

seemed to be the party's flavour. On low sofas, they didn't talk but watched, or grew bored because there was nothing to watch. Even the pairs who stood in low conversation near the walls were all the time half watching. The dancing in the centre room was continuous but never thick. Sally from Texas was there. "Hi," she called.

"That's the Carp, she's dancing with," Olga whispered, beside him in the kitchen, squeezing his hand as she reached with the other for the bottle of bourbon he'd hidden on a top shelf. All about the house were hidden half bottles of scotch and bourbon, brought by guests who knew they wouldn't otherwise get any: others carried them in their pockets. "The long sloppy one," Olga whispered. "You'll never guess what. He offered to repay her for typing his thesis for him by screwing her. Let his pants down to tempt her. And what d'you think? He's hung like a dormouse."

"What am I hung like?"

"Darling..." She paused to think. "An Aberdeen Angus."

Gradually Morrison recognised others from the party where he'd first met her. The sulky boy who'd been making a cache of beer. The long-haired blonde whose arse he'd pinched. Dr Hans Ifitz.

"There's Socrates," Olga whispered, nodding at a black-haired slouching man. He was taller than Morrison had imagined but broad too. He suggested a huge but flabbily filled sack. "I've got him real mad tonight. You know what, I've decided he doesn't even *love* me, he's just fascinated because he can't make me any more. It's never happened to him."

Socrates seemed deeply involved with a thin six-foot blonde, dancing with her in an overhanging soft bear hug, his big jowly face drooped on her shoulder.

"That's Tania," she whispered. "She's a Ukranian princess or some jazz. She's just crazy about him. He can have her any day, breakfast, dinner, supper. That's how I know he's mad with me. Christ, you don't think he'd waste time with Tania for any other reason. Excuse me," and she passed on quickly to meet the same broad boy who'd taken her away from the other party – Jimmy Pool the footballer. When she crossed to him he put out a six-inch-wide hand to ruffle her short brown hair in a way Morrison didn't like.

As he watched her, sometimes dancing, sometimes moving

bouncily about the party, she seemed far livelier than these other bored, watching people. To them, he saw, she was a joke. The ironic rightness of this delighted him: that he should be having a passionate affair with a girl they thought this about – but it made him like them no better.

"So!" Dr Ifitz said, appearing unexpectedly beside him.

Delicious. Neither knew what the other knew. Dr Ifitz was cool, even surly, but there were a hundred possible reasons besides that he'd recently disturbed Morrison making love inside a public porpoise, and as a result nearly been murdered by him.

"You have read my manuscript?"

"Hard at it," Morrison said. "Should reach page twenty any day."

"You are a fast reader," Dr Ifitz said. "You have met Butch?"

And there, sure enough, hidden on Dr Ifitz other side, was Butch Steiner. Now he put his head forward into view.

"Sure. He's my problem student," Morrison said with a merry laugh. He didn't feel merry. He was shocked to find them here together and disturbed by the way he could still only see Butch's head, peering past Dr Ifitz, so that it was less as if he was here in person than as if Dr Ifitz had produced his mask. This impression was increased by the fact that Butch was staring at him with an absurd fixed grin and, untypically, not speaking.

"How are you, Butch?" Morrison shouted, against the music, louder at this moment.

"Fine," Butch said and grinned some more.

"Well that's great," Morrison shouted, unable to stop himself moving round Dr Ifitz to make sure that the whole of Butch Steiner was here. "When're you coming to see me?" he asked, reassured by his complete body, arms and legs.

"I'm working on a story."

"Well that's fine," Morrison said, his stomach already floating, as when an elevator gate clicks before its downward lurch into space. "I could do with some light reading . . ."

"It's called *The Letter*," Butch Steiner said. "It's about this grad student who asks his professor, a real nice guy, he thinks, to write him a letter of recommendation . . .

"Don't tell me, you'll take away the suspense," Morrison shouted and strode away into the party, suspended between fury and horror, barging between dancers to reach a far wall

227

and look for Olga. Presently he saw her, talking with animation to a boy in black leather jacket, guessed he was one of the Prairie Flyers, a local red-neck motor-cycle group. This one had shoulder length golden hair and thick golden stubble. A second later he saw Olga hurry out with him, hand in hand, and from the street heard the roar of an engine. He was taking her for a ride.

Minute after minute passed and they didn't come back. Close to his conscious mind, but never quite reaching it, rose the astonishing possibility that they might *not* be coming back. He moved about the party. He danced with the long-haired blonde whose arse he'd pinched and who recognised him, "Hi there," with the merriest friendliness. As she wriggled against him he was momentarily excited, but left her abruptly to stand across the room from Dr Ifitz, smiling and waving at him, at the same time muttering filthy curses. At last he heard the thunder of an engine and they arrived in a rush, creating a small stir by the door. For the next ten minutes he heard her moving from person to person in the party, telling them.

"Chased by the cops ... Ninety ... I certainly need one of those. Going right out to get me a sugar Daddy to buy me one ..."

In a dark corridor between rooms they passed.

"I lost you, honey. I thought you'd gone."

"You did?"

"Honey, you didn't mind me going for a ride with that pea-brain?"

"Me? Mind?"

She came close and took his hand in both of hers. "Honey, we're going right home and you're going to beat me up."

Morrison raised his eyebrows. "Just as you like ..."

"I mean it," she said seriously. "Don't you want to?" she said, turning her head away coyly.

"How about the footballer?"

"I'll fix him. Give me two minutes and I'll *sure fix him,*" she said through closed teeth.

Down the passage to her apartment she began to run and Morrison pursued. She was through the door a second before he could catch her, and when he reached her room lay panting on her bed. At once he pulled her to her feet and began to drag her clothes off.

228

"Give over, these things have fasteners," she said, holding in her stomach and fumbling. She was too late and her skirt came free with a sharp rip.

He threw her on to the bed and beat her across the stomach with his belt and across her arms when she put them there to protect herself. She moaned and he beat her across the breasts. She shouted to him to stop and stood up to fight him, tears of anger in her eyes, and he threw her down and held both wrists above her head and struck at her buttocks with his other hand as she squirmed. Using the flat of his hand he caught her several stinging blows across the face, which made her scream, "Stop it," and struggle to fight him again, then start to moan and blubber. He hit her with genuine disturbing anger. Still more disturbing, a moment came when he was horrified by what he was doing.

He made violent love to her. Sadistically aroused, he thought, he despoiled her. But behind this cheery assessment persisted the appalling memory of a moment when he'd pitied her.

"Enough?" he asked.

"Oh God, I love you," she said, clinging to him, pressing her tear messed face against his chest, giving a sudden shoulder-to-heels shudder. She moved her head away to stare at him. "Oh my god, do I love you."

Morrison fetched himself a whisky sour – beating a sharp tattoo on Sally's door as he passed – and sat across the bed, sipping and offering her sips.

"Some hours ago, Miss Hopping, you were in real trouble . . ."

"Oh yeah," she said distantly. "Yeah, yeah," she said with returning enthusiasm, sitting up on the bed, staring bright-eyed at him. "Honey, I gotta sorta confession . . ."

Who is this person? Peterson thought. Where does he come from and how do I know about him? Why do I make him behave as he does and never suffer? His phone rang.

It was late on Sunday, a freezing winter night outside, the snow hard and shining under a high moon. He lifted it quickly to stop his family answering downstairs, but didn't at once put it to his ear. Faintly he could hear a voice down there. "Who's that?" it said several times, tiny and far away.

"Peterson speaking."

229

"Darling, it's me, Jill." His heart pounded. "Darling, it needs rescuing."

"What does?"

"*It* does. The bush baby." His chest heaved. His heart flooded with happiness. Even if it was bad, he would soon know. He thought it might be good.

"Where are you?"

"State City. Darling, I'll explain, but could you come quick and save it. Just for a start it hasn't any money."

"How shall I find you?"

"The Sheraton, darling. On Main. Darling, I'll book it in your name, shall I? I'll say Mrs Peterson's arrived early."

Peterson drove west through the bright frozen night. The moon shone across mile after mile of snowy prairie, and rode ahead of him down mile after mile of icy road. He wouldn't let himself guess. She'd called for him, that was enough.

Sometimes he wondered what dull-spirited people could have settled here – flat-faced northern farmers, who only cared about the astonishing crops this black soil would grow. Too phleg-matic even to be astonished – like their cows, noticing only this vegetable luxury they'd stumbled waist deep into as the removal of some obscure irritation. Hard to think of them as adventurers. Hard to believe that 150 years ago the six foot grass on this vast prairie had really hidden Indians, law a far away untrusted theory, their guns and six-day labour the only protection for their families. The country they'd tamed had been unkind to them. Too easy now to wonder how they could have born to settle out of sight or thought of any rise in the ground greater than ten feet, surely making plain even to them the terrifying simplicity of their lives : birth, corn, death.

Sometimes he remembered how he'd told Nancy that a visiting publisher needed to see him early next morning before flying to New York, about a possible movie-sale. For half an hour he'd stood about the house, acting uncertainty, irritation, hope, using his slight but real reluctance to go out into thirty degrees of frost to give his performance a genuineness he'd had to admire. It had been a more perfect excuse than he'd expected because Nancy had been afraid he *wouldn't* go, had urged, persuaded, sulked, while he'd acted reluctant, her feelings for him balanced between a new respect, even love, that he might really be going to make money, and the familiar contempt

230

because he was going to let the chance slip. At last he'd gone, with a nicely judged show of ill-temper at the way she'd forced him.

He made one ten mile detour to cross a state line to stop at a twenty-four-hour package-liquor store and buy champagne.

She sat on the edge of a big green-satin-covered double bed, looking small and alone. She smiled at him but didn't stand. She suggested a naughty child who isn't yet sure whether its punishment has finished, reminding him that he must first ask her what had happened on Friday.

"Darling, you've come."

"Right," he said, smiling cautiously.

"I didn't think you would."

"Why's that?"

She was oddly quiet, as if she'd recently used up so much emotion that she hadn't any left.

"Don't know," she said, puzzled. "Just didn't expect it."

He sat beside her. Presently he began to touch her up encouragingly.

"Darling, not yet," she said. "Soon but not yet."

He was glad to be reminded that Friday still had to be explained. "What happened?"

"Darling, I was kidnapped. True. By the forester. I think he went a bit mad."

"That was why you didn't call?"

"Right," she said. "That was why I didn't call."

"Did he just drive you away?"

"Well first he attacked me." She grew more excited. "Christ, I didn't know what was happening. I really thought he might murder me. Hey, look at this," and she pulled up her skirt to show a four-inch purple and black bruise on the inside of her thigh. "And this." She yanked at her jumper to show another on her shoulder.

"He did those?"

"Must have. I found them later. All the time he keeps swearing at me and calling me a whore. You know that old wedding ring of mine. First thing, he drags it off and flushes it down the john. Look, gone." She held up her hand. "Darling, I'm afraid I'll need another. Well, it *is* a bit embarrassing. Darling, it's sorry, it really is."

"Nothing to be sorry about," he said. "You couldn't fight a two-hundred-pound All-American forester."

"Right, I couldn't, could I?" she said.

"What happened then?"

"He drove me away," she said. "God knows where. Hundreds of miles. To some awful motel – well two actually. Then it got all confused. It didn't know what it wanted. It's really truly sorry."

He hugged and kissed her.

"Hell, you try being kidnapped," she said. "It does give a girl a thrill."

"How did you get here?"

"Oh, it came to its senses and escaped. That's all over now."

"The forester?"

"Yes, darling. We shan't be seeing each other any more. He knows the lot. Darling I had to tell him. He made me."

He forced her back on to the bed and they lay kissing and clinging to each other.

He sat up. "Nice room you've fixed for us."

"It's a pleasure, darling."

"Did you call me from here?" He grew curious. "Did you fix it before or after you called me?"

"After, of course," she said. He believed her.

"Well no, before actually," she said, grinning cautiously at him. He loved her for telling him.

They made love. "Hey, we're cool. I'd almost forgotten."

They drank champagne, "You're sweet, you really are," and lay naked, wriggling their toes, and went out to dinner at an Italian restaurant Raphaelo used to take her to, and came back to the hotel and made love. "Hey, we're real groovy."

Next day they called room service for coffee and croissants and presently he went out and bought champagne and pistachio nuts, and they lay nibbling and sipping till around ten-thirty when they made love. Later they went out to a bar she and Raphaelo had sometimes used and presently he called home and said that the movie discussions had grown complicated and he'd have to stay another night.

That evening they drank dry martinis in a revolving thirtieth-storey bar, so dimly lit that on the way to their table he caught his foot in another drinker's stool, half tumbling him out, and still couldn't see if he was young or old, or even be sure he

232

wasn't some cigar-smoking dyke. They sat, giggling and holding hands across the table, looking out over the icy moonlit city.

"You know something?" she said, "You're the only person I can be myself with."

The martinis were almost pure gin and they became quickly drunk. "You know what, you're the first person I haven't felt lonely with. I usually am, even with other people. That's Jill's secret. Don't tell anyone. It's the only thing that really bugs me!"

They went to an Italian night club she knew about and watched Greek belly-dancing compèred by a New York Jew.

"You're special," she said. "There aren't many special people."

"Style's what matters," she said. "It's not what you do but how you do it. As if you didn't give a shit."

It described her perfectly, he thought. Drunkenly, he thought it the most perfect truth he'd heard. Drunkenly, he knew that it was the only way to live, the way he too could live.

Packing next morning, he watched her stuffing one large and both small hotel towels into her case. "Just what I needed. My mother'll have a fit when she sees the hotel name on these."

"For something special?"

"Hell no," she said, and went on packing. "A mistress gotta collect her trousseau somehow."

In the days which followed they drove together about town or walked together across campus with less caution. Sometimes Peterson believed he was learning to live with style. At others he realised that it was because the forester had gone.

"He's in a forest, darling, meditating. Raphaelo told me. Poor forester. He was a nice guy really. What did he wanta get mixed up with a girl like me for?"

"Surely it was you who got mixed up with him."

"Say, you're right. I forgot."

In the evenings he tried to make his excuses to Nancy with more careless boldness, and sometimes believed he was learning not to give a shit. At others, as he watched her listening with hard indifference, he found himself reduced to a dumb horror, every word he'd been planning to say gone from his mind. If he didn't rush it, he told himself, he was sure he would learn soon.

One night – when he was supposed to be at a concert of percussion with lights – he lay on Jill's mattress bed, on the

233

floor of her orange fish-tank room, a little sorry to have missed this interesting performance.

"We could still catch the second half," he said. "Concerto for triangle with seven conductors," making it a joke but giving her the chance to agree.

"You're putting me on," she said, turning different views of a new shirt to the mirror. "Like it?"

Presently, because the problem had been discussed that day in class and interested him, he said, "So did he ever get over his oedipus complex?"

"Who?"

"Lawrence."

"SHIT," she said, loudly and explosively.

At once he was ready to laugh at his question – or, now that she'd come into the open and told him how all book talk bored her, to defend himself.

"Well I do find it interesting," he began.

But she seemed to have forgotten him, stood quite still, looking at the carpet, then cautiously feeling with both hands round the buttocks of her jeans. "Thought so. That's my last pair."

"Have they split?"

"Have they *split*!"

"Let's see."

"Hands off," and she went out, still hiding the crack. Had they really split or had she invented it to cover her accidental honesty?

Daily, at least, they made love. The score on the wall grew, making a sensational leap when she added the seven – or was it eight? – from State City. M.P., forty-eight. OTHERS, a half. She added nothing to this line for her two motel nights with the forester, and he avoided asking her whether she should.

The happy excitement it gave them was as great. But there were changes. Sometimes it seemed to him that they turned to it slightly desperately, from a period of silence and abstraction. At these moments he felt that they were trying to stay at some high point of happiness which was necessarily in the past.

One day, though he laboured and laboured, he failed to come. He was worried by this till, lying still and deflated beside her, he realised that she *had* come and might not know that he'd failed. When she didn't mention it he became increasingly confident. After this, he failed about every third time but oddly it

234

didn't make him unhappy. Now, he told himself, he knew from real experience that the giving of love was more important than the indulgence.

Another day he failed to enter her. Amazing. He pushed and shoved but couldn't get in.

"Don't worry, darling, it's not your fault."

He rolled off her. "Why's that?"

"I had a douche. It's always like that for twenty-four hours after. Destroys the natural lubrication or something."

"Why didn't you tell me?"

"We're so good, darling, I couldn't believe it."

Crossing campus on foot to see her one bright icy afternoon, the air so cold that it hurt his lungs, he was astonished to hear bagpipe music. As soon as he came on to the quad he saw the piper, tall and thin, going with long strides up and down the concrete sidewalk. He stopped to watch. What could it mean?

The music moved him in a way nothing had since that folk-singing woman in his park. Again it seemed a noise from a world he'd forgotten. He heard it coming distantly over cloud-hidden moors. He heard it among the bursting shells and mud of the First World War trenches. He heard it at a statesman's funeral: the massed regimental bands, creating something greater than themselves, a sense of man's insistent but pointless courage, a noise of heroism. As in the park, he was astonished that no one else seemed to hear. Why weren't they drawn irresistibly to it by a power they couldn't control? Instead, the few he could see – it was the middle of a class hour – passed distantly without even turning their heads.

The piper wore kilt, white shirt and short plaid jacket, but no coat or cloak, and this increased the sense that he was some illusion. How could he wear so little in this temperature? He crossed twice in each direction, then went out of sight between the Schmitt Chemical Building and the James Wilberforce Potter Hall of Dramatic Arts.

Jill was gay and excited. "Guess what, the tadpole's stormed the Persian citadel."

"Your roommate?"

"Right. At three-thirteen this morning. I can tell you to the minute. God what a lead up. You'd think the world was coming to an end. One thing, I shan't take any more wall-bashing from her. Hey, lover, why the gloom?"

235

"It certainly isn't gloom." He told her about the piper.

"Christ, those things make me sick to my stomach."

"All right," he said, "but suppose for a moment they didn't," and he explained to her what the piper made him feel.

"Yeah, yeah, I reckon I get it," she said, absentmindedly unbuttoning her blouse, edging out a soft tan shoulder and rubbing it thoughtfully.

He watched for a moment, then kissed her.

"Sorry, lover. All that carry on last night – I haven't been able to concentrate all day."

Her phone rang, they rolled apart, and she reached out a long bare arm for it while he lay with his head on her other bare shoulder.

"Sure, Jeff," she said.

"Well not right now, Jeff," she said. "Tell you what, I'll leave it at Oak Street then you can pick it up. Bye.

"Oh dear, that makes me feel kinda bad," she said.

"Who was it?"

"The forester, come back to collect his phonograph. Says he's missing it up there." For several minutes she lay still, looking up at the ceiling. "He sounded sad."

"I don't blame him."

"All those trees."

"The ones he's living in."

"The ones he'll chop down instead of me. Thousands and thousands. That's what I've done. All by myself I've demolished several forests." She lit a cigarette.

"Hell, it's a nice phonograph, too." She puffed smoke at him. "Hell, he shouldn't have come and asked for it, even if he is all washed up."

Peterson waited for her to explain.

"He sure shouldn't," she said, stubbing out the cigarette, rolling over to bite him sharply on the shoulder.

Presently when they made love he noticed that she put her hands one under each buttock, forcing them up in an even more violent rhythm than before.

"Oh yes, oh yes, oh baby, oh yes," she cried out. "Oh I love *you*." They lay still.

"Hey, you remember I owed Raphaelo fifty bucks," she said.

"Ah ha."

"He's let me off half. Isn't that just like the sod. Can't

236

make a decent gesture and let me off the lot, but has to let me off half because he needs someone to play with."

Christmas came and he told her there were three days when he couldn't see her: Christmas day and the next two, when he had to go to parties. It didn't matter, she said. She'd be going home to her parents. But she wasn't spending the whole vacation there. No sir. She'd be back just when he told her. She'd have them drive her back.

Separated from her, he missed her but not so painfully as he'd expected. As the days passed his need to see her again increased pleasantly and by the third he had moments of fairly desperate longing. This longing seemed to centre upon their soft bellies rubbing together, and for this he sighed – cautiously.

But his quiet three days with his family worried him. He ate good food, read a little, slept eight hours a night, and, when he found nothing else to do, worked on his final lectures. On Christmas day he got quietly drunk and at the parties on the next two evenings, rather drunker. How appallingly boring she would find it. He scarcely said one thing which interested him. He certainly didn't do one thing which excited him. He could see just how boring his life *was* and yet he'd spent fifteen years leading it and finding it bearable. He was worried that he might again find it bearable.

He didn't sleep with Nancy. Six weeks, now, he realised one night, seeing her lying propped and padded in bed, the soft light on her chain-mail hair style giving him a moment's desire for her. Was it really possible that she hadn't noticed?

"Hi," Jill said.

"Hallo," he said, laughing with happiness to be with her again.

But three days had left her in a different mood, which he couldn't at once define.

"Nice Christmas turkey?" he asked.

"Oh that," she said. "I didn't go."

"What did you do, then?"

"Hung around here."

He was astonished. All these three days when he'd been imagining her a hundred and fifty miles away she'd been on campus.

"Was it fun?"

237

"No."

They kissed. She shivered and came closer to him and they kissed and hugged each other with more enthusiasm. He felt happier, but also more anxious.

"You should have gone."

"Darling, I was a bit desperate," she said, "and that's your fault." She gave him several small punches on the chest.

"What *did* you do?"

"You really want to know?" She thought for a moment. "Well Christmas Day I decided to read both your books again. But that just made it worse. It wasn't your goddam books I wanted. So I went to this party."

"How was that?"

"Different pad, same people," she said. "All these guys trying to make all these chicks. I felt a bit left out."

"And next day?"

"I had a hangover. Not much. You wait. Just enough to stay in bed till four in the afternoon. Then I get up and decide I'm damn well not going to any party tonight and I'll read your books. Darling, I'm sorry. They're nice books but I just couldn't make it. So I go hunting for Raphaelo to offer him some more of my money I haven't got, but he's out, so I get a bottle of brandy and come home and start drinking. Just a small glass at first, then another. And presently, you know what? I start cursing you. Out loud. Truly. Calling you the filthiest things I can think of. After that I start to swill it down and go out into the street and walk up and down really cursing you to hell for coming and making me fall in love with you."

"Darling, I'm sorry," he said smugly.

"So you should be." She kissed him quickly. "Christ, I don't remember it all. The bottle got broken. There was a policeman – he was nice. You know what, he was so nice, right out in the middle of that icy block, I start telling him the whole goddam story."

Peterson suppressed sharp alarm.

"So he takes me home, but about four am I'm back knocking at Raphaelo's door, and he's real kind too and gives me coffee and doesn't even take a buck off me – hasn't time, as a matter of fact, seeing he's got some Polish princess bedded down waiting for him. Then he calls a cab and sends me home and the next I remember I'm back here in bed, waking up with the sheet

238

all covered in vomit and the worst goddam hangover I ever had in my whole life. And that's the day my parents are driving down to visit me."

On that day, Peterson thought – but he couldn't even remember what he'd done that day.

"So I stagger around, trying to clean up the mess. But half way I have to go back to bed. Oh god, am I ill. I'm off that stuff, I really am. And then they're hammering at the door, half an hour *early*, so I scream, 'Coming,' and run six times up and down the passage emptying a spray of air freshener, and lock myself in the bathroom and get the roommate to let them in.

"When I come out, my mother's sniffing about the apartment, trying to work out what it is – she's got a real nose for anything that isn't washing-powder bright, only she's half suffocated by all that air freshener – and my father's curled up in a chair reading *your* book – or rather, reading that nice inscription you wrote."

Peterson controlled a jerk of fear.

" 'Who's this?' he says.

" 'Oh, just a teacher of mine,' I say.

" 'Seems a nice kinda guy,' he says, turning to the picture.

" 'Oh, he's all right,' I say, casual like.

" 'What's that?' my mother says, pointing straight at the score on the wall where I've forgotten to pile up the pillows. That really gives me a turn. I tell them I'm checking off books I have to read for my courses. Top line: Marine Psychology. Bottom line: Others.

" 'There's no such subject,' my mother says.

" 'You're kidding,' I tell her. 'You think fish don't get psyches, just like everyone else?'

" 'It certainly looks like a pretty interesting kinda course,' my father says.

" 'It sure is,' I say. Wasn't that smart of me, darling?'"

"It was," Peterson said, avoiding saying that it would have been smarter to remember the pillows.

"And then they give me this giant hotel Christmas dinner: turkey, English plum pudding, the lot. And I have to look like I'm enjoying it and not like I want to vomit every goddam mouthful all over the plate."

She stopped and they sat quietly side by side on her settee.

Sometimes he looked at her, but she looked at the floor, as if still remembering that Christmas dinner too clearly.

"Darling," she said, looking at him. "It's getting a bit desperate."

He moved his hands to grip her soft arms above the elbow and pull her to him. She let him do it but stayed limp. Undoing some buttons, he lifted her shirt over her head. She sat slumped, shoulders rounded, her delicious podgy, upper half bare except her fine breasts held in by a strong white bra.

"Darling, what are we going to do?"

"Shall I tell you?" he said, attempting a lecherous chuckle. It wasn't a success.

But to his surprise she let him. "Come on, quick, quick," she said, dropping off her skirt and bra, getting under the sheet, lying curled away from him, head snuggled on to the pillow. "You always did have good ideas."

Three days had sharpened his need, but also, he now realised, created doubt. Could it possibly have been so good? Could he ever again dispense pleasure with such male assurance? He could.

"Oh Jesus," she shouted, so loudly that he hesitated a second, thinking he'd really injured her. "Oh yes, oh yes, oh baby, oh baby," she cried, as he worked faster to correct his error. "Oh yes, oh Jesus Christ." He gasped and sweated and came with the greatest pleasure and relief.

She clung to him. "Darling, don't ever leave me. Darling, that's an order."

Presently she padded naked down the passage for a Coke.

"You see, darling, it gets worse."

He sat up, serious and concerned, though slightly hurt that, despite the fine way he'd made love to her, her mood was now back where it had been before.

"I don't need you less but more."

He listened, flattered, but anxious.

"Still love me?" she said.

"I certainly do," he said, shaking his head at the wonder of it.

"Not as much as I love you," she said.

"You think that!" he said. How wrong you are, he implied. At the same time he had the strange feeling that it was an admission she would have liked him to make. And did he love her quite as obsessively as he had a few weeks ago? — it wasn't important. He only had to think of his life without her to know

240

how much he loved her. The idea made his chest tense and his stomach lurch downwards – and gave him a second of sharp pain in his anus. Very strange. But it certainly proved how truly and desperately he still loved her.

"Darling, what shall we do?"

He shook his head. He had no answer, and a desire to avoid the question.

"You see darling, you've got other things : your home and your family. And I've only got you."

At once he understood – was astonished that he'd failed to understand before. Till now he'd accepted their unspoken agreement that their affair was for pleasure, without commitment. Now he saw what a far harder condition this had been for her than for him. Because she loved him she'd been pretending to him that it wasn't – pretending to herself, too, no doubt.

"I'll think of something."

"Oh you're sweet," she said, kissing him gently.

Words like divorce he still kept out of his mind, but they floated in its vicinity. Soon he might think them. Already he thought them, and at the same moment felt a new need for her. Even before she was asking for it, he made love to her again, with desperate, self-annihilating desire. How shockingly wrong of him, he thought, close to climax, to use her in this thoughtless way. But shortly afterwards he was depressed by many problems : family, children, money, house, job.

For two days they didn't meet. Under grey skies he walked about the frozen campus, across white drifted lawns, down sidewalks where gusts of icy wind whirled snow ahead of him, as light and dry as dust, worried and thoughtful. How happy he was to love her, he thought, avoiding any connection between this and the unhappy worry she was now causing him.

The weather grew colder. On average, the *Flatville Messenger* told him, the 25th, 26th and 27th January were the coldest days and he carried about with him this idea of the year descending into still more deathlike winter.

Glancing back on the first morning as he was about to cross a street, he saw Ric Schuster, thirty yards behind him. He waited, then became unsure whether this figure – in overcoat and woollen hat, with scarf wrapped round its mouth and nose – was Ric Schuster. To his surprise he saw that it had also stopped, though what it was doing there, resting one gloved

241

hand on a parking meter, the other on its hip as it stared forward but came no nearer, he had no idea. He turned away and crossed.

Three blocks later, glancing back, he saw the same figure standing watching him. It was in the same attitude, one hand on a meter, one on its hip, but seemed further away. He was still less sure that it was Ric Schuster. He found his car and drove quickly home to lunch.

At five that afternoon, in a back street of stores to the west of campus, he saw it again – now much closer. This time it stood in a different and worryingly familiar attitude, arms folded across its chest, but because of the gloomy winter dusk which had been gathering quickly, and seemed even as he looked to move in more intensely like a surge of fog, he still couldn't be sure who it was.

As he stared at this silent watching figure he became certain that its face was twisted in a laughing sneer. Now it seemed astonishingly close to him, but the dusk had become so deep that he couldn't distinguish any feature. There was something terrifying about this silent figure watching him. The more he stared at it, the more uncertain he became of its size. Now it seemed a normal six-foot person, now eight or even nine feet. In a weird and breathing way it seemed to shrink then grow as he stared at it, each time getting slightly larger. He struggled to turn away, but couldn't. At the same time all the other people passing on the sidewalk seemed to become low and far away. leaving him alone in a conflict he didn't understand with this giant figure. At last, with a heavy shudder and an effort of will which made sweat break out in his hair, he turned away. The dusk seemed lighter as he dodged and pushed along the crowded sidewalk.

Eleven next morning, a fine frosty day, the sun bright in a clear blue sky, everywhere the dazzling white of ice and snow, he saw him again. Nothing odd about his size today. If anything he seemed small and inconspicuous among the hurrying students on the sidewalk. Today there was no doubt that it was Ric Schuster. That head lowered as if to butt a world he despised but needed. Peterson turned and strode back towards him.

"Hallo, Ric."

By the time he reached him he was staring into the display

242

window of a camera store. He turned and glared but didn't speak.

"Did you want me?"

"Can't a guy look in a store window without some goddam professor sneaking up and propositioning him?"

"Now look . . ." Peterson began.

Ric Schuster gave several sharp barks of laughter to show that it had been a joke, and glared again, leaving Peterson in further doubt about whether or not it had been.

"Why don't I drop in and see you some day," Ric Schuster said, surprising Peterson, who had been on the point of making exactly this friendly suggestion.

"You know perfectly well you're always welcome . . ."

"Aye know perfectly well, do aye," Ric Schuster said, in parody English. He glared again. "So why should I come and tell you I'm in trouble if you don't believe a goddam word of it?"

"I do my best . . ."

Ric Schuster laughed a lot, with something close to genuine amusement at the way he'd provoked Peterson into this untypical rudeness.

"What would you think?" he said in an angry jeer, "if I came and told you I was going to end it all?"

"End . . . ?"

"This whole shitting fuck-up."

"Just the fact that you came and told me . . ." Peterson began, evasively but sincerely.

"Proves I'm a nut," Ric Schuster shouted triumphantly. "Doesn't it, eh? Professor Peterson."

"I didn't say that."

"You mean it."

This was so nearly true it left him without an answer. Also he was alarmed to find Ric Schuster moving closer to him, instinctively took a step away from this stubbly, shifty-eyed face.

Ric stopped. "Come here. I've something to say to you."

He moved cautiously closer.

"You wanta take a trip?"

"A trip?"

"That's right, shout it all around. Hey, guys," he said, turning left and right to passing students, beginning to shout himself. "This guy has something to say to you all."

More angry now than he could bear, Peterson turned away.

243

He'd only gone a few yards when Ric Schuster was beside him, gripping his elbow with both hands.

"You like to?"

"I certainly might be interested," Peterson began, still walking. He'd planned to add: at any other time, if I hadn't so many worrying problems, but was distracted by the way Ric now dragged him to a complete stop, even turned him half round.

"You would?" He seemed totally sincere. His eyes met Peterson's, making him realise that till now he'd been glaring at his chest. "Hey!" he said, with real admiration for Peterson's incautious acceptance.

"You see," Peterson began to explain, but stopped, impossible now to withdraw – as he must later.

"I'll fix it. You leave it to me. Bring Nancy. Sure. I'll bring Judy."

As he drove home, the whole incident grew more disturbing. Was it a real invitation or another test of his trust? Was it real admiration, Ric had shown when he'd agreed to come, or joke admiration, to show up his pathetic need for it? Was the biggest joke that he needed this admiration so badly that he was going to let it trap him into this trip? Did Ric plan to have the trip raided? There were times when he believed Ric hated him enough for this, even if it damaged himself too. Or was the joke the contrast between his keen interest in this frivolous trip and his boredom with Ric Schuster's real-life problem? two minutes ago this so-called friend was frowning with mock concern at the prospect of my suicide. Now look how quickly he forgets such a bothersome detail. Peterson ate family supper abstractedly, and went out soon after to walk the three blocks to Hickory Street.

"We sure are grateful for the interest you're taking in our son," Mrs Schuster said.

"We know he's a difficult boy," Mrs Schuster said, "but we sure believe his heart's in the right place."

But their eyes were on the television set where a war was being fought in a jungle.

"Why don't you switch this goddam thing off, Henry?" Mrs Schuster said, watching it.

Watching it, Mr Schuster said, "Yeah, why don't we do just that – unless Doctor Peterson's kinda innerested."

244

"Not at all," Peterson said – but a bomber screamed, anti-aircraft shells slammed, "Oh my, just look at that," Mrs Schuster said.

When it was clear that his answer had been lost, Peterson said, "There's nothing special been troubling him lately?"

"Who?" Mr Schuster said.

"Why, Ric, of course," Mrs Schuster said. "Who d'yer think he's talking about?"

"Oh Ric," Mr Schuster said, and they were quiet as an American sergeant, notepad in hand, checked a ditch of enemy bodies.

"Now isn't that just the most disgusting thing you ever saw?" Mrs Schuster said.

"The problem," Peterson said, "is to know if what he tells you is the truth or a fantasy. When I first met him he told me that a law case was being brought against him for statutory rape."

"He told you that!" Mrs Schuster said.

"Well, whad'yer know!" Mr Schuster said.

In quick succession cartoon animals, long-haired actresses with little girl faces, immaculate housewives in ideal kitchens, appeared in states of euphoric wonder at the products they were advertising. Nursery rhyme tunes followed each other with scarcely a gap and a huskier than husky languid voice said, "You'll just love, love, love, this soft warm, soft warm, soft warm . . ."

"Why don't we kill this?" Mr Schuster said.

"Hold it, Henry," Mrs Schuster said, "I'm just crazy about that Standard Oil man."

"Is it true?" Peterson said.

Now they both turned from the screen to stare at him as if they'd forgotten what he'd been talking about.

"Doctor Peterson, you got to look at it from our point of view," Mrs Schuster said. "Just what would you do if your son stole your new automobile, right the second day after you had acquired it?"

"Did he do that?"

They didn't answer.

"What did you do?"

"You tell us what you'd do," Mrs Schuster said.

"It hasn't happened to me."

245

"You're in luck, boy," Mr Schuster said.

War returned. A six-man patrol crept through a swamp. Tension built. A parrot screeched weirdly, the section leader gestured his men on to their faces in the squelchy undergrowth, overprofessionally, as if he'd learned it from a lifetime of jungle-war movies.

"There are times when I feel helpless," Peterson said.

"We sure are grateful," Mrs Schuster began, and stopped, as if she'd recognised the stuck-record quality of this repetition. "For christsake, Henry, can't we turn that lousy thing off," she said.

But now he was listening intently to a political commentator. "Back in this war-torn capital, inevitably there are those who see today's developments as one more step in the ever-growing escalation . . ."

Suddenly it seemed to Peterson that, far from disagreeing about the television, they were in the most refined agreement that it mustn't be turned off, because there was something about their son Ric which it must help them not to tell. For a second he believed this was something sinister, as if they would suddenly show him that he wasn't dealing with a real human being but with one who was part ape, or had only half a head. A moment later he knew that this was only their own narrow attitude to any abnormality. Somehow he must force them to tell him what they didn't dare tell him, to prove that they shouldn't be horrified.

"Ever since I've known your son I've felt handicapped," he began. "No one will tell the truth about him." But he couldn't go on. They were both watching him again, in appeal, almost in terror, it seemed. Accidentally he'd suggested that *he* was going to explain to *them*, not what was wrong with Ric, but what they'd done to deserve such a son. The idea that he'd ever thought them dangerous or vicious was laughable. Instead, it was they who were lost children. Her big round moon face, his little rabbit-toothed moustached face, stared at him with the same anxious message. Help us, they said, to admit how little we understand, to give up the intolerable responsibility of pretending to be adults, which we never asked for.

"Back to Washington for the latest news flash from our Middle East Affairs commentator. In just sixty seconds: 'Plague Strikes Refugee Camp.' But first: Get this new, tan-

246

today, pay-tomorrow, sun-vacation package deal . . ."

"I have to go," Peterson said.

They stood, now hopelessly confused.

"We sure do appreciate . . ."

"It certainly has been good of you . . ."

He hurried out into the night, appalled by their need and his own uselessness.

His home was silent but he knew his family were in. He had the sense of them each in their own rooms, busy with their own affairs. They were like isolated parts of some complex machine. Now they buzzed quietly but at any moment one might begin to chatter and flash. Quiet and isolated as they were, he believed that they all knew he was home again, had heard the door slam and were listening to his hesitation in the downstairs hall. The idea that they would soon be all around him, terrifying him by what they knew about him – and by what he could understand about them – was unbearable. Silently, a step at a time, arms spread for balance, he began to climb the stairs.

He was half way up, lifting his feet with elaborate care, when he knew that above his head one of them was already on the landing, watching his astonishing ascent. Perhaps they were all there, in a row, staring down at him with giggles which had congealed to horror. He didn't dare turn. Twice more he lifted a foot, now shivering continuously, to place it noiselessly – then with a stumbling rush and thunderous bumping which echoed through the whole house, he reached his study, slammed the door and stood, weight on one foot, drawing in his breath with a hiss of agony against the pain of the other where he'd bruised his shin. When he could listen again the house was totally silent. Perhaps they hadn't been watching. Gradually he grew aware of them, each isolated in their own rooms, heads raised, not buzzing for a moment as they wondered what that astonishing noise had been.

Hurriedly he pulled the manuscript from his shelf and began to read.

Tonight Karl tried to make love to me – oh, it was more frightful than I can ever describe. What was so frightful, apart from his cold reptilian approaches, was that I wanted him – wanted him desperately. And then I didn't let him. Oh god . . .

247

I seemed driven by something outside myself. "You don't want me," I screamed at him. "It's just medicine. It's part of the cure. All you want is for me to stop bothering you so I won't disturb your work."

Even after I'd seen how this made him curl up with hate for me, he went on trying. He still gripped my wrist. I tried to break away. Karl is determined, that's one quality I've never denied him. He'd decided to make love to me – what an ironic phrase – and he wouldn't easily be diverted. Even though I knew that my words had produced a deep shudder of revulsion at this bony object, this ugly thing of tendon and grey skin, which he was still amorously gripping, he held on.

I don't know how it would have ended. For ten, fifteen seconds, a long long time, we stayed like that, Karl gripping me, as if desperate to make love, me straining away and sensing through those cold fingers the disgust he felt for me. It wasn't till I started to tell him I knew what he was feeling that he finally let go.

He let go because it was true. Karl respects truth. He is probably the most honest person I've ever known. Was I right to try to match his honesty? Or was I driven mad by his terrible, literal mind which listens only to my words and not to my whole soul which cries out, love me?

I'm calmer. Perhaps it's the calmness of desperation. Perhaps it's because the plan I've written of before, the hope for our future together, seems to have come closer. Did I manufacture this whole horrible scene to bring it closer? Did I need to prove, in the flesh – sinister, ironic *double entendre* – that Karl has never truly desired me physically? That in yet another sense we're in the same boat.

That terrible scene tonight has encouraged me to believe that there must be – is – a way to save our life together.

Tonight all is quiet. For many years the last two nights will be remembered: the nights of the Great Water Riots. How brutish. How typical of our centre of culture and learning.

No one knows how it began. A fraternity pantie raid probably. Nothing sensational the first night. A hydrant used to shatter all the first-floor windows of a sorority house. Several foolish arrests, two police cars overturned, half a dozen policemen drenched – how frightful that they should stand for our

248

country, a disgusting growth, as horrifying to ourselves as to all who see us, grotesque, grinning, gun-carrying, imbecile, like vicious overgrown children . . .

Somehow it seemed to catch the imagination. Perhaps the terrible hot days we've been having produced a kind of madness. Days when you long for evening, and when evening comes the temperature drops one degree, from ninety-five to ninety-four. Nights when there isn't a chance to sleep but only of wild and fearful dreams from which you wake soaked in perspiration, more tired than before.

Already the streets were full when I came back from campus. For several blocks I had to push my way through thick crowds. What was happening, I asked, but no one knew. I see now that nothing was happening. They'd gathered to *make* it happen.

We'd finished supper before we began to hear anything. Suddenly, out there in the dusk, there was a great roar. Horrifying, because it was unplaceable. Mid-afternoon on a winter Saturday, I'd have known it was a football crowd : sixty thousand blockheads, indulging themselves in sport hysteria. At first the idea of sixty thousand people roaring out there in the dark didn't occur to me. When it did I was still more horrified.

I peered out through our windows, but could see nothing. Maddeningly, Karl nibbled crackers and sipped coffee, dabbed at his thin lips with a paper napkin – how that gesture makes me see him at seventy-five, his hands all blue veins, his thin lips bloodless. I stood on our front doorstep.

Here it was more terrifying. A great surge of brutish sound, rising up over the house roofs, ending in isolated screams – Then I was walking. I remember no conscious decision. I only know that I was filled with exasperation by my husband's icy coffee-sipping calm and had to escape. I'd gone a block before I knew that I was also going to Bobby. Because Bobby was out there in that roaring, idiot crowd. Because he was in danger.

It seems absurd now, but at that moment I was convinced. His danger wasn't just a faint possibility with the odds a thousand to one against; an extra logical step, as valid as any daytime academic logic, made the connection between this frightful roaring and Bobby seem not just conceivable but certain. They were roaring because they had him out there, mocking him. He was their victim. Because he embodies all that is good in our university and country and they stand for all that is bad, they

249

couldn't have failed to discover him. He couldn't have failed to offer himself.

I could see them, tossing him among them, striking him, roaring with bestial laughter at the way he was putting up his hands to save his face, ducking his head against their blows, but never striking back . . .

I was hurrying forward along the sidewalk, not even in sight of the crowds, though their roaring now seemed only a block away on all sides and the police sirens were howling continuously, when a car slowed beside me, the passenger window was rolled down and a great flabby something struck me on the knee.

I'd stepped forward as the car slowed, thinking they needed directing. I stopped, astonished, not understanding what had happened. It had been so unexpected that at first I didn't even connect the car and that strange soft blow on the knee. But a second later I realised that the indistinct movement I'd seen inside had been someone reaching forward from the back seat to throw it out through the front window. The window was going up and the car accelerating away before I realised that my knees and legs were soaking.

My shoes too. When I moved they squelched. It had been a balloon full of liquid. How disgusting and horrible and pointless. Tears came into my eyes at the thought of my spoiled stockings and shoes. What had I done to them that they should do this to me? How could I go to find Bobby in such a mess? I was soaked to the skin. I caught a faint odour. The balloon had been full of urine.

I cried aloud then. I stood in that dark street, sobbing and crying, unable to move, my feet soaked with this revolting infected fluid.

At the same moment, 200 yards ahead at the street end, I saw them for the first time. They seemed to move in a surging howling scamper, as if all off balance, and a great hissing sheet of water followed them. Then they surged screaming back into it and were gone in the direction they'd come from. And all the time I stood there, sobbing and alone. The few people who passed paid me no attention. I even saw one of them cross over to pass on the other side.

I forced myself to turn for home. As soon as I moved, the sickening liquid in my shoes must have started to warm up and

250

grow volatile because its hideous odour rose all round me. It
choked me. I cried out and stumbled and fell onto my hands
and knees and vomited. Kneeling and retching, all I wanted
was that they should drive past again to see what they'd done.
My mind was filled with the idea of them in that dark car.
It had been too dark even to see how many. Most horrifying had
been the way they hadn't even laughed, but had done it like a
necessary but disgusting duty – like squashing an insect.

I was only a block from home when I made the most alarming
discovery of this whole evening. I was relieved to be coming
home. I was glad to have been prevented from finding Bobby.
Why? Not because I didn't still believe he'd been in danger,
but because I already dimly understood that to go near him was
to increase his danger. With a shudder of terror, I realised that
I'd come a step nearer to discovering how Karl and I might
save our lives together.

Thank god Karl was in his study, so that I could reach the
bathroom without meeting him. Though strangely, my shoes
and stockings seemed less wet than they'd felt out there in the
darkness. I spent an hour, showering, and disinfecting myself
and everything I'd been wearing.

My plan . . . Our mutual guilt . . . Must die . . .

Again the manuscript ended in heavy erasing among which
only isolated words survived.

Peterson pushed it away and sat nipping the ballpoint pen
between his front teeth. Presently he wrote :

What is this new mad scheme, Morrison read, which my wife
Martha (change name) has got into her head. At first I didn't
take it seriously. Now I know that I must take it VERY
seriously.

From the first I knew that tonight would be a bad night. I
didn't realise how bad. I'm far more disturbed than I like to
be. My hand reaches for the phone to call "I.". I draw it
back in alarm. Certainly I must not do this while she is awake.
I should do it when she sleeps. Shall I then want to do it . . .?

At six o'clock she came to me with something to say – that
was easy to tell. A hundred times in the last twenty years she
has come like this. (Six o'clock is a favourite time. Instinctively
she seems to know that I am at my least tolerant with an
empty stomach. It is a challenge to her, to force me to live

251

nervously when all my physical instincts favour a predigestive calm). On only fifty per cent of these occasions, perhaps less, do I have the patience to let her say what she has come to say.

Often I never know whether she has said it or not. Her devious mind, of course, never lets her start with it. But sometimes I think she is genuinely convinced that her introductory ploy is her real anxiety – believes that she is cleverly putting first what she cares about because she knows I don't expect it till third or seventh – or that she is putting it first because she knows that I know that sometimes she will believe that I know that she is cleverly ... The possibilities are wide.

Tonight she seemed desperate to try to make me say some phrase, but determined not to provide me with the exact words. I was willing to say it. I became quite interested in the detection of what it was from her hints. Guilt was involved, I became certain. I was in some way to make a comparison between our guilts. "But, Karl, how do we *know* that we do right?" she kept asking. "How do we *each* know?"

"Oh I get it," I began, believing I'd solved the problem, about to call out the answer, pleased by my intuition. We are equally guilty, I was going to say.

Though I believe I was right I can't be sure because at once, in the most vicious way, she began to attack me for withdrawing my name from the Ad Hoc Committee's letter of resignation. And for defending what I'd done by inventing a totally false homosexual passion for a student. The cleverness of this ploy was that she doesn't believe it's false. But here I out-clevered her. I didn't let her go on saying it was false, as I would probably have done if it were real and I wanted to withdraw from the confession. I loudly and angrily (but a bit phonily) defended it as real – thus, hopefully, convincing her it was false.

Suddenly she broke off. "So what are we going to do?"

We've been through this phase often before. I know that I must say nothing. There is nothing to be done, but it is vital not to say so. There is, indeed, no problem which needs action – our worst scenes have been provoked by my telling her this. Then she begins to scream, "What do you mean, just *go on*? How can we just *go on*?" It makes her desperate that I won't admit a crisis. Crises are what she lives for. Neurotic self-abuse. Unless we are having an emotional crisis she feels dead.

But tonight, scarily, I felt that she didn't want to scream

252

like this. For the first time she seemed more assured that our lives *were* at a crisis, than I was assured that they weren't. I even caught myself on the edge of screaming at her, "Life consists of going on. That's its horror, don't you see."

Then it came. Her insane suggestion. I was in control again. I knew it was insane, and knew that the most insane thing I could do would be to tell her so.

Together we must – I can hardly write it for shame at its absurdity and for shame that till now I've taken it seriously. Together we must eliminate our problem: Bobby Schneider. Only in this way can we come together again. Not only shall we do away with this desperate turning to another for the love we can no longer give each other. We shall be brought close again by our mutual guilt.

The terrible absurdity of this idea tempted me to shout it down at once. Good sense saved me. I saw that this was no casual idea, thrown at me as much to provoke as to be taken seriously. If I laughed or shouted her down there were two alternatives: she would bury it and cease to tell me about it. A new barrier of hate and distrust would have been created. Or she would grow wildly obstinate about it.

I began to discuss it with her in the academic way which is the only way to make her listen. "Can we create love like that? Negatively." I said.

"There's no other way," she said.

"Suppose we do what you suggest and are left hating each other," I said. "For example, suppose I feel that you have forced me into this course of action because you believe that I love him more than you love him. Shan't I then feel resentment towards you?"

"It's our only chance," she said. Terribly, I heard a new tearful gratitude and love for me in her voice, for talking to her about it so reasonably.

"What if we attempt what you suggest but botch it?" I said. "You must agree that we have relatively little previous experience . . ."

"Karl, we won't," she said.

Frighteningly, every few moments as we talked like this, I could hear the words I was saying from outside. I could hear myself acting like a madman. I could hear how convincingly I

253

was acting. The gentle, reasonable, totally mad logic I was using.

At this point (Peterson wrote), to Morrison's annoyance, the manuscript became less continuous. There were half pages, pages with isolated paragraphs at their centres, and pages which seemed not to follow from the ones before. Hard to tell if this was accident or intention. He read them with growing surprise at his own fascination.

Tonight we discussed ways and means: guns, poison, auto-accidents. We had been doing it for half an hour when, glancing up at her, I realised: my god, she is happy. For the first time for five, ten years, she is actually enjoying what she is doing. Is it the secret planning, the elevation of life on to a more intense level? Or is it just that I am working with her? Together we are planning, hoping ... This is the more terrifying possibility because it shows how easily I could have been giving her this satisfaction all these years.

An hour later the subject had not changed. We were going in circles. I'd even found myself restarting her (us) at the beginning to see how often I could do it without her noticing – I glanced up and saw myself. I realised that for the last ten minutes I'd been discussing it not just with perfectly acted sincerity, but with perfect sincerity. I'd actually started to think as if we were going to do this insane thing – a gun of course seemed most practical, though hardest to escape with. I caught myself actually approving the symbolic appropriateness of this weapon. At the moment I came to myself (I use the phrase hopefully) I gave a heavy shudder, and she noticed, and asked in the kindest way (kinder than I remember for many years) if I was feverish and would like an iced drink ...

How terrible to play a game like this with her, because to her it is not a game. The longer I play it with her (to help and please her) the more seriously she takes it. The surer I am that all her hopes are becoming based on it. The more terrified I am about what she will do if I take it from her ...

She has bought a gun from a State City dealer – using another name, getting it sent "General Delivery". This evening she showed it me. "A Browning thirty-two," she said, with a professional casualness which horrified me. How had she learned

254

to say it in that off-hand way, to offer it to me, butt to my hand, not as women normally touch guns, with alarm and cringing (proving, if proof were needed, their symbolism), but with a strong grip of the carriage, as if she'd been handling them all her life?

But the true horror was my own feeling about this gun and its purpose. I was erotically aroused. It happened so suddenly and spontaneously that I could only sit confused and silent, staring at it, my whole consciousness concentrated in that throbbing bulge in my pants which she surely *must* have seen.

What does it mean? Do I, too, secretly want him dead? Has she, with a woman's intuition (something I've never admitted) discovered this? For the simple sexual thrill of killing him? That would not be too difficult to bear. Because he is too innocent to live? To save myself the awful compassion I feel for his yet unlived life? This too I might accept. Because I secretly need Martha's love as much as she needs mine? If I believed this . . .

I really love that man . . .

His repose . . .

Because of my love for him I have had to tell him everything. Suppose he had found out that I wasn't – and he would certainly have found out from Martha. Anyway, I wanted to tell him everything. Only now do I understand how I have come to rely on his – what word can I use? Guidance? He gives me little. Presence? I see him once a week. Support? Wisdom? . . .

I am alone again . . .

I am frightened . . .

Every man his cave, Morrison thought. They've been creeping back there together and, to make it chummier, not admitting it to each other. It was a deliciously cosy tale. But some personal implication worried him, and he began to stride about his study, two and a half paces each way, looking half consciously for objects to stumble into, obscenities to shout through wall or window, gestures of any sort to escape an appalling moment when he'd been about to lapse into introspection. A thought! He stood still, his eyes flashing above the fuzz of carrotty hair which enclosed him from cheek bone to Adams

255

apple, settling on his desk. Pen. Paper – the total irony of it. He was actually suffering a spasm-like desire to write it down.

But what? Peterson thought, helplessly. He recognised all too clearly what he'd done: rushed at his problem, pretending to believe that at the last moment an inspiration would solve it. To write down what? Or, to be accurate, to fail to write down what – failure was allowed. But failure implied the possibility of success.

. . . all through the night, on black coffee, pulling at his hair, crying, chuckling aloud with admiration at his own acting – at the way it had recently compelled him to rip up two sheets he'd actually liked, Morrison wrote . . .

What?
Presently, deviously, Peterson began to write:

The Boy is a married graduate student, he (hero) read, Morrison wrote. He has a nice wife he used to love, and a nice thesis he doesn't give a shit about, and a nice apartment he can't afford so his loving parents pay for. The Boy has nice friends too. Especially this nice professor and his wife.

The Boy is crossing campus on his way to see these nice friends. They sure have been good to him. Oh my . . .

Take this professor. No one else likes him much. They say he gets his graduate students to do his research and publishes the results under his own name, and that's how he's making quite a literary reputation. They say he's stiff and cold and believes in standards of behaviour like the one's *he's* got: politeness, custom-made suits, an aristocracy of the intellect, all that crap. The Boy knows better. The Boy's seen this professor sit there with tears in his eyes while he reads his (The Boy's) shitty poetry. The Boy knows there's a great warm sentimental core inside that cold dried-up human being. To The Boy, he's an insect man, all the blood and intestine inside, skeleton outside. There's a kind of a battle going on all the time between this cold shell of a man and that soft core which keeps trying to ooze out through the cracks, if only it had the courage. It sure hurts The Boy to watch this battle.

256

Or take this professor's wife, and the way she's made a set at The Boy ever since she first caught sight of him. Some folks think she's about as bloodless as the professor – and a good deal less intelligent. The Boy knows better. He's had her sit listening with big wide eyes to every half-arse comment on life he has to make – like it's the pope who's speaking and he's about to connect her person-to-person to god. The Boy knows you've only got to treat her warm and friendly, and touch her up a trifle – metaphorically – and all that love she pretends she doesn't want to give comes out like champagne from an uncorked bottle – only more sickly.

The Boy remembers how she's taken him to coffee at the "Y", where she can pretend she's a student again, where she's *behaved* like a student. Kept flopping her head about or listening to him with it held at forty-five degrees, propped on an elbow. Got her skinny arms and wrists all over the table among the mugs and ashtrays.

The Boy is on his way to see these friends of his. He's walking across campus, and it's one of those nice summer days when you can't actually breathe because you're afraid when you get this steamy stuff inside you – what they call air down here – it'll start to boil and come out in jets through your ears. So The Boy walks slow, just in case, if he conserves his energy, he'll be able to get there before he passes away. But this isn't the only reason he walks slow. He walks slower and slower because he's thinking.

So just why have his friends The Professor and His Wife asked him to drop by and see him this afternoon? All right, they've done it before. All right, there's a dozen things he can imagine either one of them wanting to talk to him about. Somehow, this afternoon's invitation hasn't suggested any of them. It's come from His Wife by phone. That's odd to start with. She must have been planning it:

"We'd love to see you for a drink this afternoon."

"You would?" he says – thinking, why "we"?

"It's been a long time."

"Yeah?" he says – thinking, has it? and, why the excuse?

There's an uneasy pause before she says, "Do you think you can come?"

"I reckon I *might*," he says, giving the word a kick to keep her guessing.

257

Another pause, crackling with ideas. "Oh fine," she says, and hangs on. It seems she sure needs an answer.

"I'll look forward to that," he says at last, because, oh christ, he doesn't really want to hurt her.

The Boy knocks at the door. He's an hour late. She's there at once, and The Professor's behind her in the sitting room doorway. A reception committee. Things sure are organised tonight.

"Hi," he bellows at Mrs Professor.

"Hi," she shouts back, and stands gaping with horror at this accident he's tricked her into. When the echoes have died down, The Boys hear The Professor say, "Do come in."

The Boy sits on the edge of a settee. Some polite but interesting observations follow: the seasonable weather, and if a thesis comparing works of literature created above seventy degrees farenheit with those created below seventy degrees farenheit would show interesting results.

"If you keep mice above that temperature their life span is reduced by a third," Mrs Professor says brightly.

There sure isn't any indecent hurry to satisfy our baser appetites. In fact it's ten minutes before The Professor extracts himself from his fascination with the literature/temperature/ mice syndrome and offers The Boy a glass of sherry.

Sherry! How much of a self-caricature can you be!

"Delighted, I'm sure," The Boy says, trying to avoid an English drawl. The Professor goes to the sideboard – no *petit bourgeois* hiding of the booze in the pantry for this professor – and pours three very small glasses – not to dim the intellect – from a *decanter*.

At this moment something mischievous gets into The Boy. He humps him off that arse-torturing settee-edge where he's been posed like a talking monkey on a barrel and crosses to the sideboard.

"Hey," he shouts, too close to The Professor's ear for his comfort. "Make that a bourbon on the rocks."

They both stand quite still. They become petrified. They're figures from a tavern in Pompeii, caught in action, preserved in archeologist's cement – saying some long lost commonplace from nineteen hundred years ago. The Professor has the decanter in one hand, and the other's stuck out rigid three inches above the sherry glass he's about to pick up and pass. The

Boy's staring down at this hand, metaphorically licking his cement lips. At first The Boy thinks the explanation's simple. It's because of his mannerless and plebeian request. About five seconds pass before The Boy realises there's another possible explanation. Because what The Professor's staring at, and what The Boy is staring at, right there among the bottles and glasses and decanters, is a nice clean, blue and brown, slightly oily, small-calibre automatic pistol . . .

Okay, any guy can keep a gun around. Even professors get burglarised. Maybe The Boy would have thought nothing of it – if he hadn't seen how The Professor was staring at it. And had the impression that what really shocked The Professor was that *he*, The Boy, had noticed it. Or maybe there was anyway something sinister about that gun, laid out there among the glasses and decanters, not at an angle as if slung there casually after the last job The Professor had wrapped up, but neatly aligned, with just sufficient space for it. Just like it was an integral part of the sherry ritual.

If The Boy's shaken, The Professor's groggy. The Boy can tell by the way – when at last he succeeds in moving – he hands him *a glass of sherry,* and only several seconds later gives a start and half reaches out his hand to change it as he rehears and understands The Boy's request for a bourbon on the rocks.

Well this sure is a nice start to a convivial drink, The Boy thinks. But he hasn't seen a thing. There's more to come which is really going to make his hair stand on end – only it's cropped short to disguise him as an all-white, All-American boy.

"You may wonder what that's doing there," The Professor begins, taking the bull by the horns.

"Not especially," The Boy says.

"Did you wonder why we asked you for a drink tonight?" Mrs Professor tries.

"Hey, no?" the boy lies.

To The Boy they're like two frightened sheep who keep trying to get out of a field. Each time they rush for a gap he appears there and shouts "BOO" and they scamper back into the middle and stand bleating in a plaintive kinda way before they make a new rush.

A whole lot of mighty devious talk follows, about relationships, and the ethics of responsibility, and ethics in general – wife, son, daughter, mistress versus society – and about reality

– if reality's purely personal, where does the authority for morality fit in? It's all so devious that The Boy is just about persuaded a genuine academic discussion is going on, like the sort that generally bores the pants off him and he takes such a lively part in. Only right down deep at the bottom, this boy's a suspicious guy and he guesses there's a bit of high level intellectual jiggery-pokery going on. Or, to put it another way: let's not let our right lobes know what our left lobes are thinking.

All of a sudden, in a rather scary way, they're right back on the personal level: something The Boy can understand, though maybe he'd rather he couldn't.

"Don't we *all* want love?" Mrs Professor says. "To give it and receive it?"

"Isn't it our moral duty to act so that we increase the world's sum of loving and being loved?" The Professor says.

When he says this, Mrs Professor looks at him like he's the dumb boy in her class who's got the right answer, word perfect, for the first time. Like she doesn't know what to do with herself to show how pleased she is with him and with herself for the clever way she's taught him.

Suddenly The Boy gets the idea. Christ! How stupid can you be? It's as clear as daylight, as obvious as the air you breathe all the time but can't see.

"Hey," he shouts. "You're going to shoot me. To increase the sum of love in the world."

Somehow they don't like this. They don't deny it, of course, but they're pretty goddam worried by the way he's phrased it.

"That wasn't what my wife said," The Professor says.

"You're being intentionally perverse," Mrs Professor says.

"I doubt if you're trying to understand," The Professor says, just like it's an obscure point of textual criticism he's explaining. "It isn't the action that matters but the motive."

"You can't have been listening," Mrs Professor says.

Now The Boy can't stop himself from telling them. "Right, right," he cries. "I've got to understand because otherwise you don't dare. I've got to agree because you just don't trust your own minds. Because the person whose cynical good sense you really trust is me!" The beauty of it fairly staggers him. "You're wonderful. You really are. All two of you. Say, let's draw for who pulls the trigger. Or could we fix it so we all do it together? With string? Or mirrors?"

As The Boy goes on he becomes uneasy at the way they aren't responding. The Professor keeps watching him as if he'd like to interrupt, then glancing at his wife, as if he'd rather *she* did. But she just looks at the Professor and keeps making odd jerky signs at him, with her eyebrows, then her whole head.

Presently The Professor doesn't look at The Boy either, but starts making his own jerky signs at his wife, with *his* eyebrows and head. They're like a goddam deaf and dumb team. They've been carrying on like this for several minutes before The Boy gets it. The moment has come, only they're each leaving it to the other. But neither of them can do it because it isn't like they planned it. The Boy won't play the game the way they want. They're really cross with him for the way he's arguing merrily – and not showing fear or resignation, or solemn understanding, but – even when he believes it really may happen – getting the best sick laugh out of it he's had for a year. This crossness with each other – and him – is the most genuine emotion he's detected the whole evening. He's about to tell them so – "Hey, you're learning, there's hope yet" – when the entertainment goes sour on him.

He stands, "So long," and leaves them there, not even knowing how to stop him.

The Boy strolls away, whistling, singing even – the university football hymn is a particular favourite just now – for as long as he can get enough steamy air into his lungs to work with. The whole incident has really set him up, given him a genuine kick . . . when BANG.

Loud, but indoors and muffled. The Boy doesn't have to be told what made that noise. He even stops whistling and stands still and listens. There's a moment when he almost goes back. But no. Recently someone's been talking to him about illusion and reality and the possible lack of an ultimate moral authority. The Boy strolls on, considering these points.

"Miss Foringer, did you find Christ symbolism in this passage?"

Vacation was over. Peterson was taking his class, first of a final exhausted spurt to the end of the semester. Miss Foringer turned her attention back from the Christmas-card snowscape on campus to the text of *Room at the Top*.

"You know what passage we're discussing, Miss Foringer?"

261

"I sure do," Miss Foringer said, and returned to silence, leaving him uncertain whether it was true. Miss Foringer had repose. Knotted up with embarrassment at her own stupidity, as she must be, not a sign of this showed. She circled her head with absent-minded sensuousness to lay a sweep of golden hair behind one shoulder. Only when she set her chin in her hand and began to use her little finger to tickle out snot did he detect anxiety.

"Miss Steiner?" Peterson asked, letting Miss Foringer escape as heads began to turn.

"No," Miss Steiner said. It was how she'd treated him for the last month, as if her knowledge of his private life made his opinions on English Literature no longer valuable to her. She never looked up, rarely took a note, and when she did convinced him that it was merely evidence of some new defect in his character – as if she hadn't gotten enough, for heavensake.

None of it mattered.

There in the front row, arse down in her seat, white levis and rope-soled sneakers thrust into the gangway, sat Jill, gazing at him through those big dark-framed glasses, with the faintest smile, saying clearly to him : if only they knew what we know. He'd been half way through the classroom doorway, already noticed with sinking despair her empty place, when she'd come past him from behind. "Sorry I was such a bitch."

"Doesn't matter," he'd said, in ridiculous automatic answer. However long he'd thought, no words could have told her his relief. Only then had he realised how desperate he'd been.

How idiotic of him not to have seen that she'd been using the first weapon to hand to punish him for her three bad days at Christmas – days which she knew logically he'd had to spend at home but for which she was still mad with him.

"It *does* matter," she'd said, tipping her head on one side to look at him with comic soulfulness but half real apology. "Is it forgiven?"

In the doorway, unseen by more than a dozen of the class, he'd taken her soft hand and pressed it to his side, and moved in a daze of happiness to his teaching desk.

"Who agrees with Miss Steiner?" he asked, exposing her with a courage he usually lacked. Miss Steiner driven into isolation by the others, threatened a ghastly explosion of righteous wrath – he didn't care.

The bell ended his class when he was in full flow of provocative questioning. Thirty seconds later they stood together outside the doorway, looking into each other's eye with happy wonder.

"Tonight?"

"Of course." He'd need a new excuse for Nancy.

"In the library? I'm kinda sentimental about that place."

A gush of unbearable longing for her filled him. "In the library." He'd find an excuse all right. A snippet of biblical wisdom came to him. If the spirit was willing, though the flesh was weak – in the circumstances the inverse might be more appropriate. Instantly, and with no apparent connection, he saw himself as the passing class must be seeing him, middle-aged, scrawny, besotted, pathetically snared by this juvenile broad . . .

How pathetic *their* judgements, he thought. How they failed to understand that he knew all they knew about Jill and still loved her. That their love was mutual. That the word love was an insult to their varied, subtle but entirely tender feelings for each other. So much more varied but more tender since this worrying break . . .

"Hi." It was Ric Schuster. "Thought I'd find you here."

"Not a difficult guess," Peterson said coolly.

"Right," Ric cried. Nothing would disturb his renewed enthusiasm for this adventurous, broadminded English professor. If he sounded sarcastic, that was his limey sense of humour. "All fixed for tonight," Ric said. "Can you make it?" He gazed up, a dog waiting for praise. "Judy's coming."

"The problem is . . ." Peterson began.

"A friend of mine's lending us his apartment," Ric said, his hope scarcely bearable to see the ball he'd brought lifted, sniffed . . .

"Tonight's a bit awkward," Peterson said. "I'm afraid Nancy's not too keen," he said, each remark taking him one more plunging step down from the bright elevation Ric had put him on. "Unless Jill would like to come," he said, recovering desperately.

He explained it to her.

"And you weren't going to ask me?" she said.

He explained he'd always half consciously had her in mind.

"So you're Jill," Ric said.

"Right, right."

263

"So you're bringing Jill?" Ric said, his eyes moving from one of them to the other.

"He sure is," Jill said.

"If you don't mind," Peterson said.

"Mind!" Ric said, gave an address and left them. Every few steps he looked back over his hunched shoulders. "Well well," he said at the stair top, raising his eyebrows. Down several stairs and almost out of hearing, he said, "Well well well."

"Do you know him?" Peterson asked her, moving her into a recess behind a fire hydrant, where they went into a deep open-mouthed, rib-crushing, mind exponging kiss. They sighed, gasped, clung together and cried small tears of happiness.

"I seen him around," Jill said.

At five o'clock Peterson was about to close his office when a half familiar girl stood in his open doorway. She wore snow boots and a furry hat with furry ear flaps. She was a small furry pixie, with all a pixie's self-sufficient sexlessness.

"Hi," she said.

"Hallo," Peterson said, only now recognising Ric's girl Judy. "It's been a long time."

"Three weeks," she said. She sat in his chair. Everything about her seemed to have changed into this small hard adult.

"We'll be seeing you tonight?" Peterson said, with a cautious grin of conspiracy.

She shook her head, looking down at the furry gloves on her knees. Now at last he recognised the sense she'd often given him of a responsibility she was too young for.

"Ric and I are breaking up."

He was far more shocked than he could explain. "But when I saw him this morning . . ."

"I guess I'm telling you because I daren't tell him," she said. "I just don't know what he'll do."

He listened with anxious concern. It didn't occur to him to tell her that in a few weeks she'd see it in proportion. That she lived in a world which had abandoned the romantic hypocrisy that human relationships could be stable. He understood that such an idea would be useless to her, and that she might be right, because the failure of one relationship implied the failure of all.

"Oh why does he give it to him?" she said, abstracted again.

264

"For the trip?" Peterson guessed.

She didn't answer.

"Who gives it him?" Peterson tried.

She sat silent, as if wanting words to prove she hadn't said it but not finding them.

"Anyone can see he wants to destroy himself," she said. "But not this way."

It reduced all she'd said to the secondhand. She was a little girl from downstate, shocked by drugs because her mother – closely advised by god – had told her to be.

"But we take them all the time," he began. "There's half a per cent of alcohol in fresh-baked bread. Starve yourself for three days and you'll have a vision."

She watched him.

"Why pick on this instead of alcohol? It's an arbitrary Anglo-Saxon preference; mindless activity against meditation and dreams."

The more she watched and said nothing the more uncertain he became. Was she agreeing or merely reserving wiser arguments?

"Ric's not an escaper," she said. "Or else he's doing it to hurt someone, and he doesn't like hurting people."

He was left wordless. Was she back again on the homestead: the boy I marry shall be a clean-living, god-fearing boy? Or did these totally improbable ideas about Ric show an understanding of him he'd never some near?

As he reached the door of the Humanities Library, the terror of that evening before Christmas when her chair had been empty came back to him . . . And there was her chair, occupied by someone else. Fear flooded him – but receded fairly reassuringly as he saw her five chairs further along the table.

At once she was on her feet, slipped past him into the corridor with only the briefest smile, went ahead down the stairs.

From opposite sides they sat quickly into his car. "Let's go," she said, and he accelerated away with a hiss of tyres on the icy road.

As soon as they were moving she slid close to him, gripping his arm with both hands, giving a big shuddery snuggle.

"Darling, I think I'm being shadowed." She lifted her face in the darkness to give his ear a tickle with her tongue. "Darling

265

why don't you use fruit-flavoured after-shave? – hey, and soap too, then I could lick you all over."

"Who's shadowing you?"

"It's a long story," she said, and paused as if considering whether to tell him. "Darling, I haven't been quite straight with you."

"Oh?" Already he wanted to forgive her.

"You know I told you I was once married. Well it's true. The problem is, it's still true."

How well he remembered her saying that she'd told him only one lie, and the happy sense of privilege it had given him. Though he would now have a less satisfactory memory of that moment, he was even more grateful for this new confession which confirmed once more her trust in him.

"And is he still in a monastery in North Australia?"

"Oh, he was," she said. "But he wouldn't divorce me. He had a thing about me coming back. And now this Australian bitch comes and drags him out and wants to make him do it."

"She's collecting evidence?"

"Right, right."

"So that was why we had to meet at the library."

"Right," she said, delighted at how quickly he understood. "You see, he has some money, and she's afraid I might try to get my hands on it – She's darn right, I might. Darling, it's all a bit complicated. Oh yes, and she wants to marry him, poor bitch, I almost forgot that. Darling, you don't mind, do you?"

In the darkness he shook his head with sad pleasure that she should so underestimate his love for her. But something worried him. "Why didn't *you* divorce *him*?"

"I reckon I got a kick out of having him there . . . Hell, it's not as though he was exactly interfering in my life. Anyhow I never had the time or the cash . . ."

"But now that *he's* going to do it . . ."

"Darling, it's you I'm worried about."

"Me?"

"You see, frankly, you'll be the evidence."

"Who cares?" he said gallantly, his stomach lurching in alarm: citations for adultery, newspaper stories, Visiting Professor Named . . . Taking a hand from the wheel, he held her tightly against him to show her how little he cared. Or, better still, how much.

266

"Darling," she said, hugging him tightly, with an instinctive understanding which made him want to die of happiness, and distracted him momentarily as he parked, so that his front fender struck a concrete lamp stand. From six feet above, the glass globe fell in a rain of fine fragments over his hood but left the bulb up there bare and still alight.

"Well just fancy that!" she said as they sat giggling, then hurried out of the car, slamming the doors, and chased each other into the house, striking playfully at each other's arses.

Ric Schuster stands at the far end of the one-room apartment, holding a small green bottle, watching them.

At the sight of that bottle, Peterson's heart pounds. For the first time what he's going to do seems real. He feels wild-eyed. Like an animal his eyes dart, left and right, around the cluttered apartment of bamboo screens, Mexican rugs and six-foot photo-copied faces of movie stars, looking for escape. He senses that there may be other people present, hidden in closets or behind bookshelves. Though he doesn't look at Ric, he knows that Ric is watching him. And Jill is watching him.

Now he believes they may have planned this, though just what they've planned he doesn't know. But when he makes himself look at them he is more alarmed to see that neither of them are taking any interest in him. Ric has uncorked the bottle and is sniffing it. Jill has picked a record from a pile near the phonograph and is reading the sleeve. "Hey," she says, then nothing more, so that they wait moment after moment in the after-sound of that exclamation which she's probably forgotten she made.

He hunts for a question which will set what's happening in a world he knows about, but the only questions he can think of, hopelessly disclose his cowardice. Worse, he seems to have lost the power to judge whether they do or don't. Suddenly the question he knows he must ask is, Who gave it you? but he knows that this, besides letting them guess his cowardice, will show how poorly he understands the proper secrecy of what they're doing.

"Is it easy to get?" he asks.

"I reckon. If you got the right friends," Ric says. "Like you have." He recorks the bottle and throws it into the air and watches it turning over and over and stoops quickly to catch it near the floor.

"Watch out that's our trip," Jill shouts, in what she pretends is mock alarm but may be real.

"Like *I* have?" Peterson asks.

"Ever heard of Dr Ivan Heinz?"

A clicking of ideas occurs in Peterson's head, but not comfortingly. Now he knows there's a pattern, but he still can't see it. Clearly Ric can see it. Jill, too, perhaps. He feels childishly stupid and childishly ashamed of showing his stupidity.

"But is he a friend of mine?" he asks.

"He sure thinks the world of you," Ric says.

A terrible warm comfort fills Peterson. So Dr Heinz admires, even trusts him. He struggles against his happiness, trying not to care, trying to believe it's another of Ric's lies, and at the same time hunts for an oblique way to ask just which of his qualities Dr Heinz admires most: his courageous affair with Jill, or merely his talent as a writer – the second would somehow be a disappointment. He has found no suitable question when Ric brings two glasses of water to a low table and drops a white pill from the bottle into each.

"Pure asprin," he says, watching them there among the full ashtrays, cactus flower in a milk-shake carton, paper plates with the dried tomatoe, mustard and melted cheese of cheeseburgers.

"Why only two?" Peterson says.

"I'll come if Judy comes," Ric says.

"Come on," Peterson says. "You've got to lead the way," making it a joke, but now at last taking hold of what is happening by a handle he isn't too confused to hold.

"Yeah, come arn," Jill says. Together they call at him to come. Peterson is glad of Jill's support, not caring if it's another part of their plot – to persuade him they're separate, when they're together.

Ric fetches a third glass and drops a white pill into it. Peterson is deeply suspicious. It's quite unlike Ric to be persuaded. Never before can he remember him chosing self-indulgence instead of self-injury.

They watch the pills in their glasses crumble to tiny mountains of snow-white powder, swill them into opaque sediment, look up at each other and drink.

For forty minutes they wait. Far longer than it ought to take.

268

"Spiked," Ric says. "What would you expect? Well, man, now you'll really have something to tell the folks."

But he's less offensive than usual, as if he can't entirely hide his excitement, as if he's still hoping for a sign and can't concentrate on making a good job of his sarcasm.

"Why did he give it you?" Peterson says.

"Ask him," Ric says. "He's your friend."

"You been before?" Jill says.

"Sure, I've been," Ric says. "It's great. Well, isn't it? Eh? Aren't we all having a great time?"

They laugh a little.

"It's the American thing, didn't they tell you?" Ric says. "Get rid of the responsibility of being yourself – and quick. Adjust to a state of mind which doesn't see your extinction as terrifying – hey man, now you're talking. Get a grip on some alternative hope to the social/commercial rat-race which death makes so futile."

He improves as the trip becomes more certainly a failure.

"Experience a universal love, and try to sell it to everyone else, so you can get included in *their* love. Oh boy, could we do with some of that."

After a full hour it begins.

First his eyes, as if they may smart soon. As if they're getting big and orange-coloured.

Then his mouth, an odd taste at the back, as if glands long dried up are starting to secrete again. Then the back of his neck. A sense of pressure. And, when he puts his hand there, what's this astonishing mat of hair? Dense, thick, an inch deep. Amazing. Slightly tingly. Has he lived all his life with this astonishing growth right here where his skull joins his neck?

"Oh ho, here we go," Ric says. It's caught him too. He isn't sarcastic.

"Wooo!" Jill says.

"Go with it," Ric says. He becomes obsessed with this phrase. "Let go there, man. Go with it." At any other time he would be maddening, because of the way he keeps repeating it, or because it's something secondhand he's been told to say, or because he'd be mocking the people who'd told him to say it, or mocking you for trying to follow his advice. Now he says it with concern, as if he's anxious about you and wants to help.

"Woooo – hooo!" Jill says.

It comes in surges. At moments he's going, high, high. There's no other word for it. Rising, rising. But at others he believes he's as clearheaded as ever, looks around and sees it happening to *them*. They sit there, staring forward and down. They don't notice they're being watched, because they're lifting, going away, attending to the take-off inside their own heads.

"Gee!" he says.

"Oh boy!" Jill says.

"Hey, man!" Ric says. For a moment they're all together, understanding each other's astonished delight.

It gets faster. It's getting out of control. It's doing things to his mind which begin to frighten him. He clings to control of his mind by a slim hold. Panic comes close. By keeping very still he may avoid it. A tiny movement and he'll topple into it. The panic in his head is *about* his head.

It's expanding faster on one side than the other. There's a terrible blockage which won't let the other side grow. He can see no way of escape. There seems no end to this terrifying swelling of one side of his head and the appalling blockage of the other. Tiny and far away at the very back corner of his mind, something tells him that later this problem won't seem alarming. He doesn't believe it. What he believes is that the growing difference in size between one side of his head and the other is going to make it burst. There's a second when he realises that if he doesn't keep quite still, holding and holding to this tiny core of faith in his sanity, he's going to start crawling round the apartment trying to bury his head under its rugs to get away from the awful thing that's happening inside it – and knowing that he *can't* . . .

"Oh my, oh gee," he says, as he's been saying before, but for a different reason.

Far away and hazy, he hears Ric say, "You all right?" So he must have said it differently, showing he's in trouble. I'll soon be fine, he wants to say, to reassure himself, but the sentence is too difficult. He knows he won't have any control of the tone of the words. They'll croak or squeak, or some do each.

Still holding on, he stands and moves with difficulty, because his legs are shivering, to a stool at the kitchen end of the room. Holding, holding, he sits there, looking down at the formica top of a table. The pattern on the Formica swirls and moves. It hasn't just one pattern but two. They're one on top of the

270

other about a quarter of an inch apart and they're both swirling. He watches them, fascinated. Why has he never looked at a Formica table top before? The other side of his head expands. He's high.

He's let go. He's gone with it. He's plunged . . . Dimly the feeling is familiar. Something which has happened lately . . .

He goes back to the settee. He wants to be with Ric and Jill. He's sorry he went away from them. They grin up at him and go away where they came from.

Now he looks at things. Everything he looks at gives him pleasure. He realises that for twenty, thirty years he hasn't *enjoyed* looking at a single thing. He looks at the cactus flower in the milk-shake carton on the table. It has many little red heads. As he looks at them they move. They twirl and bend. They're alive. It's as if he's looking at them through a rising flow of hot air.

He turns to Ric and Jill to tell them. Christ, nothing like this has ever happened, he wants to say. That flower, it's as if I'm seeing it through rising hot air. He doesn't say these things. Partly he'd find the words hard to say. Partly they wouldn't be true. They'd be a cold extraction from the real truth. The flower, and the words he won't say about it, seem at once symbols, and the most vivid example of the difference between life and art. Life is the flower and the way he sees it. "Christ, look," he says, and points at the flower and they look.

"Yeah, YEAH," they say because they've seen it too.

Everything he looks at his eyes settle on and see truly. They feel its shapes and colours. For thirty years he hasn't been seeing things but classifying them. On the wall there's a painting of a woman's face in big mauve and orange patches of colour. He's classified it as he came in: painting of woman's face. He's even had feelings of a kind about it: ugly, crude, oversimplified, a distortion of a human face. Now it's three-dimensional, but not in the way the phrase made him expect. It advances and retreats, never all of it in focus at the same time. It's in hot air too. But the bits in focus are more vivid and beautiful than he'd ever thought possible. That great orange jaw – Or more hideous? He no longer knows which. He only knows that he sees it . . .

Dimly he's reminded that he's often lately seemed to suffer this sort of uncertainty . . .

Ric switches on the television – he's classified that too. It's

271

showing new aircraft. His eyes fix themselves on it. There's nothing else in the room but this small rectangular moving picture. A new jet liner. Its pointed nose protrudes much further ahead of the wings than its body extends behind them. The wings aren't important, just this enormous long neck and narrow head and pointed nose. Christ, why has he never seen a plane like this before? Why have all the planes he's been seeing been like the planes he's always been seeing? The significance of that machine – it's begun to move itself about now – with its tiny head no wider than its long neck, the things it suggests to him – which he can't and *doesn't want* to put into words . . . "Dinosaur," he says to Jill. "Jung. Hang on to that . . ."

A vertical-take-off machine. It rises and hovers with dangling legs, menacing, and evil. Never has he seen anything which so revolts him. It's a giant mechanical wasp. Ric switches off the television. Above it, in a small glass-fronted box, is a human skull – it's been there all the time – later he connects it with the apartment owner's motorcycle-cult. His eyes fix on the white bones of the skull, the empty eye sockets, the long teeth rising into the jaw bone. The horror. He stares and stares, held by the horror . . .

"Let's make some coffee," Jill says.

"Yeah, let's," he says.

Neither of them moves. After five minutes they look at each other and giggle with total understanding of their failure to make coffee. Her face. He's always thought it pretty. Never before has he seen how beautiful it is. Christ how beautiful. It's become flushed and wide cheeked, like an excited child's. The colour of that flush: deep red because of her tan. The softness of the skin. And her lips. Their curve and set, oh god. He doesn't even want to kiss them. Just to look at them. Her eyes. Round, dark brown, wide. The creases where they smile. At each corner, three little creases. God how lovely.

"Hey," she says. "Coffee." Together they stagger carefully to the kitchen end of the room. They have a fine time making a mess of making coffee. But all the time they're down there, giggling together, he's aware of Ric, still sitting at the other end of the room, feels his aloneness, his pain at being left out of jokes and love they have in common.

Jill watches the water rushing into the sink. Never has she

272

seen water like it. She shows it to him. They stand together, staring at this flow of hissing, bubbling water.

He spoons coffee into the coffee compartment while she holds it. The coffee flows over his finger. The way it flows – he wants to go on and on seeing it flow. He puts in spoonful after spoonful to watch it flowing over her finger. Three grains are left behind on her finger : two small and one large. The perfect appropriateness of those grains, their relative sizes, the triangular pattern they form . . . The smell of the coffee. Never has he smelt anything like it. He fills his lungs with it. Saliva runs like water in his mouth. It takes them about forty minutes to make a pot of coffee.

"Your minds are expanded," Ric says, and gets hung up on the meaning and beauty of the word 'expanded'. "What are you going to do with them?"

"Play chess," Peterson says. He's been staring at these chessmen, set out on a board on a shelf. He and Jill sit alongside the shelf to play. Are the pieces set out right? He tries to concentrate on the concept of the correct ordering of chess pieces before a game, and becomes fascinated by the knight. The way he rides the neck of his horse. The grip he has, as if engaged in some deep sexual penetration but, because his head is turned sideways, as if at the same time listening anxiously to its heartbeat.

"Are they set right?" Jill says.

With an effort he forces himself to consider. "Hey, no, my bishop's a queen." It's the funniest joke they've ever heard. They roll around in their chairs.

She picks up a pawn to move it, and holds it, studying it, fascinated.

"Let's not play chess," he says. They go back to the settee.

"We don't think they're very nice people we're playing with," he tells Ric. It's another incredibly witty crack. Never has he been so brilliant.

He puts paper on the settee, on the opposite side to Jill. Ric has made him think he should use this trip. His novel has problems, especially one problem, which he now may solve.

On the other hand, he doesn't want to lose a moment of this sensational experience. And he is anyway unsure whether he wants to write in their presence. There is a basic contradiction about writing in public, a suggestion that it's possible to live

273

and at the same time indulge this compensation for not living. Either the writing will fail or they will resent – rightly – the fact that he's going away on this compensatory private trip, when their adventure should be in common.

He compromises, keeping the paper on the seat, ocassionally putting down his hand to write there. He writes, "Think about my story and see if new ideas come." Nothing comes.

Presently, on a fresh sheet, he writes, "Still thinking about whether I should be making these notes."

On a third sheet he writes, "Thinking about thinking, about thinking (about thinking?) . . ." And later. "Back to base one – wondering why I'm doing this and if I should be. Pen has rainbow point."

On another sheet he begins, "Back to that story," and presently, "No better. Mind won't take hold of it."

Unexpectedly the second sheet now reappears where he reads, "Still thinking about whether I should be . . ." Something clicks in his mind. An idea. He knows, too, on which sheet he should write it – the third – but he can't find it. The sheets begin to get badly muddled. He gets some on to his lap. He gets some back on to the settee. Now some are on his left as well as on his right.

"Having fun?" Jill says.

Indeed he is having fun. At the same time that he's anxious to find the sheet to which to add his first useful idea, he's deliciously amused by his own inefficiency, by the chaos, near snowstorm proportions, of the papers he's turning, shuffling, inverting and letting slip to the floor. Arbitrarily he choses a blank sheet and writes.

"Idea : each time you reread a sentence – about an experience – it's a new experience. So writing becomes the constant revising of one basic descriptive sentence."

Nothing follows for a long time. Perhaps nothing can. "Preoccupied with why I so enjoyed that private party with my papers," he writes.

He stares at his two sandals, which he's put on the table, among the ashtrays and dirty cheeseburger plates. He writes, *"Who is Morrison writing about?"* He knows he must underline this because it's central, but he's forgotten why it's central. Instead, he becomes preoccupied with his two sandals. There they are on the table. They are Maurice Peterson and Peter

274

Morrison. The incredible appropriateness of this astounds him. He crosses his feet. Now Maurice Peterson and Peter Morrison have changed places. It leaves him aghast. He *knows* it's significant, but just why is tantalisingly beyond his grasp. He strains and strains to reach it, but at the moment when he almost has it, he becomes unsure whether or not it *is* significant.

He collects the sheets he has written on, and a lot of blank ones he can't separate, folds them and puts them in an inside pocket of his jacket. The significance of that! With the power of a revelation he sees that he has spent his whole life folding up little sheets of paper and putting them in an inside pocket. In a single act he has summed up his character. Jill is watching him. She has understood too.

The unnecessariness of it appals him. He wants to take them out and spread them about. Look at them, see what's written on them. If you laugh it's because of your own anxious defensive lives. Now he knows how he can live in future. He has gripped the message life has been offering him, for months, perhaps ever since he came to this country.

Ideas race in his mind. Every idea is greater *in* itself for being greater *than* itself. And greatest of all is the solution to this, his greatest, everyone's greatest, problem. How to live without shame. To learn it he has had to make this trip, THIS AMERICAN TRIP – he no longer knows which he is thinking about. He can no longer distinguish the difference. He no longer believes there is any difference.

No effort will be needed. Just an understanding, which can now never be taken from him. Secrecy is shame and shame is secrecy. Because he no longer has any shame – because he sees that it only exists if he believes it exists – he need not live secretly. His whole life will be public. His affair with Jill. No longer will he want to hide it . . . The thought is formed before he understands it. Before he remembers that from today there must be more, not less secrecy. That some people, Nancy perhaps, may not be able to live in this exposed way.

From today he is to be followed, spied on, photographed. Again he glances left and right to the closets and bookshelves. He looks at Ric and Jill. They are watching him.

Now he sees in their faces an amusement they can hardly hide – at the way they have tricked him? Why else are they watching him like this? At any moment they will make a sign.

275

They are only failing to make it because these moments of anti-cipation are so delicious they cannot bear to end them. – A shape over there on a bookshelf, seen out of the corner of his eye. He holds it there, accepting it, as he has learned to accept shapes. If he wanted he could look fully at it and classify it, as he's been classifying them and thus losing them all his life. Seen sideways, but truly, it's a head.

It's a head and it's watching him.

Something changes. Now he can't look at it. Because even if he did he'd see, out of the corner of his eye in another part of the room, another head. Already he *can* see it. It makes him duck his own head. Because beyond it he can *just* see another.

Now he knows that they're all round the room, watching him. He remembers the sense he had the moment he arrived that there were other people present. They've shown themselves. All round the room they've put up their heads. Some are in full view, some behind the bamboo screens. The head which he first saw, right in front of him, if he could ever make himself look at it, is Dr Ivan Heinz'.

Of course it's his. How could it not be – the logic seems obvious—since he organised this trip, provided the acid? Has he not been in the background, organising – the significance expands – judging, ever since that evening at the Golden Nite? Even before . . .? His owl face has been watching benevolently, malevolently, Peterson has no idea which.

Once more there is no feature he can hold on to. The chin grows and recedes. The eyes swell and contract to pin points. The bushy grey hair stands on end and lies flat. Now it sneers with scorn. Now it flattens with boredom, now it contorts with disgust at this supposed human being it's watching.

Its expression changes faster. And, more terrifyingly, he knows that the expressions of all those other faces watching him over desks, bookcases and tables, through bamboo screens, are chang-ing in time, at the same increasing rate. They are becoming, have all become, His face. At the moment of this discovery which fills him with a more terrible fear than any before, he stands to put on his coat.

"What's this?" Ric says with surprise.

"Where are you going?" Jill says in alarm.

But he knows, as clearly as if they'd told him, that this

276

is mock surprise, mock alarm, made genuine by the disappointment they fear if he escapes. They even try to hold his arms. "Hey, you mustn't go." With silent desperation, eyes on the ground, because he daren't look up at those faces which are now convulsed with laughter at his panic, he fights them off, runs out of the apartment, stumbles down stairs to the street.

The street is freezing and quiet. It must be late. He doesn't drive; he has sense enough for that. He walks the seven blocks home. He doesn't feel the cold, but he has an idea that it may be doing strange things to his extremities. His toes. The top of his head.

He watches the street lights. They are amazing. Why has he never seen them before? High above the streets, in a narrowing pathway, they stretch into the distance. He seems to become nothing but a moving pair of eyes, following the street lights. Eyes, and behind them fear. Fear with eyes.

He lets himself in. His house is hot and smelly. It must always have this smell. He remembers now that it does. Cooking bacon and cedar floor-polish – he can detect a dozen other details in this frowsty smell of his overheated brown house. He hurries up the stairs. The stairs lights are on, but every room is dark. He climbs to the attic room of his youngest daughter, Myrtle. It is she he must see – he can't explain why.

The horror. He daren't move. He stands quite still in the doorway. From here the stair light falls on one small open hand laid out through the cot bars. And, inside the bars, on one piece of white face. Below is black, black shadow. The blackness of blood.

He runs forward. He leans over her cot. The blood goes. But she still lies white and unmoving. He leans right into the cot, putting his ear close to her face to hear her breathing. She is breathing. He stands. His chest heaves a great sigh of gratitude.

Her eyes are open. He's woken her. She lies staring up at him. He smiles at her to tell her of his gratitude and love. She doesn't smile.

He leans down into the cot, in case she can't see him smiling and smiling at her, watching to see her face break into a happy smile. It moves. Its features shift and bulge. She is about to smile. She is about to *howl*. He no longer has any idea which.

277

He only knows that his own face is held down here, grinning with terror at the face of his daughter, which is seething like something putrid. At the moment when he knows she is about to wake the house with a terrified scream he tears himself away, and runs downstairs, out into the street.

He stands in the freezing street. It's a black and moonless night, lit only by the narrowing paths of street lights stretching away towards the distant prairie. He hurries back to the apartment.

They are sitting where he left them, Ric in the chair, Jill on the settee. He might never have been away. They don't even seem particularly interested that he's come back. It's as if they have passed through some fear for him which has left them beyond caring. He has made it too difficult.

He wants to call out, Ric, Jill, look, I've come back, it was all a big mistake, this is where I want to be. This is where I *have* to be. But they sit staring at the floor, dreaming their own dreams. When they smile at him they aren't seeing him. He's done something which has cut him off from them.

He has destroyed their faith in him. They offered him trust and he has run away from it. They cried out with love but he transformed it into its opposite, a plot against him. He has run back to his family, where he can give, not be responsible for receiving, love. But he has run from his family too, because they no longer believe in his love for them. His place is not there nor here, it is outside in the freezing streets, with the lines of street lights, leading away over the icy prairie . . .

He watches Ric. He has never watched him before. How he gives himself away! Those eyes, which are always on the ground except when they flicker up in what he believes is a bitter snarl, but in fact is the most transparent call for love. Love me, trust me, let me show you how I can love you if you'll only trust me. He might be saying these words. Every five seconds the right corner of his mouth twitches. It must always have twitched like that. How has he managed to see it twitching for months, but never see it? How has he sat here for six hours, with Ric and refused to notice that all this time he has been feeling only one thing? Judy hasn't come. Judy won't come. At last I've succeeded, as I shall always succeed, in making it impossible for her to love me.

His eyes. He has never seen such miserable eyes. For months

278

he has been exchanging concepts with this boy, rejecting the only concept Ric was trying to convey because he was doing it not with words but with those miserable self-hating eyes. Their creases. They are grotesque. A country of grotesques ... His American trip ... His hand is touched.

Jill is touching his hand. It's the first time they've touched since they made coffee. It's the most exciting touch he can remember. Every nerve in the back of his hand feels her soft touch. When he turns it over, every nerve in his finger tips senses the slight gritting of his rougher skin on her soft skin. He wants to go on and on touching her. The lightest touches of their fingers say things to each other ... How can he bear to touch her with this glorious love and understanding, in the presence of Ric's unhappiness? He takes his hand away and turns back to look at Ric, asking her to turn too. He believes she has understood.

The misery, oh god, the misery. His whole chest and heart are filled with the misery of being Ric. The pain. The hopelessness. Trapped in a body and mind he hates ... Jill is touching his hand.

He turns to her. Surely she has understood ... But now he sees, by the smallest turning of her shoulders away from Ric, that she has indeed understood. Don't look at him, she's saying. Look at me. I haven't told you before, but your simple-minded obsession with that conceited boy is the one thing about you I can't take. He stares at her, believing for a second that she may be right. No. She isn't right. Her face tells him.

In the most revealing way her face has changed. It tells him all about her. Her total selfishness. Love me, it says, not because I love you but because I love being loved. That little smile around her mouth, under the down of her upper lip, isn't of love for him. It's a little anticipatory smile of the self-love she's going to feel when he makes love to her.

It's the smile of a cat before a meal.

It's seductive, too, because it says to him, come arn, we're in this together. You love for yourself too. He's still holding her hand. His feelings about her hand are unbearable. He longs to go on holding it. To curl up inside it. But he is so horrified by the idea of Ric watching, that the touch of her hand is making him shiver continuously. At any moment he believes something in him must break, he'll scream ... Then he sees

279

that he was wrong about her flushed, round-cheeked, school-girl face. Its smile is loving. The other was a joke. It's smiling for the love she has for him, and the loving joke she's been playing on him. He looks back to Ric, in time to see Ric stand.

Ric stands slowly. There's never any doubt about what he's going to do. He's going to cross to the door and leave the apartment, but judging by the time it has taken him to stand he'll be about an hour doing it. He's leaving because he can no longer bear to watch their love.

He may go out with a jeer, but that will be so unimportant that it will scarcely be heard through his loud pain, which seems to echo around the room. His cry for help . . . At once Peterson tries to take his hand away from Jill. Look, I love you too, he wants to call to Ric. We both love you. Jill doesn't let go of his hand.

Looking at Jill, he sees that the joke, if any, is that she was never joking. Minute after minute the struggle goes on. Sometimes he can turn his eyes away from her to see Ric starting towards the door. More often he can only stare into her face, at her cat-smile of conspiracy under her downy upper lip. He is still looking at her when, with a ghastly crackle in his throat, he says, "Don't go."

"Let him go," she says.

"Don't," he calls.

"Why the hell?" she says. A second later he isn't even sure whether she's said these things or just meant them so clearly that she didn't need to say them.

I'm fighting for my life – the phrase arrives in his mind, clear, isolated, no need to define, qualify or argue it. Because one defeat implies every defeat. Fighting for Ric's life, too, but now, in his own struggle, even this becomes unimportant. Wash after wash of sweat runs over him. To live or die. To act or curl up. In this lies the essence of his choice as a human being, the essence of the choice of every human being. Ric reaches the door and goes.

"We must go after him," he says.

"Aw shit," she says. She's won. She can say what she likes about Ric now. But at the same time she says it with an edge of anxiety, not yet fully trusting her victory.

He tests it. "Of course we must."

"*You* go then," she says. Now she's no longer anxious. She

280

means it. If he wants to follow, let him follow for all she cares. But she knows he won't. She watches him for his smile of total understanding at his failure to go after Ric.

He knows she's won. He understands totally. But he won't smile.

He makes love to her, but he won't smile.

What love. Down, down, down. Marvellous, annihilating, terrible love. He kills every thought of Ric with his love. He dies of love. Down down he goes into the softness of her hand, into the great pit of blackness of her belly. She has grown vast to receive him. Does she cry out when she receives him? He doesn't know. His ears are closed, his eyes are shut as he sinks into her.

From midday when he woke, Peterson thought of the evening. He sighed with boredom. How could he bear to speak to anyone except her – or perhaps Ric.

Together they had been to a place which made the world of other people seem frighteningly grey. He would start the sort of useful interesting sentence of his daily life and let it trail into nothing because he hadn't the energy to put something so dull into words.

Together they had shared indescribable things, some bad, more good.

Four or five times he stood in his study door, knowing that now, impetuously, he must go to her. He didn't go. Evening came. Oddly, he had prepared no excuse for Nancy. To take action was no longer a compulsion. He'd learned to live with the need to act, watching it, but not acting. Did he even want an excuse, or was he half in love with his own painful need for her? Questions no longer needed answers. He could turn and turn them, watching them.

Half an hour before he should leave, he stood in the doorway to the television room and spoke to Nancy's back, where she sat sipping coffee and watching television with his neighbour's wife.

"The University Experimental Theatre Group want my help," he said with a small laugh. "A modern verse drama . . ."

"Christ!" Nancy said, but it might have been about a chihuahua held up to the camera by its owner in Mexican fancy dress.

"Oh isn't he just darling," his neighbour's wife said.

281

The phone rang.

"Aren't you going to answer?" Nancy said.

He moved sideways, watching with more and more surprise the back of his neighbour's wife's head which she hadn't for an instant turned from the screen, as if to avoid a rudeness she wouldn't be able to hide.

"We've lost him," Mrs Schuster said.

He couldn't speak.

"We know you were his friend."

It isn't happening, he thought. I'm still tripping.

"We'd like to thank you so very much."

I'm not even sorry, he thought. I don't even feel I ought to be sorry. All I feel is understanding. I understand why he did it. I understand that she is in real pain, but must hide it with these conventional words, because she doesn't believe that anyone else can ever believe in her pain for this boy, who they all know she was ashamed of.

Now he waited for the inevitable questions: we just wondered if you could throw any light . . . the suspicions she was ashamed to show: you say you last saw him that very evening . . . growing bolder as it was proved, to any fair-minded listener, that she was right to be suspicious. He didn't fear them. He didn't blame her. He understood the part he'd played and her need to accuse him. He felt the pain of every part of it. His understanding excluded fear or blame. He guessed that, even if there'd still been the chance, he wouldn't have tried to interfere, bcause it would only have produced a different network of pain and misunderstanding in which he might have lost his own understanding.

Her questions didn't come.

"Knowing how much you meant to him, we felt he'd want us to tell you right away . . ."

He walked about the house.

He stood watching the backs of their heads, so firmly turned to the screen, though they must have known he was behind them. A good thing because he wouldn't tell Nancy yet. At present he could bear no more understanding – when she grew restless and turned he told her.

"Ric. The boy we went to the Stardust with."

"Why ever did he do that?"

"Christ knows," he lied.

282

She was silent, watching a borzoi, while its owner, in hooded jelaba and rimless glasses with steel earpieces, explained its diet. On the edge of her mind hung the admission that she'd always thought him an unstable, not to say, frankly, offensive boy. She said, "I thought you had a date to write a verse drama."

"I'm rather shaken."

"You look it." Clearly he saw the pattern of the things she'd been saying to him all their life together. Outspoken, hard, they reached back, year after year, anything gentle an impossible admission of emotion. Phrases of manly joking hostility because only with these had she ever been able to show love. Years ago the love had gone, but he had no idea when because there had been no need to change these phrases of manly joking hostility.

"I wish I knew what to do." He wished he believed there was anything he should do. He wished he wanted to believe . . .

When he came at last to the library it was closed.

He walked about the streets. He saw the lights leading away over the icy prairie, and remembered how he'd wanted to follow them. For an hour, remembering her warning, he stayed away from her apartment. To go there at this time of night would be conclusive evidence. But he could call her. How idiotic to have frozen all this time before realising it. He dialled from a pay booth and she answered quickly.

"Darling, I'm sorry I was late. Something terrible's happened."

"Ah ha?"

"Ric's killed himself."

"Say! No!" she said.

"It's true." He paused, expecting her to go on exclaiming but she didn't. If she'd asked him questions – how? when? – he'd have known what to say, but it was as if she'd been able to act this single exclamation of surprise, and the silence which followed was her true comment.

"Could I come round?" he said.

There was an odd pause. "Better not."

"Because I might be seen?"

"Yeah," she said, as if it was an idea he'd conveniently given her. She said, "I'm a bit upset."

"About Ric?"

"Partly."

"About the way I stood you up at the library?"

283

"Could be."

He believed her. Quickly he rejected all the arguments – Darling, it was hardly my fault. She was upset and she blamed him. How absurd to imagine that his innocence could change that – though it might increase it.

She said, "I wouldn't be very good company."

"Oh," he said, unhappily. Dimly a worrying memory stirred.

There was several seconds' pause. He was disturbed to realise that there had never before been pauses like these in their phone calls. Always she'd hurried merrily into gaps. Often they'd stumbled over each other to fill one.

"What about tomorrow?"

"Okay."

"Same time, same place?" But how wrong to suggest it after tonight's failure. "Or shall I come to your place?"

"Okay."

"It won't be dangerous?"

"Dangerous?" she said, as if she didn't understand. "Oh I don't think so."

It puzzled him, but, knowing her far wider experience of the secrecy they must now practise, he didn't doubt that there was a good reason why her apartment would be safe tomorrow though today – and yesterday – it had been unsafe.

She wasn't at his morning class. He wasn't surprised. Intuitively, she'd known that they must stay apart till evening. How he approved of her sense of the clean way people should meet and know each other. True, it was all she ever thought about, but she was right there too. A surge of love for her filled him as he opened class discussion on *The Naked Lunch*.

That night he was fifteen minutes late at her apartment. There was no answer when he knocked. He pushed the door and was surprised when it opened. A piece of paper dropped to the floor.

"I don't like being kept waiting. J."

He sat on her mattress-bed on the floor. He picked the copy of his first novel off her shelf and began to read. A sudden agonising pain in the wrist of the arm he was leaning on tumbled him sideways. He'd accidentally set it against the scalding central heating pipe.

After half an hour she came. "Hi," she said. She moved

284

briskly about the apartment, taking off her boots, hanging her coat in a closet. She sat on the settee.

He stood and kissed her on the cheek. He held her by the wrists to lift her to him, but she didn't lift. When he let go she let her arms fall back onto her knees.

He sat on the bed. "Sorry I was late!" It was a joke. He would prove that it must be a joke.

She shrugged.

"Where did you go?"

"Out," she said. "It's not important."

"Isn't it?"

"I really *don't* like being kept waiting," she said, looking at him with an expression he didn't know, big-eyed, but not smiling, as if she had things to explain to him but must do it carefully to keep them straight to herself. He would have apologised now if he hadn't done it already – and if another worrying memory hadn't disturbed him. Surely she'd once said, "I like *you* keeping me waiting." Couldn't he picture her saying it, bouncing beside him, turning away her head as if to hide some secret happiness, but not successfully because it made her too happy?

"If you want to know, I had four large bourbons," she said.

"Why ever did you do that?" But he was relieved. It explained the slightly dizzy way she sat, as if something had hit her and she wasn't yet sure of the damage. He lifted her more firmly. He must take control. She needed his care as well as his love. This time she let him bring her to sit on the bed, but when he tried to kiss her she moved away.

"Darling, something's happened."

"When?" He'd meant to ask 'what?' but at the last moment shied from the direct question.

"Last night. No, the night before, really."

"On the trip?"

"Mm hm."

The way she said it, with sad apology for the sort of girl she was, which wasn't really sad or apologetic, brought back all his love for her. Now he forced her to kiss him. She resisted, then let him. He grew excited. His need for her became desperate. She began to need him too, he knew from the way she kissed. When he paused she moved away.

About to move after her, he asked instead, "What happened?"

285

Now it couldn't matter, because his love and need for her – not to mention her confirmed need for him – could overcome anything. He guessed now that their affair had been discovered. That she was afraid some foolish thing she'd done to make it public would drive him away. How little she understood his love. Together they would stand, in public. It was a decision which he'd made at some time during the last forty-eight hours without ever thinking about it. Again, as on the trip, he saw that she was beautiful. Her beauty amazed him. So did his luck, his love. Her round cheeked face, her bright eyes, the slight down on her upper lip . . . Rather abruptly, so that he didn't understand for a moment what was happening, she reached a pen from her lamp table, pushed him forward on the bed and leant behind him.

Turning, he saw her stretch to their score marks on the wall, and, opposite OTHERS, where there was still only the forester's half, made a big red stroke. Still leaning behind him, she sucked the end of the pen. "Let's be frank," she said, reached again and made two more big red strokes.

"So!" he said. Till he knew what it meant he felt nothing but numb fear. "Who?"

"Need you ask."

Less because it seemed likely that because they scarcely knew anyone else in common, he said, "Raphaelo?"

"Mm hm."

He was deeply relieved. He'd feared some new lover. All the disparaging things she'd said about this old one came to comfort him. "Love!" he remembered her saying. "He doesn't know what the word means."

Looking at her as she watched him anxiously, he felt not the smallest anger. How could he, when his heart overflowed with pity and forgiveness?

He never doubted what he must do to show her his forgiveness. He felt chiefly impatience that she seemed to want an interval of sternness, but he understood and pitied, too, her need not to have this lapse made unimportant by too quick forgiveness.

"When?" he asked.

"Last night."

"So you weren't at the library at all?" This idea alarmed him more than he understood.

"Oh, I was there," she said. "At first."

He believed her. But another disagreeable idea came. "So when I didn't come you called him?"

"Darling no, it was chance, it really was. We just met."

"Outside the library?" A question now came which was so unpleasant that for a second he blocked it. But he had to know. "So he was here when I called?"

"Mm hm."

He understood the odd way she'd answered. "Were you . . . ?" he began, but this question he no longer needed to ask, as he remembered her rolling away from him to reach a long tan arm to answer the forester's call.

"Did you enjoy it?" Surely here he was safe, the first and only man to satisfy her.

"You want a frank answer?"

"That's why I asked."

"Oh yes, I enjoyed it," she said with resignation, but a slight distant smile.

He thought of the final shame of asking for a comparison and rejected it angrily.

"Oh, I reckon I don't remember what it felt like," she said. "I was howling too much."

Suddenly something about that little hovering smile round her mouth maddened him. He gripped her wrist and dragged her to him. He started to pull open her blouse. He tore at it roughly, breaking a button. He pulled at her skirt and the zip split.

"Hey, let up," she said, struggling to help him but too slowly.

He made love to her with hard anger. He didn't sink into her but lay roughly on her, hurting her and wanting to hurt her. When she tried to scratch his back he held down her wrists onto the pillow above her head. When she tried to bite his shoulder still holding down both her wrists with one hand, he pressed on her neck with the other till her eyes bulged, her mouth came open and she began to make salivary retching noises in the back of her throat. An instant before he came, he let go. He'd been afraid he was hurting her.

She lay gasping. Presently she said, "Why did you do that?"

"Because I wanted to." It was a lie. He knew he'd never wanted to hurt her but only understand she wanted to be hurt.

287

"Enjoy it?" he asked casually. He was sure he didn't care. He was sure he would never again care.

She watched him as he lay beside her, looking at the ceiling. She shook her head, as if with dizzy wonder at herself. "The best."

She said, "All that bourbon, perhaps." But she couldn't escape. What she'd said first had been the truth.

She lay beside him, sometimes looking at him, sometimes getting the sheet into her mouth and chewing it.

"What's that for?"

"It's all confused," she said. "It always chews its sheet when it's confused."

"Perhaps it's always confused except when it's being laid," he said.

"Hey!" she said, looking at him with big bright eyes. "I reckon you got something there."

He didn't answer, or look at her. He began to enjoy this new off-hand way of treating her.

"You see," she said, puzzled, "I reckon it never really believes there's anything it can't get. Not if it wants it badly enough. That's the way it was with my parents. I just had to scream and scream and then I got it."

"Raphaelo?"

"Mm hm," she said.

But he was irritated by their continuous discussions of her life, loves, and psyche. It would have been nice, he thought, if she'd ever asked about his.

She leant across and kissed him on the forehead. "Darling, it was a nice trip," she said. "The nicest."

At once and without trace his sham off-handedness disappeared. He lay rigid. Though he hadn't been moving before, he had the impression that he'd been threshing casually about. He understood, but couldn't believe her. She was telling him their affair was finished. It was the unfairness he felt most: just after he'd fucked her better than ever before.

"Don't ever leave me," she'd said. "Darling, I'm around for the whole of your life, if for one purpose only," she'd said. "Jesus, I really *love* you," she'd said. It took time to believe that she didn't feel these things any more.

They'd been such confident things, not just about what she was feeling then, but about what she'd always feel. It was hard to accept that they'd never referred to any time in the future, that even when she was saying them she'd known she was

288

entitled to, not because they would always be true but because at that moment she felt them.

"Now you gotta admit I'm neurotic," she said smugly.

Each moment the gap she was making in his life grew. For months, she'd been a background to every thought he'd had. He'd been loved. Now he was no longer loved. Already he felt an outward shrivelling. So he wasn't the person he'd rashly thought himself, had actually started to grow to be.

"I meant it," she said, as if honestly puzzled. "All of it."

"What does he think?" Surely there was a chance she was deceiving herself.

"Raphaelo?" she said. "Oh he's being nice. He's actually listening when I talk to him. That's a change."

Peterson half smiled.

"Frankly, I think he'd become a bit jealous."

Peterson gave a sour laugh.

"Darling," she said. "I don't want to be a bore, but I need some sleep. You see I'm moving tomorrow."

He watched her, guessing.

"That's right, the forester's old room. Might as well save rent while I can."

He dressed. She needed love too, he thought. More, perhaps, than he did, so that as soon as she had it she had to hunt for more to prove to herself she could win it again. The idea wasn't much comfort.

She wanted it so badly that ultimately she wanted its opposite, could only love those who wouldn't love her, so that she could go on wanting it. How absurd, he thought to have believed he could satisfy her. He'd merely experienced the improbable luck of an amateur playing against professionals.

"Darling, I tried," she said. "I really tried."

It hurt him more. The idea that she'd used him for an experiment in psychic consistency. The idea that she'd brought effort, not desire, to their affair – surely it couldn't be true.

Most clearly he saw that, with her wider experience, she'd known things were ending and rushed to get there first, to avoid being left loving and not loved. It seemed no contradiction that this was also the state she most wanted.

Nor was this idea much comfort.

Now I'm really unhappy, Peterson thought. Outside as he

289

K

sat at his study desk, the evening grew dark early. Heavy cloud pressed in. But it had also grown warmer so that he guessed it was close to thawing out there in his black garden.

All day there'd been a great weight in his chest, but he hadn't played the Verdi operas he'd played four months before. They held the romanticism of hope – of a time when he'd half wanted his pain because it might be cured.

The idea that he'd never make love to her again, the empty years ahead, it was unbelievable. But he believed it. He put his head in his hands and groaned. In life he'd found one girl only. Till he'd met her he'd forgotten love and not discovered sex. How could he hope to find another? He didn't want to hope to find another.

Late in the evening he wrote to her:

"Understand is a big word but let's stay with it. What I understand is that you must run fastest from what you can't fault, but still doesn't make you happy. Because the fact you can't face is that there may not be any happiness. That the whole thing's an illusion. And that what's wrong with your civilisation isn't that it's *cultivated* this illusion but that it hasn't systematically uncultivated it.

"There wasn't much need once. Life was too obviously short and unpleasant . . .

"It's the new American dream. First the West, till there wasn't any more. Then to be rich and successful till you saw through that. Then to be happy. Wait. There's worse to come. American women were allowed to dream too – equal rights. Who said men were logical? It's nonsense. They have doubts all the way. They keep looking left and right and wondering if it's worthwhile. They avoid seeing the point because they suspect it may not *be* the point. Not women. Singleminded, blinkered, logical. If happiness is the object, let's get it. Not just some but plenty. Not poor quality stuff but the happiest happiness. Happiness for *me*. I owe it to myself. The one thing they can't allow is that the whole thing may be an illusion. Because when they've got it they won't want it.

"So that's how I see you: the American female, rushing blinkered towards your private discovery. Gaderene swine towards a cliff top, say. It's a good image because the big discovery is just emptiness and the long drop. Also because all the grunting and jostling gives the right idea of the sort of fun you have on the way – I'm being offensive – or rather inaccurate and so not offensive enough. There are resting places, which you try to convince yourself *are* the top, where you genuinely try to feel happy. But the minute this happiness falls below your ideal – perpetual ecstacy – and you're bored or at best contented, and the idea suggests itself that there may not be such a thing as perpetual ecstacy, you start to rush still more madly, on and up towards the top, because somewhere up there there *must* be happiness otherwise what have they all been telling you."

As he wrote there were strange scratching noises close to the house which he couldn't understand. He thought it might be snowing, but the single light he could see out there through the blackness was clear. Perhaps it was raining. He left the letter and went to bed.

Nancy was there, already asleep, he thought. He undressed in the bathroom and climbed carefully under the sheet. She didn't stir. From the darkness, without any warning, she said loudly, "Early tonight."

It was so unexpected that he gave a convulsive start.

"Not particularly."

"Having trouble?"

He lay rigid, his heart pounding. What could she mean? Surely it wasn't possible that she knew. The care he'd always taken. No no, it was impossible. It was his guilt. The obvious meaning became clear to him.

"With that play . . . ?"

She didn't even speak, just gave one sharp bark of laughter. With total conviction, he knew that she knew. For weeks, months, she'd probably known. Each evening when he'd carefully explained where he was going she'd been secretly laughing at him – not even laughing because she despised him too much.

No wonder she'd said no word about his untypical continence. She'd been laughing, despising . . . Most terrible of all was the idea that he might now try – actually wanted to try – to make love to her.

For ten minutes he lay shivering with this idea. That he might try – and she might refuse. He got out of bed and hurried to his study.

He put on pants and sweater and sat at his desk. Odd and

panicky feelings came to him. It was as if he'd reached some point where there was no way to turn.

"Understand is a big word," he read, "but let's stay with it . . ." He scrumpled the pages violently and forced them deeply into his trash basket.

He sat staring out of his window. The single house light across his garden had gone. Perhaps it was later than he thought. Outside there was nothing except black night, and those strange scratching noises. He felt trapped. He felt that they had driven him into this corner which made him panic, and that it would be their fault if he did things which surprised them. He stood. He didn't know what he was going to do, but had an idea that it might be in the bedroom where Nancy lay, not even bothering to think about him . . . On his desk, in a neat blue pile he saw his notebooks.

Staring at them, his thoughts moved out across the town to that fish-tank apartment room which he knew so well. Or was it there that he would surprise them? – but tonight, he remembered, she wouldn't be there.

His eyes refocussed his notebooks. He wanted to refocus them but struggled not to. Obscurely he felt the importance of this struggle, because he would never again be given so clear a choice between living and dying on the one hand, and dying but staying alive on the other. The longer he hesitated the better he knew which he would choose.

Presently he sat and drew the notebooks towards him. Later he opened and began to read them. Still later he began to write :

"Some hours ago, Miss Hopping, you were in real trouble."

"Oh yeah," she said distantly. "Yeah, yeah," she said with returning enthusiasm, sitting up on the bed, staring bright-eyed at him. "Honey, I gotta sorta confession. Didn't I tell you I was divorced? Well it's true. The sickening thing is, I'm married as well. To someone else."

"And your current husband's plotting to shoot us in bed together," Morrison said hopefully.

"Honey, it's not as easy as that. He's a Turk . . ." She looked up with a hurt smile at his explosion of laughter. "He's in jail and the Turkish Mafia want me to bail him out – for five thousand bucks. You see, I'm financially responsible for

him. I married him to get him an immigrant's visa. Honey,
I really *needed* that money."

"The five thousand?"

"Christ no, the seven-fifty I got for marrying him."

Morrison grew more and more charmed. "Does he have
to be bailed?"

"Honey, it's not just the Mafia. It's the State Department.
They've been here this morning at dawn – well eleven, I guess.
You know what I'm like then. They don't even say who they
are, just stand around asking impertinent questions, like when
did I last see my husband?and why am I down here at school
under another name?

" 'Look,' I tell them, 'what would you do if every goddam
time you were asked you had to say you were Mrs Kusingouppi.
They don't seem to buy that one. Then they see your photo, the
one I cut off the back of your jacket when someone wasn't
looking. 'Who's this?' they say. 'A teacher of mine,' I say.
That really makes them mad. They think I'm stringing them
along. I guess it's your hat. All this time I'm shivering in just
a blanket and not another thing. You know what? When I go
to the bathroom one of them comes and stands outside the door
to make sure I don't escape. That really scares me. I'll tell you
what saves me. I make them some Greek coffee in the pot I got
to prove to Socrates what a good Greek wife I'd make. When
they see it they say, 'Who gave you that?' 'My husband,' I say,
quick as a flash. 'Oh, so it's a real marriage,' they say."

"This husband," Morrison said, "do you happen to have met
him?"

"Of course, honey. Didn't I tell you, I married him. That's
when I met him."

"For the first time?"

"I was broke, honey, I really was."

"And the last time?"

"Yeah, yeah," she said, suddenly impatient at his slowness.
"He was quite sweet, actually."

Morrison laughed loudly and asked for more, suppressing
the first tenuous desire to lay her again.

"They've only just gone when these Mafia come on the line.
They've been calling ever since. Christ, they're *real* scarey. They
don't ever give their names. They just go on and on. 'Pay up,
kiddy.' When one gets tired he turns me over to another. 'You

293

just pay up, girly, and we won't be troubling you.' I'd pay if I could. I really would."

Around five am he drove home. Over the grey streets and acres of empty grey parking lot, out across the prairie, a pink dawn was coming for another day of mind-confusing heat. The air was still tepid from yesterday and the thermometer in his porch read eighty-eight as he leant against the doorway, jabbing with his key. Bending to peer for its hole, he found himself staring out through his porch's insect mesh to his neighbour's house, where for a hopeful instant he believed he'd seen her little-girl face with halo of curlers as she lifted the drapes to check on his movements. "I'm the wife of the Chairman of Home Economics," he sung, now bass, now soprano – as he stumbled, drunk with tiredness, around his grey house. At the stair head he paused to face Don Quixote in his niche, stared hard at him preparing something offensive, but when it didn't come, passed on with a threatening snarl. Three hours later Winnie was shaking him out of deep sleep.

"Call for you."

"Morrison here." Elbows on the desk, cheeks supported by both hands, one of which also held the receiver, he considered whether he might lay his head down there among the silted papers and still answer, tried it experimentally, half slipped off his chair and was startled to hear his neck give a loud but entirely painless click.

As a result he was fully half awake, turning it cautiously left and right, realising with relief that he could still feel his toes, when he heard her say, "It's me, honey."

Only silence could show his surprise.

"Honey, are you there? It's me, Olga."

"I'm here. Where are *you*?"

"I'm at home. At least I will be. Could you come over?"

"You know what time it is?"

"Darling, things are getting bad."

"Any time," Morrison began. "Any day, ever ready to serve . . ."

"You're a chum," she said and to his surprise, but secret delight, hung up on him.

He staggered about the house, dressing, washing, and drinking coffee. In under-pants only, he found himself in the bathroom, holding a steaming cup in one hand and a toothbrush in the

294

other. How had it happened?... In half an hour he was ready. His phone rang.

"Coming, coming," he said into it experimentally.

"Well that's sure good to know." The voice was male. It was Butch Steiner.

"Excuse me, I have an appointment," but the temptation to listen for more was too great.

"I won't keep you, Professor Morrison. I got just one thing to say. That story I said I was writing for you. Well it's a load of crap. I'm not."

"You just thought I'd like to know..." but it was too good to interrupt.

"No I didn't, Professor Morrison. I just reckoned *I* wanted to tell you. Another thing I want to tell you is how I won't be writing any more stories for you. I'm dropping the course."

"Oh come now..."

"Because I don't need it any more. You've really helped me."

"Yes?" Morrison became curious.

"By not giving a shit."

Morrison became suspicious. "What about?"

"Me."

The astonishing idea occurred to Morrison that he was only partly being sarcastic.

"All the rest do. I make them. It's too fucking easy. Not you. You don't give a shit about my personal problems."

"Well now..."

"Or my writing."

"Oh, come now..."

"You wouldn't give a shit if I went out and shot myself."

"Are you planning to?"

"You can't even make yourself *sound* interested. You don't care *which* I answer."

Morrison gave it up. "If you say so."

"Well frankly, I don't give a shit whether or not you give a shit."

Idly, Morrison began to make puns.

"That's what you've taught me. Not to give a fucking shit what you or any other fucker thinks."

The focal point of our faecal conversation, Morrison thought; the odour of ordure...

295

"So even if you cared you wouldn't be getting to know what I plan on doing."

"Maybe," Morrison said. "Hey there, you listen to me, Butch Steiner . . ."

But now there was no sound in his receiver. For the second time in forty minutes he'd been hung up on.

"Honey, I had to get out." Even now she didn't seem properly back, but stood in her doorway, as if to stop him passing. "The moment you left they began to call again. It was just as if they knew. Was that scarey!"

For the first time he believed she might be more frightened than enjoying herself. "Where did you go?"

"To my old chum Socrates. I reckoned he might know what to do. Hell, it's the same part of the world. Greece, Turkey, what's the difference? And what do you think? He's high as a kite. Stoned. Totally useless." She paused to stare at him, big-eyed, a little uncertain. "So then I try some too. Gee, that really is something. You interested?"

They drove across campus, past sidewalks thick with students hurrying for their nine o'clock classes. Weird to see this different world busily beginning another day. He had the odd sensation that he and Olga in his noisy red Triumph, though not invisible, were unseen because all their eyes were on the ground. In a northern suburb, close to the ghetto, they went down outside cellar steps.

"They keep moving around. This is where they were last. You wanta see a real meth-head's room?" Without knocking she went in.

Gradually the room came clear and he saw four people among what looked like the refuse of a furniture warehouse from which everything of value had been sent out. Two boys lay full-length on a double mattress a quarter covered with newspaper. A girl squatted cross-legged against a wall, her long black hair hiding all but a thin vertical line of her face. Spread in a yellow armchair, legs wide, like a big pale sack was Socrates.

The yellow chair was the only whole piece of furniture in the room and looked improbably clean and neat till he saw a single coiled spring rising through a split in its seat exactly between his legs. No doubt he was sitting in this sprawled way to fit round it. His big white arms with fine black hairs were laid along its

296

arms and his hands hung with soft fingers over their ends. Only this chair rose more than a foot from the floor, and the rest of the room was unevenly littered with open cardboard boxes of books, crockery and old clothes. Among these stood empty half bottles of vodka and opaque plastic jars of male toilet lotions.

"If it isn't Olga come back for more," Socrates said.

"You're telling me," she said. "Come arn, gi'me."

"What a wonderful thing a head is," the further boy on the mattress said.

"He's really away," the nearer boy explained.

"For getting all mixed up," the first said and went on grinning at the ceiling. After a long pause he said, "And turning all back to front."

The long-haired girl put white pills in metal-foil, crunched them with the heel of her shoe against the wooden head of an African tourist carving, shook the powder in a small bottle till it dissolved, and passed it to Socrates. Olga turned up her forearm, wrapped a rubber tube round her upper arm and tightened it till the vein inside her elbow stood out. Socrates filled a syringe by rubber fountain-pen sack, gripped her wrist, dabbed the vein with after-shave lotion and pressed the point at it.

"Getting blunt," the long haired girl said.

"Sure way to spread syphilis," the nearer boy on the bed explained.

"What are *you* doing with scar tissue?" Socrates said, still poking and pressing.

"It gives him a symbolic thrill," Olga said, but now it went in and she turned quickly away and bit her lower lip.

Her pretty tan arm, Morrison thought, the way she holds it, fist clenched, turned up to him, the way she sucks in her breath with that quick hiss of pain. That great white sack of a man doing it to her, the way he's now drawn an inch of blood up into the tube before squeezing it back into her vein and she's turned to watch it happening – I could never have invented anything so deliciously nasty. Then what were those other feelings in his chest, these tears behind his eyes which he never remembered before? And what was this astonishing palpitating hard?

297

Distracting himself with an effort which surprised him, he said, "Is it acid?"

"What d'you think we are, addicts or something?" the girl said.

"If you want a love-in you've come to the wrong witch-doctor," Socrates said. "This is no paisley peep-show. This is for real."

"Speed," the near boy on the bed explained.

"You wanta mess your mind up or something?" the far boy said.

They were all laughing at him, Morrison was sure, and laughed with them, then, from the serious way they went on looking at him, had the even odder idea that they might not be laughing.

"Any doctor will prescribe it," Socrates said.

"It's just not healthy, your attitude," Olga said.

"Who prescribed it for you?" Morrison said, an improbable suspicion starting.

"My shrink," Socrates said. "For slimming. My problem is self-induced sloth."

"Your shrink?" Morrison said, much more suspicious.

"He calls them Conception Pills," Socrates said. "His sense of humour stinks – but then he's German."

"What's his name?" Morrison asked, now really alarmed.

Socrates turned his big doggy but lecherous eyes on Morrison. "You've seen him at parties. He's at every party you've ever been to. Dr Ifitz . . ."

"Christ, I knew it," Morrison shouted.

Mixed in this loud shout which was far noisier than he'd meant and filled the low basement room, was delight of the sort that pleased him most – at his own appropriate misfortune – and defiance. They, too, seemed aware that something accidental and interesting had happened, and watched him. With an odd feeling of finally tipping out of control, he rolled up his sleeve and held out his arm.

High in this sense, a high he now realised he'd been climbing to for weeks, perhaps months, he scarcely felt the needle and gave himself to a moment of coldness round his heart with a heavy shiver but no hesitation. More with impatience. Sitting among the cardboard boxes, his head starting to buzz, he understood again that the battle was on, that since he'd laid Sally from

298

Texas he'd returned to pretending there was no battle, but that he could never again deceive himself in this way. He was impatient for it to start.

And there, squatting on the mattress corner, was Olga, grinning like a cat. All of them, back with their heads as they'd been before he'd come, now sat with fixed grins at what was happening inside. But Olga's was different. It told him that the battle wasn't news to her, that what *would be* news to her – but he certainly wasn't going to tell her – was that *he* now knew it. Her grin – how had he failed to understand? – was entirely about his ignorance. Little did she know ... The buzzing grew louder and now came a sense of great digestive comfort, as if he'd just finished the most satisfying meal he'd ever eaten, but with none of the weight of food. His molars clamped together. The corners of his mouth twisted up. He was grinning too.

In half an hour he caught the rhythm. His feet beat the floor. If there wasn't one in the air his mind invented it. They beat as if they could go on beating for ever. Let's go. For the first time he understood. His whole mind and body demanded it. Let's go, let's go.

It was a grin of action and power. All morning he grinned at her as they drove about town. She grinned back, then turned away to grin to herself, but uneasily, sometimes glancing at him. Little did she know ...

As they drove he had the dizzy sense of being in control but only just. Downhill they were going, without brakes, cornering with screaming tyres as he swung the wheel to avoid each new collision. As they went his mind shouted with delight but he made no sound. And she was shouting with delight too, he knew, but he watched her for the moment when she would shout with fear.

They were on the platform of a grain elevator, looking across 100 miles of shimmering prairie. They were at the university airport, the brown field stretching to the horizon in banks of mirage, the little red planes crossing and recrossing the blue sky, like a pre-war summer air-display. But no one could find the pilot who was to take them up. Come arn. Let's go.

They were in another basement. The small white pills, crushed in silver foil, the inch of blood in the syringe, her hiss of pain, her teeth nipping her lower lip, her quick glance to be sure she was being watched. What are we waiting for?

299

Always he watched her grinning at her private joke,
They were on the uncompleted frame of a six-storey apartment building. Concrete floors, concrete stairways, but no walls,
only a seventy-foot drop an inch from his toes to the baked
mud field. Railyards, a car cemetery, highway hoardings, the
neon fringe of service stations, gaudy and drab, rural routes
lined by the untidy ranch houses of prosperous citizens with
horse riding and sail-boat hobbies . . . Let's go, let's go.
Sometimes there were two cars, sometimes three. Sometimes
she was with him, sometimes not. She was with him as they
touched a hundred, already ten miles out of town on the eastern
interstate. He'd rolled back the hood and she held herself up
into the airstream, her eyes half closed, her short brown hair
quivering like something mechanical, but she still grinned.
"Hey, these Turkish Mafia, shall we fix them?"
"You're right, let's go."
He pressed the pedal to the plates. Hundred and five, hundred and ten. He drove with a sense of invulnerability. Nothing
could stop him. Tiredness was inconceivable. Monotony – how
could he ever be bored when every idea in his head so delighted
him. Fear – if the car tilted, swayed, smashed, the seconds before
impact would provide such an understanding about life that he
believed he would reach extinction without one instant of regret,
going out as he was meant in an explosion of total conception.
Seventy miles from town, they stopped at a pay booth and he
called home.
Winnie answered. Winnie, whose love for him prevented her
ever giving him one smile or word of approval . . . Lillian came.
"I've been called away, dear. Urgent. A possible film
contract . . ."
"Your pyjamas . . ." she began.
Pyjamas historical, pyjamas racial, pyjamas social, classes who
wore them, age-groups who didn't. Pyjamas philological – what
a word – pyjamas erotic – nylon, rubber, corduroy. The astonishing habit of taking off one lot of clothes to go to bed in another,
the fact, as clear as any of these, that she'd ceased to think
about his pyjamas before she'd said the word, that they'd emerged
as a meaningless exclamation, a sort of gasp of fright. Each of
these possible directions for pyjamas to lead him came at the
same instant, each fascinated him. Holding them all in his mind,
he could choose from them as if they were labelled drawers in a

300

chest, knew that while explaining the contents of one he could hold in his mind the knowledge of the contents of all the others and of where this one fitted into the total pyjama pattern . . .

"Your dress rehearsal . . . ?"

In his mind came the total pattern of his excuses to Lillian. The first inspired invention, the development of the fantasy – Nine Oh Eleven, Apartment Oh Seven – , the moment when it had become self-propagating, seducing him into the invention of quite unnecessary dress rehearsals, performance dates, to set himself these challenges for later scrambling escapes. The moment when he'd guessed that for weeks Lillian had guessed they were excuses, that for weeks her perverse love for him had made her chiefly anxious in case his invention so involved him that he *wouldn't* be able to escape. Even now he believed she wished she could withdraw her question in case it brought him to a stuttering silence in which neither of them could go on pretending . . . An instant later, devastating in its final authority, he saw that Lillian *had* believed his excuses.

It was a far worse shock. She'd taken this ludicrous joke about a play seriously. And he understood that he'd wanted to make it ludicrous to humiliate her, by making her believe his more and more absurd story.

"Hey," he began. It was so utterly marvellous that he had to tell her, lay before her in their complementary perfection these two alternative explanations, show her how, with a tiny flick of the mind he'd changed from believing one to believing the other. Poised for him to use, a thousand words of explanation were ready to flow out, perfectly chosen, with perfect emphasis. She – and he – would gasp with lunatic joy at his lucidity . . . Olga was jolting him, had seen him struck silent in admiration of his own mental fluency.

"It's postponed, dear. Later. Much later. Don't worry. Love."

Mid-afternoon they were on the State City expressways. Those bastards. He'd fix them. He felt no alarm, just invincible power. To pick up any word they said and argue from it, leaving them bemused. He didn't even want her to repeat the story. The instant they'd spoken he'd see it laid before him as tidy as a diagram, each point at which they might be lying labelled with the alternative truth. Teeth set, grinning and grinning, he knew his power, knew, to make it more powerful, its possible limits. When she offered him white pills he swallowed two quickly. "Which exit?"

"Honey, I'm not sure."

"What's their address?"

"You don't imagine they wave that around, do you?"

He swung sharply into the right lane, cornered into a side street and parked.

"What's their phone number?"

"Honey, they're an underground organisation, didn't I tell you?"

A glorious shout of laughter began inside him. "So when these guys arranged your second marriage they just materialised, up through the sidewalk . . . ?"

"It was fixed by a friend, but he's in Afghanistan. I once met one of them at a bar. I think he was at the wedding – I don't remember much. I was a bit stoned."

Marvellous! Through the underpass, on to the opposite lanes of the expressway. Eighty, ninety.

"Honey, they have cops in this country – Hey, where are we going?"

"South."

"Oh yes?" she said. "Hey, yes, YES." She gripped his arm with both hands, staring up at him. "Not South City?"

Still holding his arm she stared ahead, giving her head little shakes of wonder. The rightness of this choice grew and grew in her mind, he knew, from the way she now dropped his arm but kept glancing at him with happy but increasingly fearful excitement.

All the hot summer night they drove south. It was the most astonishing night of his life. They scarcely spoke, but seemed locked in intense contact. They were locked in a fight – he could think of no other word – which had no movement or words but seemed pure conflict. He knew almost nothing about it except that they were together in this rushing night, alone at last – of course they fought. Sometimes he had the sense that she had grown enormous beside him. She filled the car. She filled the whole dark night he was driving through. The white headlight cone he followed was a single tunnel through the great black night of her, but it grew narrower all the time as from all sides she flowed into it. She was filling this tunnel in rolling waves of black fog. The vision was so intense that when the lights of a passing car broke it, he was astonished to see her, small and contained by his side, for an instant couldn't connect her with this other great person he'd been driving through with growing panic.

Then she was going far away, leaving him alone, and this filled him with a different alarm. Faster and faster she dwindled to a doll, a pebble, a tiny point. He must go after her, but he *wouldn't*, but he *must*. Astonishingly, above the car noise, he heard a straining groan, and realised it had been forced from his own chest.

By dawn they were in another country. The priarie had gone and there were low hills with shabby homesteads. The small towns they went farting past at eighty on elevated interstates were a washed-out, dusty purple. There were outcrops of rock in the fields – but as always no people, as if Americans could only bear to touch the earth by machine.

"Honey, I need a shower."

He swung down an exit road, cruised along a motel complex : Holiday Inn, Howard Johnson, Starlight Motel, Sunshine Motel . . . He parked by an office window, booked and paid.

But he couldn't sit there while she showered, walked about the nearby shopping centre. The sun rose beside an A and P food liner, red and round, through the ruins of a forest, but the air was already as soft as tepid cottonwool, he realised, when the automatic doors of an IGA breathed an air-conditioned sigh at him. McBrides ahead. Suddenly he'd gone in, was buying a razor, holding up the five green stamps with a wonder he tried to share with the red-head assistant – with thickly coated acne – but she avoided his eyes and hurried to her coffee machine. And there, like a miracle offering from the New World, just when the problem had become serious, were whole shelves of pressurised shaving foam. Regular, mentholated, oil-based, jumbo, – the foam of your choice – he bought one arbitrarily, carried it back . . .

"Look, a genuine American miracle." He put it on the dressing table.

She stood naked in the shower doorway, arms raised to saw her back with a scarlet towel. Bare soft shoulders, soft arms, breasts as neatly round as half grapefruit – but twice the size – held taut by her raised arms . . . "You never heard of con-centrated shaving foam? Just *where* were you dragged up?"

303

Sweating from his stroll, he pulled off his shirt, undid his shoes, let his pants fall.

"What do you want with that stuff anyway, you old hedgehog, for christsake . . . ?"

At the same instant they were both lunging for it, but his pants, still round an ankle, hindered him, and by the time he was free of them she had the cap off, met him with a jet which went half over his head, half into his hair. Nothing to do but take her by the wrist, closing his eyes against more jets which now went flying around like a scented snowstorm and throw her on her back on the bed. Her grip shaken loose, he grabbed it, stood beside her, still holding her down by one wrist, playing it on her like a fire extinguisher.

But now she didn't struggle, lay squinting at it piling into a nine-inch mountain on her stomach, "Hey, look at that," gave a soft squirm of her arse on the bed. He let go her wrist to change aim to those fine grapefruit – at once she was off the bed, snatching it from him, beginning to squirt him from neck to knees.

He stood still, letting her do it. He stretched luxuriously, arms bent above his shoulders, leant an elbow against the wall. Now she was covering his private parts in a dripping foamy mass. Through it a great erection rose.

"Hey, down there," she shouted.

He gave a huge eye-closing yawn. She squirted it into his mouth.

He choked, spat, gripped her, knocking the can across the room and pushed her onto the bed. The white foam slithered and squelched between them. He wallowed in it.

"Now I need another shower," she called from the bed.

Working carefully in the bathroom, he didn't answer.

"You great brute," she called. " – hey, what you doing in there?"

"Shaving."

"Christ!" She padded to watch. "Good Lord!" It really shocked her. "You might have asked permission."

"You think so?"

Presently it was gone. Gobs of foam and curly carrotty hair blocked the basin plughole. Though it was slyly done, it was a victory, he was sure. Why should he want a beard now? The time for acting was past.

304

"Like it?" he asked, as if he cared.

"I'll be letting you know," she said, back on the bed, smoking with one hand, working the screw cap off the pill bottle with the other where she'd propped it on her navel. "Try some of these. They're remarkable."

They swallowed three each, drank coffee at the drug store and drove south.

The country changed again. They were between heavy green trees, with trunks wrapped thickly in green creeper, and branches hung with streamers of pale moss. Mile after mile these trees shut them in, and he only once saw, half hidden, a line of low shacks with Negro children playing on the dusty ground.

Abruptly, mid-afternoon, the trees ended and stretches of grassy water reached to the horizon with circling flocks of small white birds, and red-winged blackbirds perched on reed clumps, and once a white heron up to his knees who paused from fishing to watch them. By early evening they were crossing the lake causeway. First the outer suburbs of ranch houses and bougainvillaea, then the noisy streets of street cars and the bright lights of the city. His excitement grew. The preliminaries were over. They had arrived.

"Honey, I don't care where so long as I can get a tan." At the heart of the city's tourist strip they registered in an extravagant hotel with roof garden and swimming pool.

"Mr and Mrs Maurice Peterson," he lied. It was unplanned, as if at the moment he'd spoken the words had been fed to him.

Shivering with exhaustion, his jaws, if he relaxed their set, knocking together, he lay on his back on one of the twin beds. The sheets were mauve, the carpet black, the towels in the bathroom scarlet.

"Why did you do that?"

"Isn't adultery illegal in this country? You should know."

She laughed, playing with the small bottle of pills, not opening them.

"Maybe you've forgotten, I have an identity problem."

"You sure do," she said, unscrewing the lid to sniff them, glancing quickly at his naked face. "*And* you're a marine biologist."

Dawn came as Peterson wrote—the strangest he had ever

305

known. Hour after hour it seemed to hesitate, more night than day. Out there in his grey garden something astonishing had happened. He began to see that every branch and twig was hung with ice. They sagged in shapes they'd never taken before. They formed a crazy world of giant ice combs.

Presently there were several heavy rolls of thunder which shook his window, and a bright flash of lightning above the telegraph wires, hung also with a fringe of four-inch icicles. A strong wind began to blow and almost at once rain was falling hard, splashing on the concrete paths, blowing in a sudden gust against the house. Then there was quiet again except for the softly falling rain and the slight swaying of the big ice-covered fir across his garden.

Noises below in the house, the high tones of surprise as they noticed too. In a gap of silence he hurried down for coffee, fetched it from the kitchen – its doors wide where they'd run out to look – carried it up to his desk. At nine the trees began to break.

All day as he wrote their branches broke. First a single crack, echoing like a shot from the houses round the park, then a fire-like crackling of splintering wood, overtaken quickly by their downward ice-coated rush. Each time it happened he broke into sweat. Sometimes a heavy thud as they hit the ground, once a hollow clonk as one struck a car roof. At ten his lights went out.

Through the half-light day, in a room which now grew colder each hour, he wrote on.

Strip was the word, every second doorway a glimpse of another naked girl in g-string with frilly tassel hung from each nipple, in the shop windows do-it-yourself sequin-covered strip-kits, each with its bottle of spirit gum, down both sidewalks the sluggish stream of tourists, hung with cameras, clustering to peer, sucking bright red drinks through straws, wearing comic moustaches and straw hats. Others came slowly past in Surreys with fringed canopies and top-hatted negro drivers, obstructing whole streets of others who sat in traffic blocks of loaded buses, their engines throbbing diesel fumes. It delighted him even though he now walked in a dizzy haze of exhaustion, no pills for four hours, tonight he must sleep.

And it delighted her, "Come arn, come arn, you dog-on-heat,

306

I'm hungry." When they reached Dino's, "Now for some serious sensuality."

But she couldn't eat. Bouillabaisse, she had one mouthful. Pamplone in a bag, she undid one brittle end of the baked paper and picked at a fishy shoulder. "Must come down to enjoy all this goddam food," she said, making him certain that she'd swallowed more when he'd last seen her playing with the pill bottle.

Exhaustion crumpled him but she talked with a bright alertness, as if she'd just woken, as if her talking worked on her like an added drug. "So there I am, bopping along, thinking all the time he doesn't know I've seduced his roommate, not once but half a dozen times . . ."

Avocado à la Créole, crab meunière – if she was too high to eat, he was too near collapse. Suddenly he was laughing at their total inability to force down one more mouthful of these delicacies – food he'd missed for two years in this country of salads floating in vinegar, butter-soft steaks without flavour, deep deep fried Kentucky chicken flavoured with old old brown oil. But she stared at him in surprise. "What's so funny about that?"

He shook his head, words coming into his mind only with terrible effort, one at a time, unconnected, as if the last two days and a night had exhausted the supply.

"Only guy I've known who was a real sensualist. 'Doesn't that *smell* good,' he'd say. 'Feel that,' he'd say. And when you felt it, he'd say, 'No, *feel* it.' It was indecent, it really was. If you knew what was going on. It was like he was having one public orgasm after another."

"*You* knew?"

"Sure I knew. Well one night when I'm low, I call this guy up. I've always kinda liked him. And he comes over and we agree, why go out to see who's around when we can do it ourselves, so let's not pretend we're having an affair, but just go to bed for the fun of it.

"Well what do you think, right at the start, when he's just getting inside, we both have the giggles. He just can't go on he's giggling so much. We lie there side by side, getting these great bursts of giggles. In the end we never do make love. Just go to sleep. Explain that."

Like a huge static weight, his ideas shifted an inch as he pushed at them, then rolled back. He believed he understood.

307

More accurately, he believed there were attitudes in his mind which could have led to understanding if he could ever have shifted them.

"Hell, we both wanted the same thing, what was wrong?"

"That's it," he said, and at once forgot why. Instead, he began a rapid erection, wanted to hurry through the meal and back to their room, wanted her desperately but with a sharp alarm that unless it happened quickly he might die of exhaustion first.

"That was right after I come back from this Freedom Summer lark," she said. "I reckon I was a bit unbalanced."

She described the trip. She described how she'd gone on this boy's motorcycle because of this other boy who was the expedition leader, who she was crazy about. She described her discovery that he only liked black girls and how she'd worn dark make up and had her hair frizzed. "You know what he told me : 'Honey, give up. They *smell* different.'

"You know what really scared me. I found I was starting to *believe* all that freedom jazz. I mean, it's one thing a guy refusing to screw you, but when he starts screwing your mind instead – then it's time to quit."

Back through the old-town strip he staggered while she bounced gaily. Piles of vomit in the gutters among the corn husks, melon rinds and beer cans. Now it was a better carnival. A party of five, arm in arm, in paper hats, singing and striding, none of them ever wanting to go in the same direction at the same moment so that their shoulders must be suffering continual heavy jerks, though because they were drunk they would only feel the damage next morning. But an abortive carnival, coming to its climax in patches instead of as a whole.

As soon as they reached their room she shut herself in the bathroom and he waited, arse propped on a table. Five seconds later he was toppling, eyes shut, head already sunk as low as his shoulders, only saving himself by a wild lunge forward. At this instant she came out and as a result they seemed to slam together in a more violent kiss than he'd meant or she'd expected.

They swayed about, sat, then lay on her bed. Tonight he must extend these preliminaries to prove that he could, but, lying on her, both still dressed, he again found his eyes shutting, his mind drifting into dream. The longer he persisted the less

308

excited he became. Even the decent erection he'd started with dwindled, collapsed.

The moment this happened he felt a panic which set his heart racing and he tried to make use of this different excitement as a substitute for the others. But it passed quickly too, and they lay side by side, looking at the ceiling, not moving. Her head was on his arm above the elbow – sending it to sleep, as if it had taken this decision independently. Her elbow stuck painfully into his lower ribs. The longer it stayed there the deeper the hole it seemed to be making, one inch, two inches, a great crater in his side.

"Honey, let's sleep."

He woke with a shock, cut her short with a big mouth-stopping kiss.

"Honey, you're exhausted."

"Say that again," he said, reblocking her mouth, at the same time unbuttoning her shirt.

She held it together and rolled away. When he came after her she turned her head away. "Honey, there's a problem."

"Problem?"

"You won't believe it. You can't possibly."

"Why not?"

"Freud and all that."

"Try and we'll see."

"I've forgotten The Pill."

It was good news, there was no doubt. Now he could be loving without the alarming anxiety that he might fail to perform, or fall asleep on the job. At the same time his escape seemed too lucky. Was she testing him? Droooping and crumpled as he was, he knew he should protest loudly, pull at his hair, glare at her with blood-shot lecherous eyes, blame her for her idiotic mistake – but could he blame her? Suddenly he realised that he was really worried: not because she'd forgotten it, but because she was apologising.

"You could hardly be expected ... We were just driving round town."

"That's right, I couldn't, could I," she said brightly. But something seemed to worry her again. "Anyway, there was only one left. So, Professor Morrison," giving his chest a punch, "you'd have had to let up anyway. And about time! Hell, even the best machines gotta rest once in a while."

"Is that so?"

"Honey, what'yer want, a blood bath or something? Look, you stoopid old biologist, it's fertilisation we gotta fix, not ovulation."

He told her the story of the rich son in Paris and his bills to his father for duck-shooting.

"Trust an Englishman," she said. "A comic story for every occasion. It's sad, damn it. Suffer, can't you. I am."

The odd thing was, she didn't seem to be.

"Honey, I'll get some tomorrow. Promise."

"Don't you need a doctor's prescription?"

"You think a little thing like that's going to stop me?"

"How long's the gap?"

"Five or six days. We might cut down on it."

For the first time he understood the seriousness of what she was saying. He was shocked and still more determined not to show it. "Why not let me add them when I cable my bank? 'SEND URGENTLY, TWO THOUSAND BUCKS, TWENTY-ONE PILLS.' It's the new currency, didn't you know?" Five or six days alone with her, unable to lay her. That was bad, bad. He told her the story of the Chinese keeper of owls and the lizard.

She groaned and went to the bathroom, grinning back from the door.

He meant only to take off his shirt, but at once he was dragging off the rest of his clothes in a frenzied rush, as if his body had finally rejected the control of his mind. Shivering heavily, though the room was at seventy-five, he fell into bed, pulled the sheet to his hair and began to dream.

She was beside him and they were driving through a great forest with trailers of moss. The trailers grew thicker, began to reach out across the road. "Come arn, come arn," she said, encouraging him, but not hopefully because they both knew that the strength which had been in his beard had been transferred to these trailers of Spanish moss . . .

He woke, astonished to find the lights still on, the room silent. Could she possibly still be in the bathroom? He tried to call her but no sound came, convincing him, from his experience of other dreams, that he hadn't woken but was still dreaming. Because he knew this, he was now certain that he'd woken. Again he tried to call – and shocked himself awake by an awful straining croak in his throat – proving that he'd still been asleep. The lights were on but the room wasn't empty. She was sitting on the edge of her bed, grinning down at him. He believed she'd just said something to him and was waiting for an answer. He grinned and closed his eyes . . .

A second later he knew she'd turned out the light and the room was black. Distant sounds came from the street five floors below, insulated by the double windows and closed drapes. The air-conditioning hissed faintly. Now the ideas of the night before came back and she began to fill the shut-in black room. Her great black shape flowed into every corner. He struggled to breathe. She was filling all the air space. Somewhere at the centre was her head, deeply sunk into her hunched black shoulders, a great black bat . . . He woke in a heavy sweat, his heart pounding. There she was, in her bed, dimly visible, the sheet wrapped under her arms like a sarong, showing all her bare creamy shoulders.

But as soon as his eyes shut she was coming up out of the bed, filling the black room . . .

He thought of the two bottles of pills, the Conception and the Anti-conception pills, the ones she's brought and the ones she'd forgotten. He must count them to find out if it was true that she only had one left. He was counting them. The bottle was full. Thirty, forty, fifty, she'd lied – but he'd only dreamed he was counting them . . .

Now he was truly out of bed, bumping his shin on a chair as he felt his way to the bathroom – he stood dead still in the blackness, his bare feet on the soft bathroom pile – they would be the wrong pills, of course, the Conception pills. It was the Anti-conception pills he must count, the bottle in which she claimed there was only one left, which she claimed she'd left behind. His heart quieter, he slept better, remembered no other dreams, though he saw her in bed when he woke with a shock of relief. Her bare shoulders, rounded and soft, but at the same time strong, as if the foundations of this heavy softness were square; the mauve sheet tightly wrapped below her arm-pits, the mauve pillow half hugged, half under her head – had there been some reason for his sense that she'd been missing? For several minutes he hunted for it. At moments during the day his mind went back to hunting for it, but he didn't find it.

All morning she slept heavily. Twice she stumbled to the bathroom to pee. All the way there she kept her eyes shut, feeling for wall and door. On the way back, padding across the black pile, she stubbed her toe on the bed leg and gave a low moan and got quickly into bed with a violent snuggle and several throat-clearing snorts as she pulled the mauve sheet right over her head.

He went out to breakfast and came back. She'd turned on her other side, only a three-inch patch of her short brown hair showing.

He went out for coffee and walked about the town. He was excited by it and hated it. Those five paper-hatted tourists, arm in arm, red-faced, singing and jerking at each other's shoulders. Germanic, of course, like so much that wasn't Jewish or Italian. Why did they seem more inflated and cruder than anything he could remember even in a Munich beer garden? More worrying, why, after two years of immunity, did he now care?

The square with *more* paintings, in *more* chocolate-box styles than he'd ever seen. The tourist stores in rows – streets of nothing else. Marble eggs from Italy, four-inch-diameter candles from Sweden, pottery from Spain, baskets from Greece, not an American item – except Genuine Old Southern Candy. He tried some and it was so sickly he wanted to vomit.

It was the hints of Europe, of course, that made him remember and compare. Less easy to explain why it now tightened his chest with an anger he'd learned to laugh away before he could remember. Why, more sickening, it filled him with nostalgia, a feeling he'd never admitted, and honestly believed he didn't suffer. He drank two iced absinths and went back to their hotel. She was still asleep.

He went out for lunch. While he ate, a more humid heat settled on the town and now every step was a sweaty struggle. More Americana: a toy Colt .45 in a case. "Authentic replica in durable plastic of the early model revolving-cylinder percussion hand-arm widely used in the Great War between the States and in the early days of the Old West . . ." Identical street signs, in blue and gold ceramic tiles, with crests of blue and gold castles: "When this city was capital of the Spanish province which bore its name, this street was named Calle Real . . . Calle Major . . ." He was filled with longing to be there again, in a

312

country where there was real history which had put its mark on real people. And with fury that they could tidily sterilise their European past into this dead information for tourists to acquire but never feel. With relief he reached the cool hotel, rose to their air-conditioned room, stood staring at her empty bed.

Bathroom empty, a scarlet towel and some mauve Kleenex on the black carpet ... He realised that he'd been planning to put right the disturbing things she'd said to him last night by saying some disturbing things to her when she woke. Tray with empty coffee cup and half eaten croissant by her bed. Half hidden under it, a folded sheet of paper.

"Sorry to slug it, darling. Where are you? I'm going to hunt. Love O."

He checked the pool. He checked the downstairs hotel foyer. He lay on his bed, reading the room service menu and hotel facilities sheet. It gave him an idea and he switched the television set to Channel Two: view of the roof-garden – so that worried moms could watch for when their kiddies sank – and there she was, on a deck chair, flat out in the sun. He bought a swimsuit at the hotel shop and went to join her.

"Good sleep?"

"Sure sure." But she seemed to tell him it was bad taste to interrupt the important business of tanning herself.

"Where did you go?"

"Shopping. One swimsuit – like it?" It was orange with a pattern of white paisley. It fitted deliciously across her tight belly and swelled gloriously over her fine breasts.

"And one bottle of pills." She fumbled in her purse to show it. "What did I tell you?"

He laughed, better pleased than he was going to show.

"Honey, I know the way you feel."

"You do?"

"Well if you don't you ought to," she said and oiled her front and lay on her back, reading, but carefully holding her book so that it didn't shade any flesh. It was a new book, he thought, but she was already two-thirds through.

"Hey, oil my back."

He gave a sharp laugh, and oiled it. She lay on her front, reading and soaking up the hot sun.

No alternative, he put on his swimsuit and swam, and sat by her, and swam again. But he was afraid he'd burn. His skin,

313

a light orange with freckles, suggesting the carrotty colour of his missing beard, turned scarlet easily, then pealed to a baby pink with bigger freckles. After an hour he grew impatient.

"Coming to see the town?"

"Why?"

"About a million of your countrymen come here each year to gape at it."

"You'd sure make a good salesman."

She was obstinate in a way he didn't remember. He oiled himself and lay on a towel. The sun seemed hotter than he'd ever felt it. His mind died in it. He dripped sweat which evaporated at once on top but soaked his towel below. His heart thundered. He understood the self-destructive thrill this must give her. Too late, he became amazed that he'd let her force him to stay – dressed and left her. In half an hour, as he drank absinth at a bar, his shoulders, chest and the front of his legs were glowing. In an hour he didn't want to touch them. In two hours he was making only the most careful movements to stop his clothes touching them.

That night they went through the gay streets of the tourist quarter to watch several strip shows and eat at the Sea Horse. Once, before they went out, and once when they came back, he saw her holding up the bottle of meth pills. But he didn't believe she was taking them.

He slept little, turning all night from one raw shoulder to another, and woke early, but again she slept late. He dressed and walked about the town. Several times the night before, and now again, out in the mind-fogging heat of the day, hurrying from shade patch to shade patch, he remembered his family.

Paralysis prevented him from calling them. But it was different from the compulsion to behave outrageously, which had so often made him feel less than a self-controlling person. More than once he came to a halt on a side walk, blocking a lean-jawed farmer in scarlet Dayglo hunting cap, a Florida matron in curlers and Bermuda shorts: *christ,* what was happening to him? shaking his head like a wet dog to get the tepid cotton wool out of it. Was he actually feeling sorry for them?

After each of these moments he found himself hurrying back to the hotel to see if she'd woken or was still asleep, hugging that mauve pillow. After each of them he understood clearly

314

that although four more days without laying her would be painful, to leave sooner had ceased to be possible.

All the time, now, he watched her. The way she moved her hands, her head, her neck, the texture of the soft brown skin below her arm where it joined her back. It gave him the feeling that till now he'd only seen her out of the corner of his eye, bouncing cheerily beside him, looking up at him with those big brown eyes, had even made love to her looking the other way. Now he thought all the time of her wide soft feet, and big soft arse, and tight belly and soft but strong tan shoulders above the sheets, looked for them quickly as he came back to his room for the third time that day, lightly belching crab salad. Again her bed was empty.

Empty coffee cup and crumbs of croissant, but no note. He switched the television to the roof-garden channel. There she lay, distorted and grainy but distinct, soaking up the sun. He made a move towards his wet swimsuit in the bathroom, but at once felt new pain in his raw chest and shoulders. He lay on his bed and dozed.

Ten minutes later, when he looked again at the silent moving picture her chair was empty. So was the chair beside hers. She was standing at the far edge of the pool and a young man stood beside her. He recognised a blonde young Scandinavian who'd been in the chair beside hers on the afternoon before. He hadn't spoken and he remembered having no thought about him, but realised that he must have watched him. He'd been burnt as brown as an Indian, but his hair had been a bleached pale gold. There's been pale gold hairs on his chest too. It was the contrast of these with his dark brown skin that he'd stared at, and the little silver cross on a thin silver chain which had hung among them.

For several seconds it seemed coincidence that they were standing there together at the edge of the pool. They didn't speak or seem aware of each other. Then she must have said something to him because she was smiling at him. At once they both dived.

Morrison went by elevator to the roof-garden and stood in the arcade of the bar where he couldn't be seen. They were still in the water, a yard apart.

"Hey, that's real cute," she said. "Do it again."

He did it: a backwards dive with a flip which turned him in the air and let him into the water as smoothly as a slim fish.

315

"I wish I could do that," she said. "You teach me?"

The Scandinavian neither answered or smiled.

She swam away from him. "What I need," she said, "is a great lecherous inflatable negro to follow me around with a tray of dry martinis."

Morrison went to their room and stared at the screen. They were on the near edge of the pool, and she was shaking back her hair and brushing water from her thighs and he was watching her, letting himself drip. They were on their chairs and the waiter was taking an order from them, then holding out his tray to them in turn. The Scandinavian signed.

"Christ," Morrison said. "CHRIST," he shouted. He got off the bed and strode up and down, sometimes breaking into a wild laugh, sometimes widening his eyes to the extreme outsides of their sockets. "It's happened," he shouted. He threw open both sets of hotel windows, letting in a gush of oven-hot air. "HEY," he shouted, high across the roof tops of the tourist quarter. Five stories below on the street, a trickle of window gazing tourists, moving slowly from store to store in the humid afternoon, didn't look up. He slammed the windows. He sat on his bed. He stood at the mirror, staring at his reflection, his stubbly orange jaw, his eyes getting wider and wider and WIDER. "Goddam it, I think, I think, *I think* I love her."

He hurried to the roof garden and stood under the arcade by the bar, where he could watch but not be seen.

"What I need," she said, "is a dish of caviar sandwiches and some Pol Roger '59."

"You do!" It was the first time he'd heard the Scandinavian speak. He had no foreign accent. He spoke with lazy assurance.

"That's right," she said coyly, got off her chair and went with a backwards look of mock offence, to stand ten feet away, looking out over the city roofs to the great suspension bridge, the vast sluggish river. Mock flight. It was a demonstration performance. The Scandinavian didn't follow her, as, of course, she'd hoped he wouldn't, and she soon came back.

"I was just thinking, what we need is some parachutes. Psychedelic ones. Just imagine landing among all those tourists in my paisley bikini on a paisley parachute." The bright diverting fantasy.

The Scandinavian watched her, sipping his drink.

316

"I once got involved with some jumpers."

"You did?"

"Yeah, yeah, but that's a long story." The hinted past of adventure and glamour . . . Her soft oiled body. Her soft wrists and little brown hands. Christ, it's really happened.

Night came and in the park the branches still fell. Dimly across his dark garden Peterson could see his neighbour's television antenna sprawled about his roof, as if a vast heat had suddenly softened its metal, a big dead metal spider. Then he couldn't see it. He wrote by candlelight, his knees wrapped in a blanket. Once the gun-like crack of a heavy limb came close beside his house and the tumble of crashing ice rushed past his grey window, making him jerk away, leaving something hanging there at an angle, a gutter perhaps.

Sometimes police sirens howled down distant streets. Then there was silence and no branches falling but only a stirring wind. Then complete windless silence so that he grew aware of all those trees out there in the park, straining to hold up their loads of ice, straining, straining, till with a sudden splitting crack one of them could bear it no longer.

A new noise. Across the park, then on some far away street, chain saws had begun to work. Their engines chattered like two-stroke motor cycles so that each time one started he found himself waiting for it to drive away and grow distant, but it didn't He imagined his neighbours using them, in hunting caps and lumber jackets, playing northern frontiersmen . . . Out there she lay, in the arms of someone who didn't love her. What he, who did love her, could have given her tonight, in darkness, the world breaking apart around them. Tears of regret formed in his eyes and clogged his throat. Suddenly, a revelation he'd somehow missed before, the inescapable self-contradiction of this hope became clear. It was *because* he loved her that he could never give her what she wanted.

Soon after this, a change occurred. Though Peterson could not escape from his own damp-eyed symptoms they began to sicken him. He wrote:

Morrison stood quite still at the centre of the thick black pile of their cool hotel room, thinking. Presently he went to the

317

bathroom and took one meth pill. In ten minutes, as if this time they knew what to do, his jaws clamped.

Gaily she came down at sunset and shut herself in the bathroom. Gaily, they went through the warm darkness to dine at Bee's, a still more expensive restaurant. Tonight she meant to eat properly, she said. "You know what, I'm really getting to like this place."

Moules marinières, she slurped it down and sat, little brown hands on the table edge, glancing hungrily at the steaming plates as they went past. He sipped his own and pushed it away. But at once he called for the menu again, cancelled all they'd ordered, led her through it section by section, improving, adding.

"Hey, what's the idea?"

"You deserve it."

Instead of the modest but promising dishes they'd chosen he led her each time to the most expensive, most fattening.

"Sure, I deserve it, but why now?"

"Now I know you'll appreciate it."

But he wouldn't say their names, rejected the others in turn, left her each time to look up at him, big-eyed:

"Could I?"

"Of course."

"Oh gee!"

"That's the time I pick up this pilot," she told him. "He's Estonian. Is he beautiful! The most beautiful guy I've ever seen. Too bad his mind's the size of an ant's egg. Actually I can't really tell because he only speaks about twenty words of English and five of them are 'You fly with me Miami.'

" 'Sure,' I tell him, because I think he's kidding. I get a real shock when we drive out on to this airport and get into a great sixty-seat airliner, just him and me. Turns out, it's his job to ferry them back when they get to the wrong places."

She described his apartment in Miami and how he'd left her alone all day to go to the beach, but taken her out to expensive meals in the evening. "Honey, it was sheer boredom. All those fine guys sunning themselves. What else could a girl do? Also, it *was* a bit spooky, being kept like that. He didn't even touch me. I got the idea he might be planning something really horrid. Hey, maybe he was just romantic. Didn't touch me because I was so pure. Funny, I never thought of that."

318

She seemed genuinely surprised. "What a filthy mind I've got," she said smugly.

A delightful idea came to Morrison. Her round fish-eyes. These delicious fish dishes she was gulping. The appropriateness expanded. To eat and be eaten : her life story.

"You know, I reckon I've really come down at last," she said. "About time too," taking a huge sloppy mouthful, so that she had to use the tip of her tongue then her napkin to collect some grey drips of spicey sauce. "Mmmm."

But oddly she didn't seem it. Her face wider and more flushed than ever, now seeming as young as a schoolgirl's, she talked with the same self-intoxicating fluency.

"That's the first thing that happens after I leave West State University. Kinda shakes a girl's confidence. Yeah, didn't I tell you? I was finishing school there. What a place! Not like Bigg State. That's civilised. There's a real town only a hundred and fifty miles away. West State there's nothing for *five* hundred. They didn't play at things up there, like giving parties for instance. Got straight down to the job. If you passed someone in the street you didn't just know who he was screwing right now. You knew who he'd been screwing last month. And the month before. And the month before that. You could make a damn good guess who he'd be screwing next month."

"Sounds delightful."

"Oh it was," she said, but with less enthusiasm than he'd expected. "What a place to start a nice married life. Yeah, yeah, didn't I tell you?" and checked herself, realising too late that she'd shown him that for an instant she'd forgotten who she was talking to.

"What was that like?' '

"Fine, fine," she said. "Till it wasn't." But a new dish had come. "That's a long story," she said, through a steamy fork load of lobster Neuberg.

Close to saturation, she pushed away a heap of broken shell, but her eyes still swivelled to passing plates. If only, if only ... "Was I ever in Las Vegas! I was a change girl at Diamond Bill's. What a place. All those horrid old men having orgasms all round me as they lost their fortunes. Maybe I was jealous ... Only had to see one guy win a jackpot. You seen it? The money doesn't come out all at once. It goes on pouring and pouring. And this young guy stands there with his hand still

319

on the lever, as if he can't understand why he isn't allowed to go on pulling it. Then all these old women come crowding round, giving him advice, and then go away again because they aren't really interested, and anyway they got their own levers which still need pulling. And he still doesn't do a thing till one puts out a hand. So he hits it, real hard, on the wrist. He doesn't even look to see whose hand it is but just stands with his belly real close to the machine." She shuddered. "And all the time that goddam machine's still vomiting cash." It really upset her.

"Matter of fact I got to know that guy later," she said and smiled to herself.

"Rum Baba? Baklava?"

"Hey?" she said, and gave him a sharp glance as if he'd restarted some suspicion. "Oh well, okay."

"Cassata Siciliana?"

"Come arn now, what *is* this?" But when it was brought she absentmindedly sprinkled on nuts and took some slippery pink and emerald spoonfuls.

They drank at a bar ten foot wide with a narrow platform behind the barman's shoulders where a young almost breastless negress took off her clothes to music, only interrupting the routine to sidle through some black curtains to change the record. The climax of her was to turn her arse to the audience, naked except for a vertical red strap, bend at the knees, draw her buttocks apart, look over her shoulders, put out her pink tongue and blow a rubbery fart. Morrison laughed loudly but it was less funny the third time. Next came a big-thighed, huge breasted white girl, whose act was to make her enormous floppy pear drops fly in circles, their eight inch tassels suggesting the propellers of a twin engined aircraft. She circled one, then the other, then both. As an encore she circled them in opposite directions. Morrison clapped wildly. At the bar the three of the audience of five who weren't at that moment drinking turned to stare at him.

"Honey, did I ever tell you about this girl friend of mine who had these enormous ones. I mean ENORMOUS. Well she's laying this New Zealander six times a night, so she says — he's my boss at the office, by the way. And I get to thinking, hey, what's she got that I haven't. You know what? I almost get them stuffed. It's a fact. I spend nights studying the litera-

320

ture. The trouble is, I can't afford it, so there's only one way. Get to know the doctor, then maybe he'll do it free – hey, why do I always get my life in such a mess? There I am, dating one boy – yeah, yeah, but he's not important – trying to make the grade with this New Zealander – only the trouble is after the good time he's having all night he can hardly keep his eyes open daytimes – I'm really sorry for that guy. And at the same time trying to seduce this horrid young Roumanian doctor. That's when Socrates turns up. Hell, do you blame me?"

They went six miles by taxi to the neighbouring parish where the laws were less strict and the Oh Golly Club showed a transvestist strip show. A pretty blond girl-man began, "If you don't all clap nice and loud we're going to lock all the doors and then you'll all have to stay here and join us." The audience of college girls, businessmen and their wives, and tourists on night-life tours, tittered. "There, I thought that would get you going." Morrison applauded wildly as a great white man with flesh as soft and wobbly as a woman's, stripped to g-string – surely too tight to hide anything – and well filled bra. Slightly clumsily with his big male fingers, he undid this at the centre, disclosing – another bra. When he'd disclosed five more, he minced to the back of the stage, fumbled with the hooks of the seventh, and flapped it back to show his podgy but quite flat white chest as he whisked off the stage with a gay squeal.

"Honey, I don't think I like this."

"It's wonderful."

Mr Laura Spark, world famous contralto, was beginning her act with an aria from Carmen. She sang with a heavy German accent.

"Did I ever tell you about the time I went with this boy who stole cars? That was splendid, it really was. Each time he came to take me out he'd bring a new one. Then half way through the evening he'd get bored. It always happened at the same time, right after the movie. So we'd find another. That was just after I finished high school. My parents liked him a lot. Hell, he was a nice guy. He wasn't a crook or anything. He just had a thing about big new expensive cars. When he got a glimpse of one he liked I'd see his eyes turn and he'd forget I was there. You won't believe it, but I got jealous. I got to thinking when he was laying me, he's not really noticing *me*, he's just thinking about the next Cadillac he's going to knock off."

321

L

They drove six miles back to town and looked through the open street windows of the Jazz Hall. On a platform directly inside, the band of old negroes played, showing great rolls of purple flesh at the backs of their necks. Beyond their knees the audience were wooden and two dimensional, each with nose, mouth, two ears, two staring eyes, keeping improbably still and upright. Even when they clapped, their arms seemed wooden. Unable to believe that their music could do this to anyone, these warm old men turned their big black heads to joke out through the windows. "Come on in, man. You get yerself a cold out there, yes sir."

"You ever been laid by a spade? No, you wouldn't. Well one time, before I met Socrates . . ."

At three they came back through the warm streets of hot-dog-munching, beer-can-tilting tourists in false moustaches to their cooler hotel room. Coolly she kissed him on the cheek. "Honey, thanks, I really enjoyed that."

But now, as a second precaution, she acted a stumbling exhaustion, let her clothes drop all round her, except her panties, wouldn't look at him as he dropped his own, casually disclosing a fine hard.

"What's all the staring for?"

He gripped her wrist, stood holding her while she struggled to escape.

"Now then, Professor Morrison," she said, jokey and arch.

He gripped harder.

"Hey, that hurts," she said, peevish and squirming.

He reached for her other wrist. "Look, what *is* this?" she said, keeping it away from him.

"Come on then," he said.

"Honey, grow up. Didn't I explain?"

Sick with anger, he let her go and watched her all in one movement jump into bed, curl violently towards the wall and pull the sheet over her head.

A second later she propped herself up to look back at him, "Honey, I'm real sorry," and snuggled under again.

Continually, in his dreams, he crossed the three feet between their beds to lay her. Mostly she pushed him away. Once her bed was empty. Once she sat up suddenly, as if she might still be asleep. "Honey, don't you remember," she said gently. And he remembered and went back to bed. Sickeningly, in his

322

dream, he was grateful. When he woke, he lay astonished at the happy gratitude he still felt because of the kind way she'd sent him back to his own bed.

He dressed. Improbably, in this holiday town, a crowd of quite different people were going to work in the streets below. He found the small bottle in the bathroom and swallowed two pills. Today he needed to think.

Soon his head hummed busily, his molars clamped, his mouth set in a grin. But he could think only of her soft arms and wrists, her soft bare back, oh god her naked back ...

All morning, as he walked the streets, there was this astonishing soggy lump in his throat, which he last remembered when his father, ex-company sergeant-major, had hit him with a belt for damage to a cucumber frame which he hadn't done, and he'd wanted to tell his mother but known that he must never let himself. Behind his eyes were these astonishing tears. His heart pounded with a soft floppiness, mmpff, mmpff as if in exact imitation of the despair of his mind.

Right on the surface of this was the desire to go to her and tell her that the time for pretence was over and there was nothing in the world he wouldn't give her. At the moment when he actually heard in his head the words of love and surrender he might use, and imagined the sort of pity *and disgust* she would feel for him, his mouth fell open in a low groan and he stopped on the spot, blocking the sidewalk. He seemed to feel every fresh carrotty bristle on his face, creeping about it from earhole to earhole.

Mid-afternoon, her bed was empty. He took three more pills, switched the television to Channel Two and lay sometimes glancing at it, more often grinding his teeth at the ceiling. There they were, side by side, soaking up the sun. That silver cross, nestling in those pale gold hairs. Her soft tan back, slightly shiny with sun oil. They didn't bother to talk. He was filled with a desire he never remembered before, to expunge a whole incident from his life. Those sixty seconds when he'd let her see that he was suffering. The moment when she'd sat up in bed to tell him something COMFORTING.

"Why don't you suffer," she'd said. "I am." But right at the core of any suffering she ever did must be the consciousness that she was enjoying it. Cautiously he began to like this idea. All right, she'd made him suffer, but she'd neatly fixed herself

323

so that she *couldn't*. Because it was the state of mind she most wanted, she would *never* be able to have it. His grin got bigger. He turned to the screen, able to bear to look again – their chairs were empty.

Yes!

He looked for them in the water and beside the pool. Yes, YES.

He jumped from his bed and stood close to the screen – and backed away from it, wild at the way it blurred when he wanted to get close enough to see round its edges to search the whole roof garden. All the way up in the elevator he seemed to hold his breath till he could be sure.

Not in the water. Not at the bar. Not gazing out from any of the parapets over the sun-drenched city to the suspension bridge above that huge curl of river. He checked each twice. The second time he checked their chairs they were occupied by two gross women with gold wristwatches and dimpled red flesh between their two-piece swimsuits. All the way down in the elevator he seemed to hold his breath till he could be sure that she hadn't come back to their room by some different route. She hadn't.

He stood at its centre, his head buzzing and buzzing. With a wild leap he switched off the set. Suppose she'd come back and seen it on and guessed what it had shown him . . .

An idea came to him: that other bottle of pills. *The* Pill, on which she'd once said her life depended. In the bathroom, the beauty of that accidental double meaning so delighted him that he could only stand staring through the clear glass of the little bottle, at the cluster of small orange pills inside, like the eggs of a fishes' row – on which her life might really depend. There should be twenty-one, till the day after tomorrow, or the day after that perhaps, when she could start taking them again. But just suppose there wasn't twenty-one. A muffled click somewhere out in the corridor froze him. Quickly he tipped them into his hand and began to count them back into bottle. bottle. "Eighteen, nineteen, *twenty*."

He lay on the bed. His head hummed like a top, buzzed like a bee.

He'd miscounted. He hurried to the bathroom, poured them on to the black formica surround of the mauve basin, formed them into fours – Form fours, a shout from his past, his

324

father a military man retired at Battersea... Five groups of four. Not one too few, not one too many – or had he accidentally made one group of five? He checked, rechecked, and poured them back into the bottle.

He'd dropped one? He went on his hands and knees on the black pile carpet, ducked below the mauve basin, peered behind the mauve john. A new muffled sound outside made sweat start heavily, but he didn't move... The total appropriateness of being found by her, on hands and knees, peering behind the mauve john... There was no other sound and five seconds later he was out in the corridor, softly closing the door.

He walked about the town, but had little memory of how he got from place to place. Her soft oiled back. That little silver cross in those golden, but slightly sun-dried hairs. The gay but loving words she would say as she played with it there... At one moment he was in the square, circling the bronze horseback general on his plinth. "The Union must and shall be preserved," his rearing steed, hat raised from that lean determined face, pigeon sitting on his horse's flowing tail, so much the same colour against the bright sky that it seemed a part of it. You dangerously deluded, not to say unpleasant fool, he thought. Just take a look around.

Later, though when it began he had little idea, he was going from window to window of the antique stores. Pieces of eight in a tray, cutlasses and bayonets in an elephant's foot, Arab flintlocks with curved stocks to fit under the arm – for firing from moving camels? And there it was at last, leather holster green with mildew, but still functioning he felt sure as he examined it on the counter, broke it open, clicked the hammer, saw the point of the striker emerge.

"Would this be a genuine example of the revolving-chamber hand-arm, extensively used in the Great Civil War between the States?"

"It sure would," the store keeper told him.

"Not to mention the early days of the Old West?"

"Right, right," the store keeper cried happily.

"And would it still shoot?"

"It sure would," the store keeper said earnestly, but with growing suspicion at these selling points so improperly supplied by the customer. "You planning on doing some hunting?"

"No, no," Morrison said truthfully, because he had no idea

325

what he was planning, only knew that once again he wasn't a person but an outer-directed victim. Ten minutes later, a heavy parcel in thick brown paper under his arm, he was checking out of a supermarket, paying for two big green notebooks.

A parcel now under each arm, one heavy, one less, he stood in a sporting-goods store and ordered a box of .45 shells. Correctly he should have bought two only, but the order might have seemed suspicious, and now he was compulsively cunning too. He would need it to survive. Was that another discovery?

Back through the crowded streets of clanging streetcars – the business day of citizens again surprising him at its end – to their hotel room. "What you got there?"

She came out of the bathroom and stopped towelling herself with the bright red towel to stare at him. "Presents?"

He could only laugh.

"What's so funny?" She watched him with more interest than for several days. "For your family?"

He laughed a lot and put the parcels under his pillow and sat on his bed to stop her coming near them. She shrugged and towelled herself, but several times as she dressed he saw her eyes straying towards them, gauging whether she could grab and open one before he could stop her.

Tonight they were to dine at A's, best known and most expensive tourist restaurant, with the exciting reputation for treating its customers most rudely, as if it were their privilege to be allowed this sample of an older better world – But, half way there, he called a taxi, drove her to a dress shop in the modern town.

"Hey, what *is* this?"

"Don't you want a new dress?"

"Sure I do," she said doubtfully.

For half an hour she tried them on, turning in front of the mirror to look at herself over her shoulder, cocking her head left and right, pushing their sleeves up above the elbow to show off her soft tan forearms, pulling them down to her little brown hands.

"You know what, this'll be my first dress that's been *paid for* since . . ." but she couldn't remember, broke into delighted laughter. "Oh yes," drawing back her head, half closing her eyes as she admired herself. "You like it?" turning to him,

326

becoming suddenly still at the sight of him watching her. "So what's going on?"

"Cheap," he said, and called for others.

"Hey yes," she said, catching sight of herself in the mirror as she came out of the dressing closet. "Yes, yes," turning to look at herself over her shoulder, in this elegant, all black dress with puritan neck and long black sleeves to the wrist.

"Phoney," he said, but she didn't seem to hear, let herself be led absentmindedly back into the closet by the saleswoman as she stared at him. "Say, what *is* this?"

He chose one in huge clashing rays of emerald and orange with an orange sun at her stomach and little emerald bows on her shoulders. He was delighted. Now it was sophisticated if outrageous, now a little girl's party dress. She hugged his elbow. "Honey, thanks." She bounced ahead of him, head erect, swinging its skirt. "Do I feel good!" But, waiting in the line on the sidewalk outside A's, she stared at him again with big eyes. "How much *did* that cost?"

Huîtres Rockefeller. Coquilles Saint Jacques.

"Did I ever tell you about the guy I made impotent? That was real spooky. Hell, yes, I know it's meant to happen: the American female and all that. I never thought she was *me*. He doesn't just try and fail. He starts to say he's not feeling like it tonight. But he takes it for granted he can go on sleeping in the same bed. I ask you! Is that hard on a girl! Funny thing is, I've been planning on leaving him, but when this happens I can't. We go on living together a *whole month*. Matter of fact, that makes me feel kinda smug – didn't know I could hold out so long."

Scampi. Calamares.

"Hey, why don't *you* eat?"

"Not hungry." It was true. When he put a piece in his mouth and chewed and chewed it became limp and flabby but he still couldn't swallow it. There seemed some physical barrier in his throat which made it impossible to force this flavourless unneeded substance down into his stomach.

She gave him a sharp glance, but only for an instant. "Whole stuffed woodcock in Madeira sauce. Oh gee, could I?" Tonight she was even gayer. "Say, you don't think that's the effect I have on all men, do you?" A look of big phoney, but half real, alarm came on her face. "Come arn. Tell me it isn't

327

true. Oh shit, wouldn't that be fate – for *me*. Christ no," she said, reassuring herself. "Hell YES," she said. "Just remembered this teacher I had at West State."

Silently, with concentration and care, he encouraged her. Delight was too careless a word. Tonight he was anxious that some false word shouldn't make her stop.

"My English teacher," she said. "I took quite a fancy to him the first time I saw him. So I fix a date to discuss my work with him. 'In my office?' he says. 'Hell no,' I say. 'I can't concentrate in an office – can you?' So we agree to meet outside the Union – but he doesn't turn up. That's his big mistake. After that he's really had it. In a big way."

Presently as she talked he knew that they were at the centre of a stage. Though she didn't talk loudly, all around them the tables of tourists had begun to watch. At the side of the restaurant, vacant-eyed waiters watched. They'd no idea what was happening but they knew it was real. And she knew they were watching and fed on it. She was marvellous. She was alive. She filled out that absurd emerald and orange dress, so that she seemed physically bigger than all these shrunken people around. It was as if she was the only person wearing colour because they were all in drab grey. Her round face, dark from the sun but flushed with blood, made theirs seem anaemic, as if every one of them suffered from poisoned livers or chronic constipation.

And he was performing too, not in her defiant talkative way but in the way he listened to her which alternately filled his buzzing head with waves of love and admiration for her, and made him give great hidden shouts of murderous laughter. It was because she sensed this that she performed, sensed that he was high as a kite, stoned as a newt, but more alive than he'd ever been, so that he could actually *feel* his chopped-off carrotty stubble growing again.

"Well next time I get it fixed to meet him at this friend's apartment. I'm not giving him a second chance. The moment we're alone I start getting my clothes off. Don't think I've ever seen anyone so startled. When I give him a good kiss it's like I'm kissing some guy under hypnosis. Yeah, he kisses all right, and how! But it's like he doesn't really believe it's *him* doing it.

"So I let him have a break, and he runs down the passage – I reckon he's hunting for the bedroom – hell, people have all

328

sorts of hang-ups – or he likes getting undressed in private – he's unbuckling his belt as he runs. After about two minutes I get suspicious and go after him. And where do you think I find him? Stark naked, squatting on the john, with his arms round his knees, crying and shivering. All he'll say is, 'I can't, I can't'."

All the time, as he listened he was aware of those two parcels under his hotel pillow, the heavy, and the less heavy. Astonished at his earlier obtuseness, he saw clearly the choice they offered him. Clearly he saw that they offered no choice because he'd chosen.

"Soufflé au Grand Marnier avec crême de Saint Bernard. That's one thing I've longed for all my life. Hey, honey, you'll be broke. Honey, you will let me know when you're broke, won't you . . . That was the first time I was unfaithful to my husband. You like me to tell you about my husband?"

"Of course."

"Well, soon as I get home, I say to him, What would you do if I told you I'd been seducing someone? He just laughs. Poor guy. He doesn't begin to believe it. You know what? Getting my husband to believe what a bitch I am is one of the hardest things I ever have to do. He just *won't* see it."

I've chosen, Morrison thought, but goddam it, I wish you *hadn't* met someone who knows what a bitch you are. *And* is going to do something about it. But at once a new and devastating picture occurred to him. What would she do when she finally faced that genuine six-chamber revolving hand-arm which had won the West? Laugh at his old-fashioned accusation as he stood there, pointing it at her, with his absurd newly sprouting beard, a figure from nineteenth-century melodrama, "Madam, you've been unfaithful to me. You shall pay the price," finally admitting to her that his emancipated expedition into her brave new world of sex without guilt had been an act, because he'd reverted to an old world, lousy with rural value judgements, clogged with pre-Pill moral attitudes. Even as he pulled the trigger she'd be laughing.

"You see, he worshipped me," she said. "Okay, he knows what all our friends do. Okay, he knows what he's done before he met me, and what I've done before I met him – well most of it – well let's say a good ten per cent of it. But our marriage is

329

different. Nothing can upset that. The trouble is, he got me and Zen about the same time.

"You know, we used to spend whole days out in the country looking at the goddam grass. We didn't even *talk* about it. Hell, I tried, I really did. A whole year I tried. There were even times when I thought I saw what he meant about the goddam grass. I just couldn't make it.

"The douche is the first thing. That's a lucky accident, really. I get this itch which scares me silly because I think it's syphilis. So off I go like a bat in hell to the doctor, and he tells me, all you need is to wash a bit more, young woman, and makes me buy a douche. I'm pretty relieved, I can tell you. But the next time after I use it I can't think what's happened because my husband can't get in. It's okay again after twenty-four hours and it isn't till after I have a douche again that I realise what's going on. After that I just keep right on douching. You've never seen a girl with such a hygienic vagina. Hell, yes, we used to have quite good sex, but I'd gotten to being goddam worried about being treated like I might break. Too holy to touch.

"It really upsets him, I can tell you. I see he's just longing to go off and have a test run on someone else, but he's really fixed himself there, because that'll upset our precious marriage.

"The problem is, I get impatient. Hell, a girl can't hold out for ever. And one day I get to thinking he may be reckoning we can go on being married *without* sex. He's so mixed up he may even persuade himself it's better that way. Just as soon as I get that scarey idea I know I'll have to do something desperate. So I start an affair with the first guy to hand, who happens to be an old chum from my home town. I don't take any chances this time. Seduce him right in our marriage bed, right around the time my husband's due home from his classes.

"He believes it then okay. Hauls me out of bed, and cracks me across the face, left and right. Oh gee, did I have the two biggest black eyes you ever seen. You know what? Just as soon as he does that I remember why I love him and begin to wonder if the whole thing isn't a big mistake. Can you believe that?"

Morrison said he could, and ordered Greek coffee. When it came, with two little pieces of green Turkish delight for each cup, he sent the waiter for a plateful.

"Didn't last," she said gaily. "Next minute he begins to cry and say he's sorry and hopes he hasn't hurt me. That really finishes things." She stared at him with her big round eyes, as if noticing him for the first time for half an hour. "So that's the story of my life. Like it?"

Morrison passed her the plate of Turkish delight, finely quickly. "Mmmm. Have some."

"What's this?"

"An Oriental delicacy."

"You're kidding!" She ate a piece tentatively, on the end of a tiny silver fork. "Mmm. It's good." She ate three more pieces quickly. Mmm. Have some."

"No thanks."

"Hey, would I be able to live on Turkish delight? Vitamins and all that jazz. Because if I could . . ."

Late that night, back in their hotel room, he moved the parcels from under his pillow to the drawer by his bed, and half covered them with the room's Gideon bible. As he shut the drawer she came out of the bathroom and smiled, telling him they both knew that she meant to see inside those parcels. But what she didn't know, he thought, as he lay fully dressed on his bed, not the smallest chance that he'd sleep tonight, the meth humming and buzzing in his head, was how and when, and whether she'd like it when she did.

Presently he could hear her breathing. It was the most regular breathing he could remember. He remembered the way Lillian breathed, now quickly, now slowly, the way her whole body sometimes gave a convulsive jerk as she fell asleep – or she'd suddenly push herself on to her elbow, gasping for breath, as if in some dream she'd been suffocating. Olga's breathing never changed. Because her mouth was open he didn't hear her breathe in, only the soft regular puffs as she breathed out.

At three in the morning he was driving round town. On a far outskirt he reached the entrance to the lake causeway. Should he cross? He liked the idea of her waking alone in their hotel room and explaining how her husband (misregistered with a cleverness he had to admire) had been unexpectedly called away and left her no money. He liked the idea of the police failing to trace a Professor Peterson at Bigg University. He didn't like it enough.

He could hear too easily the amusing story it would make.

331

If there was one thing he wasn't going to be, it was another amusing story in her gay life. He swung the car back into the city and drove fast, alarmed that he'd unconsciously planned this escape, alarmed that he'd left her alone. As soon as he opened the bedroom door he heard the soft regular puffs of her breathing.

At dawn he was near the river. Past the brewery, silent but smelling strongly, as if in the warm night it had breathed a cloud of malt vapour around itself, across a hundred yards of railroad siding, the nearer he came the more astonished he grew at its size. This great block of water, a mile wide, thirty, fifty feet deep, moving every moment of the day towards the ocean. It was magnificent. It gave him a better idea of this enormous country, drained by six, seven rivers as large. When he reached the wharf he saw that, far from moving sluggishly, it went with a heavy rush, every part continuously disturbed by swirls and eddies and small gurgling whirlpools. Now they were lit pink by the rising sun but by day it would be the murky grey of used soapy water. Above it, the suspension bridge seemed no longer something of the earth but of the sky. Its ends planted in the city, far from the banks, it stepped across the river without effort or calculation.

Back through the square he came, that lunatic general raising his hat to the Union he'd helped preserve. But today he was fine in his pathetic conviction, fine that he should salute this city of vice, fine that the city should seem less wicked than vulgar, as grotesque and unfrightening as a wicked city in a German fairy story.

Old Southern Candy, "Bella the beautiful, SEVEN times nightly," all the time as he walked he was aware of her, sleeping up there above it, her soft but strongly built shoulders, the mauve sheet wound tightly below her more-than-life-size grape-fruits, her innocent breathing. She was fine too. He grew more and more conscious of her, seemed to see her up there suspended in some hammock or sea shell, a figure not from myth or legend, history or tradition, but from some pantomime parody of these. Finest of all, that he, a European, was going to make her pantomime real.

He swallowed more pills. In the night the bottle had grown low, and he was alarmed that they were running out. He re-corked it without counting. There would be enough.

332

But he grew impatient, began to check her room more often, around twelve was surprised to find her half dressed. Oddly, he felt that he'd surprised her too. It was as if she'd been dressing fast for some purpose which was no longer possible, so she could now dress more slowly, but she sometimes forgot and began to dress fast again. Had she hoped to be gone before he returned? When she used the bathroom, he checked the drawer by his bed. The two parcels, still shop-wrapped, lay as he'd left them, half hidden by the Gideon bible, open at Ecclesiastes 12.

"Take me to The Admiral's, honey. It's *the* place."

"They've been telling you?"

"Yeah, yeah, this guy I met at the pool. He's quite an expert."

Marvellous. He felt all the happiness of the action restarting after the long night.

"We just gotta go there before we leave."

"So we're leaving?"

"Well one day I suppose we shall." But it was a slip, he was sure. "While I've got *some* skin left. Before you're arrested for debt."

The more she said the more certain he became that it had been a slip, and the more delighted at the defiant way she played, not just to win the game but to win every point, arranging to use him as her bread ticket to the end.

They lunched in a courtyard, below trailing morning-glory, among cool green tanks of giant gold fish.

"And when your husband slaps your face, what does your chum from your home town do?"

"Do?" she said. "He doesn't *do* anything. He just stands and gapes, as if some dead eye dick may have just shot off his testicles but he doesn't dare look see. The funny thing is, as soon as my husband hits me, I completely forget that guy. I get quite a shock when he gives a little cough to show he's still there and says he thinks he'll be going."

Morrison ordered champagne.

"He still writes," she said dreamily. "Christ no, not him! My husband. He hopes I may come back, poor sod. Hey, as a matter of fact that other guy writes too," she said gaily, as if reminding herself of one more undeserved happiness in her life.

"Do you write to your husband?"

"Sometimes."

333

"And tell him he's a poor sod? Or let him go on hoping?"

"Honey, you wouldn't be bitching by any chance?"

"Christ no," Morrison said, as truthfully as he knew how.

"Didn't I tell you, that's what he wants to hope?" she said She thought about it. "Anyway, a girl can't tell when she may be in trouble." She thought some more. "Or when she may need to be in trouble. Oh gee!" capturing a final mouthful of smoked eel before the plate went, gaping at the twelve-inch rainbow trout on its silver dish which had replaced it.

"What does your second husband feel about the arrangement?"

"Feel?" she said. "Hell, he's an American citizen, wasn't that what he wanted?"

"I just wondered."

"Oh shit," she said, "you know what Turks are. Now I come to think of it, he'd probably have liked me as a wife. In fact he did make one improper suggestion right after the marriage. I wasn't having any of that. Just played dumb and slipped away before he got up any more courage."

Morrison paid the large bill and left a twenty-dollar tip. He was pleased when she stood staring from it to him and from him to it, so that he had to push her forward out of the courtyard away from the three bowing, chair-shifting waiters. Opposite was a cemetery and she was still staring at him as they crossed into it. "You're crazy, you really are."

Shrugging her shoulders, bouncing ahead, but still glancing back, she'd gone twenty yards down the centre path of whitewashed vaults and family tombs before she seemed to see them. "Hey, what are we doing in this goddam place?"

"One of the sights of the city."

"They can keep it." But she seemed half fascinated, led him in a wide sweep which took them along remoter paths. It grew quieter and soon they could hear no motors and only the occasional distant clanging of a streetcar.

The further they went the greener and prettier and quieter it became. All around were yellow-green tropical trees and below them went the lines of white tombs. The soil was sandy and there were carpeting patches of small mauve flowers. Soon the tombs became more dilapidated. Now some were of old unwhitened brick and some totally covered in dusty creeper with bright blue morning-glory flowers. Others had collapsed, show-

334

ing dark openings, or were tilted at odd angles because the ground had sunk.

They reached the cemetery wall, made up entirely of rectangular openings for coffins. The bottom row had mostly sunk out of sight, many of the middle rows had lost their plaques or fallen open, showing grey bones inside, the top row was twisted and penetrated by the roots of the trees which grew above. These formed a twenty-foot dense but elongated spinney, going in both directions, as if surrounding the whole cemetery. Here blue jays squawked, and above, puffy white clouds drifted across blue sky.

Never had he seen anywhere like it. She receded, became unimportant, a dancing, irritated doll on the extreme edge of his vision.

"Native of Liverpool. Died 1857."

"What a place to make love." She seemed to be near a wall-tomb, peering in.

"Native of Hamburg. Native of Genoa."

"Would that give one a kick – hey, what's the time?"

"Perished of fever. Samuel and Maria Brown, their son Harold, their daughters Charlotte, Ruth, Sarah, Margaret, all being natives of Hull."

"Christ, come arn. I gotta get back for my tan. The sun's going to set."

She changed in their bathroom, grabbed a towel, and hurried to the roof. He lay on his back on his bed. He didn't switch the set. There was no need. In his head ideas went in a beautiful circle of understanding, so beautiful that he often laughed aloud, then stopped quickly, not to interrupt them.

But at once he had to be sure, hurried to the roof. There they were, lying side by side, the sun shining on their oiled brown backs. Their heads were turned towards each other, their cheeks pushed out of shape against the cushions, but they didn't speak. There was nothing to show that they knew each other.

At five their chairs were empty. He'd expected it, but fear gripped him. Suppose they were escaping. Impossible for her to leave town in her swimsuit, but suppose she'd already hidden clothes in his room. He walked the hotel corridors, end to end of their soft mustard pile.

Now he strode down them with long soft strides, a highland shepherd, now he sauntered, a seaside cockney. Now private eye,

335

now lecher, now philosopher, now nothing but a grinding of teeth with exasperation that he seemed less and less to be any-thing except a succession of compulsive poses – unless at last he reached some core in this exasperation at his own coreless vanity – The time . . . He'd forgotten, came at a wild run to the elevator, pressed the wrong button, stood mad with anger at its slow descent when he needed to rise, widened his eyes terri-fyingly at two small crew-cut boys who now rose with him.

"Say, mister, would your name be Mister Fish?"

She lay on her back on her bed, dressed but eyes shut.

"Honey, I'm not feeling so good."

"Too many eels?"

"Shit no," but she didn't offer an alternative.

"You go and eat. I reckon I need some sleep."

He dressed carefully, new nigger-brown dacron trousers he'd bought himself, new sky-blue sea-cotton shirt, admired in the mirror this gay tourist-wear, topped by the foul fuzz of his new beard. All the time she lay still, eyes shut. At first he watched her for the flicker of eyelids which would tell she was checking him, then didn't trouble. She would never fail herself – and him – so trivially. He'd gone three blocks through the warm night when he remembered his parcels in his bedside drawer.

At once he turned back and came to their room, steadily, but not hurriedly because now he had an increasing sense of a pat-tern which he couldn't escape. Her sudden unconvincing illness fitted easily. More obscurely, so did his failure to remember the parcels till he was three blocks away, though they'd been in his mind for the last thirty hours. He sensed that whatever he found must fit too – but rushed the door, seeing in the final second as he turned the key, her standing directly inside, hand reached towards him, holding that foreshortened weapon. She wasn't there.

Wasn't on the bed. Wasn't in the bathroom.

In his bedside drawer the Gideon bible still covered those two shop-wrapped parcels, "Remember now thy Creator . . ."

Admiration again filled him. To have opened them would have been an impossible admission that he could ever again interest her. A moment later he saw her note. "Feel better, darl-ing. Going out to hunt for you. Hungry. O."

He loaded the gun. Far too clumsy for his pocket, he put it in the paper bag from his new clothes. One of her nylons lay on

336

the black carpet and he took this too. Standing in the corridor outside his closed door he swallowed the last four pills and posted the empty bottle down the mail-chute. Too late he wished he'd labelled and addressed it to Dr Ifitz. Put a message inside – but no, there'd have been no need for a message. In the strangest way, he felt that Dr Ifitz would have known both whom it came from and what message the empty bottle carried. Beyond this, he saw that he *had* mailed it to him. The message it carried was in part of thanks, of course, but not of a hypocritical sort which would insult both their intelligences. More it was a message of recognition. Now I know you, Morrison wanted to tell him. So I know why I wanted to destroy you and see that this was not so much wrong, as a mistaken estimate of my ability.

The moment he reached the ground and the elevator's metal doors slid back he saw them, framed in its square opening, drinking cocktails at a table in the hotel bar. He wore a cream tropical suit with yellow tie. She wore that child's party dress of emerald and orange he'd bought her. At the instant he saw them they were laughing gaily, then stopping suddenly to stare into each other's eyes. The bar was cut off from the hotel's foyer by a wrought-iron grille and perhaps it was this which had given them false security, but he was disappointed.

A second later he saw how rightly defiant it was that she should sit here with her new man, risking him finding her if he came back, but hoping for the triumph of watching him go blindly past. Her laughter was laughter for this new lover, more beautiful than any yet, but it fed, too, on the chance that at any second they might be discovered. He went blindly out into the night, came back by the hotel's side door and sat at a table in a dark corner of the bar.

Side by side on the table he put his paper bag and his absinth frappé. He didn't touch either of them.

All evening he seemed to sit at bar tables, gun and drink untouched in front of him, watching them. There was no hurry. It wouldn't be right to deprive her of this final night when she believed her last lover was hunting her along the same gay streets that she was bouncing, crazy with love for her new lover, that at any moment the two might meet. But it wouldn't be right either, to lose her.

Crazy with hope too, as he was at the start of any new

337

affair, he now realised. It was this that made her jump in with both feet, making each time a bigger splash. If it had all been a big joke to her, why should he have cared? What ultimately saved her – and incidentally destroyed him – was that she played as a joke what she was deadly serious about, because she was the biggest romantic of all.

It was Saturday night in the tourist town tonight, the carnival at last set for a climax. Surreys passed continuously, carrying bland-faced parents with crop-headed children in striped T-shirts, middle aged women with frizzy blonde hair and big mottled arms coming out of tight cotton dresses. The crackle of transistor-pop mixed with the hoof clops as they came close behind, then faded quickly as they passed ahead into the blare from a dozen open doorways. Along the sidewalks moved wide sluggish streams of pale-fleshed people, chewing, munching, sucking through multi-coloured straws at bright red fruit-clogged hurricanes, or spooning pistachio-green cherry-studded ice from scarlet sundaes. In and out of them, bumping, slopping, apologising, he strode and dodged in pursuit.

Sometimes they seemed to hurry too, as if she was actually flying ahead in that gay dress, and it was only by luck that he saw them turn at the far end of a street. At others they lingered and he found himself dangerously close, forced to stare obsessively at trays of opaque Old Southern Candy or the scarlet cone of a do-it-yourself nipple-cap. Early in the evening they went to a strip show and he sat in a back row.

He watched her performing as she'd once performed for him. What could it all be about, this continuous pouring out of thousands and thousands of gay words? Just their quantity astonished him. But of course he knew: the story of her life. He felt a moment's dangerous pity for that cream-suited dummy, so sex-assured, from the uninhibited north, who was never going to be asked the story of *his* life. But contempt too. Why should she ask him?

Again there was a girl with propeller udders. She spun the left one, steadying the right so that it only joggled lightly. She spun the right, steadying the left. And now, because they were sitting up front, he saw her head haloed by this flying tasselled breast. Applause, laughter, and out they went, her arm round his waist, her head on his cream-suited shoulder.

Then they were eating in a candlelit courtyard and he left

338

them to move impatiently past doorway after doorway, each with its group of tourists peering in at more huge swinging milk sacks. Again it was the quantity which impressed him, doorway after doorway, sack after vast sack, as if something had been sown in a climate too hot and moist and grown into a bloated self-caricature. Again he saw the whole country in this overblown way. Mountains and mountains of flaccid but cleanscrubbed flesh seemed to surround him. Size had become a quality in itself. Bigness, independent of what was big. An acorn-squash, water-melon civilisation.

Now it was impossible to hurry, the whole district blocked with slow-walking, sucking, laughing people. A dozen, twenty great streams of them moved through the hot damp night. At each turning when he hoped for space to walk fast and take deep lung-filled breaths, he met a new one coming bulging and swaying towards him. It was as if he was trapped in some gluey substance, and, each time he raised a leg or arm to escape, sank deeper. Panic began, he must hurry back to their candlelit courtyard while he still could . . . He heard the music of pipes.

He stood listening, knocked this way and that by the flow he was blocking, steadying himself at last, six feet out in the street. It came again, above the rumble of engines, the blare of other music, the heavy chatter and gabble of these hundreds of moving people, distant but unmistakable.

He ran, stopped, ran again, stood still, wild with frustration that he still couldn't tell its direction. Now he was at the centre of a cross-roads, facing the flashing headlights of a thickly embedded car, twisting his face in angry impatience at its blaring horn, not because he cared about this mechanical howl but because it stopped him listening. Clear and sharp, over all their heads, down the wide street from the north, he heard it.

Three blocks he struggled and pushed till suddenly on all sides people were falling back, leaving him alone. Right ahead, they were advancing on him, and as they came this space cleared continuously. He'd been looking for a great procession. Instead they were tiny, dwarfed by the crowd which followed them, and which seemed to be forced forward under its own momentum so that it was all the time on the point of overlapping them. By some strange effect of the lighting, this following crowd seemed also to fill the street in depth like a black shadow, reaching half way up the houses and looming above them.

In front came five boys in white shirts, carrying lanterns. They jumped and romped and turned each other by their free arms. Next came a strange girl in uniform and plaid beret. She was both brightly alert and dowdy. She didn't frolic herself but when they paused, shouted to start them again. The pipers followed: two stout middle-aged men, blowing hard. They wore kilts and tight plaid jackets and were bald with puffy red knees and pale jowly faces.

Last came a ragged group of boys and girls, jumping awkwardly, as if they didn't know how to dance and were embarrassed to be there at all.

But in his head the music sang. He wanted to shout and jump as high as the roofs. When he saw the lifeless faces around him, as if this was just one more tourist curiosity, he felt less anger than disbelief. How could their spirits fail to leap up at this music which held the essence of heroism? In his mind he saw some single piper, crossing a moor, cloak swinging, sword at side, his music calling through the mist to every distant granite hovel to men to come out and be great. And they came, and he came with them, ran forward to join – and saw in front of him a dozen embarrassed boys and girls, sniggering at two red-kneed, bald-headed businessmen, stars of the local Hibernian Society.

When they reached a cross-roads they tried to go ahead but the girl in uniform and beret ran at them, poking at their ribs with a small cane, pushing with her hands at their arses to turn them left.

It was fifteen minutes before he could force his way back to the restaurant. They were gone. From bar to bar he hunted them. Sometimes he hurried in, then out again. Sometimes he sat drinking beer. He was in despair. Next to him a slim cold girl with hair so short that her head was like a sick child's, told her boy, "Three years I was married. That really cramped my style."

Was he the only person who hadn't been told? He bought them both drinks, started an argument about where they should go next, saw the exact moment when her boy committed himself too angrily to MacNeil's for Old Time Song, so that he couldn't change his mind when she chose this new face with its weird orange scruff, because at least it was different from college boy after college boy who tried to please her . . .

340

Down the street he ran her.

"Say, what's all the hurry?"

"You really want to know?"

Into the courtyard of Mike's for hurricanes. Dark and thickly set with crowded tables, but at the centre a big fountain of coloured water. In a corner he crushed her against the hut which housed the old-time organ – she was so slim he could have broken her ribs. Olga had made him forget slim girls – put his mouth on hers, chewed her lower lip, bit her tongue, all the time staring above her head with wide open eyes at that great tumbling of coloured water, now deep maroon, now pale green, and feeling through her slim back the wheezes and clonks of the instrument inside – When who should be standing watching them, six feet away, but her recent boy.

"Hi there."

Let her lead him dizzily to a table.

"What's in that goddam bag?"

"A long barrel, six chamber, revolving-cylinder hand-arm, of the type much used in the winning of the West . . ."

"You think you're quite a smart guy, don't you?"

Ordered two ten-inch glasses with dark floating fruit, and liquid that shone a deep red in the fountain's light. "Hi there, what's yours?"

But her recent boy just stood staring at them, as if still too horrified by the way he'd followed them to admit he was here, as if some terrible explosion might be brewing in his gentle heart.

"Oh, forget him," she said.

Left her sitting in front of those fruitier than fruity drinks to pee – it had been as sexy as chewing blotting paper – mounted a wash-basin – Olga had spoiled him for thin girls – climbed feet first out through the toilet window, was running hard the second his heels jarred on the sidewalk for the hotel park.

Out across the city he roared, his tiny farting red car passing narrowly between converging trucks, cutting across wide convertibles, their boy drivers hung with girls at their necks like heavy bibs. The Oh Golly Club. Where else would she take him?

Lights going down for the last performance as he came in, a babble from backstage, as chattery as women though gruffer, then the pretty girl-man with pageboy wig and bony knees:

341

"This afternoon I washed my bosom – what's that ma'am? You did too? I should hope so. You didn't have to put it through the tumble-drier after." But already he'd checked the audience, was pushing his way out. Absurd to be here when there was somewhere so much more obvious – so obvious that it seemed she'd actually told him to look there. Those open wall-tombs ... Back across town he raced.

Again he noticed the quietness of this polite residential district of big white houses and big cool gardens. From The Admiral's courtyard the dinner-time conversations hummed faintly, rising to occasional bursts of laughter which seemed hardly to reach the bigger night outside. With a jump and scramble he was over the cemetery's closed iron gates, only a small rip in the crotch of his new trousers. He hurried forward.

He turned left and right, hunting for that area of broken wall where he became increasingly sure he'd find her. He went more slowly. He stopped.

Rushing at him as if he could suddenly block it no longer came terror at where he was. It came from all directions so that he wanted to shut his eyes and block ears, then run wildly to escape. All around him these white tombs which tilted in the sinking ground, seemed to lean towards him, cutting him off from the world of living people. In the moonless night they seemed to glow faintly and he grew aware of the thousands of bodies they held. Soon it would be impossible to escape. Soon he wouldn't want to escape.

A moment later he saw a movement. He saw another. He began to see them everywhere, but never when he was looking at them. Soon he was shouting, "Hi, you there," as he ran stumbling towards them, first in one direction then another, then not shouting because of the heavy shivering of his jaw which made his teeth bang. But he'd teach them. Trying to frighten him. Because now he sensed that he was in the grip of some final test and that if he passed he would never again doubt that to survive was to fail, even though to die was *not* to succeed but a sick joke ... A happy picture came to him of those polite diners in the courtyard of The Admiral's, falling into worried silence as they'd heard him howling out here in the graveyard. But, strangely, he knew that he was howling *for* them, not against them ... Twenty yards ahead, he saw a movement of a new sort: a pale figure appeared, paused, then crossed into

342

the darkness. A second later she followed. She was harder to see in her coloured dress. She seemed to cross in a single quick sweep, as if moving with spread skirt, her feet just above the ground.

He stalked them. Sometimes they were far away at the end of a path, sometimes so close that he could hear them whispering. As much because it rustled as for any purpose he was certain about, he left his paper bag on the steps of a vault, pulled the nylon over his head and took the gun in his hand. He had a clear picture of himself, human to the shoulders, head like a fleshy eyeless slug.

In arranging it he'd lost them. He ran wildly again, reached the cemetery wall, began to go up and down those open tombs, peering into them, stopped, struck by a parallel, those dozens of little drawers in his mind into which pyjamas – any subject – seemed of its own momentum to arrange itself, so that he knew the contents and relationship of every one – these hundreds of little drawers, some blocked, some bone-filled, in one of which she and her lover ... At once a new idea came to him : start firing into one, see them bolt like frightened rabbits from another, or realise that miraculously he'd chosen right, their bodies jerking about in there as he poured in shell after shell ... Glancing right he saw them again, poised on the top of the iron cemetery gates, saw her hold out a hand for help before they both jumped outwards. But an instant earlier he'd seen something else : a paleness above her shoulders which meant she'd turned to look back into the cemetery – fear? curiosity? – or to make sure he'd seen them leave?

By the time he jumped from the gate their taxi was moving. Back through the tourist quarter he raced after it. The carnival near climax now, clubs poured out streams of men in bonnets, and women in boaters; schoolboys on a first drunk sang, "When the Saints ..." in a swaying line; caught clearly in his car as it stood at a traffic halt, as if it were being sung directly in at its window by someone he couldn't see, a calypso, "Lemon tree very pretty," he moved the shift – "Lemon tree very sweet" – felt a memory stir which he'd no time to trace as he jolted forward with a hiss of burning rubber. They'd escaped while he was stopped, but he'd guessed their direction, cornered fast into the quieter square, making for the coffee house. A hundred yards before he reached it he saw them, arms round each other's waists, going up the ramp which led past the brewery to the river.

Over the railroad tracks he followed them, staying far behind, but came closer when they reached the water. To his right the bridge crossed the sky, vast but frail in the night. They turned away from it. Dark warehouses rose to his left, then a corrugated fence which left only a six-foot gap along the wharf edge. After twenty yards this turned sharply.

Here he waited, peering, withdrawing, peering. Something had distracted them and they seemed to stand close together, looking down into the water. Again he heard their low voices. Then he knew they were clasped together, his arm round her shoulders, her arms round his neck, her head back, eyes shut . . .

They were coming again. Close to him they paused, standing with their toes on the edge, once more looking down at something below. And now, more strongly than ever, he believed that – on a level she half knew about – she'd arranged this moment : that she even sensed this slug-headed figure close behind her in the darkness. Hand in hand with that poor Dane, her fingers actually locked in his, wanting desperately to love him and be loved by him, that she was nevertheless quite unable to warn him, because her whole being was caught up in the excitement of what might be about to happen, because it was this danger which made her love him and need his love, because to avoid it would create more than a momentary anti-climax – would betray all she lived for.

Beyond this, with new clearness, he understood that she was laughing at him because she didn't believe he'd dare, but at the same time was desperate for him to dare. Because it would make the best of all the gay stories of her life, and it didn't matter whether or not she lived to tell it.

The funny thing was that neither her laughter because he wouldn't dare, nor the romantic fulfilment it would give her if he did, was going to stop him. Carefully he set the gun on the gravel. If the laugh was on him it was on her too. Carefully he came upright, hearing the creak his left knee often made when he straightened it under weight, noticing her start but still not turn. Now he shared so strongly her excitement that he seemed to merge more and more closely with her, began an urgent erection . . . He lunged and heaved.

A hand in the small of each of their backs, he heaved with

344

the greatest force he dared use, one job he wasn't going to mismanage, but his lunge was almost too violent and he tottered on the edge as they went, arms thrown up, out into the darkness. His recovery took him a step backwards, so that in an instant they'd fallen out of sight and he heard only her descending scream.

On and on it went, far longer than he'd expected. It told him that she'd again outmanoeuvred him. It wasn't a scream of terror. There was nothing self-deceptively romantic about it. Finally it proved to him that she didn't want truly to suffer, but only enough to enjoy it. Any desire he'd believed she had for real suffering had been *his own* romantic invention. His final push into the night, intended to jolt her into true suffering, had only given her the ultimate erotic thrill.

No splashes as he'd expected, but a noise he'd never heard before. Hollow and metallic, like a big muffled gong, echoing out across the river, with an undersound like a wet slap. Peering into the darkness, he saw why. Close to the wharf a dark shape presently formed itself into a cylindrical floating tank. It was this they had been staring at, must have hit.

A waning moon rose and Morrison still stood there, now staring down at that big floating cylinder, spinning slowly in the moonlight, as if some weighty blow had set it in motion, now staring out beyond it at the gurgling, bubbling river. Already he would need to search far down it towards the ocean. He searched and saw nothing.

He groped by the corrugated fence for the gun.

He moved beside the river. He couldn't have hurried if he'd wanted. Exhaustion gripped him. Even to stay upright seemed to put a dangerous strain on his heart. Above everything else he wanted to lie down where he was and sleep and sleep. But he knew he must struggle on. As he went he had the strangest illusion. Out of the corner of his eye that great mile-wide block of moving water seemed to be flowing backwards, upstream, into the heart of the continent. Now, too, he half saw on its surface, a dark floating object, first far out in the middle, then close to the bank, then in several places at once. The river was accepting her, carrying her back to her country ... How right, he felt – in a final spurt of understanding which seemed as if it might be his last so that in future his mind would experience only confusion – that it should accept her. The water, her

345

element – out there, that pop-eyed fishy look he'd noticed from the first time he'd met her at last no longer seemed a deformity. It was he who had proved landbound, unacceptable ... But as soon as he looked directly at the river its empty surface gurgled and rippled correctly towards the ocean.

Dawn coming, he made their few possessions into a newspaper package, paid the bill and left town. He must not raise suspicion. He needed time. But he needed, also, to go back for that second parcel. He did these things with dogged exhaustion, forcing each movement with an effort of will which seemed to kill a small part of him, but without mistake.

Two thousand miles west, he booked at a cleaner than clean motel – décor, plastic Tyrolean – on the edge of a desert, where, ten years earlier, he might have watched the fireballs rising which had probably meant the end of any civilisation he understood ... Born in Battersea, of army stock ... They would rise again.

Here, too, he was at the heart of scenic wonderland, that bluer than blue, sunnier than sunny, playground of the people he had fought. Playground and people were one, because they were making a playground world, where happy adolescents could spend their lives in guilt-free innocence, living in pure sensuality, dying in pure orgasm. He felt no anger or envy, though surprise at his own lack of adaptability. Driving past sign after sign directing him to wonder-canyon after wonder-canyon, he even projected a Freudian footnote on their playground obsession with these natural features – he had more serious work.

So, on the third morning, after many hours' sleep and an hour-long careful wash, he sat at his Tyrolean desk in a sunny window and opened the first of his big green notebooks. Pen in hand, he paused, the familiar explosion of shame rising inside him that he should actually be about to write! Now, when he had acted, emerging a man – if a dead one – from her fishy womb, how could he bear to make this new retreat to his own booky womb? But somewhere in his mind an idea lurked, took shape, was born.

There was a lot to write, but he mustn't hurry. Above all he must write it well, because the biggest irony could yet be that they would accept what he'd written and reject what he'd done. Here was the only excuse for his projected masturbation. That

346

it would lay the best of smokescreens so that, when he finally disappeared they'd pity him, not realising that they should cheer.

He had several days, perhaps even weeks. Before he became ensnared in that astonishing system of procrastination they called justice, so appropriate because it perpetuated the faith that you could buy your way in and out of happiness, of life itself. You had to be able to. There weren't such words as "can't" or "no". Nanny had forgotten to say them. The gas chamber, the electric chair, what grotesque but proper nightmare ends to the big illusion.

They'd probably even find him money.

But no, Morrison thought, glancing at his motel bed where a small lift of the mattress showed the resting place of that fine antique hand-arm, much used in the Great Civil War between the States. Finally, abused, disabused, self-abused he would act again. An older, melodramatic, guilt-infested but heroic civilisation would outwit them yet.

Morrison was dead, Peterson wrote, at work on his third novel (Morrison wrote, at work at last on his final and posthumous novel). To his own disgusted amazement – but secret delight that he should truly be the victim of such a sick joke, Peter Morrison (revise name) was at last dead.

That was the trouble, Maurice Peterson thought, nipping the ballpoint pen with his teeth till they made tiny pits in its shiny blue plastic, furrowing his forehead in what he imagined to be a look of profound concentration but in fact suggested a sheep
. . .

Morrison wrote on.

347